"At every level, this is a thrilling book."
—The Drood Review of Mystery

In a small town in upstate New York, amidst the bustle of the Women's Rights Convention of 1848, history was in the making. And so was murder . . . Critics and authors agree that mystery's ingenious new sleuth Glynis Tryon is "A HEROINE WORTH CHEERING FOR!"*

Praise for *Seneca Falls Inheritance* by Miriam Grace Monfredo:

"A wonderful evocation of time and place, a heroine worth cheering for, and an involving, well-crafted plot—a recipe that any mystery reader can savor."

—Stephen F. Wilcox, author of the
T.S.W. Sheridan and Hackshaw mysteries*

"An exceptional first novel . . . from its exciting opening right up to the revelation of a well-concealed murder in a gripping courtroom scene."

—Edward D. Hoch, former President,
Mystery Writers of America

"An engaging mystery . . . Monfredo has given us a taste for a dynamic time in the history of women's rights."   *—Mostly Murder*

"A page-turning suspense story . . . historically authentic and cleverly entertaining."   *—Publishers Weekly*

"Blends history and mystery in an unconventional murder story."   *—Rochester Times-Union*

"A meticulously researched, first-class mystery that evokes, with charm and vividness, rural life in the Empire State a century and a half ago."   *—Buffalo News*

"Exciting . . . entertaining reading, equal parts murder mystery and historical novel . . . The success of *Seneca Falls Inheritance* rests with the fully drawn character of the poised, plucky librarian Glynis Tryon."   *—Syracuse Herald American*

"The genius of Monfredo is to teach 'herstory' while absorbing the reader in a good old-fashioned mystery . . . Write more, Monfredo."   *—Newsday (NY)*

Berkley Prime Crime Books by Miriam Grace Monfredo

SENECA FALLS INHERITANCE
NORTH STAR CONSPIRACY
BLACKWATER SPIRITS
THROUGH A GOLD EAGLE

NORTH STAR CONSPIRACY

Miriam Grace Monfredo

BERKLEY PRIME CRIME, NEW YORK

NORTH STAR CONSPIRACY

A Berkley Prime Crime Book / published by arrangement with St. Martin's Press, Inc.

PRINTING HISTORY
St. Martin's Press edition / August 1993
Berkley Prime Crime edition / May 1995

The Penguin Putnam Inc. World Wide Web site address is
http://www.penguinputnam.com

ISBN: 0-425-14720-7

Berkley Prime Crime Books are published
by The Berkley Publishing Group,
a member of Penguin Putnam Inc.,
375 Hudson Street, New York, New York 10014.
The name BERKLEY PRIME CRIME and the BERKLEY PRIME CRIME design are trademarks belonging to Berkley Publishing Corporation.

PRINTED IN THE UNITED STATES OF AMERICA

10 9 8 7 6 5 4 3

For my children, Scott and Shawn and Rachel,
and for Liz and Nancy,
with love

ACKNOWLEDGMENTS

I am grateful for the numerous fine libraries—public, academic, and specialized—in western New York: their resources and their helpful staffs have greatly enriched *North Star Conspiracy*. Those are the Rare Book Division of the Rush Rhees Library, University of Rochester; New York State Historical Association, Cooperstown, New York; also The Rochester Public Library, Rundel Memorial Building, with special thanks to Wayne Arnold, division head, Local History Division, and Lucie Miller, assistant division head, Literature Division; The Strong Museum Library, Rochester, New York, and assistant reference librarian and archivist, Carol Sandler. Also Frances Barbieri and Bill Leonard of the Seneca Falls Historical Society, and Betty Auten, Seneca County historian.

For their assistance I would like to thank Conley Edwards, reference archivist, and Sarah Huggins, reference librarian, of The Virginia State Library and Archives of Richmond.

I am indebted to those individuals who have made unique contributions: Dave and Diane Hutchinson, owners of The Maxwell Inn of Naples, New York, which was once a station on the Underground Railroad; Joanne Woodard, Deputy Commissioner of the Seneca County Board of Elections, Waterloo, New York; Bob Rosenberg, Cherry Hill Stables, Spencerport, New York; and Alex D'Angelo of Bordeaux.

My daughter, Rachel Monfredo, of the Boston Museum of Fine Arts, gave generously of her time and professional skill in handling American material culture questions—no matter how small or how strange, or at what hour of day or night she received them. My father, Horst J. Heinicke, M.D., contributed medical information and his spirit-raising flowers. And dear friends Nancy and Ray Leary lifted me over the last hurdle.

Finally, for his invaluable assistance and support, I wish to thank my husband, Frank Monfredo, who gave limitlessly of his legal expertise, trial experience, and problem-solving skills. *North Star Conspiracy* owes much to his creative suggestions.

AUTHOR'S NOTE

The major characters in *North Star Conspiracy* are fictitious. However, actual historic figures appear from time to time; the interested reader may find them listed with annotation in the Historical Notes at the novel's end. The characterizations of Elizabeth Cady Stanton and Susan Brownell Anthony are based on the author's interpretation of Stanton's autobiography, *Eighty Years or More: Reminiscences 1815–1897* (1898). Also Volume I of *History of Woman Suffrage*, edited by Stanton, Anthony, and Matilda Joslyn Gage (1881).

The 1854 newspaper articles that are excerpted in the novel may be found in their entirety in the above cited *History of Woman Suffrage*.

The issues raised in Chapters 16 and 17 have their bases in actual legal arguments of the time period and, with one obvious fictional exception, refer to authentic Commonwealth of Virginia and/or United States Supreme Court decisions. Additional information may be found under Court Cases in the Historical Notes.

My apologies to Seneca Falls for taking some liberty with the topography of the town, describing the Seneca River-Canal more as it appears today than in 1854. I wanted to simplify for the reader what was at that time a complicated system of river, canal, islands, and an industrial and residential area known as "The Flats," which no longer exists. However, the location of the river and streets described in the novel is essentially the same as in 1854.

The Underground Railroad was the name given a vast, silent conspiracy, conceived and operated by humanitarians who defied a law of the land because they believed it violated the inherent right of human beings to be free.

—ARCH MERRILL, *The Underground*

PROLOGUE

❧

*Gone, sir, gone, with her child in her arms, the Lord
only knows where; gone after the north star.*
— HARRIET BEECHER STOWE,
UNCLE TOM'S CABIN

OCTOBER 1841

CLOUDS FLEW OVER a pale waning moon, trapping the fugitives in darkness. The clouds were thin, insubstantial as moth wings, yet they swept the woods with shadows. Lanterns held aloft by pursuers swung arcs of light over their steaming horses, but those fleeing on foot dared not burn even their meager candles. They crept forward blindly.

The child could barely make out her own hand groping before her. She and her mother, and her mother's man, inched forward over tree roots, stumbling through brush that lashed their legs like braided cowhide. The child thought she had never been so cold. Where were they, that her breath smoked in the air?

As the child looked to the sky, the clouds flew on; the moon emerged, a milky, lopsided light. The man hesitated, his neck craning upward. Behind him, the child and her mother waited while he strained to find the North Star hidden behind snarls of bare branches. Finally he shook his head, pushing the blanket-wrapped infant in his arms at the woman.

"Cain't see it! Hold the young-un whiles Ah look from that place." He pointed through the trees to a small grassy clearing. "Got to make us a reckoning."

"Hurry, Sam!" whispered the woman. "They's close behind. Hurry, y'hear?"

He nodded once, and vanished. The child stared at the spot where the man had just been, then dropped the heavy knapsack she carried; under her bare feet leaves shifted with rustles like those of the plantation mistress's crisp petticoats. The infant gave a sharp cry, and the woman quickly put it to her breast. The child leaned against the woman's hip. It seemed as though they had walked forever. She didn't know why.

She held a blurred memory of the night she had been lifted from her straw on the dirt floor of the lean-to. Carried by someone, someone who ran with her and pitched her into a wagon; her mother's hand pressed against her mouth: "Hush!" She remembered the sacks that covered her, their mildewed odor, their coarseness scouring her skin. The jouncing sway of the wagon. A boat sliding through dark, wind-dancing water. Caves that smelled like chalk and dripped rain from long stone daggers hanging overhead.

The child now rocked from one foot to the other, digging her toes into the leaves for warmth. She pressed her forehead against her mother's waist. "Ah's so tired, Mamma," she whimpered. "When'll we stop?"

"Hush, chile." The woman's fingers patted her daughter's lips. "Hush. It be soon. Stationmaster back there, he say next safe house be north side of these woods. Near town name of Seneca Falls." Her hand moved gently; the child felt it stroking her cheek. "Sam find us that Drinking Gourd star, baby-gal, we be on our way."

Above them a night bird screeched, beat its wings, and rose to hunt. Shivering, the child wrapped her arms around herself. Then sucked in her breath at another shrill sound, somewhere behind them.

Dogs baying.

"Mamma?"

Her mother's hand clamped over her mouth, voice frantic in the child's ear. "Hush, now!" She tapped the child's cheeks roughly. "You hear me, chile? Hush!"

A tall shadow slipped through the trees. The man. "We got to run, Ama! Run fast. Fast!" Sam's breath hissed like steam escaping a kettle.

"Where?" The woman sagged against a tree trunk, the infant still at her breast. "Where'll we run to?"

Moonlight suddenly flowed through the trees; a silver river that spilled over branches to flood the woods with metallic sheen. The dogs' howling came closer. Now the child could hear the crackling snap of branches, the thud of horses' hooves. Her mother pushed the infant into the man's arms and, grabbing the child's wrist, started to run. Shackled by her mother's grip, the child stumbled behind. She didn't know what they were running toward; she knew only that a terrible evil pursued them. Devils. More terrible than the baying dogs, or the horses . . . more terrible even, her mother had said, than death.

Just behind her, the child heard the heavy panting of dogs. The ground seemed to shudder; when her legs buckled, it reached up to snatch her. Dropping to her knees, the child saw giant horses lunging between tree trunks, and she threw her arms around her mother's legs while the horses reared over them. Hooves sliced the air inches from her face.

Sam thrust the infant at her mother, then stepped away to grab a thick fallen branch; leaping at the horses, he swung the branch before him like a blade that slashed cane. Still clutching her mother's legs, the child felt herself dragged forward as her mother lurched, screaming, toward Sam.

At the crack of rifle shots, the child ducked her head; she heard her mother gasp, then felt a weight press her body face-down into the ground. The sharp bite of gunpowder made her eyes tear.

The child tried to open her eyes but the tears made her lids stick. The sudden silence of the woods confused her; why was it so quiet? "Mamma?" she whispered. "Mamma?"

A moldy earth smell under her cheek made her wonder if she were back in the plantation root cellar. Then, through a throbbing noise in her head, the child heard the snuffling of horses. She strained to get up, but pinned under something heavy, she could only roll her head to one side. Blinking the tears back, she forced her eyes open. Nearby, three dogs with sad, wrinkled faces stood watching her. One of the dogs whined, pawed the ground at her shoulder, and touched her cheek with its cold nose. She couldn't remember why she had been afraid of them.

A warm trickle slid down her cheek. Her hands lay trapped underneath her, but she wriggled one free to wipe away the sticky wetness. It smelled sweet. When she touched her fingers to her tongue, they tasted like the iron rim of a water bucket.

Above her she heard a voice. A devil's voice.

"Fool! Damn fool! Did you have to do that? The Man's not going to be happy, good property destroyed. And shooting so wild—you likely killed that kid with the others."

The child knew the voice. Steady, low-pitched, like drum beats pulsing after dark behind the lean-to.

"Naw, she fell 'fore Ah hit 'em." An unknown voice. Rough. Like small stones crunching under boots. "What wuz Ah s'pose to do? That black demon liked to have killed us. And the stupid bitch wuz in the way."

"You better be right about the girl, or we don't go back. Ever."

The child felt the weight pushed off her. Hauled to her feet, she was shaken roughly. She squeezed her eyes shut and clenched her teeth, afraid she would cry. Afraid what she would see.

"This here the one we want?" The rough voice again. "This mulatto kid?"

"Yes—she's the one."

"Hey, kid. You's goin' back!"

The child opened her eyes. Lit by lantern flare, two faces, white devil faces, seared their images on her mind with a ferocious clarity. She jerked her gaze away from the faces; then she looked down.

Sam lay crumpled over his branch, his neck twisted, his open eyes blank. Next to him, the blanket-wrapped bundle was a silent grayish mound flecked with dark splotches. Her mother sprawled like a rag doll with a stain spreading across her back.

"Mamma . . . *Mamma*?" The child felt herself hoisted onto a horse in front of a devil.

More terrible than death, her mother had said.

Frantically clawing the heavy mane, the child twisted it around her fingers like rope. The starless sky descended as a monstrous bird of the night, closing her inside its dark wings.

ONE

❧

The wife who inherits no property holds about the same legal position that does the slave on the Southern plantation. She can own nothing, sell nothing. She has no rights even to the wages she earns; her person, her time, her service are the property of another.
—ELIZABETH CADY STANTON, FEBRUARY 1854
ADDRESS TO THE LEGISLATURE OF THE
STATE OF NEW YORK

FEBRUARY 1854

A LONG WAIL of warning blew from the steam whistle of a New York Central locomotive, two passenger cars ahead of the one that librarian Glynis Tryon occupied. In its own way, she thought, it was as desolate a sound as the moonstruck howl of a wolf. Or the cry of a night bird caught unawares by dawn.

Glynis shifted restlessly on the unyielding seat, then clenched her teeth when the motion of the train rounding a curve of track jerked her body back and forth. A minute later the car once again settled down to a steady *clack-clack-clack*. She turned to her window, watching the stale-snow gray and bark brown of winter move past, relieved of drab sameness by shoots of red-osier dogwood, sumac fruit's burgundy velvet, a few parchment-colored oak leaves still clinging to otherwise windstripped limbs. Silver glittered from the surface of frozen ponds. Beside the tracks rose great stands of evergreen, the remainder of dense forests that once covered much of western New York, their needles fringed with snow. Mile after mile.

Glynis felt yet another strand of hair, loosened from its thick topknot, bounce against her coat collar. The whole knot was coming unpinned; she had a vision of her head sprouting reddish-brown snakes like that of a Gorgon. But her hands, despite woolen gloves, were too cold for her to even think of trying to fumble with hairpins. The railroad car was furnished with but one woodstove, and the passengers alternated between being red-hot and half-frozen.

Glynis glanced at the neat, unfashionably bobbed brown hair of the woman on the seat facing hers. Susan Brownell Anthony looked deep in thought, squinting nearsightedly out the window. Her deepset eyes—the left one slightly crossed—were shadowed, but the thin nose and prominent jawbone thrust with firmness against the harsh light. She sat erect, back ramrod straight, although Glynis guessed the woman must be as exhausted as herself.

Beside Susan, Elizabeth Cady Stanton snored softly, her chin nestled into the collar of her coat, curly hair hiding the deceptively cherubic face. By the time they arrived back in Seneca Falls, Elizabeth would bustle off the train while her companions dragged themselves behind her. All three women were in their mid- to late thirties; Elizabeth alone had the recuperative powers of a ten-year-old.

Glynis leaned back to rest her head against the upholstered seat. They had just completed a two-week siege of Albany. The first New York State Women's Rights Association meeting had been held to coincide with the state legislative session; the legislature, however, had all but ignored them. This despite Elizabeth's powerful speech on behalf of working women and suffrage. And despite Susan's ten-thousand-signature petition of support gathered by sixty women in thirty counties of the state, during one of the coldest winters in recent memory.

So had anything really been accomplished? Glynis saw herself many years hence, feebly tottering into the legislature, *still* asking men in government to grant women the rights that they themselves enjoyed.

But no, she thought, probably not: it was unlikely, no matter how long she lived, that she could ever overcome her terror of public speaking. Try as she would, shyness always wrapped its chill fingers around her throat to clamp off her breath and render her mute. It never failed to embarrass her.

Her head suddenly jerked forward, then back, accompanied by a shrieking whistle and the screech of iron wheels grinding on iron track. As the train ground noisily to a halt, sparks darted like fireflies. Glynis could barely make out the squat building of the Auburn railway station through clouds of engine steam, while travelers on the platform below moved like disembodied ghosts through dense fog.

"Are we home?" Elizabeth Stanton yawned, peering over the high collar of her coat.

"Almost. Last stop before Seneca Falls," Susan Anthony answered, shifting on the seat to smile at her companion. After a few days spent with the Stantons, Susan would go on to her home in Rochester.

Tired though she was, and dispiriting as the legislature's reception had been, Glynis remained grateful for the days spent with Elizabeth and Susan. She rarely saw them anymore, since the recent expansion of her library had made scarce any time for women's rights activities. Still, by summer she should have things more under control. Then—

"Glynis?" Elizabeth's voice broke through her thoughts. Glynis started, and looked up to meet the keen brown eyes.

"Where were you?" Elizabeth laughed. "Not here, certainly. I asked how plans for a Seneca Falls theater are coming?"

Glynis tried to conceal an involuntary moan by clearing her throat. This did not deceive for a moment Elizabeth Stanton, who laughed again, and said, "I see."

Glynis smiled and nodded. "Vanessa hasn't made up her mind whether to purchase an existing building or build a theater. She's rather in a dither over it." And expecting Glynis's library to furnish her with answers.

Elizabeth turned to Susan Anthony. "You've met Vanessa Usher, haven't you?"

Susan hesitated. "I'm not sure . . ."

"Oh, if you'd met her," Elizabeth chuckled, "you'd be sure! Vanessa Usher is not forgettable, wouldn't you agree, Glynis?"

Glynis would agree.

"Miss Usher," Elizabeth explained, as Susan looked puzzled, "believes her role in life is one of bringing culture to the outposts of civilization—namely western New York. Which is quite laudable of course. I just wish she'd expend some of that prodigious energy, and money, on social ills as well."

"Those don't overly concern Vanessa," Glynis said. "In any event, I've asked Niles Peartree to send some theater renderings when he has the chance." She turned to Susan. "Niles is my landlady's son—he owns an art gallery in New York City. Vanessa insisted I contact him. She's very determined about this project."

"Determined" seemed a feeble characterization of Vanessa's iron will. Glynis stifled a sigh, and felt a fool for having been drawn into yet another of the woman's elaborate enrichment schemes.

"I just hope," Elizabeth said, "that Vanessa manages to lure the traveling theater troupe back to town. I thoroughly enjoyed their performances last fall—although some of the players struck me as a trifle odd."

A *trifle odd*, Glynis thought, was a polite understatement. But Vanessa had been enchanted, promising a theater if the troupe would return.

As waiting travelers now began to board the train, Glynis noticed two men standing back away from the passenger cars, their faces strangely grim as they scanned the windows. But they must have seen something, as both suddenly moved to enter the car. Glynis realized those were badges she had seen glinting on their coats. She would have recognized the Auburn police constable—so who were these men? U.S. marshals, most likely. But why were they here?

Her gaze went to the back of a young Negro man, seated across and up the isle from her. When the man had boarded at Syracuse, Glynis noticed that he wore wool trousers and jacket but no overcoat, despite a temperature well below freezing. And now the marshals appeared and strode down the aisle to stand beside him.

"You got papers?" asked one of them, resting his arm on the back of the man's seat. The marshal stroked his short beard and waited.

The interior of the railroad car became wholly still.

"I *said*," the marshal repeated, "have you got papers?"

The young man started to rise. "I don't need papers," he protested. "I'm free, two years now." He said this with conviction, although his face betrayed fear.

The marshal brought his hand down on the man's shoulder

and pressed him back into the seat. "Is that so? Well, I got a printed handbill here, says you sure are not free! Says you got an owner down in Georgia wants you back."

Glynis chewed on her lower lip and calculated the distance to the exit. Too far. Although she had heard of this kind of thing happening, she herself had never seen it. And she didn't want to now. Why didn't someone do something? But then, she thought, how could anyone prevent U.S. marshals from carrying out federal law?

Elizabeth Stanton, who had twisted around in her seat to watch, abruptly got to her feet and stepped into the aisle. "Officer," she called, as she went toward him, "I'd like to see that."

So quickly did Elizabeth move when she reached the marshal that she had the handbill in her grasp before the man could react. When he reached out to grab it, Elizabeth swung away from him, stating, "I do not see the slightest resemblance between the face on this," she held the handbill aloft for other passengers to confirm, "and that young man sitting there."

Glynis stared at the handbill sketch. No; there was no resemblance. Most of the passengers quickly looked away, to stare out the windows or to study the floor. Uneasy shuffling echoed the length of the railroad car.

"Ma'am, I think you better go back to your seat," the second marshal said. "This isn't your concern."

"It most certainly *is* my concern, and everyone else's on this train," Elizabeth shot back, "if you mean to take this young man—this *free* man—back to Georgia. You cannot just—"

"Mrs. Stanton!" Susan Anthony had in the meantime stood and now moved quickly toward her friend. "Mrs. Stanton, come back and sit down. Please. There's nothing you or I can do about this. Not *now*."

Susan's voice sounded steady enough, but Glynis could see her hands trembling. And could almost hear the wheels of rhetoric whirling in the woman's head, composing letters to newspapers, abolitionists, senators, President Pierce. . . . Susan Anthony felt as passionately about the Fugitive Slave Law as Elizabeth Stanton, and she was at that moment just as angry—Glynis knew from the way her jaw thrust forward. But Susan was one to choose her battlegrounds prudently, and she must recognize that she couldn't fight on this one.

"Both you ladies, get back in your seats," the bearded marshal directed sharply. "I'd hate to have to arrest you for obstructing the law."

The marshals hauled the young Negro to his feet, nudging both Susan and Elizabeth back up the aisle as they did so. Glynis drew in her breath. And exhaled with relief when an elegantly tailored man, three seats ahead, stood to firmly grasp Elizabeth's arm. It was Seneca Falls banker Michael Olivant; Glynis hadn't even seen him board, so concerned had she been with the marshals.

Olivant escorted Elizabeth, lips pursed and no longer protesting, back to her seat. Susan followed, skirts swishing in her haste.

With the two women again seated, Olivant nodded to Glynis. "Afternoon, Miss Tryon," he said; then he turned to watch the marshals leave the train with their prisoner. From the window, Glynis saw the Negro being hustled onto a buckboard as the train began to pull slowly out of the station. For a few moments, a nervous silence vibrated inside the car; then gradually, a few voices at a time, conversation resumed. Sheets of newspaper rustled loudly. Glynis wondered if anyone else felt as ashamed as she.

Elizabeth's eyes glistened; she pulled a handkerchief from her purse and dabbed at them furiously, while Susan remained tight-jawed and silent. But at least, Glynis thought, Elizabeth had attempted *something*. The four-year-old federal Fugitive Slave Law said that all Negroes accused of being runaways, justly or not, could be sent south without even the opportunity to speak in their own behalf. It was without question an unjust, Draconian law. However, it *was* the law. Shouldn't they work to change it, rather than break it as so many abolitionists urged? But if she believed that, then why did she feel that all of them, herself included, should have interfered with those marshals? Kept them from taking that man into slavery—whether he was freed or not?

The smell of damp wool and pipe tobacco made Glynis glance up at Michael Olivant, who stood in the aisle beside her seat. He had leaned over her to stare out the window and, like the women, he said nothing. His pleasant, even-featured face had remained impassive throughout. Only his fingers tapping the upholstered back of Glynis's train seat revealed emotion. She couldn't be sure he even knew he did it.

Elizabeth finally said, "Thank you, Mr. Olivant. I apologize for my rashness—though not for the sentiment provoking it. I just tend to hear my heart before my head."

Straightening, Michael Olivant slowly nodded at her. He started to move up the aisle but turned back to say, "I've been in Albany recently on bank business, Mrs. Stanton, and heard about your speech to the legislature. I want you to know I agree with what you said—about the laws having to do with women and their wages. Employers *shouldn't* be obliged to pay a wife's wages to her husband."

"Well, Mr. Olivant," Elizabeth replied, her smile obviously forced, "I wish we had you in the New York Legislature."

"As a matter of fact," Olivant said, "it's something I've been giving some thought to. Running for office, I mean. I believe our district assemblyman should be challenged this next election."

"My dear Mr. Olivant." Elizabeth now smiled spontaneously. "Please do sit down and join us."

SEVERAL WEEKS LATER Elizabeth Stanton bustled into the library, marching straight to Glynis's desk to firmly place on it a newspaper clipping.

"I received this in today's mail from a friend in Albany. She thought I might like to see what our visit there inspired. Read it, Glynis. Read it and ... well, if your initial response is the same as mine, you won't know whether to laugh or cry. I myself have decided not to waste any tears on such drivel."

Glynis picked up the clipping, which was from the March 7, 1854, *Albany Register*:

WOMAN'S RIGHTS IN THE LEGISLATURE
While the feminine propagandists of women's rights confined themselves to the holding of Conventions, and speech-making in concert rooms, the people were disposed to be amused by them, as they are by the wit of

the clown in the circus, or the performance of Punch and Judy on fair Days, or the minstrelsy of gentlemen with blackened faces on banjos, the tambourine, and bones. . . . [But] people are beginning to inquire how far public sentiment should sanction or tolerate these unsexed women, who would step out from the true sphere of the mother, the wife, and the daughter, and taking upon themselves the duties and the business of men, stalk into the public gaze, and by engaging in the politics, the rough controversies, and trafficking of the world, upheave existing institutions, and overturn all the social relations of life. . . . It was never contemplated that these exotic agitators would come up to our legislators and ask for the passage of laws upholding and sanctioning their wild and foolish doctrines.

Two

&

Life's but a walking shadow, a poor player
That struts and frets his hour upon the stage
And then is heard no more.
—SHAKESPEARE, *MACBETH*

AUGUST 1854

GLYNIS CAME DOWN the front porch steps of her boarding-house to the stone path lined with mignonette and fragrant, three-foot-high, blue and white heliotrope, then turned south on Cayuga Street to walk briskly along the hard-packed dirt road. Seven-thirty on a summer morning, but as unlit by sun as twilight. Strands of smoke gray mist wreathed her ankles; now and then the mist separated to swirl upward with the swinging motion of her long linen skirt. Her eyes mirrored the gray of the mist, and wisps of red-brown hair, loosed from the topknot hidden under a wide-brimmed hat, brushed her cheeks. One hand gripped the shoulder strap of a book bag, the other clutched stems of pink and white phlox. Now and again she sniffed at the blossom clusters.

Ground fog lying over village and canal all but obscured Seneca Falls's six churches. Only their steeples were distinct, rising sharply from the mist like heaven-bound arrows. Their cast bronze bells, tolling the morning hour, vied with canal boat foghorns: the bells rang bright, seraphic, the heralds of Jehovah; the horns sounded requiems.

Glynis shivered in the dampness, despite the road heat rising through her high-laced shoes. Small wonder this fog, she thought; for the past week, it had been unusually hot even for early August in western New York. Hot and oppressively humid.

The Seneca Falls markets had just opened when she reached Fall Street, the wide dirt road that passed through the center of town. Proprietors were sweeping wood-plank sidewalks. Their storefront bins swelled with rainbows of blueberries, blackberries, purple mint, cherries, radishes, carrots, yellow and green beans, and pale-brown husks hiding golden corn. Already farmers were leaving for home and fields. Huge wagon wheels rumbled behind the sturdy-legged draft horses.

Glynis tried to ignore the smell of cinnamon buns coming from the bakery shop she approached. The shop's crisp white curtains had been drawn back, the better to entice passersby with not only smell but a view of the trays bearing plump, nut-studded buns, ginger biscuits, apple-and-spice muffins, crunchy sugar-dusted rusks . . . Averting her eyes, Glynis hurried past the shop windows to continue down the street.

Stopping to first shake dust from the hems of her skirt and underskirts, she then pulled several sheets of paper from her shoulder bag before entering the two-story, white-framed building that housed the offices of *The Seneca County Courier*. She began to push open the door but hesitated, standing for a moment to gather resolve. As Seneca Falls' librarian, she wrote a monthly book-review column for the newspaper, but recently the *Courier* had begun to publish some of her pieces on women's rights. These pieces, however, appeared under the pen name Sebastian P. Japes.

"Your items will get more attention if readers think they're written by a man," the *Courier* editor had insisted when Glynis first submitted the columns. "Otherwise nobody will bother to read them."

After the Japes column had appeared several times, Glynis somehow worked up enough courage to challenge the pen name. Ephraim Penrod, the editor, said, "No; we keep the name. It's perfect! Look at these outraged letters—every male in town wants to know who this jackass Japes is, selling out his fellow man."

Glynis protested as strongly as she was able—which, she reflected, clearly hadn't been able enough, since the editor stood firm. No pen name; no columns. She had consoled herself that at least he printed them, and she would just have to bide her time. But now, she informed herself with firmness, she'd bided long enough. She determinedly pushed the door open to step inside.

"Good morning," Glynis addressed the top of the editor's

balding head; Ephraim Penrod sat hunched over his desk, which stood squarely in the middle of a large front room. "Ah, Mr. Penrod . . . I wonder if we might discuss my women's columns again, and the name—"

"No need to discuss it, Miss Tryon," the editor interrupted. "It's a fine name: Sebastian P. Japes. Has character. We keep it!"

"But Mr. Penrod—"

"Miss Tryon, this is a newspaper, *my newspaper*, not one of your ladies' magazines. Now, do you want to see those columns of yours printed in it or not?"

Glynis silently debated this; after she gave the editor a reluctant nod, she backed quickly out of the office, berating herself for cowardice. Hypocrisy. Lack of moral fiber.

When she left the building the sun had appeared, flat and red and round, as if drawn by a child's hand. Heat burned through the mist, sprouting parasols on Fall Street like toadstools after a rain. Before crossing to her library, Glynis pulled forward the floppy brim of her hat—she couldn't risk more sunburn, certainly not more freckles—while fumbling with the flowers from her boardinghouse garden.

From behind her came the slowing *thwock-thwock* of hooves. She turned to take several quick steps backward as a black Morgan horse eyed her straw hat. Several passing women smiled coyly up at the Morgan's rider from under their parasols; these smiles were lost, however, as the rider was looking elsewhere.

"Morning, Glynis." Cullen Stuart, Seneca Falls' constable, drew up on a rein. The horse's muzzle swung away from the hat.

"Cullen. You're at this end of town early."

"Looking for you. Found out I have to ride to Waterloo today for a court hearing—those four runaways that were picked up here by U.S. marshals a couple days back."

Glynis nodded. Immediately after their capture, Cullen had wired the slaveholder who claimed to own the runaways, since the runaways swore they had been manumitted just a week before. A reply to the wire had not yet arrived, but until one did Cullen hoped to delay a forced return south. He straddled a fine line; the Fugitive Slave Law provided imprisonment and fines for law officers who did not enforce it. Cullen could delay only so long.

"I hope those people are released," Glynis said quietly. "What do you think?"

Cullen shrugged. "Can't say. But I'll see you when I get back." He paused, looking down at her.

She knew he wanted something said about their conversation of a week ago. But she couldn't. Not in the middle of Fall Street with half the town passing them. And she still wasn't sure what she was going to say to him anyway.

"Then I'll see you when you get back, Cullen. And . . . well, be careful."

He frowned slightly, nodded, and flicked the reins. The Morgan moved forward. Glynis stood watching man and horse maneuver around carriages congregated in the road, then turn west toward Waterloo. Cullen looked back only once.

A BREEZE OFF the canal through the tall library windows made the desktop papers quiver; as well they should, Glynis smiled, gazing down at a drawing of three witches rising from a hidden pit behind a tree sprouting crowns and scepters. Netherworld trapdoors, wings, balconies, and Elizabethan canopies stretched before her. When he said "All the world's a stage," she thought, the man knew what he was talking about.

Glynis stood to study the theater renderings: the drawings, photographs, and black-ink lithographs that spread across her desktop overflowed onto her worktable and chair. Who would have believed the number of stages built in the Western world? And these pictures were only representative. Sent by Niles Peartree from New York City, they'd arrived three days before.

Glynis sighed and smiled to herself again; could a small town in western New York be ready for this? And why had she let herself get entangled in another of Vanessa Usher's lofty projects?

The library door swung open. Vanessa herself swept across the pegged wood floor, exuding a pungent perfume that smelled remotely, Glynis decided, like something her landlady used to repel mosquitoes. Perspiration glossed Vanessa's smooth pale skin and she sank slowly, as though gravely ill, into the chair opposite Glynis's desk; Vanessa was not so weak, however, that she neglected to lift her hoop frame before she settled.

"Something terrible has happened, Glynis." Her voice was a stage whisper projecting clear through the wood-beamed ceiling. "I can hardly bring myself to talk about it."

Pausing to spread her skirts artfully around herself, Vanessa then gazed upward, suggesting a death-bed confidence. Glynis waited. The "it" could be anything, and she dared not even blink: Vanessa could transform herself, with lightning speed, from someone who resembled a dark-haired Botticelli angel into a remarkable likeness of Lucrezia Borgia. It was worth watching.

"I just don't know what I'm going to do," murmured the angel. Silence. Then, "It's those wretched cur cousins!" snarled Lucrezia. "Glynis, you might *say* something—I feel as though I'm talking to the Sphinx!"

Glynis moved the drawings from her chair to the desk, and sat down. "All right, Vanessa—what have the cur cousins done?"

"They're challenging Aunt Rebecca's will!" Vanessa leaned forward, frowning. "Our lawyer says he's just received notice from the Surrogate that they've filed an objection. And until it's cleared up, the will can't be probated. Do you know what that means?"

Glynis nodded. "No money."

"Exactly! No money. Glynis, do you think Mr. Merrycoyf's a competent lawyer? I mean, shouldn't he have kept the wretches from doing this?"

"Of course Mr. Merrycoyf's competent. The wretches—the *cousins* must believe they've a chance of getting your aunt's will thrown out. On what grounds are they contesting it?"

"Undue influence!" Vanessa snapped. "As if Aurora and I would try something like that on Aunt Rebecca. She'd have to have been feebleminded—and she certainly was not!"

No. Rebecca Usher had not been feebleminded. Eccentric, possibly, like her niece—though Vanessa's sister Aurora was not in the least odd—but neither Vanessa nor her aunt was witless. Nor, so it seemed, were the cousins.

"So what does Mr. Merrycoyf say?" Glynis asked. "Will this rigamarole take long?"

"Long enough, if I can't buy the church before the theater troupe comes back. What am I going to do?"

Glynis recognized this as a rhetorical question. To get what she wanted in the past, Vanessa had moved heaven and earth.

But Vanessa, having finally spotted the theater renderings, abruptly stood to bend over Glynis's desk. "These are splendid, Glynis. When did you get them?"

"A few days ago. It seems converting a church into a theater isn't unheard of—after all, they're more or less alike in form and function—though it can be a big job." Glynis tried but couldn't resist adding, "And expensive."

Vanessa scowled and stared off toward the windows. Watching her, Glynis tried to imagine what scheme was being hatched, and how she could avoid—

"Glynis, I've just had an idea."

Glynis held her breath.

"Michael Olivant is president of Red Mills Trust, which foreclosed on the church. And Red Mills is Aurora's and my bank—we even have a few shares of stock in it that our parents left us. So why shouldn't Mr. Olivant lend me money to buy the church from the bank, as well as extra money to convert it, on the strength of my aunt's estate? I could put up the inheritance money as . . . what do you call it? In a poker game?"

"Stakes," Glynis said. "I think you better call it *collateral*, Vanessa, when you talk to Michael Olivant. But how can you rely on Rebecca's will? If it's being contested?"

"Oh, we'll get the money! Those scoundrels can't prove any 'undue' influence. It's just the delay that's maddening. But Mr. Merrycoyf says no matter what happens, Aurora and I will get at least half the estate."

Vanessa hesitated, her fingernails making sharp little clicks on the desktop. Glynis could only guess at what was being calculated.

"That might just be enough," Vanessa said at last, smiling, "to persuade Mr. Olivant to let me buy the church . . . with his money! I'll simply have to convince him, that's all, and worry about *my* money later. With a loan we can go ahead. We have to. I won't disappoint Tavus Sligh and the troupe when they get here—I promised them a theater. The contractor can start work if we come up with a plan. Which apparently you have!" Vanessa's arm swept over the drawings. "But it does look very complicated."

"Oh, I should think it will be," Glynis agreed. "*Very* complicated."

Vanessa's eyes widened, but her response came swiftly: "Then I'll just have to let *you* deal with the contractor, Glynis." This said with a drawn-out sigh of regret. "Especially since now you know all about theaters. And you're so much better with little details than I am."

With this disposed of, Vanessa turned to leave. Glynis watched the door swing closed behind her, then sat back to take a deep breath as she usually did after a session with Vanessa. A potent scent lingered.

GLYNIS GLANCED AT the clock on her desk: five-thirty. At noon, her assistant Jonathan Quant had finally returned from the rail station, hauling the crates of books they'd been expecting. The entire afternoon had been spent sorting and cataloging.

Across the bright open room, the walls of which were lined with bookshelves built to just below the windows, Jonathan bent over his desk to peer myopically at a file card. His curly hair resembled a rat's nest. Glynis wondered how anyone as precise in his work as Jonathan could be so careless about his appearance. He always looked as though he'd just climbed from bed: shirt rumpled, neck-cloth askew, frock coat—when he remembered to wear one—so wrinkled Glynis questioned whether it had ever known a pressing-iron. His trousers were too short. His boots were scuffed.

On the other hand, he bathed regularly. Was unfailingly cheerful. And he possessed the compulsive curiosity of the true librarian. These were qualities Glynis had hoped would compensate for his personal disarray. She also had assumed, because he was intelligent, that he would learn he couldn't expect regard from library patrons if he looked like an urchin. She had been wrong. The patrons adored him.

He seemed very young. But at twenty-four, he was the same age she had been when, twelve years before and newly graduated from Oberlin College, he'd arrived in Seneca Falls.

"Jonathan," she said, crossing to his desk. "I need to leave now. You can close at six."

Jonathan looked up, his eyes magnified by spectacles to soft water-blue globes. "All right, Miss Tryon—I'll finish these before I go." He smiled and gestured to the neatly stacked books beside his desk, already sorted in alphabetical order. Small columns of file cards marched in precise, uniform ranks across his desktop, aligned perfectly as if by ruler with the blotter edge.

He was wiping his pen on his trousers as Glynis left.

When she stepped outside the cool stone building and climbed the few steps to Fall Street, the air seemed sweltering. She paused for a moment to get accustomed to it, looking down at the walled canal section of the Seneca River, which ran below the library and parallel to Fall Street; beyond the village, the smaller canal joined the Erie system. Most shops and offices were on this, the canal-river's north side; the south side was lined with mills and factories. Residential streets stretched down both long shallow slopes to the riverbed.

From where she stood, Glynis could just see the steeple of a white church on the river's far side. *Former* church; she forced back what she felt was an inappropriate smile.

Six years before, it had been discovered that the church's minister frequently patronized Serenity's Tavern. His had been a clandestine patronage, as the tavern served also as a brothel. His congregation was so shocked—as was indeed most of the town—that although the minister left Seneca Falls, his flock left the church as well. The white clapboard building stood empty.

The bank foreclosed, anxious to resell it, but as Michael Olivant commented: "Who wants a used church?"

Vanessa Usher did. "Just because the church can't serve as the Lord's house of worship anymore," she reasoned, "doesn't mean that Apollo can't be served quite well."

Glynis felt somewhat responsible for Vanessa's choice, which was why she consented to undertake the theater research. "It will be less expensive to convert the church," Glynis had argued at the time, "than to put up a new structure."

She hadn't really cared what Vanessa did with her money, but Glynis liked the little church and knew the bank was considering razing it to sell its land.

Now, as she crossed Fall and started up Cayuga Street toward her boardinghouse, she reminded herself to talk tomorrow with building engineer Ian Bentham. After a long absence, Bentham had returned to Seneca Falls that spring to start a contracting and building firm.

Some parts of the church, Glynis believed, should be saved: especially two stained-glass windows, purchased and shipped from London by one of the church's founding members. Friedrich Steicher was dead now, but his lovely windows should be preserved. It was he who told her in confidence that the building could be used as a hiding place for runaway slaves. He had had installed, without the knowledge of the congregation, a tunnel that led from beneath the altar through the church basement to somewhere along the canal towpath.

Glynis now saw that a section of that tunnel could be used as a platform trap to raise and lower actors from the stage. Not a purpose, to be sure, that the former church member had in mind. But it was likely one he would have enjoyed.

Her steps slowing, Glynis pulled a handkerchief from her sleeve to blot her moist face. This summer had been without doubt the hottest she could remember. Every move she made sent rivulets of perspiration down her back; her white lawn blouse and cotton stockings clung like a second skin. The whale-boned bodice dug into her ribs, making it difficult to breathe. And the stiff underskirts tied around her waist weighed a ton. If the heat continued one more day, she would dispense with the dratted things altogether. It was absurd vanity anyway, and women should be ashamed of themselves for enduring such agony. But they all did. Where is it writ, Glynis asked herself daily, other than in *Godey's Ladies Magazine*, that waists be like that of a wasp, hips appear roundly fruitful, and breasts not move when the rest of one's body did? It felt, she imagined, a good deal like being encased in a suit of armor.

The sensibly comfortable bloomer costume—tunic and pants—had not lasted long. The ridicule the bloomer occasioned, from the press and the pulpit, had discouraged even the hardiest feminist. Its only supporters, other than the women brave enough to wear it, had been a few members of the medical profession. The bloomer had died a swift and noisy death. Glynis still grieved.

Just ahead on Cayuga Street was her landlady's shingled house, inherited from one of her deceased husbands. Harriet now perched on the front porch railing, cleaning string beans. Glynis noted the lack of a certain rigidity to her landlady's torso; Harriet obviously had had the great good sense, and self-confidence, to dispense with vanity.

"You look warm, Glynis. Lemonade's in the kitchen."

Glynis paused on the path at the bottom of the porch steps, breathing the fragrance of heliotrope. Harriet's other boarder, Dictras Fyfe, moved slowly in a wicker rocking chair, an ebony-knobbed cane resting across his knees. He lowered the newspaper he was holding. "Afternoon." He gave Glynis one of his sweet, unhurried smiles and raised the *Courier* again, until only the crown of his thinning gray hair showed above it.

Behind Mr. Fyfe's chair, Glynis's white terrier, Duncan, yawned and stretched and got to his feet. He came forward a few steps, waving his tail, then slumped to the porch floor again, where he lay blinking down at her from under his shaggy brows.

"Too hot, isn't it, Duncan?" Glynis leaned against the porch railing, watching the deftness with which Harriet removed the string, snapped each bean in half and dropped it into a tin kettle on her lap. All in one smooth rhythmic motion.

Without looking up, Harriet asked, "Long day?"

"Very," Glynis answered, going up the stairs to sit on the top step. "Vanessa made an appearance."

Harriet nodded. "That would make a day long, all right."

Mr. Fyfe lowered his paper again to smile at Harriet. The

woman was a good head taller than Glynis, who considered herself average height. Harriet's thick dark-blond hair was shot through with silver; recently bobbed, it swung around her shoulders, around her level hazel eyes that ordinarily viewed the world with composure. A beautiful-looking woman, Harriet; she must now be in her early sixties. And the survivor of three husbands.

"Here—first good ones of the season." Harriet reached toward Glynis with a fistful of beans. "Try some. Oh, there's a letter for you from Rochester," she said, glancing toward the house. "Looks like your sister Gwen's handwriting."

At the sudden rattle of an approaching carriage, all of them turned toward the road. Duncan roused himself enough for a perfunctory bark when a slender man in white clerical collar reined in his trotter and jumped from the runabout to hurry up the front walk. He repeatedly patted his smooth-shaven face with a large white handkerchief.

"Reverend Eames!" Harriet slipped from the railing to extend her hand. "Hot afternoon to be making calls."

The minister nodded, out of breath. "Sister Peartree . . ." he gasped.

Glynis and Harriet both stiffened, alert, at the single word "Sister." Dictras Fyfe's chair stopped in mid-rock, the newspaper sliding from his lap.

Reverend Eames looked at Glynis and Mr. Fyfe; his kind, worried eyes traveled back and forth between them as if undecided about something. Finally he turned to Harriet. "Sister Peartree," he said quietly. "Since you have stock in the company, I thought you'd want to know that an unscheduled train is expected in tonight. Unloading probably four or five pieces of unwrapped cargo at the station."

Harriet nodded, immediately moving to the front door. Glynis thought Reverend Eames was being unduly cautious— surely he knew that both she and Mr. Fyfe understood what he meant: runaway slaves were coming into Seneca Falls and would need clothing provided by the Underground Railroad's "stockholders." The runaways would be hidden at Reverend Eames's church, a station of the Underground, and Harriet and others would take food and the clothing there as soon as it became dark.

On the other hand, Reverend Eames probably did have reason to remain so cautious. Several weeks before, a Pennsylvania minister had been sentenced to serve five years in a southern prison—for doing nothing more than what would be done in Seneca Falls that night.

Reverend Eames nodded to Glynis before walking quickly to his carriage; he must have a number of stockholder messages to deliver. As the runabout clattered off, Glynis heard Harriet inside, climbing the stairs. For clothing stored in the attic, Glynis guessed. She experienced a sudden sense of disquiet, and even shame. She'd never involved herself in the Underground's activities, simply looked the other way. But since the train incident last February, it no longer seemed simple; she could still see the young Negro man being hustled onto the buckboard. To intentionally break the law, however, did not seem simple either. Not simple and not right.

She bent to pick up the forgotten kettle of green beans and went inside.

THREE

*I was free, but there was no one to welcome me to freedom.
I was a stranger in a strange land.*
—HARRIET TUBMAN

AN OLD MAN walking slowly down Fall Street the next morning stopped now and then to wipe a handkerchief over his face. He carefully refolded the handkerchief each time, then slipped it back into his trouser pocket before he walked on. Limping a little, as though his feet hurt, the man scuffed his worn boots along the dusty road; his black face was crisscrossed with lines, like the boots. As he walked, his eyes never lifted from the road, as if he observed each step forward with care. As if he had learned all too well the need to be careful.

The roads of these here towns all look near the same, he decided. Same as the ones I seen south. Difference is, here I got a name—and it ain't "Boy!" Moses Rawlings. That's who I is now.

In sleeves of coarse cotton, his ropy arms with muscles like tight round knots hung at his sides; he reached up once to pat the paper in his shirt pocket. This here says I ain't Boy no more.

At the southwest corner of Fall and Clinton, Moses Rawlings looked left to a small brick building. He rounded the building, saw red-painted hand pumpers through its open windows, and found an office in the back of the firehouse, as he'd been told.

Inside, a tall rangy white man stood behind a desk, shuffling some papers. The man's face, though not old, had a weathered look: snow and sun, frost and burn carved deep. His sand-colored mustache, like his hair, looked thick and soft as the Master's shaving brush. Watching him, Moses Rawlings thought: This one stands like a man who knows he don't have to "yes, sir" nobody.

The rangy man looked up from the papers. "Morning," he said. "You looking for me?"

Moses pulled off his cap to twist it in his hands. "If you's the constable, Ah 'spect Ah am."

"Yes; name's Cullen Stuart. What can I do for you?" His smile seemed real enough. Friendly even.

The old man's shoulders untensed some, and he eased the document out of his shirt pocket. "Ah come by to show you my freedom paper. Got into town here a while back, and they says you's the man to see."

Cullen Stuart came around from behind the desk. He took the paper, wrinkled as though it had been folded and unfolded many times, scanned it briefly and handed it back. "Seems O.K. to me. You plan on staying in town?"

"Ah b'lieve Ah might do that, if Ah finds work here."

The constable turned to his desk to shift the papers around. "I assume you came into town . . . alone?" He didn't look up, didn't wait for an answer, only said, "I heard our livery stable owner just lost one of his grooms. You any good with horses?"

Now he looked up, straight into Moses Rawlings's eyes.

He knows about us, the black man thought. He knows— and he's gonna act like he don't. Moses Rawlings had heard about this constable, that's why he'd headed here; still he knew he could never be too careful. Maybe when he got to know this white man better, he'd trust him with the real reason he'd come to this here town of Seneca Falls. But not yet. Too dangerous.

He nodded at the constable and said, "Ah's real good with horses."

Cullen Stuart bent over his desk to write some words on a piece of paper. "You give this to John Boone. His livery's about halfway down Fall Street toward the river bridge. He'll be glad to get a man so soon."

He held out his hand. "Good luck, Moses Rawlings. Hope you get the job."

THE NEXT AFTERNOON an orange-red sun, the Lord's oath of another fiery day on the morrow, had begun to drop in the western sky when Moses Rawlings steered the trotter along the canal towpath. Time to head the carriage back to the livery stable. When John Boone had seen the constable's note the day before, he'd hired Moses right then. Put him to work before he'd had time to find a place to sleep even.

"You can bunk in the tack room with Zeph," Boone had said. "Until you find somewheres. You know how to handle a rig?" Moses said he did. He'd spent all yesterday afternoon and all this day driving ladies around Seneca Falls. He'd never seen so many busybody, skinny women. Must be the cold winters up here, he thought. They never gets warm long enough to store meat on them bones.

The night before, he'd shared the tack room with a young black boy, name of Zeph Waters. Moses didn't ask the boy his age, though he wanted to; didn't ask him the time of day after he got a sullen stare in answer to his own extended hand. Boy never said a word the whole night. Mad at the world, that young-un looked to be. Handsome boy just the same.

Moses had just now come from the smithy. Big black-skinned man that smith was, name of Isaiah. Man stood over his forge, coals purple-hot, sweat runnin' off him like the river at flood. He asked this Isaiah, Moses did, the thing he'd come to ask. Smithy just looked at him hard; said, "What you want to know that for?"

Now Moses he was done for the day, just delivered the last lady home safe. The Lord knew he was weary!

Behind him, he heard a sudden pounding: the hammer of horse's hooves coming up fast. Moses steered his trotter to the side of the towpath. A pistol cracked, the bullet passing directly over the horse's head; the startled trotter broke stride, trying to run. Moses's hands gripped the reins and he pulled up hard. A long whip uncoiled, snaking out and over the carriage, striking first the old man's hands, then the trotter's neck.

The whip struck again, forcing the horse and carriage closer to the canal. Moses fought to keep the carriage wheels on the towpath. Over and over the whip came down. Though his hands hurt something fierce, Moses had to concentrate on keeping his horse off the edge of the canal wall. *But that horse he's spooked bad. Somebody trying to kill me? Why?*

Suddenly, though Moses couldn't look around, he knew. He knew who it was. Him! The devil still lived—let loose on this land . . .

Moses never did see the rider coming up alongside.

CULLEN STUART GLANCED at John Boone; the livery owner's scowl had deepened as he watched his drifting carriage bob against the canal lock. A lasso thrown from the towpath finally caught. The carriage heaved in the water to begin a jerky approach toward the men pulling in the line.

"Dammit to hell!" The livery owner's hand tightened around the harness of his trotter. "Good carriage wrecked!"

Cullen thought Boone ought to thank his lucky stars for the mule escape hole—an opening built into the canal wall from which led a wooden ramp. The escape hole and ramp had allowed the trotter to climb out of the canal and up to the towpath. He'd been found munching grass.

Moses Rawlings had not been as fortunate. He'd been pulled from the water but not in time. Cullen glanced toward Dr. Quentin Ives, who stood with the men positioning a stretcher beside the body.

Cullen shook his head and looked away. "I sent Rawlings over to you," he said to John Boone, "because the man said he could handle horses. Looks like he was wrong."

Boone's scowl deepened still further. "That's what I can't figure. 'Cause he *could* handle horses. Never saw a man better. Damn strange he got himself into the canal."

Boone walked away, leading his horse. After a few yards he paused to look at the smashed carriage now dripping on the towpath. He kicked at a wheel, swore, and kept walking.

Cullen watched the men with the sagging stretcher hike toward Fall Street. "I suppose there's no question that Rawlings drowned?" he asked Dr. Ives.

Ives shook his head. "No, I don't think so. The body's pretty badly bruised, lot of contusions around the head and hands. But the carriage must have done that . . . like the welts on the trotter's neck. And the man probably couldn't swim, even if he was conscious when he hit the water."

"All right, Quentin. You'll make out a death certificate to that effect then? Cause of death was accidental drowning. We ought to bury the poor fellow fast, the weather being warm as it is."

"I imagine there's no chance of locating any relatives?"

"No . . . I doubt it," Cullen said slowly. "Rawlings had just come into town. I remember his manumission paper said he was freed some place in Virginia . . . Henrico County. Never heard of it."

He wasn't supposed to know that runaway slaves had come through Seneca Falls two nights before. There was a good chance Rawlings had traveled with them, then stayed in town while the fugitives continued north on the Underground route. That happened sometimes.

Even if the runaways were family of Rawlings, what could they do? With the help of the Underground Railroad—and Cullen knew almost every church, every house, every Quaker farm involved in this silent conspiracy—some luck and fast horses, by now the fugitives might be close to a Lake Ontario port. And ships that would take them across the water to Canada. Freedom.

Cullen mounted his horse; he sat staring at the canal for a time, then turned the Morgan toward the firehouse. He'd finish the paperwork still on his desk, then head to the Peartree house. And Glynis.

For the past days he'd tried not to worry about it. About what she'd decide. He should *know*, she'd been a part of him long enough. He was afraid he did know . . . and that would be that. She was stubborn. She'd listen, she'd look at him with those beautiful smoke eyes, catch her lower lip between her teeth and try not to cry. But she wouldn't change her mind. Never had, not about this. Stubborn. But he couldn't let her put him off any longer. He needed an answer.

ON A CAST-IRON settee, between clumps of white pinwheel daisies the size of saucers, Glynis sat with Cullen in the Peartree back garden. Behind them, the setting sun gleamed red through a clump of shaggy-barked birch. Glynis wondered how long it could stay so hot; the entire village of Seneca Falls had a wilted look. Everyone was out of sorts, exhausted from the unrelenting heat.

She shifted to rearrange her limp drooping skirt. That

morning she'd left the boned bodice and the underskirts in her
wardrobe cabinet, and she felt peculiar: unshapely and angu-
lar, the hourglass become linear. But definitely cooler. And
rather pleased with herself.

Cullen had just told her about Moses Rawlings. "Rotten
thing to happen. He was a nice old man. From somewhere in
Virginia—a Henrico County. Here he was, free for just a few
weeks, and then this . . . accident."

Glynis's fingers plucking off faded daisy heads paused in
midair. Cullen's tone said something other than his words.

"It *was* an accident, wasn't it?" she asked him.

"Yeah, sure. Must have been. Quentin Ives thinks so. It's
just damn peculiar, Rawlings driving that carriage into the canal, what with Boone saying he was a good horseman. Course
something could have spooked the horse, Rawlings just lost
control." Shrugging, Cullen sat forward to study the parched
brown grass.

Glynis shivered at the delicate flutter of ghosts: six years
before, a drowning in the canal had set in motion a terrible
circle of death. But this was different.

Cullen leaned back, thrust his hands into his pockets, and
stared up through a screen of birch leaves. His voice sounded
offhand. "So . . . have you thought about what I said a while
ago? Come to any decision?"

He didn't move, didn't even look at her. And he sounded as
if he were asking about the weather! Had she *thought* about
it? What else did he suppose she'd been doing?

Her irritation ebbed. Cullen wasn't being casual. He was
like that—not wanting to expose how much something mattered. She should know by now.

But after struggling with herself for days, and nights, she
still was unable to make sense of how she felt.

A week ago, he had started with, "Glynis, something has
come up," as though some minor detail had made him late
that night. Not a warning of what was to come.

"Remember Allan Pinkerton?" Cullen had gone on. "When
he came through town a few months ago? Got a letter from
him today."

Glynis recalled Pinkerton as a brusque, vigorous Scotsman,
interested in Cullen's reputation for keeping order in Seneca

Falls. He was also interested in Cullen's experience with train robbery on the Rochester–Albany–New York Central lines. More interested still in the fact that for the past few years, there had *been* no robbers on those lines. Pinkerton had seemed impressed.

"Why the letter?" she had asked, oblivious as to what could be the impact of several pieces of paper.

"Pinkerton's going to open another office of his Chicago detective agency. In Cleveland," Cullen had told her. He seemed to look at her in a very odd way—she *had* noticed that. Then, "He wants me to start it up and run it a while. Maybe stay there."

She couldn't have heard . . . Cullen leave Seneca Falls? No. No, he couldn't be considering that. What was he saying? Her mind seemed to be slowing down like an engine running out of steam; it wouldn't track, wouldn't move beyond his "maybe stay there."

He continued talking; Glynis heard his voice, but not his words. She had never considered the possibility that Cullen might someday not be there. He always had been. For the twelve years she had lived in the town, Cullen had been there. A widower—his wife and child killed in a wagon accident a year before she'd arrived—he had been withdrawn, almost distant, the first months she'd known him. Her own shyness had kept her distanced, too, from almost everyone. But slowly, both with the caution of the once-wounded, they had moved toward each other.

Cullen was, among other things, her best friend. He couldn't leave!

She had interrupted him to say this. He stopped talking, studying her with an intensity that was not at all like him. It was so unlike him that she didn't finish explaining all the reasons why he couldn't go. To Cleveland. Practically the frontier.

"Glynis, listen to me," he'd said then, in a quiet, unfamiliar voice. "I'd rather not go alone. Not without you."

She'd felt blood drain from her face, leaving her lightheaded. Detached from herself. "Cullen, I can't go *with* you. It's too far to travel back and forth, and there's my library, and besides, what would people say?"

She was babbling, she knew. And that probably was not what he meant. What he had meant . . .

He had nodded; his face had been pale, his eyes so dark, almost black. He *had* meant marriage.

And now, a week later, she remained just as confused. She thought he understood that marriage would not be discussed, that that was a tacit agreement between them. Her decision not to marry had been made years ago—a choice that involved a great deal of pain, and long before she met Cullen—when she decided to go to college. Yet here was the painful decision to be made again. A decision forced on her; to live without him, or marry and follow him to Cleveland.

What about her job? A job she liked, certainly as much as he liked his. She couldn't marry and keep the kind of position she had now. Women couldn't do that; they just couldn't. Men wouldn't hire married women, not for anything more than menial labor—in mills, factories, on farms to pick crops, to watch their children and do their laundry and cook their meals. And why should she leave a place where she'd finally put down roots, deep roots, with people she cared about, to traipse off to Ohio?

Because she was a woman. That's what it boiled down to—because she was a woman, she had to make the choice. How many times had she heard Susan Anthony say that? And it was true. Cullen could have it both ways: a spouse *and* a vocation, in any town he chose. But not her. Marriage meant the end of a woman's freedom, even if the man was as good a man as Cullen.

She didn't know what to say. All she seemed able to do was sit there and look at him, while desperately forcing back tears. She bit down on her lip. The tears came anyway.

He knew. She didn't have to say anything; he knew. He got up abruptly from the settee, and began striding toward the house.

She couldn't let him just go! "Cullen, wait . . ."

He turned and took several steps toward her, his face expectant. But she couldn't . . . couldn't say it.

Without seeing, she stared at her hands gripped in her lap, and shook her head. "I wondered how soon you'll be leaving?"

His face went blank. As though he'd forgotten about that. Then, his voice hoarse, he muttered, "That depends. On how soon Jacques Sundown gets here."

Jacques Sundown? What was he talking about?

Cullen cleared his throat. "I didn't tell you I'd finally tracked Jacques down. Through Pinkerton's agency."

No, he hadn't told her. Jacques Sundown: Cullen's former deputy. His father had been French, a fur trapper, and his mother a Seneca Indian; Jacques Sundown's Indian name was "Walks At Sundown." He had left Seneca Falls very suddenly six years ago. Just dropped out of sight, without saying good-bye to anyone. Without saying anything. No one knew why he'd gone, or where. Over the years they had stopped looking for him. Had assumed he didn't want to be found, or couldn't be found.

"Jacques is alive?"

Cullen nodded. "In Quebec. I wired him he could fill out the rest of my term as constable. Heard from him yesterday. He's coming back, probably be here end of the week. I hadn't planned to leave that soon . . . well, for obvious reasons. But under the circumstances, now I think I will."

Glynis began wiping in distress at her eyes, and felt something soft . . . petals? . . . brush her face. She looked at her hands, then down at her lap. White with crushed daisies.

"I'll see you before I go, Glynis. To say good-bye."

Cullen walked quickly around the corner of the house and out of sight. A few moments later she heard the sound of hoofbeats. She held her breath, straining to listen.

Then they were gone.

FOUR

~

So sorrow's heaviness doth heavier grow
For debt that bankrupt sleep doth sorrow owe
—Shakespeare, *A Midsummer Night's Dream*

September 1854

GLYNIS SAT HUDDLED in her muslin undress over a mug of
coffee in the Peartree kitchen. Glancing out the window at a
pale sunrise, she propped her elbows on the table and pressed
the fingers of both hands hard against her temples. The dull
ache in her head would not go away. It had been there for
days. The queasy stomach struck last night.

She lifted the coffee mug, then set it back down more
firmly than she intended. Drops of coffee spattered over her
undress and, dabbing the stains with a napkin, she decided tea
would be better anyway. Chamomile tea to settle her stomach.
She looked at the tied bunches of herbs hung to dry from
beams at the end of the large rectangular kitchen, and wondered if she had energy enough to get up and boil water. She
doubted it. The four-legged box stove sat under the herbs with
a neat pile of firewood beside it, but first she'd have to go
fetch another bucket of water from the backyard well. The
thought overwhelmed her.

Now September, Cullen had been gone little less than a
month. It seemed like a year. She had seesawed back and
forth between anger at him for leaving and anger at herself
for letting him leave alone. The anger was frequently interrupted by spasms of anxiety: What if she had made a terrible
mistake? What if Cullen never came back? This possibility
had appeared all too probable the day they said a very
strained and brief good-bye. Or just as bad, what if she came
to believe she *had* made a mistake and wrote to tell him so,
and he didn't care: he had found someone else. Some woman
in Cleveland who didn't give a tinker's damn about choices

and independence and freedom. And what, she now wondered, was so attractive about these anyway, without Cullen?

She found herself constantly tired, as though each move she made required climbing uphill. Every part of her body ached—even her bones hurt. And she feared she had diagnosed her condition: acute melancholia. The reason for her mother's death, or so the doctors twenty years ago had said. . . .

She had to *stop* this. She wasn't her mother. Her mother who, after bearing three healthy children—Glynis and her younger sister and brother—had had two stillborn babies, lost an infant of fourteen months to whooping cough, then a young daughter to Genesee fever. It was the last tragedy that sent the thirty-year-old woman to her bedroom; she rarely emerged from that self-imposed prison. In retrospect, many years later, Glynis realized her mother believed the deaths were somehow her fault—and never did emerge from the opium haze under which she survived for another three years.

Glynis inwardly cringed, as she always did remembering her mother's slow death, and reached out to grip the edge of the sturdy table. She told herself the remedy now was to just go through one day at a time. Or as Harriet put it, "Live today and stop worrying about how much worse you might feel tomorrow; tomorrow might never come." Harriet had offered this cheery bit of counsel with a fairly unsympathetic attitude. Well, what could she expect from Harriet? Who had married three times!

Glynis pushed herself from the table and started to get to her feet, then moaned and collapsed back in the chair. How would she ever get through *this* day? The performance and dedication party for The Usher Playhouse were not until evening, but before that she had to survive one last *Midsummer's Night Dream* rehearsal. Thanks to Vanessa Usher. And Felix Mendelssohn.

The last thing in the world she wanted to do was perform. But Tavus—Octavius Sligh, Seneca Falls' new, self-crowned emperor—demanded the Mendelssohn and Glynis's flute. Vanessa's hero, Tavus, and his traveling theater troupe had some weeks ago returned to Seneca Falls from their tour of the southern states. And how remarkably fortuitous, Glynis reflected, that the troupe's arrival had coincided exactly with closure of the Red Mills Trust loan to Vanessa and beginning of the structural conversion of the church.

Building engineer Ian Bentham was not only making the conversion possible, but now said the theater could probably be ready by mid-October. Glynis had thought it would take at least six months.

A hall floorboard creaked, and Harriet appeared in the kitchen doorway. "Morning. You're down early for a Saturday. Couldn't sleep again?"

Glynis nodded.

"Thought I heard you," Harriet said, "prowling around upstairs in the wee hours."

"Yes, I finally decided I might as well get up," Glynis said, getting quickly to her feet; she did not want to hear another well-meaning "let-time-take-care-of-it."

"And now I really have to get going, Harriet. It's a long day ahead."

WALKING TOWARD THE river bridge in late afternoon, Glynis felt her head begin to throb again. The dress rehearsal, an unmitigated catastrophe, had just ended. Actors had tripped over their lines and one another, Tavus Sligh had bellowed constantly, and Vanessa had wept the entire time. Moreover, Vanessa's building being neither church nor theater at this point in the conversion, the dedication performance that night must be held outside—and dark clouds now threatened rain.

Glynis left the church grounds just as Ian Bentham and his construction crew began to unload a mammoth green canvas awning from a frame-bed dump cart. Tavus Sligh stood directing this sideshow in stentorian voice with Vanessa beside him, wringing her hands. When she wasn't shaking her fists at the sky.

As Glynis now waited at the south end of the bridge while several carriages passed, she thought she glimpsed Jacques Sundown's white-and-black paint gelding on the far towpath. She'd seen Jacques only once since he'd returned, and then on Fall Street just by chance. He'd merely nodded to her that day and rode on.

When she reached the other side of the bridge, the horse

and rider had disappeared. Turning onto Fall Street, her step faltered and she paused, the hair rising on the back of her neck. A stranger with a rifle in the crook of his arm strode down the center of the road, gripping the leads of two tan-colored bloodhounds. The man seemed to be peering intently at the streetfronts of shops and offices; but he then spotted Glynis, and started toward her. She noticed uneasily that there suddenly appeared to be no one else on Fall Street.

As he approached, she saw her first impression—that he was a big man—had been mistaken. He actually wasn't very tall, but heavy and barrel-shaped. His head seemed to be set atop wide shoulders, with no neck in between.

"G'day, ma'am." He gave Glynis what she supposed was a friendly enough smile, although for some reason he reminded her of a grinning stone gargoyle. One of his hounds padded forward to shove a wet nose into her hand. The man gave its lead a savage jerk and the dog, cringing, sank to the ground. With its wrinkled jowls resting on enormous paws, the hound regarded Glynis with mournful eyes.

"Sorry, ma'am." The man spoke with a pronounced and gravelly southern drawl as he touched the wide brim of his hat. Glynis nodded once and eyed the dog with sympathy.

"Name's Lyle Brogan, ma'am. Ah's a stranger heah 'bouts—could you tell me if theah's a gentleman in this town name of Farley? Thomas Farley?"

"No," Glynis answered. "No, I don't know anyone by that name in Seneca Falls."

Brogan's grin broadened, which pulled his lips away from discolored front teeth. Rearing his head back, he squinted down at her as though he thought she were lying. And she wasn't sure that if she *had* known someone by that name, she would have told him. The man was obviously a hired slave-catcher—hardly deserving of help. Besides, she did not know a runaway by the name of Thomas Farley.

She moved to leave.

"Now, s'cuse me, ma'am," he said, "but in the event you don't know this heah fella, Farley, could you tell me where Ah can find the law in this town?"

"Constable Stuart—that is, Constable Sundown's office is

at the firehouse." Glynis turned and walked away. She imagined him staring after her, the gargoyle grin fixed on his face.

A slave-catcher. The last one through town had aroused a lot of resentment; neighbors arguing with neighbors over the Fugitive Slave Law. There had been some ugly threats. She hoped this Brogan would leave before it happened again.

TITANIA'S WINGS WERE drooping. While the Fairy Queen dragged them across the stage, raindrops spattered their gauzy fabric. The actress beneath the wings seemed aware she had lost flight capability, and she shrugged several times. Finally she gave the shoulder harness straps a quick tug and, without missing her cue, trilled through a flower-covered arch: "Fairies away! We shall chide downright, if I longer stay."

Exit Titania stage right.

The actress stepped from the platform of the temporary outdoor stage to slip behind a clump of birch trees. But she hesitated, shooting a long look at Vanessa; Vanessa as Helena, now waiting offstage for her entrance cue. Titania's look was one of malice. Unconcealed venom.

Glynis saw this as she leaned forward to blot rain splotches on her sheet music. What on earth was that about? But Titania disappeared behind the birches, and Vanessa didn't seem to have noticed.

Glynis slipped her piccolo into a pocket of her black silk skirt and, with eyes still on the stage, felt around in the grass under her chair for her flute case. As her fingers touched it, the case slithered just beyond reach. She bent to retrieve it, taking the opportunity to glance behind her into the audience. Just at the edge of the seating area stood the slave-catcher. Grinning broadly at her. Before she whirled back around, his hand touched his hat brim.

What was *he* doing there? The fact that half of Seneca Falls seemed to be on blankets and wooden chairs behind her didn't explain why the slave-catcher Brogan should be among them. Unless he thought he was going to find the unfortunate Thomas Farley there.

But she had just heard her cue and didn't have time to think more about Brogan. Raising the flute to her lips, she felt raindrops tap her fingers.

*"And certain stars shot madly from their spheres.
To hear the sea-maid's music."*

A long roll of thunder obscured Puck's next line. Glynis heard a few chuckles, but sensed from the rustling behind her that some of the audience were preparing to flee. Next to her, the violinist grabbed for his case.

The rain held off for a time. But the threat remained and, without even turning around, Glynis could hear the audience thinning with a swish of skirts and petticoats. Some pessimists had already gathered under the awning that sheltered the food tables and punch bowls. Nonetheless, the performance was well into its third act before the heavens opened.

"Midsummer Nightmare is what we've got here," yelled the violinist as the company dashed to the awning. Rain pelted down. Her flute held protectively under a fold of skirt, Glynis rushed with the others for cover.

Following the rest, Vanessa swept in under the awning; her white tunic costume hung limp and black hair dripped down her back. "That's it!" she snapped. "If anyone ever questioned why we need a real theater in this town . . ." Her arm thrust accusingly toward the platform puddling with rainwater.

Glynis went through the crowd to the food tables, where the Ushers' domestic help sliced gold and silver cakes and poured Roman punch: a frothy mixture of cherries, beaten lemon ice, champagne and rum. In honor of the emperor Octavius, no doubt; Glynis reached for a pitcher of lemonade. The rain had already let up somewhat, and she eyed the distance to the rear of the white clapboard church. Too far for a discreet dash from under the crowded awning.

From where she stood, the church still looked like a church. It bristled with scaffolding and rope, while between its rear studs an open expanse yawned like a Druid cave; but its steeple still held a bell, and its austere rectangular shape still looked New England Protestant. Only the glowing stained-glass windows reflected a certain joyfulness not ordinarily associated with Calvin's God.

"Do you think it really can be made ready by October?"

asked Aurora Usher, Vanessa's sister, emerging from the crush of people.

"Doesn't seem possible, does it?"

"No," Aurora laughed. "But let's not tell Vanessa that!"

Aurora was just as pretty in her pale, fragile-looking way as the more exotic, black-haired Vanessa, but it was hard to find any other resemblance. They were as morning and midnight, sun and quixotic shadow.

"Aurora, during the play did you happen to see a burly man with a wide hat? A stranger?"

"Yes. I saw him right before the deluge." Aurora looked puzzled. "I noticed him because . . . well, I wondered why anyone would think bloodhounds might enjoy Shakespeare."

Glynis smiled, and tried to look through the crowd. "I can't see him now. I'm surprised so many stayed."

"Oh, Vanessa put the fear of God into everyone before the performance started. You were practicing your music, so you didn't hear her going on about fair-weather friends."

Under the awning the crowd shifted, parting enough for Glynis to see banker Michael Olivant and his wife; Deirdre Olivant was a transplanted Virginian, a member of the large, Westmoreland County, Nathaniel Rochester family. Even without this distinguished background, it would be difficult to overlook Deirdre. Her height—she was every inch as tall as her husband—and the red-gold hair and Celtic coloring gave the woman a commanding appearance. Deirdre always managed to look as if she had nothing to do but dress for her husband's pleasure. Tonight the hoop frame beneath her elegant gown was immense; her corset must be breathtakingly tight, Glynis imagined, to produce an hourglass shape surely never bestowed by nature. And Deirdre carried herself with a regalness that implied that her husband was so successful she need never lift a finger or bend to a stove. Which was just as well, since it would not have been possible in that corset. Glynis rebuked herself for this meanness and wondered, not for the first time, why she rather disliked Deirdre. Perhaps it was envy.

The two Olivants were talking with Ian Bentham. Bentham looked more like a banker than did the banker, Glynis thought now, seeing them together for the first time. Olivant had an even-featured lean face, while Bentham's was round, his body stocky and well-fed. But Bentham was one of those heavyset men with surprising agility; just that morning Glynis had been astonished to see him run nimbly along an overhead catwalk. She didn't know Ian Bentham well, since he had first left Seneca Falls shortly after she'd moved there. She'd just learned he was a West Point graduate and a member of the Army engineering battalion that had built roads and supply routes in Mexico during the war. Rumor had it that Bentham had then gone to California to make his fortune in gold. Whether he had or not, no one seemed to know. Nor why he'd come back to his small hometown to start a contracting business, when his talent might have been better financially rewarded elsewhere.

Michael Olivant turned from Bentham to shake an out-stretched hand; several outstretched hands, in fact. He deserved congratulation: were it not for him, The Usher Playhouse might still be but a gleam in Vanessa's eye. And putting up money for the theater didn't hurt Olivant's announced candidacy for a legislative seat either.

Aurora had drifted away, and Glynis again glanced toward the church. The rain had stopped. People were moving from under the awning to the canal slope and towpath. Among them were members of the theater troupe, including some of the Sligh family—all of whom Glynis hadn't yet sorted out.

She went to the church's rear entrance. Scaffolding hung over what would be access doors to backstage; Glynis ducked under it to find Tavus Sligh. Turned away from her, he held a carafe of sherry in one hand, a wineglass in the other, and he stood staring at what had been the altar. The four steps that led from the altar to the main floor, steps that had once stretched from one side of the church to the other, had had their end sections removed for the creation of a stage with wings. Only the middle portion now remained. Glynis watched, riveted, as Tavus poised himself on the top step, lifting his glass to an invisible audience.

She must have made some sound, because he whirled to face her. Not in the least abashed, he smiled and raised the glass again.

She thought Tavus Sligh could pose for a Beowulf illustration. Nordic blond and blue-eyed, he affected a warrior's stance, feet apart, torso bent slightly forward as if at the ready to grasp a sword; it was not, however, a sword but an elaborately carved dagger handle that protruded from the sheath attached to his belt. There seemed about him a barely restrained energy—unpredictable and disquieting.

"Well, Miss Tryon." The voice was as full, rich and deep as a cello, and Tavus played it as a musician an instrument. "Did your flute survive the downpour?"

Glynis nodded. "It must be disappointing to have your performance interrupted that way."

"Happens all the time," Tavus said, coming to place the carafe on a plank suspended between sawhorses. "But soon we shall have a real theater. No more interruptions, right?"

He swept aside his damp Oberon's cape, which smelled faintly of sheep, to lift the wineglass. "Will you join me, Miss Tryon? We'll share the glass." His voice had become seductive. Warm as stroking fingers.

He drank with his eyes fixed on her. Glynis fought embarrassment—precisely what he expected. He probably thought a spinster librarian fair game. An amusement. She tried for what she hoped would convey majestic disdain— never her most successful expression—and turned to leave.

Tavus exhaled loudly and said in more robust tone, "You should try the stage, Miss Tryon. You have the control for it. Good posture. And wonderful bones ... take my word for it, you're the kind of woman who ages well."

That was certainly reassuring.

She nearly collided with Vanessa Usher, who came swooping through the rear opening.

"*Here* you are, Tavus," she purred. She brushed past Glynis without speaking, without seeing anyone but Tavus Sligh. Glynis left quickly.

As she started for the awning, a sudden movement caught her eye. Calista Sligh, now minus Titania's wings, stood half-hidden by a clump of white birch. Tavus's wife stared toward the church, her expression much as it had been earlier, during the play. Glynis wondered if the woman had watched Vanessa go inside. But surely Calista had by this time become accustomed to her husband. Tavus gathered women the way bread crumbs gathered birds. She couldn't consider Vanessa Usher a threat; Vanessa was flirtatious, but not a seductress. Cullen had once said, very unkindly—Glynis smiled, remembering—that Vanessa couldn't concentrate on anything, other than herself, long enough to seduce anyone.

Cullen. Glynis suddenly missed him intensely, in another distressing, unexpected surge of misery. She stood, trying to fight back tears before she reached the awning. Taking a deep breath, she turned to look again at Calista Sligh, whose white dress and slenderness all but camouflaged her between the birch; whose mane of hair reminded Glynis of willow branches tossing in a March wind. But just now, Calista stood motionless. How long would she stay like that? Glynis thought uneasily.

Turning toward the food table, Glynis heard a deep southern drawl. Lyle Brogan leaned against an awning support, grinning down at a short, fleshy woman Glynis recognized as being with the theater troupe. The woman's face was still heavily made-up, exaggerating her small features, and her skin under kerosene lantern light looked as green-tinged as her imitation emerald earrings. Snatches of their conversation were just audible.

"Lyle, if you aren't going to tell me why you're in this godforsaken town . . ." The woman's kohl-lined eyes fluttered up at Brogan while she ran long red nails slowly down his arm.

"Cain't say, not heah, Luella, but Ah'll tell ya later . . . now come *on*, honey!" He removed her hand from his arm. Luella tossed her head, swinging the long green earrings, and laughed at something else Brogan said. Now the red nails rested with familiarity on his chest.

"You sure about that?" Luella asked, laughing again.

It certainly did look, Glynis thought, as if Brogan and Luella had become uncommonly friendly in the short course of one evening. Did the man never stop grinning? Then, abruptly, Brogan yanked on the bloodhounds' lead. The dogs scrambled to their feet and, with the slave-catcher and Luella, disappeared into the darkness beyond the lanterns' glow.

Glynis realized she must have been staring after them when Calista Sligh, who had suddenly appeared beside her, said,

"Luella and Brogan are old . . . well, to put it delicately, let us say 'old friends.' They met last winter when we were south."

Calista's strong, husky voice always startled Glynis; it seemed to overpower the rest of her. She looked drained of color, her skin almost translucent, but from what little Glynis had seen of Calista Sligh, she usually looked that way—a little like a pale wood nymph Glynis had admired in a steel engraving. Even without the fairy wings.

"It's time, everyone!" Glynis and Calista both turned as Vanessa's voice carried across the grass. "Time to toast The Usher Playhouse."

The crowd bore down on the domestic help carrying trays of champagne glasses. Vanessa's voice, nearly drowned out, projected just enough for Glynis to hear, ". . . and Mr. Bentham has assured me that we can open October thirty-first. Allhallows Eve. Our director, Mr. Sligh—" Vanessa simpered at Tavus beside her "—has decided that our first production will be *Macbeth*."

Under her breath, Calista Sligh murmured, "*Macbeth*. How very appropriate. It has witches. A curse. And murder."

Glynis spun around, but Calista had already moved toward the bubbling champagne.

OUTSIDE THE CABIN the September night was quiet, save for the drone of crickets and katydids. Even the earlier breeze had died, so Lyle Brogan woke instantly with the frenzied howling. His eyes snapped open. He saw only darkness when he struggled to an upright position on the cot, but those were his dogs, baying wildly outside. Brogan swung his feet to the dirt floor, felt for his boots and pulled them on. Reaching for his Jennings rifle, he groped his way to the canvas that covered the cabin doorway and, pushing the canvas aside, stepped down.

His boots slid in the mud left from the earlier downpour. Brogan careened forward, flailing his arms, then regained his balance to stand gazing toward the Seneca River. Nothing seemed to be moving in that direction. But the dogs' howling continued; he could just make them out, straining at their ropes.

"Damn stupid hounds," he muttered. "Likely a cougar's got 'em riled."

He walked for several yards, eyes straining toward the dogs and the river. Behind him, a twig snapped. He whirled around, the Jennings ready in his hands. He could see nothing. He took a few cautious steps. Then, catching a quick movement from the corner of his eye, he swung to his left, rifle raised, eyes narrowed as he peered into the darkness.

"Who's theah? Ah'll blow y'all's head off if'n—"

Stepping out of the night, a figure took shape. Brogan's face relaxed. He lowered the rifle, letting it swing toward the ground.

Thus it was useless against the blade that flashed in the other's hand; Brogan saw only a glint of metal before it plunged between his ribs. When it was jerked out and thrust in again, and again, the only expression on Brogan's face was surprise. His rifle clattered to the ground. With a choking sound he fell forward, his hands clawing at his chest.

Long after the figure and its weapon had vanished, the dogs continued to howl.

FIVE

◥◣◢◤

SATURDAY NIGHT'S DOWNPOUR had led to heavy gray but
rainless clouds all of Sunday. Now Monday morning, the
sunny sky looked as if it had been scrubbed clean, thought
Glynis as she made her way across the river bridge; scoured
and polished to a bright September blue. The summery air
smelled of warm earth and new-mown hay. Cullen's favorite
month was September; Glynis remembered the Sunday picnics they had taken to the park on Cayuga Lake. She swallowed and wiped at her eyes, forcing back an aching sense of
loss, then tried to distract herself by gathering late-summer
blue and purple asters massed along the hard-packed dirt road
that led to Smith's.

She wondered why she didn't hear the ping of Isaiah's
hammer striking the anvil, or the wheeze of bellows; or smell
woodsmoke from his forge. The blacksmith usually had more
work than he could handle on a Monday morning. When she
came in view of the small gray-painted house, it seemed unusually quiet. Nothing stirred save four horses grazing contentedly inside a post-and-rail fence. One of them raised its
head to whinny.

Glynis looked around for Isaiah Smith. He must be inside.
The blacksmith was descended from one of the first Negro
families in western New York: when Colonel Nathaniel Rochester arrived in three Conestoga wagons with his pregnant
wife Sophia and their nine children—and before he moved his

family to the site of the future city on the Genesee River that would bear his name—he immediately emancipated all ten of the slaves he had brought north. Rochester left the South, he had said, to escape the influence of slavery, to give his own slaves their liberty, and to rear his and Sophia's children in a free state.

After a few more steps toward the Smith house Glynis finally spotted Isaiah, big muscular frame stretched out under a hundred-foot horsechestnut, his open, square-jawed face nearly hidden under a straw hat. From beneath the hat issued an occasional snore.

Under the spreading chestnut tree, the village smithy *lies*, she thought, smiling; somehow it didn't have quite the verve of the Longfellow original.

But Isaiah ordinarily worked hard. She went by him quietly. Avoiding his sturdy leather boots clumped with mud, which stood at the front steps, she climbed to the house porch, swept clean enough to eat from, and knocked at the open door. "Hello . . . Lacey! Anyone home?"

After a minute or two Lacey Smith appeared, a small wiry woman with skin the color of polished ebony wood, and cheeks like shiny apples. Her hair fell in a long braid over the shoulder of a coarse-woven cotton shift, the front of which had been embroidered with sprays of white daisies that looked real enough to pluck. She swung open the door.

"Morning, Miz Tryon." Lacey took the asters Glynis handed her with a nod. Her eyes flickered toward the horsechestnut. "Reckon you saw my ambitious man out there."

Glynis smiled. "Taking an early nap?"

Lacey did not smile. "He been that way since him and his poker friends finished off their jugs last night. Four horses to shoe—and him sleeping off a bender."

Glynis wasn't sure what she should say. But Lacey shook her head as if to express, "What's *to* say?" then motioned Glynis to follow her into the sunny kitchen. With the exception of a tiny front parlor, the kitchen sprawled over the entire first floor of the Smith house. At the far end, under windows with a southern exposure, stood tables covered with fabrics, scissors and knives, spools of thread, pincushions, and the other tools Lacey employed in dressmaking. Another table, set apart from the others, held yards and yards of lace; one big square lay pinned to a parchment pattern, and still had attached bobbins hanging over the cushion beneath. It was this lace for which the woman had become known over the breadth of Seneca County, and well beyond.

Lacey Smith once told Glynis the only good thing about slavery had been that, as a child in Virginia, she'd been taught by her French mistress to make *point de gaze* and *point d'Angleterre* lace. This Frenchwoman renamed her when Lacey's skill became apparent; Lacey said she could hardly remember her real name, although she'd never forgiven the white woman for taking it from her. But it was common enough practice to change slaves' names, she'd explained with a shrug.

It seemed Lacey bore the Frenchwoman no other resentment. This mistress had allowed her to keep one-third of the money earned from her lace work—she'd supposed "it was only fair." The same woman agreed to sell the young slave her freedom for seven hundred and fifty dollars. For twelve years Lacey saved. Working at night, after her other chores were done, she put aside enough to come within fifty dollars of her freedom. Then the Frenchwoman died. The woman's son ignored his mother's agreement; immediately he prepared to sell Lacey south to the canefields. The night of the woman's funeral—with the family drowning their grief by looting the wine cellar—Lacey stowed her lace-making tools in a knapsack and ran. With the help of the Underground Railroad, and her seven hundred dollars, she made it to New York State. And eventually to Isaiah Smith.

Lacey now went to her worktable. "You come about the shawl for Miz Peartree? It's not done yet."

"Oh, Lacey, I'm sure it isn't," Glynis said. "I told you Harriet's birthday isn't until November. No; I just thought I'd pay you half now. While I've got it," she added quickly, catching Lacey's sharp glance.

Lacey sat down, gesturing Glynis toward another chair. "You sure you not been talking to Doc Ives?"

Glynis flushed. Quentin Ives *had* told her that Lacey

needed spectacles. Badly. They were expensive, the spectacles, and he didn't know if Lacey could afford them. He'd ordered the spectacles anyway, telling her they'd work out the payment. But Lacey hadn't come back for them.

"Never mind answering," Lacey said scowling. "I can see from your face. You'd make a poor poker player, Miz Tryon. Anyway, I'll take your money. Not 'cause I can't pay for those spectacles, 'cause I can—just hain't found time to get into town for 'em. But I need to buy more linen thread for the shawl. You're sure you don't want cotton? It's a lot cheaper, like I told you."

"No, Lacey, I don't want cotton thread. Not for Harriet. Cotton's nowhere near as nice as linen—you told me that yourself."

Lacey nodded, a satisfied smile crossing her face. But when the front door opened, banging against the porch wall, she scowled again.

Isaiah Smith came into the kitchen, somewhat unsteadily. He tipped the brim of his straw hat toward Glynis. "Morning, Miz Tryon."

"Afternoon, be more like it," Lacey snapped. "You see those horses out there? Where you think they come from? You think they just wandered in, lookin' for somewhere to stand around—somewhere with soft grass so's they don't need *shoes*?"

Isaiah turned toward the windows, peered out, and sighed loudly. "Woman, you give me no peace. No peace at all."

Glynis opened her purse. "Here, Lacey, I think that's half of what we agreed on . . . right?"

"Looka here now, Lacey-gal," Isaiah said, turning back to them, "you gone and made Miz Tryon feel unwelcome with all that sharp talk." The grin spreading across his face would melt butter, Glynis thought.

But Lacey got to her feet, glaring at him with hands on her hips. "You get out there and fire up that forge, Isaiah. Never you mind what Miz Tryon feels—you best worry about what *I* feel!"

Glynis followed her from the kitchen; Isaiah, she noticed, didn't seem particularly chastened. Out on the porch Lacey said, "If he wasn't so good-lookin', I'd throw him out!" She smiled then, but Glynis had caught the conflict in her voice: the exasperation and the love. Then Lacey threw her head back and laughed. A laugh that rang like Isaiah's hammer. "I'll get your linen thread—same day as I pick up my new specs," she said, still chuckling. "Have the shawl ready by month's end."

Glynis walked back down the dirt road, wondering if it were true, what she'd heard about the Smiths—that their house had secret niches, concealed cupboards, and attic compartments used as hiding places for runaway slaves. That Lacey and Isaiah were part of the Underground Railroad. Glynis assumed she would never know. She didn't want to know.

IN THE LIBRARY later that morning, Jonathan Quant called to Glynis, "I think they're here, just coming down the steps."

Glynis left her desk to go through a doorway that separated the library from the Seneca Falls Debating Club room. This room could seat thirty comfortably, forty if all held their breath; it had been annexed to the fieldstone building three years before.

The small group waiting while she unlocked the outside door included, among the men, some of the area's most committed abolitionists. The women were those involved with women's rights, among them Elizabeth Stanton with her husband Henry. Susan Anthony came in accompanied by Ernestine Rose, both of them recently returned from a speaking tour on behalf of women's rights that had taken them to the largest cities on the East Coast. Elizabeth had stayed behind in Seneca Falls, having decided to forgo travel indefinitely to spend more time with her five young children. At least this was the reason she gave; Glynis believed that Henry's strong objections to his wife's absences had a great deal to do with Elizabeth's decision. Henry Stanton himself traveled extensively.

Ernestine Rose, although not in attendance at the first women's rights meeting six years earlier, had since become heavily involved in the women's movement. Mrs. Rose, a Polish émigré, lived now in New York City; it was said she had renounced her Jewish faith—her father was a rabbi—because it held that women were inferior.

When they'd all finally settled, Henry Stanton began, "I've asked you here today—" he cleared his throat emphatically "—to discuss the candidacy of Michael Olivant for the state assembly. Mr. Olivant has indicated that he would appreciate any suggestions on advancing his campaign. In other words, what might we do to assist?"

"I take it," Gerrit Smith said, "that we're all in agreement about supporting him?" Gerrit was Elizabeth's cousin—wealthy, affable, and a leading antislavery advocate.

Glynis listened to the murmurs of assent. It was the first time in her memory that men and women had met together like this for a joint political effort. Of course, the women couldn't vote in the election. And the men involved were probably not typical of most men. Still, she couldn't help but wonder if they were aware of Michael Olivant's opinions on working women's wages. As far as she knew, Elizabeth and Susan hadn't mentioned their February train conversation with him to anyone. And if they were both as smart as Glynis thought they were, they wouldn't.

"I understand Olivant's going to run as a Republican," Gerrit Smith went on. "Since the party just developed this year, will the affiliation help him? What I mean to say is, do the people of this district know that the Republicans formed, at least in part, as a response to the slavery issue?"

"That's up to us, Gerrit," Elizabeth answered, "to let the voters know. But first there are the designating petitions for Mr. Olivant's candidacy. Do we have enough signatures? Or do we need more people to work on that?"

Jonathan appeared in the library doorway and gestured to Glynis; he really looked a tad less disheveled today. Did she dare hope? She got up quietly and walked into the library, closing the connecting door behind her.

"I thought I should let you know," Jonathan said, "that the constable was just here, looking for you."

Glynis felt her heart lift, then realized that Jonathan wasn't talking about Cullen. "Constable Sundown? Where is he now?"

"He said he couldn't wait, that he would see you later. I just thought you should know."

Jonathan's face seemed guileless enough, but Glynis saw in his eyes curiosity writ large. Well, she couldn't relieve him; she had no idea what Jacques Sundown wanted.

"Which way did the constable ride?" she asked. "Toward the firehouse?"

Jonathan shook his head. "No, he rode north along the canal."

Questions from library patrons kept her for some time. When she finally returned to the meeting, plans were under way for candidate Olivant's appearance in early October at the Seneca County Agricultural Fair. Suddenly the outer door swung open and into the room stalked a gaunt, wraith-like figure. Glynis inwardly groaned: Eebard Peck would likely keep them there the rest of the day.

Eebard stood with his back to the door, searching those in the room with silvery eyes. A few strands of lank hair stretched across his otherwise bald skull.

"Havin' a secret meeting, I see," he shrilled. "About slaves, I reckon. Well, I don't s'pect you'd mind if I join you, seein's how I prob'ly got more of them folk to freedom than the lot of you combined." Eebard threw himself into a chair and folded his arms across his chest.

"This isn't an abolition meeting, Mr. Peck," Henry Stanton said, his voice amiable, "but you're welcome to stay, I'm sure."

That's very smart, Henry, thought Glynis. Better Eebard in here, contained, than out on the street ranting about exclusion from the ranks. Excluded not, of course, because he was crazy.

Eebard's glance continued to dart over all in the room, and Glynis knew those small silver eyes could glitter like sunlit ice whenever his two favorite topics came up: slavery, which, to the man's credit, he detested, and fertilizer, which he loved. Eebard could wax eloquent for hours on either subject, although Glynis would definitely give fertilizer the edge. Fertilizer had turned Eebard Peck's formerly barren farm, so he said, into a Garden of Eden. And while it was true that Eebard's land had recently begun to produce, just where exactly his herd of dairy cows and huge white Yorkshire pigs had come from was the subject of much speculation. Glynis thought it was probably safe to assume that, whatever fertilizer's other virtues, cattle and swine did not spring forth from it alone. But not to hear Eebard tell it.

The man regularly haunted the library for the farm journals to which she subscribed; he would sit at a table, running his hand across the pages of *Moore's Rural New Yorker*, punching each word he read with his index finger. He usually muttered to himself in a low staccato hum. Occasionally his voice would rise and then Glynis heard things like "Buckwheat!" and "Clover!" and "Yessiree. Plowed under, that's the ticket!"

She wondered about Eebard's affectation of a farmer twang. Once at the telegraph office Glynis had heard him dictating a wire; he spoke then like any other western New Yorker: nasal, broad *a*'s but no twang. She attributed it, like other aspects of Eebard Peck, to the eccentricity that demanded attention. The man made himself impossible to ignore.

She now saw others trying to disregard his twitching form, which looked as if it would at any second spring from his chair like a jack-in-the-box.

After another half hour of discussion, Henry Stanton said, "So, Olivant's first campaign speech in Seneca Falls will be Saturday, October seventh. Now, is there anything more we should discuss today? Or shall we adjourn and meet again next Monday?"

Eebard Peck leapt from his chair. "Now hold on," he shouted. "Just what do we all know about this here fancy Ole-vahnt? Are we sure he's agin slavery? Or is he just one of them hip-o-crites? Will he vow he'll do all in his power to wipe Satan's work off the face of the Lord's earth? And does he—"

"Mr. Peck," Gerrit Smith broke in smoothly, "perhaps you should ask Mr. Olivant those questions. And let us proceed here."

Eebard shook his head violently. "Cain't ask him," he

muttered, and unexpectedly sat down. "Man won't talk to me."

Behind Glynis someone said, "One more recommendation for Olivant." A soft chuckle followed.

Through the open window Glynis heard sudden excited voices, which sounded as if they came from Fall Street. She got up to close the window, but paused with her hands on the sill. On the road above, she could see Jacques Sundown leading his paint gelding. A man was slung face down over the horse's back.

"What's going on out there?" Gerrit Smith stood behind her, peering over Glynis's shoulder.

"I don't know. It looks as if someone's hurt."

At that moment Henry Stanton ended the meeting, and chairs scraped over the floor as people got to their feet. Glynis took this opportunity to slip outside and hurry up the steps to Fall Street where a small crowd had begun to gather around Jacques. He slowed his pace as Glynis went toward him.

"Jacques, what's happened? Who is . . . ?" She paused as two tan bloodhounds appeared behind Jacques. She now recognized the burly shape of the man over the horse.

"Lyle Brogan," she whispered, and then saw the bloodstains. "Is he . . . ?"

Jacques's flat brown eyes stared at her. "You know him?"

"Yes. Well, no. That is . . . I've met him. Jacques, is he dead?"

"He's dead." Jacques's tone, as flat as the eyes, expressed nothing beyond the words.

Jacques Sundown hadn't changed in six years, Glynis thought distractedly; the irrelevancy of this observation, however, did not lessen the shock of seeing Brogan's corpse.

Just then someone jostled her from behind, and she stumbled forward. When Jacques's hand shot out to grip her shoulder, Glynis winced more from surprise than pain. She had forgotten his strength. How fast he moved.

Her shoulder tingled and, reaching up to rub it, her fingers brushed Jacques's hand. He released her abruptly, almost shoving her away, before he stepped back.

"Got to get him to Dr. Ives." His eyes flicked back at Brogan's body. "Need a death certificate. You wait for me at the firehouse."

With the hounds pacing beside him, and the paint clopping behind, Jacques continued up Fall Street. Lyle Brogan's torso hung over the horse, his lifeless arms and legs swaying back and forth in a macabre dance.

IT WAS ANOTHER hour before Glynis managed to get away from the library, and then she set out rapidly for the firehouse. Passing the Bakery-and-Confectioner-Shoppe, she ignored the smells that normally forced her to step inside. She hardly glanced at the Widow Coddington's millinery shop with its beguiling windows of straw hats, caps of silk, bonnets of velvet trimmed with flowers and feathers and plumes and lace, all perched on white wooden forms the size and shape of ostrich eggs.

Up and down Fall Street carriages had stopped while their occupants exchanged gossip, and horses stood patiently flicking their tails at flies. There were a few excited voices, some indignant gestures, but Glynis thought the town as a whole appeared rather calm about the fact that death had just passed through. Or perhaps, because the dead man was a stranger with a dubious occupation, it didn't much care. She herself experienced no distress at Brogan's death, and supposed she should feel guilty about this, but couldn't. However, she was curious as to how he had died. From the snatches of conversation she overheard, there seemed to be an assumption that Brogan's death was accidental. An assumption no doubt encouraged by Jacques Sundown.

When she came abreast of John Boone's livery stable, she slowed her pace. Zephaniah Waters sat on a stool grooming a trotter just outside wide doors that led to the horse stalls. The young Negro's head pressed against the flank of the horse, and he didn't look up as she approached.

"Zeph . . . hello."

His head jerked up, and Zeph spun around on his stool. His startled look eased somewhat when he recognized her. "Miss Tryon." He put down the brush and currycomb, and stood with arms dangling at his sides, wrists and forearms protruding from sleeves of a coarse cotton shirt that stretched taut over his shoulders.

"Zeph, two copies of *Bleak House*, the new Dickens I told you about, came in yesterday. I thought you might want to borrow one."

The large dark eyes that had at first narrowed in wariness now became less guarded. The boy took a few steps toward her, and she realized he must have grown again. He had to be close to six feet, and he was still in his early teens.

"Have you read it?" he asked her.

"I just started it yesterday, Zeph. I can't say yet whether I like it as much as *Oliver Twist* or *David Copperfield.*"

The boy had read both. He nodded and shifted his bare feet. "I'll be by then."

"Jonathan can get it for you if I'm not in."

"When *will* you be?" he interrupted.

She should have known Zeph wouldn't set foot in the library if she wasn't there. Now that Cullen was gone, she wondered if she was the only white person in town he trusted. At least she seemed to be the only one he talked to voluntarily.

"Come by tomorrow morning, Zeph. I'll be there then."

The boy inclined his head slightly, picked up the brush, and went back to the trotter.

Glynis rounded the firehouse, hesitating before she entered the constable's office. It would be her first time there since Cullen left. She had thought Jacques Sundown would come by the library when he arrived in Seneca Falls; after all, before he'd left so abruptly six years ago, the town had been involved in a series of murders that together they'd solved. Not that she and Jacques were what anyone would call friends. But she was a little hurt that he hadn't made any attempt to see her. And the only reason he wanted to now was because she had recognized Brogan, though she couldn't see that the man's death had anything to do with her.

She rapped on the open door, steeling herself to see someone other than Cullen behind the big desk. Jacques stood in front of a wooden cabinet; motioning to her with his head, he continued to shuffle through file folders. Glynis went in and sat down opposite the desk. He certainly didn't seem to be in any hurry.

Jacques must now be in his late twenties, she figured, but he didn't appear to have aged much in the past years. Coppery skin and black hair indicated his Indian background; the name Sundown was common enough among Senecas in western New York. Jacques's father had been French, but this man's sharp features, high cheekbones, and height didn't resemble the French with whom Glynis was familiar.

Cullen called Jacques Sundown "Dagwunnoyaent"—the name of a Seneca wind spirit. And in fact, Jacques reminded Glynis of nothing so much as a powerful sleek red hawk, one that drifted idly on the wind a split second before it shot like an arrow toward its doomed prey.

Seven years before, Jacques Sundown had rescued Cullen, badly outnumbered in a violent bar brawl. Cullen said he never saw a man move so effectively so fast, and he hired Jacques as deputy that night. Glynis knew little of Jacques's personal history—it was hard enough to get him to answer for the present. She guessed it wouldn't do any good to ask why he'd been in Quebec when Cullen found him. Unless he'd changed.

Something wet and cold suddenly nudged her wrist; she looked down to see one of the bloodhounds shoving his nose into her hand. He sniffed at her skirts while his ropy tail swung back and forth. From behind the desk his companion's tail emerged to thump the floor.

Glynis bent to scratch the dog's wrinkled neck. "They seem so docile, these dogs," she said to Jacques, who still stood at the file cabinet. "Friendly. I'd always assumed they were vicious animals, but their reputation must come from their name . . ."

Her voice broke off as Jacques's expressionless face turned to her. Glynis bit down on her lower lip. She hadn't been trying to say anything profound, for heaven's sake, just break the ice between them. It had been six years! But his look said she'd either lost her wits or must be intensely stupid. Instead of years it might have been yesterday she'd last seen that look.

"I mean," she floundered, "that is ... well, *bloodhounds*. What a name!"

Jacques shifted from the cabinet to the desk chair in a single lithe movement. "Name comes from 'blooded hounds.' "

He said this slowly, as though she might have difficulty understanding. "Not bred as fighting dogs—they're not vicious. Bred special for tracking. They're supposed to be best at it— like blue-blooded people. If you believe that."

Believe that? After all the times Jacques had been called "half-breed"? But Glynis remembered she never could tell when he was joking.

"Are you going to keep the dogs?" she asked.

"Don't know."

"Well, if not," she said, "what are you going to do with them?"

"Feed them."

Why was it, Glynis asked herself, that Jacques Sundown could still make her feel like a fool? Why did she let him? "You said you wanted to see me," she said finally. "About Brogan?"

He shifted in the chair. "Stopped by the library to tell you. Some kids found the body. At an abandoned cabin up-river. I was on my way to fetch it. Thought you'd want to know."

"Why would *I* want to know?" she said.

"You always wanted to know before when bodies turned up."

"Jacques!" He *was* making fun of her. Still. "That was a different situation entirely and you know it. And it was years ago!"

Glynis realized her voice had risen when the hound lifted his head with a short bark. Jacques stared at her, and she thought something moved behind his eyes. He was laughing at her.

"How come you knew Brogan?"

Glynis took a deep breath and sat back, trying for dignity. "I met him on Fall Street, Saturday, when he asked directions to find you—in a southern drawl."

"Didn't find me. Never saw him before today."

"That's strange," she said, frowning. "He wanted to see you because he was looking for someone named Farley. Thomas Farley, I think he said."

"You know him? Farley?"

"No. But I'm sure Brogan was a slave-catcher, so this Farley might be a runaway he was tracking." She looked down at the bloodhounds, now both sleeping at her feet. Hard to believe these sweet-tempered dogs inspired so much terror; although from what Jacques just said, only the men behind the dogs were to be feared. "Do you need an inquest?" she asked.

"Not much question how he died. Dr. Ives says Brogan was stabbed. Looked like knife wounds to me. Don't need an inquest."

"So he was killed," Glynis said.

Jacques grunted. "Hard for a man to give himself that kind of damage."

"Well, who in Seneca Falls would want to kill Lyle Brogan?" As soon as the words were out of her mouth, likely prospects jumped to mind. No, she told herself; this didn't concern her.

"I recollect," Jacques said, "you used to be good at this 'who would want to kill somebody' business. . . ."

So he did remember. It suddenly occurred to her that he perhaps wanted help. After all, he was constable now, not simply Cullen's deputy, and he might feel at a disadvantage, having been away from town for so long. Not that his pride would ever let him say.

"All right, Jacques, I'll try," she said reluctantly, telling herself she did it for Cullen—his regard for Jacques. "Suppose Brogan had caught up with a runaway?"

"Any in town?"

She shook her head. "None that I've heard of. But things have changed here since you left." Glynis paused to think; better to not mention the Underground. "What with the railroads now, the new western states . . . the town isn't as quite as settled as it once was. People come and go, passing through, all the time. Besides, when does Dr. Ives think Brogan was killed?"

"Can't tell for sure. Probably couple days ago."

"Then whoever did it could be miles away by now. But Brogan was still alive Saturday night—I saw him at the theater performance. He left the party . . . wait . . . Jacques, I don't know exactly when he left, but he had with him a woman from the theater troupe. Luella, I think her name is— she might know something. Calista Sligh told me Brogan and this Luella were, ah . . . well, 'old friends' is what Calista said."

"That what they looked like to you?"

"They certainly seemed . . . that is, they acted like they were *very* good friends."

Intensely aware that her face flushed, Glynis glanced sideways at Jacques. No response. She couldn't tell if he understood or not.

"Would a woman have been strong enough to stab Brogan?" she asked quickly to change the subject. "I don't know much about that sort of thing . . ."

"Sharp enough knife, him not ready for it—anybody could do it. This Luella woman friendly with anybody else, you know?"

"You mean . . . ." Glynis hesitated. "You mean, could another man have been jealous of Brogan? Maybe someone in the theater troupe?"

Jacques's shoulders twitched; on anyone more demonstrative, it might have been a shrug. "Wouldn't be the first time a man got killed over a woman." His voice carried an unfamiliar edge.

"I guess not," she said, after waiting to see if he would volunteer more. "It seems farfetched, but I guess it's possible. Did Brogan have money with him, when you found him?"

"Yeah."

"A lot of money?"

"Three hundred dollars."

"That much? Don't you think that's a little strange?"

"Yeah."

"Jacques, can you be a little more . . . expansive?" Why did she bother—can pigs fly? She felt as if she were pulling teeth, one by one. With a sigh, she went on, "Well, with that amount of money, robbery couldn't have been a reason for the man's murder. Was there anything else, well, out of the ordi-

nary you can tell me? So I don't have to keep stabbing around
in the dark . . . oh. Oh, I didn't mean *that* exactly."

Heat flooded her cheeks. Jacques watched her as he might
a lunatic he thought could be dangerous.

Finally he said, "No handbill."

"No handbill?" she repeated. "What . . . ? Oh, I see what
you mean. This *is* peculiar, if Brogan was after a runaway.
He'd need a picture to show the marshals."

"Wouldn't have it on him if the one who killed him was the
runaway."

"Who took the handbill, but left Brogan's money?" Glynis
said. "That seems odd. What do you think?"

"I think I don't like it. Think I better find this Luella
woman." Jacques pushed his chair back from the desk and
stood. Unwinding from their curled positions, the two hounds
scrambled to their feet.

*Thank you very much for coming in, Miss Tryon. I appre-
ciate your time, Miss Tryon. And your suggestions, Miss
Tryon.* Ha! She could wait for him to say something like that
until doomsday!

Glynis looked at the dogs, who stood watching Jacques's
every move expectantly. "They're like shadows," she said,
thinking the hounds might bridge the chasm between them.
"What are you going to call them?"

"Dogs."

They were at his heels as he walked to the door.

HOW COULD IT be possible that Jacques Sundown had not
changed in six years? How could *anyone* not change in six
years? Glynis pondered as she went through the front door of
her boardinghouse.

Voices came from the kitchen. She recognized Harriet's,
but couldn't place the other. It wasn't Dictras Fyfe's. Toenails
clicked on the wood floor and Duncan appeared, tail going
like a metronome. Standing on his hind legs, he planted his
forepaws on her skirt and sniffed furiously. Bloodhound
smell? Then, apparently satisfied she had not brought the in-
terlopers with her, he turned to trot back down the hall.
Glynis followed him, pausing in the kitchen doorway.

Harriet turned from the stove, her face radiant. "Glynis,

look who's just dropped in out of nowhere." She gestured toward the table.

A young man's face, dark hazel eyes and expression much like Harriet's, met her with a familiar grin.

"Niles!" Glynis said, moving toward him. "When did you get here?"

Harriet's son stood to wrap his arms around Glynis. "It's a long story," he said with his face against her hair. Still holding her shoulders, Niles took a step back to look down at her. "Glad you're home," he said quietly. "I stopped by the library, but you'd already left." He frowned and ran a hand through shiny dark-brown hair.

He looked so pale, Glynis thought with some concern. There seemed to be an edginess about him; the vitality, the exuberant zest, were missing. But then, hardly anything about Niles resembled the adolescent Glynis had first met twelve years before. She had watched him grow: leave for college, then art school, graduate and move to New York City to start his own gallery. She'd watched young women watching him, laughing their self-conscious "notice-me" laughs and smoothing their hair. Niles rarely appeared to see them. His eyes seemed always to be focused on something beyond.

He must be, what, twenty-six now? Still young, to her, though he didn't look young at that moment. He looked worried. On edge, she thought again.

"How long have you been here, Niles?" she asked him. "You look as if you could use some rest."

"That's what I said," Harriet agreed. "But he wanted to wait for you."

"Didn't want to go through the story more than once," Niles said, slipping back into his chair. "I need some help—from both of you."

Glynis smiled and sat down. "Now, since when have you needed help? You were always so independent."

Harriet sighed. "Never could tell him anything." But she smiled with warmth and a look of affection. As though her son had stepped from yesterday into this moment without years or distance passing between.

Niles glanced up at his mother, held her eyes a moment, then shook his head slightly. He turned to stare out the window. "Garden looks . . . well, like it's always looked. Like home."

There was in his voice something melancholy; something that again made Glynis aware of a difference in him.

"Niles, has anything happened?" she asked. "You seem . . ." her voice trailed off.

He shook himself a little. "Mother's got supper ready," he answered. "I don't know about you, but I'm starving. Why don't we all go ahead and eat, while I tell you. What's happened."

SIX

❦

It's my duty to prepare you for a train of circumstances that may, and I go so far as to say that will, shock you.
—CHARLES DICKENS, *BLEAK HOUSE*

"THE WHOLE THING began well over a year ago," Niles said, pausing to brush crumbs of corn bread from his clean-shaven chin, "when I went to a William and Mary college reunion. Took a few canvases along to Williamsburg—some of my own work, and several Hudson River artists'—to a gallery there. I'd been in Virginia only a couple of days when the gallery owner told me that some tobacco planter, a Victor St. Croix, had purchased every piece I'd brought. And wanted more. You can imagine how I felt. My own gallery's been doing fine, but southern patrons sounded . . . I don't know . . . exotic, I guess. So I rushed back to New York, gathered up canvases, and headed south again to the St. Croix place—it's just east of Richmond.

"I'll spare you both the details of transporting, alone, three large crates of paintings from Broadway to the New York Central train station, through Philadelphia, Baltimore, Washington, and finally Richmond. I must have been mad! Still, I didn't think I could pass up the opportunity.

"In any event, I finally arrived, painting intact, at the St. Croix plantation, Jolimont." Niles stopped, then repeated the name; it rolled off his tongue like *Joe-lee-mone.* "It's the biggest farm you ever saw, hundreds and hundreds of acres, almost like a small city. Seems it's been in the St. Croix family for over a century, since ten thousand acres along the James River were given to Huguenots fleeing Catholic France.

"Anyway, St. Croix and his wife Katherine—she's his second wife—offered me a drink on the veranda. And then, out of the plantation house walks this girl . . ."

Niles hesitated. For the first time that afternoon Glynis saw real liveliness appear on his face as the memory surfaced.

And something else, unfamiliar. "Well, she's not exactly a girl," he corrected himself. "She's eighteen. And so beautiful she ... well, she just took my breath away. ..."

His voice broke off. The liveliness in his face abruptly vanished, and he stared down at the coffee steaming in his cup. Harriet's eyebrows lifted with impatience as she handed him a pitcher of cream. Niles poured the cream into his coffee and stirred, endlessly, watching it swirl; at this point it seemed clear to Glynis that his stalling foreshadowed bad news.

When he finally raised his eyes, it was to glance back and forth from his mother to Glynis. What in the world so troubled him? wondered Glynis uneasily. What did he find so hard to tell them? After all, people often fell into love unexpectedly—and that's what she guessed had happened—but it wasn't considered a crime.

After picking at a few loose threads in the linen tablecloth, Niles threw himself back in his chair. Taking a deep breath, he exhaled it heavily. "For days I've tried to figure out how to tell you this, but I guess there's just no good way." He tipped backward until the front legs of his chair lifted off the floor; Harriet's lips pursed exactly as they had when he'd done this years before.

Rocking on the chair's back legs, Niles thrust his hands into his trouser pockets. Glynis decided nothing he could possibly have to say would be worthy of this suspense.

And Harriet looked ready to jump out of her skin. "Niles!"

"All right! You're not going to like this no matter how I say it." He inhaled raggedly. "I fell in love with that girl the instant I saw her ... and she's a slave ... and she's not white. That is, she's part Negro. Mulatto, they call it—although she's really a quadroon. But none of that matters, because the law says she's a Negro if she's got *any* Negro blood. And that's the whole story!"

Niles pitched himself forward, the front legs of the chair striking the floor with a loud thump. Yanking his hands from his pockets, he brought his open palms down on the tabletop. The slap rattled the dishes. Then he hunched forward, staring at his mother.

In the hushed kitchen, shock flashed like heat lightning. Glynis turned mutely to Harriet, who had gone deathly pale, beads of perspiration forming on her upper lip. Niles's hands still rested on the table, but he'd clenched them into fists.

Glynis became slowly but acutely aware of the smell of coffee. An ordinary, everyday, commonplace smell. For what seemed an eternity, all she heard was labored breathing; they were, all three of them, taking in the very same air but might each have been on separate continents.

Harriet, at last, cleared her throat with obvious difficulty. "I doubt if that's really 'the whole story,' Niles." Now she coughed slightly, dislodging words still caught in her throat. "Surely there must be more to it?" Her voice seemed far away, as if she had withdrawn to another room.

"Well, yes!" Niles answered, his tone uncommonly curt. Why does he sound so harsh? He unquestionably realized how stunned his mother would be.

"Her name . . . her name's Kiri!" Niles said this with emphasis, as though expecting to find himself contradicted. "It means some kind of flower; at least that's what her mother told her. Her mother was a slave too. Mulatto."

Glynis thought suddenly of Jacques Sundown—called "half-blood" and "half-breed." A cruel fate, to be neither one nor the other. What could Niles be thinking of? *Was* he thinking? No, of course not: he said he was in love.

Harriet passed a hand over her eyes, then cleared her throat again. "Her name, Niles . . . it's just . . . Kiri?"

Niles glanced at Glynis, then back across the table at his mother. Glynis, seated next to him, could see tears spurt and threaten to overflow; she didn't know what Harriet could see. Niles's fingers dashed at his eyes, plucked at the tablecloth, and then were still. "Mother, she doesn't exactly have a surname," he said, his voice cracking. "Her mother died years ago, and she doesn't know who her father . . ." His voice cracked again as he broke off.

Harriet had sat very still. But now she shook her head a little, heavy silver-gold hair brushing her face, hoping perhaps to shake away his words. "I suppose," she said at last, slowly, "not knowing her father . . . that's hardly the girl's fault, is it? I wouldn't hold that against her."

Glynis had not for a moment doubted it. But Niles's immense sigh of relief stirred the charged air.

"Maybe you ought to come home more often, Niles." Glynis didn't bother to conceal the irritation in her voice. "Get to know your mother better!"

Niles gazed down at his empty plate. A sheepish smile reminded Glynis of the time he'd been caught feeding his mashed turnip to the dog next door; the detested turnip that during supper he'd somehow concealed in his napkin. Harriet had laughed, that night, at his ingenuity.

Now Glynis watched her struggle to compose herself. She knew Harriet well enough to guess the woman would search for something, anything, optimistic in her son's words.

Maybe Niles suffered from infatuation, a condition that could pass, given enough time. But since "it will pass" is what Harriet assured her after Cullen's departure—and since the passage now seemed interminable—Glynis didn't feel eager to foist this upon Niles. However, Niles lived in New York, the girl in Virginia; they were both young; time and distance might resolve the whole potential catastrophe.

Niles's next words blew that hope sky-high. "Actually, that's not quite all of it," he said, the gravity in his voice unmistakable.

Glynis's head shot up; she didn't dare look at Harriet.

"Kiri left . . ." Niles shook his head. "No. No, I mean she escaped—from St. Croix's plantation. Ran away. And . . . I've brought her here."

"Here?" Harriet gasped. "To Seneca Falls? Oh, Niles, you couldn't have."

To which Glynis added quickly, "You *didn't* encourage the girl to run, did you? You surely didn't help her to escape?"

But his expression gave answer enough.

"Niles, that's against the law," Glynis said sharply. Didn't he know that? "It's terribly dangerous for you. What if you're caught?"

"I don't intend to *get* caught," he answered, with a reckless look she had seen on him before. "But I need your help."

Harriet swiped at her wet cheeks. She shook her head again several times and stared at her son. "I don't understand," she said, finally. "I just don't understand."

"I told you, Mother. I love her. I want to take her to Canada. Marry her there."

Harriet's hard-held composure crumbled; although she wept quietly, the sound of her pain penetrated every corner of the kitchen.

Glynis desperately tried to convince herself that Niles must be temporarily deranged. At any moment he would come to his senses. How could breaking the law, to say nothing of violating powerful—in fact, omnipotent—social codes, be in any way construed as sane behavior? Surely, if he were caught, the legal system would take this into account.

Niles, shoving his chair away from the table, jumped up abruptly and went to the back door. "I guess I knew you couldn't approve of this," he said in a hot, dry voice. He reached for the door handle. "But I thought you might at least *try* to understand . . ."

He pulled the door open, but paused with his hand still on the handle.

It occurred to Glynis then—how could she have been so heartless?—that all this must be as hard for Niles as for his mother. "Niles, wait!" she called, as Harriet seemed beyond speech. "The girl—what does she think about this? Is she willing to place you in the jeopardy *you'll* be in, if you persist?"

Niles turned in the doorway; without hesitation he said, "No. No, she isn't. She was so reluctant to run away with me it took weeks to convince her. And at the last minute—well, I almost had to kidnap her. I think . . ." He stopped, his forehead creasing. "I think she's afraid my intentions aren't honorable. That I won't marry her. I don't know how she can think that . . ."

He paused, sighed, and stepped back inside to lean against the open door. "But slave women are sometimes . . . well, mistreated by white men. Badly mistreated," he said, looking at Glynis as if hoping he wouldn't have to be more specific.

She wished she didn't understand, but how could she not? She would imagine, now forced to consider it, that female slaves might be violated with impunity, without even the doubtful deterrent of legal protection. For if this legal protection was not even available to white married women against rape by their husbands, how much more vulnerable were black slave women?

Niles's voice sounded more agitated when he said, "Kiri doesn't trust easily. Any of us. I thought she would see I wasn't like men she'd been accustomed to. That I wouldn't touch her—and I swear I haven't . . ." He broke off.

Glynis believed him. She had known him too long not to. Furthermore, if he had wanted solely to seduce the girl, he could have done that in Virginia, without risking everything to bring her north. Surely the girl must realize that. Unless . . .

"You say you're in love with her," she said. "But Niles, how does she feel about you? Could it be that she simply used you to help her escape?"

"No! You don't know her or you wouldn't say that. But . . ." His voice faltered. "But how she feels? She's so afraid, now, she probably doesn't know what she feels. Other than fear."

"This speculation about who feels what is a waste of time," Harriet unexpectedly blurted. "What's important now, Niles, is what are you going to *do*? And where in heaven's name is the girl?" Her voice sounded stronger; she shook out her handkerchief, brandishing it like a white flag, then blew her nose with great dignity.

Glynis wanted to applaud with relief; this sounded more like Harriet.

"Kiri's at Reverend Eames's church," Niles said. He appeared somewhat startled by his mother's recovery, but plainly intended to take advantage of it. "She can't stay there much longer though, because more runaways are due in tonight. And there's already someone looking for her. We think he followed us. A slave-catcher."

"A slave-catcher?" Glynis repeated. No; no, it couldn't have been Brogan. It couldn't! "Niles, just when—exactly— did you and the girl get here? Today?"

Please Lord, let it have been today!

"No, not today," he said, "we got here Saturday. Right after dark. But I've stayed with Kiri at the church because she's so frightened. And I thought I'd better scout around some, see who was in town, before I came here . . . and involved you two."

"Why do you think someone followed you?" Glynis asked him, trying to ignore the scenes swarming in her mind.

Scenes that included Lyle Brogan's death. How could she be so certain Niles would never rape a woman—but so uncertain as to whether he could kill a man?

And Niles looked tense when he said, "Kiri felt sure St. Croix would send someone after her. She said he'd hired slave-catchers before when his slaves ran away."

"And have you seen anyone—has *she* seen anyone that looked like—"

"Glynis," Harriet interrupted. "I think we need to know what Niles intends to do now."

Glynis bit her lower lip. Harriet didn't know about Lyle Brogan's death, and she might not make any connection if she did. But if Brogan had been after the girl, to what lengths might Niles have gone to protect her? And if this were so, who then was the "Farley" person for whom Brogan had searched? Another slave-catcher—maybe even a southern sympathizer who served as informer for the slaveholders? Glynis had heard of such people. Could there be someone like that here in Seneca Falls? That might explain why several runaways had been caught recently. The young man on the train in February, for instance; she wondered at the time how those marshals knew . . .

"Glynis?" Harriet stared at her.

"Sorry, Harriet. What?"

"Niles wants to bring the girl here as soon as it's dark."

Well, Glynis told herself, she should have known she couldn't avoid forever the dilemma created by the Fugitive Slave Law.

Four years before, Congress enacted legislation that granted a new California territory admission into the Union as a free state, as most northerners and the Californians themselves wanted. But since a free California would upset an existing balance in Congress between the fifteen free and the fifteen slave states, southerners threatened secession. Within terms of the 1850 Compromise, the South agreed to stay in the Union, but only if the North ceased obstructing the recovery of their fugitive slaves. Hence Congress voted to strengthen an earlier, already existing statute—now known as the Fugitive Slave Law.

Cullen Stuart had dodged the issue by remaining more or

less uninvolved; he, like the majority of northerners, had no ambition to interfere with slavery where it already existed. But he would not voluntarily help southern slaveholders hunt down their slaves trying to escape north to freedom. So when he could, he looked the other way. He risked heavy penalties by doing so, both legal and personal: Cullen believed in the rule of law, and Glynis understood how much discomfort his ambivalence caused him.

Harriet felt no such ambiguity about the Fugitive Slave Law and had worked with the Underground movement for several years. But Glynis could see the woman's conflict at this particular moment. Harriet could well be assisting a situation in which, if Niles fled to Canada, she might never see her son again. But how would she feel if Niles was caught, arrested and imprisoned? And how would Niles feel about his mother if the girl whom he loved was sent back to slavery because Harriet had refused her help?

"Glynis," Harriet repeated, her usually placid eyes revealing intense distress. "I said that Niles wants—"

"Yes, I heard," Glynis said. "Harriet, I know this is difficult—but I'm not sure you have much choice. The alternatives might be worse."

Harriet nodded as if she had already determined that and simply sought reassurance. "Yes, all right, Niles. Bring the girl here," she told him. "Thank heavens Dictras Fyfe's away in Syracuse!"

"Good," Niles said readily, "I'll sleep on the porch to keep an eye out for strangers. Although I don't think Victor St. Croix knows I have any connection with Seneca Falls. Just New York City. I was careful about that—so we probably don't have anything to worry about."

Glynis tried to remember: what had it been like to be so young, and so oblivious?

EIGHT . . . NINE . . . TEN. When the front parlor clock finished chiming, Glynis went to the window, as they'd arranged, to remove an oil lamp from the sill. Against the pane the night pressed darkly; as yet moonless. After untying the yellow satin draperies, she let them fall back into place across the window. Then she returned to the kitchen, where Harriet had just finished snuffing candles. Glynis lowered the lamp wick, and they sat down at the table to wait.

The only sound other than Duncan snoring under the table was the soft metallic click of Harriet's knitting needles. She once said that if all the socks she had knit for Underground fugitives were positioned heel to toe, they would stretch to the North Star.

The lamp's light flickered dimly. Needing to squint, Glynis hunched over *Bleak House* but found she couldn't concentrate on even the intriguing character of Dickens's detective, Mr. Bucket: "there is nothing remarkable about him at first sight but his ghostly manner of appearing."

Glynis glanced quickly toward the kitchen door.

She kept seeing Lyle Brogan's limbs swinging from Jacques Sundown's paint. How could she ignore the possibility that Brogan's murder might have involved Niles and the girl?

Every now and again a floorboard creaked, or an overhead beam ticked, contracting in the cooler air of nightfall. Then her eyes flew to the door. As did Harriet's. The moon would rise soon; what kept Niles?

Glynis realized she'd dozed off only when she jumped at Duncan's menacing growl. She reached down to put her fingers around the terrier's muzzle, clamping his mouth shut. The growl just went deeper. "Hush, Duncan!"

Harriet's chair scraped loudly against the floor as the door swung open. Niles stepped into the kitchen.

He pulled someone in behind him by the hand. The someone appeared, for all the world, to be a slim boy, averted face concealed by a floppy-brimmed straw hat. A loose, white cotton shirt had been tucked into baggy doeskin trousers.

"Niles, what kept you?" Harriet asked anxiously, then gave a nervous laugh and added, in more normal tone, "We were concerned!"

Niles nodded. "Just being cautious. And Kiri needed some persuading before she'd come." His hand still clasping hers, he turned to the girl behind him, who stood with head inclined just inside the door. She gave Harriet and Glynis a swift upward glance from under the straw hat; then stared down at where Duncan, his tail swinging back and forth, had planted himself.

"Mother, this is Kiri." Niles gave the girl's hand a small tug. "Kiri?"

Kiri pulled her hand from his to remove the hat. "Miz Peartree, ma'am . . . thank you for having me." Her voice had a whispery quality, like folds of silk rubbing together, and her shoulders rounded forward slightly as if she were about to bow. Glynis fervently hoped she wouldn't. But the girl's gaze simply brushed Harriet before it returned to the floor.

Niles had been right about her beauty. Glynis wondered, when he said the girl was mulatto, if she had escaped by passing for white. But she couldn't have; her skin matched perfectly the dusky brown of her doeskin trousers. Her hair had been cropped extremely short, tight-curled as a Persian lamb's, and her cheekbones appeared sculpted, Glynis thought, high and defined as her own. She had seen a few mulatto women in Rochester and although they were striking-looking, none had this girl's fragile loveliness. The fragility made Kiri still more appealing, even if it proved deceptive— and Glynis rapidly determined the girl must be hardier than she appeared. But it could well be understood why Niles had been drawn to her. Niles the artist even more so.

An awkward silence followed before Harriet said firmly, "You're welcome here, Kiri, of course." She extended her hand. The girl seemed to hesitate, then stretched out her own with a quick, shy glance at Niles.

Niles's shoulders relaxed with a shrug; he smiled and introduced Glynis.

Kiri's head came up then, bringing remarkable wide dark eyes level with Glynis's own; she seemed suddenly taller than Glynis had initially thought. The silken voice murmured, "Niles talks of you with affection."

"Would you like some tea?" Harriet said cheerily, too cheerily, then turned to shut the door as if forgetting what she'd asked. Glynis could imagine with what effort the woman attempted normalcy.

"What are your plans now?" Glynis said to Niles when they'd sat down around the table. She noticed that Kiri watched Harriet carefully, uneasily it seemed, and Glynis wondered what had been the girl's work at the plantation. She probably wasn't accustomed to anyone waiting on her. And Kiri finally rose from the table and went to Harriet, who now stood at the stove.

"May Ah help, Miz Peartree?"

"No! Oh, no!" Harriet answered quickly. Her face immediately flushed with an embarrassment painful to see, and there followed another gaping hole of silence.

"I'm sorry," Harriet said at last, recovering her usual warmth, "of course, you can help. I'm afraid I'm a little flustered tonight." She handed Kiri the pot of tea.

As Kiri turned back to the table, Glynis saw something that might have been humor brighten the girl's eyes. However, Kiri said solemnly enough, "Ah wasn't ever a kitchen maid, Miz Peartree. So please don't fret about that."

The brightness in her look lingered after she sat down. But when she turned to Niles it disappeared, to be replaced by something more complicated. Glynis couldn't read Kiri's gaze, couldn't even hazard a guess as to what the girl thought. Did she really care for Niles? Or had he simply been her means of escaping from slavery? Or because of her distrust of white men, could she herself not know how she felt?

In any case, it surely took courage of heroic proportions to escape as she had. To leave behind all she knew. Had her life been so unbearable that she would entrust her safety to a young white man? Travel hundreds of miles with him—Niles had told of swamps and rivers and forests, camouflaged carriage-house passages, concealed attic rooms, basement cubicles and hidden cramped cupboards in farmhouses and barns, inns and churches—so that she might arrive in the unfamiliar North with apparently only the clothes on her back and the hope of goodwill from complete strangers?

And what now? Now that she had come so far?

SEVEN

❦

*"Now where," pursues Mr. Bucket, "had she been on
the night of the murder? She had been to the theayter."*
—CHARLES DICKENS, *BLEAK HOUSE*

BY THE TIME Glynis reached Fall Street the following humid
morning, damp petticoats that clung to her cotton stockings
made every step precarious; once again she thought with
longing of the dearly departed bloomer costume. From low-
hanging black clouds, rain fell as yet only in intermittent
sprinkles. But a downpour threatened. Up the road Niles suddenly appeared, riding from Boone's Livery; he turned his
horse onto State Street, undoubtedly headed for Reverend
Eames's church.

The night before Niles had outlined his plan. With the other
runaways due into Seneca Falls, Kiri would travel north to the
port of Oswego and cross Lake Ontario to Canada. She could
then wait for Niles in a Kingston church used by the Underground Railroad. In the meantime Niles would return to New
York City.

"I've sold my gallery," he told them. "Just need to sign the
final papers and arrange for my inventory to be shipped to
Montreal to the gallery I'll work from temporarily—until I
can set up one of my own."

"You've been planning this for some time, haven't you?"
Harriet asked him.

Niles must have caught the note of pain in her voice.
"Yes, Mother, and I'm sorry I couldn't tell you sooner. But
it seemed best to involve as few people as possible. The
whole thing's been a risky affair." He added, somewhat
lamely, "Besides, I didn't know exactly when we were going to make a run for it, so the details had to wait till the
last minute."

Glynis thought it just as likely that he didn't want to hear
what certainly would have been his mother's protests.

Now wiping perspiration from her forehead, she entered the library on a rumble of distant thunder.

"Morning, Miss Tryon." Jonathan Quant nodded to her energetically and went on shelving new acquisitions. "Zeph Waters looked in earlier," he said over his shoulder, "but then walked right back out when he saw you weren't here." Jonathan smiled ruefully. "I had the Dickens ready for him, too."

"Don't take it personally, Jonathan," Glynis sighed. "You know Zeph is . . . well, shy." Jonathan smiled again and bobbed his head. It was difficult, Glynis thought, to imagine what, if anything, could offend him.

Moments later the library door swung open and Zeph Waters stepped inside; he must have been watching for her.

"Morning, Zeph," Glynis said to him. "I'll get the copy of *Bleak House* for you. I've read a fair amount now—and it's rather confusing in the beginning. Dickens assumes his readers are familiar with the British court system, but of course we Americans aren't. And it's important to the story line because the novel's characters exist in a legal predicament that came about long before they were born—that is, they're bound by conditions they had no hand in creating."

Rather, she thought suddenly, like the plight of American slaves—permanently imprisoned by a past, not of their making, from which they could not extricate themselves. Because Kiri's mother had been a slave, Kiri's circumstances were fixed even before her birth.

While Glynis was talking, Jonathan, with characteristic tact, faded toward the back office after pointing to the volume on his desk. Zeph waited for him to disappear, then snatched up the book. Watching him leaf through it, Glynis recalled the difficulty, about a year ago, under which they'd met.

She had been working in her office when she heard Cullen call to her from the library proper; she found him gripping by the collar a lanky, dour-faced Negro boy Glynis knew only as "the Waters kid." The boy held a book under his arm. And Cullen looked provoked.

"Just happened to see this lad," he explained, "leaving with one of your books. Funny thing is, he shoved it under his jacket when he saw me. Since he doesn't seem to have a subscription card, did he have your permission to borrow it?"

Glynis glanced from Cullen to the boy, whose sullen eyes simply stared at the floor. Cullen took the volume from Zeph and handed it to her with a look that said, "It's up to you." The book's title was *Uncle Tom's Cabin*.

Glynis studied the boy with interest; this book wasn't something most youngsters would choose to read. He probably went to one of the public schools, but Glynis didn't think teachers would be recommending Stowe's novel to young people. Still, he'd taken only this particular book—one about slavery.

She suddenly realized the boy had been watching her with what seemed to be a mixture of defiance and appraisal; since she hadn't reacted immediately, he must be wondering what she would do.

What she did, for some reason she couldn't have explained at the time, was to say, "Well, yes, Cullen, as a matter of fact I *may* have indicated he could read the book. Obviously, there's been a misunderstanding here."

"Then he's a library subscriber?" Cullen asked, his voice as even as his gaze.

"Ah ... well, we were going to discuss that, I believe, weren't we?" Glynis answered with her eyes on the boy's face. The youngster's head jerked up to stare at her with a startled expression. But he recovered rapidly to give a short nod.

Cullen released his collar. "All right, just wanted to make sure," he said. "Sorry, Zeph. My mistake."

When Cullen left, Glynis explained the library's subscription rules without comment on the "misunderstanding," and waited for the boy's response.

"I don't have money for a subscription," he told her, his face sullen again.

"But you do want to read this book," Glynis said. "That is, I assume, what you planned to do with it."

His expression altered a little. The frown smoothed. Glynis even wondered if he would relent and smile. No. "You think

I can't read, don't you?" he asked, his tone as much amused as belligerent.

"No, I don't think that," she said. "It seems to me if someone goes to the trouble of stealing a library book, he wants very much to read it. In which case," she said quickly as he looked about to argue, "we should probably come to some arrangement."

Surprisingly, this had been arrived at without much discussion, and on his part no resistance: in return for subscription privileges, Zeph would scythe the grass around the library, and shovel snow from the walk in winter. Jobs that Glynis ordinarily hired out.

They had never again discussed that day's incident. Nor had Cullen.

As she watched Zeph now, Glynis reflected that other than the boy's grasp of material far beyond his age, she knew very little else about him. She learned from Cullen that Zeph's parents had died of pneumonia, within weeks of each other, the previous winter. He had no other family. Cullen found the boy work at Boone's Livery, where Zeph now boarded. How lonely it must be for him since Cullen left, Glynis now considered for the first time. No one else seemed to take any interest in the boy. John Boone was an irascible man, and probably a difficult employer. But then, Zeph himself was difficult.

The boy closed *Bleak House* and tucked it securely under his arm. But he stood there looking at her fretfully, his forehead creased in a frown.

"Yes, Zeph, was there something else?" Glynis asked him.

The boy fidgeted, shifting his weight from one foot to the other; then he shrugged and turned to go. But at the door he hesitated and, still frowning, he swung back to face her.

"What is it, Zeph?"

"Uh . . . Mrs. Peartree's son. He's . . . he's back in town?"

Glynis thrust away a jolt of fear, reassuring herself that Zeph couldn't possibly know about the runaway girl. How could he? "Yes," she answered, "Niles is home for a short visit."

Zeph's eyes narrowed, and he opened his mouth several

times as if to say something. But finally he shook his head, and pulled open the door. He left without another word.

BY LATE AFTERNOON Glynis realized she had spent most of the day preoccupied with Kiri's situation. She'd splattered cold tea on several book pages, misfiled catalog cards that she then immediately needed, and caught the same finger twice in a desk drawer. And she'd just groused at Jonathan; he'd returned from the post office at the general store with mail that included additional *Macbeth* scripts Tavus Sligh had demanded. They would have to be delivered to the theater. Now all she needed before the day ended would be to have Vanessa Usher turn up.

At five minutes to five the library door flew open.

"Glynis, haven't those scripts arrived *yet*?" Vanessa wailed, flinging herself into the nearest chair. "Dear Lord, how do they send the mail these days—by pigeon? I can't understand why— Oh, is that them? They're here? Well, why ever didn't you say so?"

Glynis handed her the package. "Just came, Vanessa. I thought you could wait until tomorrow."

"Tomorrow! Glynis, you don't seem to understand—while *you* may not have any sense of urgency, today is crucial. You do know what today is, don't you?"

"Judgment Day?"

"Exactly," Vanessa answered.

"Van, I was joking. I'm afraid I don't recall why today is so important."

Staring at Glynis as she might a troglodyte emerging from underground, Vanessa retorted, "The special auditions, of course. For the *Macbeth* women. You know, Glynis, there are times when I think you aren't the least concerned with elevating this town from its primitive state. We might just as well squat in caves in bearskins, beating on drums, for all you'd notice."

"Oh, that I think I'd notice," Glynis sighed. "Is your present pique to do with your audition? For Lady Macbeth, I assume?"

Who else? Certainly not one of the witches.

"Naturally, Lady Macbeth. And it's not doing my nerves

any good worrying about these scripts. Tavus is beside himself—he holds me responsible for their delay. Even though I told him it was *your* job."

Glynis became aware of Jonathan sidling up to the desk, his eyes behind the spectacles large and full of curiosity as they always became in Vanessa's presence. "Miss Usher," Jonathan said, smiling, "I'll be happy to deliver the scripts to the theater for you."

Barely glancing at him, Vanessa waved her hand dismissively. "Dear me, I think I can manage them now that they've finally gotten here. Besides, Glynis, you have to come with me. Tavus needs to see you."

Glynis groaned. "About what?"

"Well, actually, Ian Bentham needs to see you, too. We have a problem. With the money."

"What do you mean '*we* have a problem'? Van, I really don't have time for . . . *What money?*"

"The money I don't have." Vanessa inched her chair closer to the desk. "Glynis, remember you and Mr. Bentham thought it should be possible to finish the project with the bank money I borrowed? Well, what with those few little things that Tavus needed—"

"Little things like a personal dressing room for himself," Glynis responded, "and a wine cellar in the basement, no less."

"Glynis! Tavus is the director! You can't expect him to just mill around with the other actors before a performance."

"Is milling around, as you put it, something he's not done before?"

Vanessa sighed. "Yes, isn't it dreadful? He's had to until now, poor man." She recovered herself with a toss of her head. "Anyway, we must come up with a plan to raise more money. I can't go back to Mr. Olivant, I just can't, Glynis. You understand . . . it would be too embarrassing, after he's been so generous. And after I assured him we wouldn't need more."

"Vanessa, I don't understand why you keep saying 'we.' This is your problem."

"Well, no, it isn't. Not *just* mine, exactly. You see . . ." Vanessa paused, and Glynis held her breath.

"That is," Vanessa said slowly, "I persuaded Ian Bentham to let me finish paying him from our opening week's receipts." She paused again. "And also I—Glynis, Mr. Bentham really admires you, you know, so promise you won't be angry—I told him that you asked that he agree to it."

"Vanessa! You didn't! How could you?"

"You're angry."

"Believe me, 'angry' doesn't begin to cover it."

Vanessa nodded eagerly. "Yes, I was afraid you might feel that way. But what could I do? I couldn't go to Tavus—for some reason he and Ian Bentham don't get along. And now we have to come up with—"

A crash brought them both to their feet. Next to an overturned chair, Jonathan sprawled on the floor, gazing up at them sheepishly. "Sorry," he muttered. "Just clumsy, I guess."

"Just trying to overhear things that aren't your concern," Vanessa snapped. She took several steps backward and with a now honey-coated voice murmured rapidly, "I really have to go now, Glynis, dear. Shall I tell Ian Bentham that you'll be along shortly?"

"Oh yes, I'll be along, all right."

Vanessa hastily gathered up her hoop skirt and petticoats, and fled. Glynis stared after her; she felt her nails digging into her palms. Collapsing back into the chair, she looked up to see Jonathan studying her.

"What is it, Jonathan? Did you knock over that chair as a diversionary tactic? Think I couldn't restrain myself—that I'd throttle her?"

"Miss Usher really wants that theater, Miss Tryon," Jonathan said earnestly. "She seems quite desperate. But there might be a way to get the needed funds. If I could make a suggestion?"

Glynis sighed. "I pray it's something short of holding up the Red Mills Trust."

WHEN GLYNIS REACHED her boardinghouse a short time later, she found Niles and Kiri at the kitchen table with Harriet. After giving Glynis a quick shy smile, Kiri ducked her short-cropped head to resume staring at her hands, which she clasped tightly in her trousered lap. If one didn't look too closely, Glynis thought, she *might* pass for a young boy. A very beautiful boy.

Niles gulped the remainder of his coffee. Glancing at Kiri's hands, he covered them with one of his own while explaining to Glynis, "Everything's set. As soon as it's dark, I'm taking Kiri back to Reverend Eames's church— three other runaways are there now. Eames will move them all to Oswego tonight."

"How?" Glynis asked. "Isn't that dangerous for Kiri, if someone's searching for her?" Or, she thought anxiously, did Niles know Brogan was no longer a threat? But he could have heard about the slave-catcher's death in town . . .

". . . looking for a *girl*," Niles had continued. "Not a boy." Removing his hand from Kiri's to the tablecloth, he traced a line with his finger. "Eames will drive a farm wagon from here, north to Oswego. A wagon loaded with corn. And under the corn . . . ?" He grinned, looking like a fourteen-year-old again. The look, however, didn't last. "I'm catching the last train out for New York," he said soberly. "Tonight as soon as I leave Kiri at Eames's."

His mother, who all this time had said not a word, got up abruptly and went to stand at the open door, where she quietly stared out into the garden. Kiri watched Harriet closely, perhaps waiting for Niles's mother to object. But Harriet wouldn't. Or perhaps Kiri had seen Harriet's tears. As had Glynis. There could be no way of knowing when the woman would see her son again. And undoubtedly Montreal seemed to her, at that moment, as far distant as the moon.

ALTHOUGH SHE WANTED to stay with Harriet, Glynis left for the theater a few minutes later. They all agreed she should go, so as not to attract attention to the plan afoot. Plus, for all they knew, Vanessa Usher at any minute might appear on their doorstep.

Beneath still-menacing dark clouds, church bells were tolling six when she approached the river bridge. Her chest suddenly tightened, and she quickened her stride: with the two bloodhounds pacing beside him, Jacques Sundown rode his paint gelding slowly up Fall Street—going back to the fire-house, Glynis prayed.

She'd entirely forgotten about Jacques. And now realized she had no idea what his attitude might be toward fugitive slaves. Would he look the other way as Cullen had done? This was not the time to find out. But Niles knew about Cullen's departure, so Glynis hoped he recognized the potential danger from Jacques Sundown.

She turned her head toward the bridge, acting as though she hadn't seen Jacques, but just then he spurred the paint, coming straight for her. She couldn't very well ignore him. Slowing her steps, she waited for him to rein in the horse a few feet from her. "Jacques . . . did you want to talk to me? I'm in rather a hurry, I'm afraid."

For a long moment, Jacques just stared down at her; Glynis began to imagine something ominous behind the flat gaze. She fought the impulse to look away, or turn and bolt. But what could be the matter with him? Did he know about Niles and the girl? Of course not, how could he? Perspiration began to trickle down the back of her neck.

Why didn't he *say* something? "Jacques?"

"Got a wire from the Auburn marshal's office," he said, finally. "They're looking for some runaway slave. Think she might show up here."

She? Dear Lord, how could they possibly know? Glynis refrained from biting her lip, and instead cleared her throat. "Well, yes, Jacques, I see. . . . No, actually I don't. Why are you telling me this?"

"Auburn marshal's office wants help."

"You mean," Glynis began, her heart starting to pound— why *was* he telling her this?—"that you're supposed to help them track this runaway down?" She resisted looking at the bloodhounds waiting with patience on either side of the horse.

"Sounds like it. Could be somewhile before I get to that Luella woman. You see her, hear something, you let me know."

"Yes." Relief shot through her. "Yes, of course I'll let you know. But now I really have to hurry, Jacques." Turning away with a quick nod in his direction, Glynis started across the bridge. She'd have to stay clear of him somehow, until Kiri and Niles were out of town. She glanced backward; Jacques once more rode up Fall Street in the direction of the firehouse.

As she neared the half-converted church, the noise of the construction became an unholy racket. Carpenters pounded nails into floorboards. Roofers, also pounding, crawled like ants overhead. Saws wheezed through planks, and workmen shouted back and forth as though miles separated them.

For some reason, Vanessa sat sulking just outside the entry doors, but seeing Glynis approach, she darted around the side of the church to disappear behind a stack of timbers. Glynis refused to chase after her. Moments later she saw Vanessa dashing toward the church rectory some yards away. Although the Red Mills Trust still owned the rectory, Michael Olivant had allowed the theater crew to use it for constructing stage sets and storing costumes.

Glynis decided she didn't have time to fret more about Vanessa right then, and she stepped into the church.

Octavius Sligh, waving a script and muttering to himself, strode up and down the center aisle. His wife Calista's two aging aunts, and a widowed older sister, perched on sawhorses, serenely knitting or crocheting or whatever they did with their ubiquitous balls of yarn. Glynis had been introduced to them, but since all three looked exactly alike to her, she couldn't yet match the faces with the names. She wasn't sure it mattered; she couldn't think of them as anything but the Three Fates, weaving destiny through their gnarled fingers.

Some distance away Calista sat on the edge of what would be the stage, obviously studying a script. She looked up as Glynis approached her. "Calista," Glynis said, "I'm looking for a member of your company. A woman named Luella."

Calista glanced around the church. "I haven't seen her, not recently."

"Not at all? Do you remember when you last saw her?"

"I'm not sure," Calista answered hesitantly. "It could have been the other night—at the party."

"Saturday night?" Glynis asked with surprise. "You mean you haven't seen Luella since *then*?"

Calista shook her head. "No, I don't think so. Your Constable Sundown asked the same thing this morning. And I guess nobody's seen her." She looked thoughtful. "But we haven't started rehearsals yet—Luella could have hopped a train for Syracuse or someplace else for a few days. She does like her fun, Miss Tryon."

Glynis nodded to Calista and walked away. Apparently no one had been concerned as to Luella's absence. Or perhaps Jacques hadn't told them about Lyle Brogan's death. Well, it was Jacques's investigation. She'd just been curious.

Glynis looked around, searching for Ian Bentham. She couldn't find him, but through a gap in the side wall she could see members of the acting troupe scattered over the grass outside. Her own head throbbed with the construction noise. How could any of them concentrate on their scripts?

As if in answer, Tavus Sligh abruptly bellowed, "Quiet! I want it *quiet*!"

The noise diminished. Tavus tapped his foot, his face stormy. "I thought you said"—he directed this to the construction foreman—"that you would be through by six today. It is now," Tavus pulled a watch from his pocket with a studied gesture, "it is now six-fifteen."

The foreman shrugged, then grinned. "I thought *you* said you want this here building done by October."

Tavus glowered at the man before turning to point through an opening beyond which a grassy area sloped to the canal. "Company! Out there!"

Glynis, trailing the others outside, inadvertently witnessed a strange exchange between Calista and Vanessa. Although they were nearly beyond earshot, the angry expression on Calista's face appeared clear enough. ". . . and watch your step, my *dear* Miss Usher, if you're smart!" were the only words Glynis caught.

Vanessa's look of wide-eyed innocence transformed to a pout as she turned on her heel and flounced off.

The rest of the troupe assembled on the slope; pounding inside the theater could still be heard, but now at least sounded muffled. Glynis suddenly found herself the object of Tavus Sligh's annoyed expression.

"Miss Tryon," he growled, "I asked to see you some time ago."

"Ah, yes . . . yes, I know that," Glynis answered. "I'm afraid I was detained. But I don't understand why . . ."

"There is the matter of the scripts you were responsible for," Tavus interrupted. Glynis started to reply, but he went on without pause. "I suppose we can only be thankful they have finally arrived."

"Mr. Sligh, I—"

Tavus dismissed her with a wave of his hand. "Never mind, Miss Tryon, never mind. Just make certain it doesn't happen again."

Glynis felt every eye on her and wondered how she might disappear into the ground. Tavus and Vanessa must have hatched from the same egg. She began a half-hearted protest, but he turned on his heel, shouting, "Company! Time for auditions. Lady Macduff first."

Vanessa appeared, to hurry past her with script in hand and pout still in place. Glynis reached out and caught her arm. "Just a minute, Van . . ."

"Glynis, I have to audition shortly. I don't have time to talk right now. I do wish *everyone* would leave me alone."

"Unless you're auditioning for Lady Macduff, which you're not, I think you have a minute," Glynis said. "And why do *you* look so annoyed? I'm the one who should be furious. Speaking of which, where is Ian Bentham?"

Vanessa stared at her as if she hadn't the faintest idea of what Glynis meant. "Ian Bentham?"

"Yes, Ian Bentham. The man who's making your theater possible, remember? The man to whom you fabricated a story."

"Glynis, I don't know where Mr. Bentham is. I don't care where he is. I am preparing, or *trying* to, for my audition." She tucked the script under her arm in order to pass a limp wrist delicately across her forehead. Next she'll be rubbing her hands together, Glynis supposed.

But Vanessa's next words sounded unaccountably shaky.

"You do know whom I'm up against for Lady Macbeth, don't you?"

She appeared so uncharacteristically nervous that Glynis could almost feel sympathy for her. Almost. "I expect, Van, that Calista Sligh ordinarily would have that part."

She nodded. "Yes, Calista would." Vanessa's face became solemn as she twisted the script in her hands. "But Tavus is letting me try out for it," she explained. "And I do know, in case you think I don't, that the only reason he's doing that is because . . . because I'm financing the theater. I'm sure everyone expects me to fall flat on my face."

"Well, I don't think you will," Glynis said slowly. The woman never ceased to amaze her; humility was not something she associated often with Vanessa. "In fact, I believe," she told her sincerely, "that you likely will do very well."

"Oh, Glynis, do you think so?"

Glynis nodded.

"In that case," said Vanessa curtly, "will you kindly leave me alone?"

She marched off to stand on the canal towpath under a clump of aspen.

"Miss Tryon?" Glynis turned to see Ian Bentham coming toward her, his solid frame maneuvering with dexterity around the construction clutter. "Miss Tryon. Someone said you were looking for me."

"Yes, I was. I need to clear up a small matter. It seems Vanessa Usher has . . . forgive me, Mr. Bentham, I don't quite know how to say this. Ah, Vanessa perhaps misrepresented my wishes—quite unintentionally of course."

"Please, Miss Tryon," Bentham broke in, "think nothing of it. In spite of not knowing Miss Usher very well, I suspected there may have been some, shall we say, imaginative reasoning on her part. Whatever the case, I didn't believe you had anything to do with the matter. And I'm quite happy to accept Miss Usher's proposal."

"Thank you," Glynis said with feeling. "Van does get carried away sometimes."

Bentham's gaze went to Vanessa, who stood under the trees deeply engrossed in her script. "How long have you known Miss Usher?" he asked Glynis.

Too long, Glynis thought. "About twelve years," she said. "I've found over time," she added, "that Vanessa is a very interesting woman. Not a person with whom one would become bored."

"No." Bentham's chuckle was deep. "No, I wouldn't think so."

"Actually, there's something else," Glynis said. "It may be that my assistant, Jonathan Quant, has come up with a possible solution to the, ah, the shortage of funds."

Nodding, Bentham folded his arms across his chest, and Glynis could imagine him thinking: What now? "Of course," she said quickly, "it may not be feasible."

"Let's hear it."

Jonathan's idea had been to encourage subscriptions for the box seats, paying now, in advance, for the entire season; the seats might even be auctioned off at the upcoming fair. "Of course," Glynis finished, "it would depend on whether more boxes could be built in addition to the two you've already installed."

"How many more would you be thinking of?"

"How many would be possible?"

Bentham's gaze went toward the church. Glynis could almost see his mind scanning the architectural plans. Finally he said, "I'd have to look at the plans again, but I think four more might be constructed—two additional on either side of the balcony."

"So you think it can be done?"

"Yes, I think so. I'll look into it." His head turned in the direction of an urgent voice shouting to him; he smiled at Glynis and started back to the church.

She tried to guess how late it had become and looked to the sky. The black clouds still hovered, releasing occasional spatters of rain. But it would need to be dark before Niles took Kiri to the church. Another hour at least, Glynis calculated.

She glanced around her, realizing that she still hadn't seen Luella arrive. Just then Tavus Sligh bellowed for Lady Macbeth, and Glynis drifted toward the outdoor platform.

She had to concede that it proved judicious of Tavus to let several women read for Lady Macbeth; all could then see that his wife clearly deserved the part. When she'd finished and stepped down from the platform, Calista had performed a commanding Lady. No one could doubt the woman's power to induce her husband to murder his king.

The theater company, most of them seated on the grass below the platform, chattered among themselves while awaiting the next audition. They quieted with a glare from Tavus when Vanessa appeared, her script under her arm.

It took a moment before Glynis identified just why Vanessa looked different; she had tied her black hair into two long switches, which hung forward over her small breasts almost to her waist. It gave her a younger, more vulnerable look.

As she read her first lines, Vanessa's light high voice took on a breathy quality. Glynis experienced a sinking feeling. Why would Vanessa affect that sweet tone for the strident Lady Macbeth? The actors on the grass moved restlessly, as though embarrassed for the woman on the platform. How long would it be until they started to laugh? Glynis didn't think she had ever, until that moment, felt pity for Vanessa Usher.

But then, abruptly, quiet descended over the company. Their attention had focused, almost as if Vanessa had drawn into herself all available light and sound.

> *"Come thick night,*
> *And pall thee in the dunnest smoke of hell,*
> *That my keen knife see not the wound it makes,*
> *Nor heaven peep through the blanket of the dark*
> *To cry 'Hold, hold!' ..."*

Tavus Sligh missed his cue for Macbeth's entrance line. He seemed as surprised as everyone else with Vanessa's unusual Lady: An artless young woman who simply played at power—without a thought to consequence. Who said *she* couldn't murder the king, but "Had he not resembled my father as he slept, I had done't." A woman who, while certainly coveting a queen's crown, lacked her husband's vaulting ambition, which drove him to murder again and again. She, instead, went mad.

Vanessa stepped from the platform as Tavus Sligh announced, with something less than his usual volume, "Miss Usher will play Lady Macbeth."

Glynis looked quickly for Tavus's wife, whom she guessed might take exception to this casting. But Calista Sligh had vanished.

Lightning suddenly streaked in the western sky, followed by a menacing rumble of thunder. With a start, Glynis realized she should have made for home some time ago. Actors ran in every direction while she hurried around the church. Before she reached the river bridge, a horse and canopied carriage drew up alongside. "Let me give you a ride home, Miss Tryon," Ian Bentham said, as he held out a hand to help her.

Rain splashed the stones underfoot as she climbed into the carriage. Glynis suddenly remembered Luella; she had not been with the troupe watching the auditions. So where was the woman? But if no one else had been concerned, why should she be? There were certainly others to worry about. Kiri and Niles.

The night had become very dark.

A SHRIEKING WHISTLE from the departing train gradually became absorbed by the night, and the clatter of passenger cars dwindled as they disappeared down dark crisscrosses of track. The last train out. Under an overhang of the Seneca Fall station roof, three men stood together just beyond the light cast by flickering lanterns. Rain running off the eave hung a curtain between them and those now struggling in the downpour with trunks and valises.

One of the men, standing somewhat apart from the other two, extended his arm to point north. "There's only the one road that runs straight to Oswego."

"What makes you so sure," one of the other two men asked, "that there's the road they'll take?" When he and the other pulled up the collars of their jackets against the rain, badges flashed briefly.

"What about back roads?" the second marshal asked, stroking his short beard.

The first man's arm dropped back to his side. "Reverend's not expecting any trouble—he'll take the easiest way. And that's the main road."

"Sounds right," the bearded marshal agreed. "We'll head out soon as we pick up horses at the livery. They should be ready."

"What about my payment?" the first man interrupted.

"You'll get your money when we get ours. Soon as we round 'em up."

"Now!" the man protested. "I want payment now. That was the agreement."

"So what's yer hurry?" the other marshal said, grinning. "You goin' somewhere? Canada, maybe?" Both marshals chuckled softly; their laughter continued as the other man, scowling, took several steps backward.

Still snickering, the bearded marshal gave the man's shoulder a hard poke. He and the other lawman then strode off quickly into the rain.

EIGHT

Did Fear and Danger so perplex your Mind,
As made you fearful of the whistling Wind?
                                    —PHYLLIS WHEATLEY

ONLY MINUTES BEFORE Ian Bentham reined the trotter in front of the Peartree house, the downpour abruptly dwindled to a few fine sprinkles. Chased in and out of clouds, a half-moon rode before a chill gusty wind. As Bentham helped her from the carriage, Glynis clutched at her billowing skirts and ducked to avoid the wildly swaying canopy.

Her stomach cramped spasmodically with tension, as it had all afternoon; she hoped there were enough boneset leaves for tonic. But had Niles gotten Kiri safely to Reverend Eames's church? While she and Bentham were traveling up Cayuga Street, Glynis heard the whistle of the last night train out of Seneca Falls. Niles should be on his way to New York. She had heard that same whistle every night for years but never before had it sounded so plaintive. She could visualize Harriet now seated alone at the kitchen table.

"Mr. Bentham," she said quickly, "thank you for your rescue. I'd ask you in for a cup of tea, but I would guess my landlady's already retired. So perhaps another time."

Thank heavens for the mandates of propriety; not impossible to circumvent with discretion when one had a mind to, but extremely convenient when needed. Glynis liked Ian Bentham, but not near enough to trust him with knowledge of this night's clandestine activities.

She noticed some odd expression cross his face. Or perhaps it was just the moon's shadow, because Bentham nodded and said pleasantly, "Another time, then."

He waited by the bottom porch step until she reached the front door, but to her relief he then returned to the carriage. With a light flick of the whip over the trotter's rump, Bentham and the carriage began to pull slowly away.

When Glynis opened the door, the house appeared to be completely dark. After her eyes adjusted, she saw a faint gleam coming from down the hall and followed it into the kitchen. Harriet sat at the table just inside a lamp's circle of light. Her eyelids looked painfully swollen.

"Oh, Harriet . . . Niles is gone then?" Glynis slid into a chair and closed her hands over Harriet's cold fingers.

Harriet started to speak, her voice catching hoarsely. She raised a wet wad of handkerchief to her face, coughed several times, then took a deep breath. "He left just a while ago. Got the last train, I assume. I didn't see him off—we didn't want to attract attention. Glynis, I have this dreadful premonition . . ." Her voice caught again in a stifled sob. ". . . that I'll never see him again."

Glynis remained silent as Harriet wept, trying to think what she could say that might not sound banal. Nothing came to her. It could be that Harriet wouldn't see Niles again, at least not for a long time. They both knew that. Glynis's own eyes filled and she reached in her sleeve for a handkerchief. Her hand stopped in midair as she jerked bolt upright.

What had that been? That creaking noise outside the window? Then she heard what must be a branch of the birch scraping against the pane. She slumped back in her chair. It had only been the wind.

Harriet's sobs slowly quieted. Finally, she sighed and wiped her eyes. "Thought I was all cried out before you got here," she said to Glynis, her look one of profound sadness.

Glynis thought there would probably be many more tears in the next days. Perhaps forever. There seemed to be some grieving that never really ended; it just became at last more bearable. But here there could be hope.

"You know this situation can't go on," she said tentatively, still afraid of banality. "The slavery issue has to be settled. Congress meant the Fugitive Slave Law to be a compromise and instead look what's happened—it's begun to put the entire country at odds. After all, who would have thought even a little town in western New York could be touched by it."

Harriet nodded. "Yes . . . and I think eventually there will come a day of reckoning. But not soon. Likely not in my lifetime."

"But if the Fugitive Law were repealed," Glynis persisted, "then Niles and Kiri might come back here."

"Glynis, you can't believe that! All the laws in the world could be repealed, but people here will never accept marriage between whites and Negroes." Harriet paused to wipe her eyes. "In a big city like Montreal perhaps Niles and the girl could be ignored, or at least tolerated in time. But not in Seneca Falls. Not that long ago some people around *here* held slaves."

Glynis sighed, agreeing unwillingly. "But Montreal isn't really so awfully far," she said, trying another tack. "You could go . . ."

She broke off. There, outside, came the sound again. And it definitely did not sound like wind. "Harriet, do you hear anything?"

But Harriet, too, had braced, listening. "Someone must be out there," she whispered. "Can't be up to any good—not this time of night."

Glynis reached over to part the window curtains a few inches, but couldn't see beyond the blackness. Getting to her feet, she picked up the lamp and started for the door. After several steps, she shakily set the lamp back on the table. "I'm not brave enough to go out there, Harriet."

"Not stupid enough, you mean," Harriet whispered.

"But if someone's prowling around, why isn't Duncan barking?"

"Duncan's asleep in the basement. I've told you he's getting a bit deaf—"

Harriet cut her whisper off, interrupted by a sudden banging on the kitchen door. An instant later Duncan, barking furiously, hurtled from the basement stairwell. He threw himself against the door, then planted himself squarely in front of it, deep growls rumbling in his throat.

Glynis and Harriet stared at each other. "Is the door locked?" Glynis finally whispered.

Harriet shook her head.

Incredulously, they watched the latch slowly raise. Duncan, snarling fiercely, again hurled himself against the door. The latch dropped. Over the terrier's fury Glynis heard, "Miss Tryon! Open up!"

A young voice. Glynis grabbed Duncan's collar and hauled him backwards. "Quiet, Duncan. Shush!"

"Miss Tryon, open the door. C'mon, quick!"

Glynis knew that voice. She raised the latch, pulling open the door; on a gust of cold wind, Zeph Waters burst into the room. He slammed the door shut.

Duncan growled, straining against the collar.

"Zeph, what in the world . . . ? Duncan, that's enough! Enough!" Duncan's growls subsided, but he eyed Zeph warily.

"Miss Tryon, I've gotta talk to you. Something's—" Zeph stopped, seeing Harriet.

"It's all right, Zeph. You know my landlady, Mrs. Peartree. Now what's going on?"

Zeph turned to Harriet. "Your son, Mrs. Peartree—he's gone."

"What do you mean?" Harriet scrambled to her feet. "What's happened to Niles?"

Zeph shook his head. "Nothing's happened to *him*. He left on the last train. But that girl he brought into town—she's in a lotta trouble."

Harriet sank silently back into her chair.

Glynis found herself gaping at the boy. "How do you know about the girl?"

"I know, that's all." Zeph's face settled into a grim expression. "Doesn't matter how. But two federal marshals came into town on that late train. They just hired horses at the livery—I figure they're going after those runaways with Reverend Eames."

"Oh, my dear Lord," Harriet moaned.

"Zeph, what do you know about all of this?" Glynis repeated. "Is this what you wanted to tell me at the library this morning?"

"Yeah. I heard some talk at the livery last night—something about fugitives getting captured. Then old man Boone gets a wire this morning from the U.S. Marshal's office in Auburn. And he tells me to have a couple horses ready tonight."

"Zeph, why didn't you say so earlier? Oh, never mind, we haven't got time for that now."

"How long you think I'd keep my job, if I told everything I know?" he offered bluntly. "Anyway, I couldn't do much until Boone went home. But I thought maybe the girl might be with the other runaways when I saw this lady's son—" he swung his head toward Harriet "—when I saw him get on the train tonight. Alone."

He paused, looking around. "She's not here, the girl, is she?"

"No," Glynis answered unhappily, "she's not here. She *is* with the others. And now what?"

Zeph's eyes narrowed. He started to say something, then shrugged and stood rocking back and forth impatiently, staring at Glynis.

Why did he seem to think she'd know what to do? If only Cullen were here—they didn't dare confide in Jacques Sundown. But they couldn't just sit by while a disaster unfolded.

Harriet got to her feet, stumbling over Duncan who, his heroics discouraged, had curled himself under her chair. "Reverend Eames must have started out with the wagon by this time."

"Yeah, he did," Zeph said. "About an hour ago."

"That long! They could be several miles from here now," Harriet said, her voice sharp with worry. "Glynis, what should we do?"

"I'm thinking . . . or trying to." Glynis paced in front of the door, her mind refusing to be useful. How on earth could they expect to stop federal marshals?

They couldn't.

"Zeph, I heard something in the side yard—before you knocked?"

"Yeah, the carriage, I guess."

"Carriage?"

"One of Boone's runabouts. I drove it around to the side of the house so nobody'd see."

"You have a carriage? Here?" Glynis opened the back door and stepped out. Beside the stair railing, the muzzle of a big bay horse swung toward her, lips dripping white daisies. He whinnied softly, then bent again to the flower bed.

Glynis watched the horse a moment, then stepped back inside. The blur of an idea began to take shape. But to do it she'd need Zeph, and it might be perilous for them both. Being Negro increased the risk to him tenfold. And he was so young. Still, he'd made a decision to become involved when he took the carriage, presumably without John Boone's knowledge or permission.

Moreover, she couldn't do it without him. "Zeph," she said hesitantly, "those marshals will probably follow the main road to Oswego, don't you think?"

"Yeah, that's the way I told 'em to go," he nodded. "Main road north. The *long* way to Oswego."

"And isn't it likely," Glynis went on, "that Reverend Eames took the back road from the church? You know, the one that winds around farmland before it crosses the road going north. He probably wouldn't chance the main road until he had to—not with fugitives stashed in the wagon. Does that sound right?"

Zeph responded with a quick nod; obviously he'd already thought of this. Not so Harriet, who stared at her with a look of dawning comprehension. To say nothing of alarm.

"Then maybe we've got a chance," Glynis breathed. "But Zeph, this will have to include you. I can't do it alone. And maybe it can't be done . . ."

"Glynis," Harriet interrupted. "Just exactly what is it you plan to do?"

"Harriet, to explain I'd have to think—and if I think much more, I'll be too scared to go through with it. So please don't ask."

Glynis turned to the boy. "What about it, Zeph? Will you help? I'll certainly understand if you feel . . . well, that it may be too risky." Risky was an understatement.

He shifted his feet, looked at the floor, then slowly raised his eyes. "I figure I owe you," he said to her. "For the time when the constable—"

"You don't owe me anything! Something this dangerous, Zeph, you should only get involved if you believe it's the right thing to do."

Glynis, studying his face, wondered how she could expect this boy to know what he believed. It was not lost on her that she'd only just now, just this minute, made up her own mind about the Fugitive Slave Law. And this after months of internal debate. But this law no longer endangered only strangers, but a girl with a name and a face and substance. A girl whom Niles Peartree loved. And whose courage she herself admired.

But Zeph did not know Kiri, and he had grown up in a state that abolished slavery before he'd been born.

The boy's eyes now followed the toe of his boot tracing the grain of the oak floor. He looked up at last to give her a curt nod. "Let's go."

Did "Let's go" reflect sufficient resolve? Glynis supposed it would have to do. "All right," she said to him. "If you're certain." She waited. He nodded again. "Then I need to get my cloak upstairs. Harriet, it's windy out there, and Zeph's only wearing a shirt. Can you quick get him a jacket?"

Before Glynis finished, Harriet was already halfway down the hall. Grabbing the lamp, Glynis rushed up the stairs to the wardrobe cupboard at the top and yanked the doors open. She groped around inside, the clean, strong smell of cedar somehow reassuring.

"But what are you going to *do*?" Harriet called up.

"Don't ask!" Glynis's heels clattered back down the stairs. On the last step she paused, fumbling with the clasp of her black wool cloak. "I haven't thought it all the way through yet, and it's better if you don't know anyway. In case someone should . . . that is . . . if anybody asks, you don't know a thing," she completed lamely. Then, "Harriet, please don't look at me as though I've lost my mind. I probably have, but we can't just sit here and do nothing."

She reached forward to give Harriet a quick hug. "Now come on, Zeph, we need to catch that wagon. At least we have to try."

GLYNIS DREW THE hood of the cloak up around her head, and clenched her teeth as the carriage bounced over what was little more than an old Iroquois footpath. She glanced at Zeph's face, set in concentration. The boy strained in a futile effort to see the path beyond the horse; this frustrated by a moon that kept disappearing behind clouds. Gusts of wind threatened to overturn the lightweight runabout and drove the cold straight through Glynis's cloak. She clutched the hood tightly around her face. They had been making good time toward the place where she prayed they could intercept the runaways. Certainly they must be moving faster than a farm wagon pulled by plodding draft horses, and heavy with Reverend Eames, four fugitives, and bushels of corn.

Glynis shivered in the cold wind . . . or in fear. She did not find it heartening that they'd had so little time; the lack of a distinct plan terrified her with unknowns. What if the marshals reached the runaways first? What could be done with the runaways if she and Zeph did reach them in time? What if, what if . . .

She must have groaned aloud, because Zeph gave her a swift sidelong glance. "What's the matter?"

Despite his taut features, his voice sounded almost casual, as if they were out for a Sunday drive in the country. It then occurred to her that Zeph in some perverse way might be half-enjoying this. The challenge . . . the danger. Even breaking the law—with adult encouragement, no less. She winced at this last, questioning again what right she had to involve the boy in something so clearly illegal. "Those who prevent execution of the Fugitive Law are traitors," politician Daniel Webster had recently stated. And yet here they were, she and Zeph . . .

A jarring bump nearly tossed her over the runabout's side. The undercarriage gear grated ominously. "Sorry," Zeph muttered between clenched teeth. The footpath, what Glynis could see of it, had deteriorated into a series of ruts. For several minutes of rough jolting, the carriage creaked as if about to break apart, and Glynis felt severely the vehicle's lack of springs. Her entire spine vibrated by the time Zeph could steer the horse up onto the grassy roadside.

"You O.K.?" Zeph asked, drawing on the reins. The bay came to a stop.

"Yes, I think so. What do we do?"

"I dunno. We can't stay on this path—it's too rough on the gear." He stood unsteadily on the runabout's slatted floor to peer ahead. The moonlight had become more reliable, the clouds having cleared off enough to see the grassy fields surrounding them. By this time disoriented, Glynis twisted on the carriage seat, looking to the sky.

"There." Zeph's arm thrust skyward. Following his finger,

Glynis found the Big Dipper, sometimes called the Drinking Gourd, then imagined a line from the Dipper's bowl to locate the North Star.

"We could cross that field," Zeph motioned to the north, "and meet up with the other road. That'd get us there faster, but the ride will be plenty rough."

"And the carriage?"

"It'll be O.K., I think. Besides, we can't go any other way—not and catch that wagon before it gets to the main road."

Glynis looked down at the deep ruts of the footpath from which they had just come. They had left the house perhaps an hour before. If she remembered correctly, the intersection for which they were headed lay some hour-and-a-half's carriage time from Seneca Falls, under normal conditions. And in daylight.

"All right, Zeph. I guess we have no choice."

He flicked the reins, urging the horse forward. With relative ease, the bay pulled them up a shallow slope to begin a jouncing passage across the field. But at least now the wind gusted behind them. Meadow grass alongside the carriage flattened in long rippling waves. Glynis's cloak flew around her like a sail, much as if they navigated a small boat through high seas. Her stomach began to churn. She gritted her teeth and held on.

They were forced to stop several times to untangle grass wound through spokes of the runabout wheels. After one of these delays, the carriage began to jerk side to side; Glynis looked down to see its wheels mired in mud. They both got out to lead the bay over a low-lying marshy patch, and Glynis heard her shoes squelching. Moments later her feet were wet, a cold clammy wetness that traveled directly into her bones. And like wicks, her cotton stocking drew water up and soaked her petticoats. When she and Zeph at last climbed back in the carriage, her skirts were not only mud-smeared but, she would have sworn, several pounds heavier. And they had lost precious time.

The field seemed to stretch on forever. Then Glynis grabbed Zeph's arm. "Listen. . . . Do you hear something?"

Zeph cocked his head, then nodded. "Could be the wagon."

He drew up on the reins. Wind carried the distinct sound of horses whinnying. "Or," he said tensely, "it could be those marshals."

He quickly pulled the horse to a halt and, handing Glynis the reins, jumped from the runabout before she could protest. Head ducked, his hands parting field grass with swimming motions, Zeph moved forward in a crouch. Then disappeared.

The waiting seemed to Glynis like hours. Her feet felt icy, almost numb; when she tried stomping her shoes on the carriage floor, bits of drying mud flew. She strained again to listen, hearing now only wind whistling through the grass. It sounded forlorn, like sighs of despair. Above her a few remaining wispy clouds feathered across the black dome of sky, and she had the disturbing sensation of being the sole human left on earth.

Why didn't Zeph come back . . . or call out to her? Maybe he couldn't, because the marshals had found him—a Negro boy alone. What had she gotten him into?

When she felt she could not sit there alone a moment longer, she climbed from the carriage to walk up beside the bay horse. Hock-deep in grass, he stood as still as a piece of statuary in a village square. Head down with eyes half-shut, his nostrils discharged little puffs of vapor. He nickered at her softly. Glynis threw an arm over his shoulder and pressed against his rough hide; as much, she realized, for comfort as for warmth.

Suddenly the horse's head went up and his ears pricked forward. Zeph leaped from the grass.

"Found them," he panted. Pointing ahead he told Glynis, "Wagon's down below that slope."

"The runaways?"

Zeph nodded, still breathing hard. "Told 'em about the marshals. They're trying to figure what to do. Can't go on in the wagon—and they can't turn back. The marshals'll get 'em either way."

"What about Kiri? The girl. Is she all right?" Glynis asked.

"I don't think so. She's kinda strange—you better take a look. You can drop those reins, that bay's not going anywhere. C'mon!"

Glynis, with a glance over her shoulder at the horse, and

dragging her wet skirts, followed Zeph through the grass. A few minutes later she looked down a slight grade at a wagon below, piled high with corn. Reverend Eames and three Negro men stood in the dirt road, while a small figure huddled alone in the grass alongside.

Once down on the road, Glynis went directly to the girl. "Kiri, it's me. Glynis. Are you all right?"

Kiri didn't answer, but seemed to become smaller, as though she had curled in on herself. She trembled in violent spasms.

Glynis knelt beside her. "Kiri, it's all right," she said, putting her arm around the girl's shaking shoulders. She got no response.

"She been like that," one of the men said to Glynis, "since we start out. That gal, she mighty scared."

Glynis nodded at him and squeezed the girl's shoulder. "I know you're frightened, Kiri. But we'll get you out of here soon."

Reverend Eames and Zeph bent to retrieve fallen ears of corn from the road, tossing them back up with the others. Glynis reluctantly left Kiri and walked past the men to the wagon. The rear gate had been lowered and a panel removed to reveal a false bottom; she could now see a narrow space where the fugitives had been hidden. It looked to be less than a foot high. They must have been forced to lie shoulder to shoulder, flat on their backs on the wagon floor. For all that time.

"Reverend Eames," she asked, "what can we do?"

Eames began pulling blankets from the hiding space. "The men want to go ahead," he said. "On foot. And that *is* the only way they can get through now. Those marshals, by my estimate, will meet up with this road within the next half hour. But the girl . . . I don't know . . ." His voice trailed off, and he shook his head.

Zeph stared at Glynis, rocking back and forth on his feet. His dark eyes crackled: *Do something fast*! Did he think she'd forgotten for one minute that he could also be at risk?

"If the men go on alone," Glynis said, trying to cover her fear, "is there an Underground station nearby?"

"Fairly near, yes," Eames answered. "It's a church this side of Weedsport, due north across the fields about three miles. They might make it in an hour."

"So if you were to continue with the wagon on this road," Glynis said to him, "and then turn north on the main road, you might be able to provide us all with some time."

Eames immediately understood. "But what about the girl?"

"We'll take her back with us." As she said this, Glynis looked at Zeph. If it were possible, his whole body telegraphed even more impatience. But thankfully he said nothing.

Eames frowned. "If she goes back to Seneca Falls with you . . ."

"I know the danger, if we're caught," Glynis said. "But what else can we do? She's in no condition to go on—and we have to get out of here right now! But we need some time . . . a head start."

"I can give you that," Eames answered.

"Zeph, can you get Kiri up to the carriage?" Glynis asked him. "I don't know if she can make it by herself." She turned to Reverend Eames. "She seems dazed. Almost paralyzed with fear."

"Yes," he agreed, "I've seen frightened people before in this situation—though none quite as panic-stricken as she seems to be."

Zeph had at first scowled, but he went to the roadside to bend over the still-trembling girl. He shook Kiri's shoulder, said something to her, then shook her again. From where Glynis stood, Kiri appeared unresponsive. Zeph stood over her, talking, obviously trying to persuade her, still with his hand on her shoulder.

Kiri finally raised her eyes to look up at him, shifting her position as though she might attempt to stand. Glynis began to move toward her just as the girl crumpled backward; Zeph grabbed her, lifting and hoisting her over his shoulder like a sack of grain, then started with her up the grade.

Reverend Eames pointed out the North Star to the three Negroes standing beside him. They held only blankets and their small knapsacks. The looks on the men's faces, men who shortly would be alone in an unknown land, forced Glynis to look away; she had somewhere lost her handkerchief and finally wiped at her eyes with her sleeve. After she heard a brief prayer murmured, she turned back to watch Reverend Eames shake each man's hand.

"Good luck," Glynis whispered, as the men turned and started north across the fields.

Reverend Eames's faith rang somewhat louder: "God go with you."

THE DRAFT HORSES plodded ahead. Other than the comforting thud of their hooves, wagon wheels scraping the dirt road made the only sound in the darkness. Reverend Eames pulled his thin wool scarf more closely around his neck; without his white linen clerical collar he felt incomplete. But it needed to be left at home. He had become simply a farmer, getting an early start to market. The dry sweet smell of the corn behind him provided a fruitful reminder that God's hand guided this errand of mercy.

It would not often occur to Reverend Eames to question too closely what he did: the laws of men seemed frequently at odds with what he believed to be those of God. And while much of the Underground Railroad south of Philadelphia could be run by black people—often, like Harriet Tubman, escaped slaves themselves—here in the North the additional help of whites had been sought.

Ask, and it will be given you. Seek and you will find. Knock and it will be opened to you. Amen.

Reverend Eames reached the intersection without incident, and turned north on the main road; some little time went by before he heard behind him the anticipated hoofbeats. He prepared himself to lie as capably as he might be called upon to do: *Why no, I've seen no one else on this road recently. But you two lawmen might be talking about a large wagon that passed me perhaps an hour ago, traveling north. That's right; moving fast. Why yes, from what I could see of his collar, the driver was in all likelihood a minister.*

Reverend Eames's lips moved silently in prayer as two federal marshals pulled their horses alongside the farm wagon.

GLYNIS THOUGHT SHE never in her life had been so tired; it took an exhaustive effort just to pull her cloak around herself and Kiri, huddled together on the carriage seat beside Zeph. At least the wind seemed to have diminished some since they recrossed the field. They returned the way they had come, she and the boy on foot, leading the horse. Although they did not speak of it, Glynis guessed that Zeph, like herself, had not been entirely confident of Reverend Eames's ability to withstand the questioning he would likely encounter when the marshals caught up with him. It seemed best to be cautious.

Glynis glanced at Zeph over the head of the girl. As on the trip out, he stared straight ahead, concentrating on the path before them. Both soaked and covered with mud from the marshy field, neither he nor Glynis had said a word since climbing back into the carriage. At that point, teeth chattering with cold, Glynis had put her arms around the girl to draw her close, grateful for the small nod Kiri gave her; she seemed to be in some possession of herself again. She needed to be. It would be a long ride back.

The girl's head now bobbed with the unrhythmic jouncing of the carriage. She too stayed silent. But even the horse's hooves making soft thumps on the path sounded dangerously loud as they moved through the night. Glynis found herself constantly looking over her shoulder, expecting pursuers at any time to materialize.

Occasionally Zeph took his eyes from the path long enough to cast a glance behind. He did this now, catching Glynis's eyes briefly. His forehead creased with concern, or fear, or anger; she didn't know him well enough to be able to tell which. Why had she done this, placed herself and him in such peril? There had been plenty of time to consider this on the way out. It involved, she'd decided, more than the issue of slavery. More than the safety of the girl beside her, no matter how protective she'd begun to feel about Kiri.

It involved Niles. With what she knew about the youngster he had been, and the man he had become. Because she now believed there were things from which some people never recovered.

In the weeks following Cullen's departure, the sharpest pain lessened, like a wound closing over, but a dull ache remained whenever she thought of him. Or even when she didn't. It felt, the constant ache, like a new limb growing to replace her feelings for Cullen, one encased in thin scar tissue that threatened to rip open at the sight of a black Morgan horse; a shopkeeper humming a Stephen Foster tune Cullen liked; the smell of saddle soap and the charcoal-cured tobacco he smoked. The pain gradually became bearable—she hadn't wept in days—but it hadn't gone. She wouldn't get over it. She now believed, however, that she could survive.

And Niles? If something happened to Kiri, whom he clearly loved enough to give up everything for? Who of us, she wondered, can really know how another will handle grief? Her own mother, once a talented and vibrant woman, died from it. She couldn't save herself. She simply withered to a parched stalk, dried as extract of the opium poppy; a small handful of ashes when she merged with her children under the marble headstones.

And then there was Jennifer MacLauren. Lovely, golden, young Jennie, whose sunny sweetness for eighteen years shot light into even the darkest corners of Seneca Falls. When she fell in love and married Jamie Terhune, the whole town took pleasure in their joy. Jamie and Jennie; even their names went together. And then, after a single year of marriage, Jamie left for Mexico . . . for the war. He told Jennie he *must* go. He swore he loved her; it had nothing to do with that. But because she was a woman, Jamie patiently explained, she couldn't be expected to understand the blood-coursing lure of "Remember the Alamo!" She couldn't understand the concept of Manifest Destiny, or why a man had to stand up and fight for the things in which he believed. Jamie had been right about that: Jennie did not understand. How could a war be more important than she?

Every morning after he left, Jennie went to wait at the railway station. Jamie would come home that day. When he didn't come, it would be the next day. And the next. Then came the day when Jamie did come home. Some of him. The freighter engineer handed Jennie a wooden box containing her letters tied with a blue ribbon, addressed to James Terhune, Fourth Division New Yorkers; three handkerchiefs on which Jennie had carefully embroidered the initials JT; several coins with odd words; and a hickory-handled knife, its blade still bearing dark red flecks. In the box too had been a smaller box

lined with blue velvet. It held a round silver medal attached
to a red, white, and blue ribbon and a letter to her from Major
General Winfield Scott himself. She should be proud, the letter said, that her Jamie had died heroically in the great battle
for Churubusco, fought on the continental divide high above
the shining towers of Mexico City.

Jennie of course had no reason to believe this nonsensical
tale told by a stranger. And every morning thereafter she
waited for Jamie at the railway station. She still waited. A
pale fragile wraith, muttering her madness to any man leaving
the train unlucky enough to encounter her. Lovely young Jennie. Mad Jennie.

And so Glynis recognized that no altruistic abstraction like
freedom sent her out into this night . . . simply a need to keep
Niles and Harriet, whom she loved, from grief. And for herself, for now, that should be reason enough.

Drawing Kiri closer to her, she shifted uneasily on the seat,
flinching at rattles of the carriage as they headed down a long
slope. The horse had held his own, and Zeph seemed to be
letting him choose his own pace. Glynis could feel herself
gradually nodding off.

Her head came up on a surge of fear at Zeph's sharp intake
of breath. He pointed left of the path. She looked beyond him
up a treeless hill where, at its crest some quarter mile away,
a lone horse and rider had appeared, silhouetted against the
sky. While too far from the carriage for her to pick out details, the horse appeared not to be moving.

Glynis leaned over Kiri. "Zeph," she whispered, wondering
if he could hear her over the runabout's noise. "Can he see us,
do you think?"

Zeph's shoulders moved in a small shrug. He snapped the
reins lightly and the horse quickened its pace. Beside Glynis,
Kiri stirred restlessly, as if she were shaking off sleep. Glynis
held her tightly, terrified the girl would cry out, but instead
Kiri quietly burrowed down still further inside the cloak.

Suddenly, the horse above reared and began to move
swiftly along the crest of the hill, parallel to their own passage. Could it be one of the marshals? How many others were
behind him? Hardly able to breathe, Glynis watched in heart-

stopping fear, expecting any moment to see an entire posse come thundering toward them down the hill.

It then seemed to Glynis that the horse had slowed, been reined in, prepared to turn down the hill. But as abruptly as they appeared, the horse and its rider vanished to the east.

Gradually Zeph's hands gripping the reins loosened somewhat, and he raised one to pass it over his face. Glynis slowly exhaled.

But why would someone be out riding at this time of night—and had he seen them?

For a time, as they traveled at a steady pace, both she and Zeph anxiously watched the hill above and the road behind. And just when Glynis questioned whether the ride would ever end, the road began to level out. They must be getting close to home; there were the first trees of the forest that ringed the open farmland around Seneca Falls.

Kiri shifted on the seat. She had been nestled against Glynis's side, trembling only a little, her breathing shallow but even. Glynis assumed the girl must be asleep. Following the footpath into the woods, they began to pass between hundred-foot white oaks, rooted there since the time of the Iroquois. Branches loomed over the carriage to bar the meager moonlight; the boughs swayed and whispered in the wind, sweeping shadow upon shadow to darken the path. The smell of moldering earth, the humus of decaying leaves, rose from beneath the carriage wheels. Kiri suddenly pulled herself upright, whimpering softly. And just as suddenly, the whimpers became shrieks of terror.

To either side of her, Glynis and Zeph sat stunned, not knowing what had happened or what to do. Kiri screamed again and again, the sound soaring on the wind like a ghastly summons to their exact location. Rocking back and forth on the seat, the girl clawed at the cloak. Glynis tried desperately to grasp her shoulders, wrestling with the heavy wool fabric enveloping them both. "Kiri! Kiri, hush! You *must* be still!"

Zeph shot Glynis a wild look. "Stop her, will you! What's the matter with her?" he yelled over the screams. "Marshals could be right behind us . . . shut her up!"

With strength born of frenzy, Kiri struggled blindly, threatening to heave both herself and Glynis over the side of the carriage. Glynis heard hoofbeats behind them. Grappling with the panic-stricken girl, she turned to look back, then saw Zeph's arm swing toward Kiri. The slap resounded through the woods like a rifle shot.

Kiri's eyes rolled white before she fell back against the seat. Glynis held the girl's face, raising her eyelids to see if Zeph's blow had knocked her unconscious. But Kiri blinked, her lips moving, and Glynis thought she heard a soft murmur: "Mamma." Then the girl fell silent, twisting the cloak around her fingers.

The trees began to thin. The moon again lit the path and as no horses appeared behind them, Glynis decided the hooves she'd heard were her own heartbeats. Zeph glanced at Kiri once or twice, his eyes narrowed, jaw plainly set in anger. Then the last trees fell behind and they were traveling again in open land. Darkened houses and barns of reassuring solidness appeared. An occasional farm dog barked a perfunctory alarm. And Kiri slept.

GLYNIS, SEATED IN a rocking chair before the wood-burning stove, could barely keep her eyes open as she watched Harriet hand Kiri another steaming mug. The girl's hands still trembled. She gripped the mug to keep tea from sloshing while Harriet securely tucked around her a large quilted counterpane. The warm Peartree kitchen smelled of corn muffins just pulled from the oven. Glynis glanced at the clock: two-thirty.

"Thank you, Miz Peartree." Kiri's voice sounded sturdier. Her chair creaked when she snuggled down inside the quilt.

Zeph had turned another chair around; he straddled it with his chin resting on his arms. And he watched Kiri. Probably speculating, as had been Glynis, about the reason for the girl's earlier hysteria.

Kiri looked up just then to catch Zeph's eyes on her; she blinked back tears, lowering her own eyes to her lap. "Ah'm sorry about what Ah did back there," she whispered. She raised her eyes to Zeph's to say again, her voice some firmer. "Ah'm sorry."

" '*Sorry*'! That's all you can say? 'Sorry'?"

"Zeph," Glynis began, "we're all tired, so why don't—"

"No! Tired's got nothing to do with it! 'Sorry'?" he

shouted, scraping his chair across the floor as he leaped from it. "Me and Miss Tryon could have got ourselves jailed, or something worse, just to help you. Not that you'd care—you telling at the top of your lungs like you're bein' chased by hell-hounds—

"Begging your pardon for that, Mrs. Peartree, ma'am," he added quickly, his tone barely apologetic. He stood now in front of Kiri, glaring down at her.

"That's quite enough from you, Zephaniah." Harriet's mouth pursed forbiddingly, and Glynis hoped for his sake that Zeph would shut up. She herself didn't have the energy to try to calm him. And she didn't entirely blame him; Kiri had frightened her badly too.

However, Kiri sat up, shrugging the quilt to the floor, and said to Zeph, "Ah *am* sorry. Ah know what you and Miz Tryon did. Ah'm grateful to y'all, truly Ah am. But Ah remembered . . ."

Kiri's voice broke as her eyes filled. She reached down to retrieve the quilt. Glynis sat forward to say, "What did you remember, Kiri? What could have been so terrifying a memory?"

Kiri shook her head. Tears splashed down the dusky cheeks onto the quilt she was twisting around her fingers. "Ah don't know if Ah can say."

"If you do, it better be good," Zeph growled, his eyes fierce. But he sat back down again, straddling the chair. "That is, if you expect more help. You're going to need it—you're not out of this yet, you know. How long before you think those marshals are gonna figure out—"

"Zeph, be quiet." Glynis didn't look at him as she said this, but watched Kiri's hands shake as if with palsy. "Kiri, it might help you to tell us. If you can. After all, we're concerned."

She paused to fix Zeph with a look she hoped sent sufficient warning. When he frowned, she turned back to the girl. "What is it, Kiri, you think you remember? It seemed to be the woods that frightened you, but you certainly hadn't been there before tonight, so—"

"But Ah *have*." Kiri clutched the quilt around herself. "Ah have been in those woods. Or some just like them."

Snorting loudly, Zeph shifted in his chair. "Oh, yeah."

Kiri twisted inside the quilt to face him. "How would you know, big ole smart black boy, what it's like . . . like to have to run!" The tears abruptly stopped. The color of her cheeks deepened, one of them slightly swollen from Zeph's earlier blow.

Zeph opened his mouth, but Kiri rushed on. "To have to run and never stop running. Not to eat, not to rest. How would you know that, living up north here? Where you can do anything y'all want. Even say things hateful and mean!"

Astonished, Glynis glanced at Harriet, who shook her head, mouthing. Let her go on. But Glynis wasn't about to interrupt this stunning metamorphosis. Apparently Zeph wasn't either; he just gaped at the girl.

Kiri herself seemed surprised by her outburst. She placed her hands on either side of her face, pressing her cheeks, then winced, and rubbed the swelling lightly. Now it was Zeph who mumbled, "Sorry." He did not look sorry. He still looked angry.

"Do you think you can tell us now, Kiri, what you think you remember?" Glynis prompted, spurred by the sudden strength in the girl. "About the woods, wherever they were?"

"Oh, they all were up here," Kiri said. "Ah don't know if they were the *exact* same woods—" she threw Zeph a dark look "—but they were someplace around this Seneca Falls. In New York State. So she said . . . the mistress, Ah mean."

Harriet moved away from the stove and drew up a chair close to Kiri. "The mistress? On the plantation in Virginia you mean?"

Kiri nodded. "Mistress St. Croix. She told me the whole thing. Ah couldn't remember it—Ah was five when it happened, the mistress said. But now Ah remember." She paused. "Wish Ah hadn't." Her hands went to her eyes, covering them to shut out the memory.

Harriet put her hands over Kiri's, lifting the girl's face close to her own. "What happened when you were five, Kiri? Just a child . . . such a little girl to have something terrible happen."

Kiri's distraught manner seemed to calm some. "The mistress told me," she said, sighing heavily, "that my Mamma ran away from Jolimont with her man and their baby . . . and me—"

"What d'you mean 'her man'?" Zeph broken in. "You mean your father? Her husband?"

Kiri shook her head. "Slaves can't marry—don't you know that?" She looked almost as though she pitied Zeph's innocence. "Leastways not on our plantation. And Mamma's man was black. Ah'm just part black. Not like you."

Glynis saw Zeph's expression and quickly reached over to press his shoulder; he looked ready to hurtle from his chair again, whether from anger or hurt she didn't know. But did Zeph think his Negro blood something to be ashamed of? Glynis asked herself with a jolt. She hadn't even thought about it—how could she be so ignorant? Could that be where his perpetual anger lay rooted?

"Never mind the boy," Harriet said to Kiri. "Just concentrate on what you're telling us."

But Zeph refused to let it go. "So who *is* your father?" he asked the girl belligerently.

Harriet glared at him. Kiri looked down at her hands, hesitating. Then she whispered, "Ah don't know."

"That's no fault of yours." Harriet covered the girl's hands again. "But what happened when your family ran away?"

Kiri started to speak, but her voice caught as she looked at Harriet. She cleared her throat and started again. "The mistress said they were killed. All of them but me. We were running, and the dogs and the devils—Ah mean the men, came after us . . ."

Haltingly, Kiri managed to recount what her memory had finally released; what her child's eye witnessed in a moonlit blood-splashed woods thirteen years before, just outside the peaceful little town of Seneca Falls.

Tears streamed down her face; winter ice melting in a sudden thaw to reveal evil frozen beneath. All this time, Glynis thought, Kiri has had this horror within her. Not even able to identify it. What terrible shadows it must have spawned over the years; shadows moving just beyond her grasp. Of course she distrusted Niles's motives. The real wonder was that she could place any trust in him at all. Or in any of us.

Harriet knelt beside Kiri's chair, her arms around the anguished girl, her face pale as death. Glynis, attempting to cope with her own distress, turned to see Zeph's reaction. The boy sat utterly still, not a muscle moving, his eyes shut. No facial expression revealed what might be his response.

Kiri's weeping at last began to subside. Harriet said gently, "I think you should finish this now, Kiri. So you can start to put it behind you. How did you get back south?"

"They took me back. The two men. White-faced devils—that's what Ah thought they were. One of them was the plantation overseer."

"Do you know what happened to them?" Glynis asked. A few days ago she would have assumed they'd been hanged, but she wasn't sure of anything anymore.

"Ah don't know," Kiri said softly. "The overseer, he didn't stay on the plantation after we got back. Ah know he left soon after, because Ah never saw him again." She shuddered and pulled the quilt tighter. "Ah guess the other man was a hired slave-catcher—he didn't go all the way to Jolimont."

Kiri paused to again wipe at her eyes with Harriet's handkerchief. "Mistress St. Croix couldn't tell me everything. Maybe she didn't know what all happened. Or maybe the master didn't tell her."

Zeph had been quiet for so long that Glynis began to wonder if he might have fallen asleep. But then he opened his eyes and started to unwind himself from the chair, his movements slow and labored, as if he were unfamiliar with his own body. As Glynis watched him with concern, he stood and went to the door. With his hand on the latch, he said, "Have to get the carriage back before old man Boone—"

"You can stay here," Harriet said. "There's no point in you leaving—it'll be morning in a few hours."

Zeph shook his head. "Yeah, that's why I have to get back. So what are you going to do," he said to Glynis, "with her?" Jerking his head toward Kiri, he pawed at the latch to pull the door open; his hands fumbled, as if they didn't belong to him.

What could be the matter with Zeph now? Glynis wondered. He suddenly acted as if he couldn't get away fast enough. And not a word to Kiri, not a word about what he'd just heard. The boy behaved so unreadably, so much of the time, although at least she'd had a small glimpse earlier of why. But she felt too tired to attempt deciphering him now.

"I'm not sure what to do, Zeph," she told him, wearily. "But something needs to be done fast, because you're right, of course, about the marshals; sooner or later they'll be back. And we can only hide Kiri here for so long—she has to get out of Seneca Falls."

Zeph nodded without looking at Kiri, almost as if he were deliberately avoiding contact of any kind with her. "O.K. So what do we do first?"

We? He did say *we*? Glynis felt a rush of warmth for the boy. "Would you wait just one more minute, Zeph? I need to send a wire to Rochester."

She went into the hall and after retrieving coins, paper, and graphite pencil from a cabinet drawer, returned to the kitchen. Zeph stood against the door, shifting restlessly from one foot to another while Glynis studied the ceiling for inspiration. She had to be careful. If the message got into the wrong hands . . . what could she say that only her sister Gwen would understand? She glanced over at Kiri and Harriet, who both sat watching her chew on the wooden end of the pencil. Finally she bent over the table to write: Gwen Stop Changed mind about railroad Stop Arriving today afternoon train Stop Make ready guest room for niece Stop Glynis

Finishing with her sister's address, Glynis handed Zeph the coins and note, saying, "Since the telegraph office is just down the street from the livery, could you send this off for me as early as possible in the morning? Please, Zeph, be prudent—just hand it to the agent and leave."

And please, Gwen, she thought, *understand.*

She waited while he pocketed paper and coins, then asked him, "Would you be able to bring a carriage, a *closed* carriage, here tomorrow? In time to get to the rail station for the mid-morning train west?"

"Glynis, what are you thinking of doing?" Harriet asked her, worry creasing her forehead.

"I have to sleep on it, Harriet. We *all* have to sleep. So, Zeph, can you get the carriage here?"

He hesitated, as if starting to say something. A strange expression crossed his face, almost as though he expected her to read his thoughts. But then he shook his head, pulled open the door and slipped through it.

The door swung closed behind him.

NINE

~~~

On my Underground Railroad
I never run my train off the track,
and I never lost a passenger.
　　　　　　　　—HARRIET TUBMAN

AS THEY DREW near the Seneca Falls railway station, Glynis watched their ephemeral safety vanishing under the wheels of the enclosed carriage. Before they left the house, and a worried Harriet, Kiri had asked, "What if the marshals are at the station?"

Trying to reassure her, Glynis explained, "I don't think they'll be there now; they probably would have looked for you on an earlier train—that's why we've waited until the midmorning run. And remember, they may still be chasing you north if Reverend Eames outwitted them."

She hoped Kiri found confidence in this—because she didn't. There were so many things that could go wrong between there and the relative security of Rochester. But she couldn't know the unknown or anticipate the unexpected, which she hated. She always had. Her greatest misgiving concerned the unpredictability of Kiri's behavior. Although, oddly enough, the girl appeared much stronger that morning. And Niles had said she performed courageously during their flight from Virginia, a situation surely as fraught with danger as the present one.

Zeph now pulled them up alongside the squat red brick station house. When he opened the side door of the two-seater coupe, Glynis could have sworn something resembling a grin crossed his face as crinoline petticoats swelled to fill the opening. Once squeezed through the carriage door, she and Kiri stepped to the cobblestones surrounding the station house.

Again checking Kiri to make certain the girl had no dusky skin visible, Glynis felt as if she gazed into a mirror; they

must look like twins in deep mourning. Both wore black ba-
rege gowns that covered them entirely from high ruffled collars to long close-fitting sleeves, and black lace gloves, to
floor-length skirts that swung bell-shaped over the crinolines.
Bonnets tied under their chins draped black, close-woven silk
tulle veiling over their faces to just above their shoulders.
Both she and Harriet had succumbed to outrageous vanity
when they'd seen the beautiful gowns pictured in a ladies'
magazine as "the latest word in funeral fashion"; they'd had
Lacey Smith make the outfits last spring just in case someone
died—and, they told themselves, it seemed safe to assume
someone eventually would. Harriet had just spent the early
hours feverishly tucking and darting and rehemming her gown
for Kiri. When they finished dressing and retreated under the
veiling, Harriet proclaimed it impossible for anyone to identify them. And Glynis agreed; looking at Kiri now she decided that, for all she could see, it might be Queen Victoria
who stood there.

Glynis now glanced around the station yard cautiously;
there were no marshals, no one she knew in sight. But she
also saw no train, heard no distant whistle. There could be no
telling how long they would have to wait. She glanced up at
the sky; low leaden clouds threatened rain, but for the time
being they were probably safer waiting outside.

"Remember, Kiri, you're supposed to be my niece—but let
me do any talking. I'm going inside for tickets now."

She left Kiri with Zeph while she went into the station. After all, who would suspect the figure in elegant mourning
dress, accompanied by a Negro livery driver, of being a runaway slave?

"Two tickets to Rochester on the next train," she said quietly to the stationmaster in his cubicle. While he wrote the
tickets, Glynis turned to survey the station house. Her breath
caught in her throat, and she whirled back around to face the
ticket window. Banker Michael Olivant's wife had just
stepped inside; her face half-hidden by a huge Leghorn hat
dripping with ostrich plumes, the silk of Deirdre's gown slithered expensively over lace-edged petticoats. The woman had
swept through the door as if she owned the station house.
Which in fact she might, if her husband's bank still held title.

Glynis swiftly rearranged her veil, hoping against hope that Deirdre couldn't recognize her. Why should this take so long? Agonized, she watched the stationmaster nonchalantly run his finger down the timetable on the counter.

After what seemed an interminable wait, the stationmaster glanced up at the clock. "Train's running a little late, miss. It'll be about ten minutes before it comes in. You can have a seat over there." He gestured toward wooden benches lining the far wall. There seemed to be a dozen or more people waiting, all unfamiliar. Some of them directed sympathetic glances in her direction; Glynis reacted by fingering her black veil.

From the corner of her eye she caught movement just behind her and heard an unmistakable slithering. Glynis mumbled her thanks to the stationmaster and with face averted, turned to leave.

"Just a minute!" ordered Deirdre's voice.

Glynis froze. But then, "Just how late did you say the train would be?" demanded Deirdre, brushing past Glynis to interrogate the stationmaster.

Head down, Glynis hurried to the door. Several men, just coming into the station, stepped aside to avoid her wide skirts and nodded pleasantly to her.

Outside she found Kiri and Zeph standing just around the corner of the building, somewhat concealed between the carriage and brick wall of the station house.

Glynis whispered, "Zeph, I think you should probably go now."

"Just leave you alone here?" Zeph scowled. "I don't think so."

"It will be safer."

"How can it be safer? What'll you do if somebody recognizes you?"

Why did he insist on arguing with her? Glynis tried to keep exasperation from her voice. "Zeph, you're smart enough to have figured out that someone in this town must be notifying the U.S. Marshals' office when runaways come through."

"Yeah, I figured that out last night. Didn't know *you* had."

"If Reverend Eames didn't manage to resist those marshals . . . well, you're putting yourself in danger by staying here.

Livery drivers don't ordinarily wait around, and we'll all begin to look conspicuous. We'll be fine from here on out. Really."

Zeph, still scowling, stalked to the front of the carriage. But he hesitated and with his hand on a front wheel, stood looking straight ahead. He turned abruptly to come back to Glynis, his face grim. "Bad news," he said under his breath. "Two marshals just rode up—they're behind the station house. And I'm not leaving."

Glynis glanced around frantically. They were all but trapped. She and Kiri couldn't go inside, not with Deirdre Olivant in there, but several large rain drops had just hit the cobblestones. If it started to really rain?

Her fear suddenly, and dreadfully, mushroomed, when antislavery agitator and fertilizer fanatic Eebard Peck appeared around the corner of the station house. He muttered either to himself or to his mule, Glynis couldn't tell which, because Eebard kept tugging on the animal's harness. An empty farm wagon bounced noisily behind him. Glynis grabbed Kiri's arm and they ducked behind their carriage. But just as Eebard, dragging his mule, came alongside them, the mule dug in its heels. It brayed once, and settled back on its hind quarters.

Peeking around a carriage wheel, Glynis could see Eebard's eyes flash white; flailing with a stick at the animal's rump, he cursed steadily. Glynis abruptly realized she shouldn't simply crouch there, gawking in panic. Under the noise of the man's shouts, she whispered to Zeph, "Go! Create a distraction while we get out of here."

She seized Kiri's wrist to pull her from behind the carriage, then both rushed around the side of the station house, just as a whistle sounded to the east somewhere down the track.

Behind her Glynis heard Zeph yelling, ". . . and you're blocking my carriage, you crazy old man. C'mon, get that wagon out of the way!"

Eebard shouted something unintelligible, drowned by the mule's braying and heavy wheels rattling over the stones. Glynis and Kiri had stopped just short of the station's front doors; both suddenly took several steps backward. Marshals were coming around the opposite corner of the building.

Beside her, Kiri gasped and shrank back against the brick wall. Glynis tightened her grip on the girl's wrist to pull her forward to within a few feet of the tracks, and turned them both sideways, facing east and the oncoming train. "Remember," Glynis whispered, "don't say *anything*!"

She rearranged her veil, taking the opportunity to glance around. With relief she saw that more travelers had appeared, hurrying with their valises toward the station house. The two marshals followed these people inside. Glynis breathed shallowly, and heard another whistle blast from down the track. It sounded much closer.

"You all right?" she asked Kiri. The girl nodded. Glynis could now hear the whistle blowing a warning at the track crossing outside town. Just a few minutes more and they would be on their way to Rochester. But what if the marshals boarded the train?

She looked back at the station house. To her distress, the marshals had just emerged, looked around, and begun walking slowly toward her and Kiri. They spoke to others, with some gesturing and frowning, but all Glynis could make out were a few syllables here and there. The badges progressed steadily toward the tracks. One of the marshals had in his hand a rolled sheet of paper: a handbill . . . with Kiri's picture? But the sketches were rarely good likenesses. Still, Glynis fought down the impulse to run, grasping Kiri's arm firmly in case the girl had a like impulse. Then suddenly the marshals stood in front of them.

"Morning, ma'am." The marshal nodded to her, stroking his short beard. She recognized him: the same man who had taken the young Negro from the train at the Auburn station months earlier.

Glynis murmured, "Good day," and gave Kiri's arm, rigid under her fingers, a slight squeeze. Kiri's head bobbed.

"Sorry about your bereavement, ma'am. You traveling—or meeting someone, this morning?"

Glynis cleared her throat more loudly than necessary. But surely the man couldn't hear her heart pounding as loudly as she could. "We're going to a funeral, my niece and I," she answered softly, praying her voice wouldn't shake. She started to turn away with Kiri in tow.

"Please, wait just a minute, ma'am," the other marshal said. "Where is it, this funeral?"

"Ah, in Rochester," Glynis answered. She immediately knew she shouldn't have said that—but how could she lie with the tickets right in her hand? Besides, they might have somehow intercepted her telegram. And as if fate continued to conspire against them, she saw Deirdre Olivant coming up behind the marshals. The woman would very likely recognize her voice. Again, Glynis fought down the impulse to run.

And where, now, could Eebard Peck be, who would also know her voice? If the marshals should ask her to pull back her veil, how could she refuse? How could Kiri? She felt her breath shorten, panic rising. Glancing up from under the veil, she saw the bearded marshal studying her with what seemed more than casual interest. But his eyes went over her shoulder. And behind her, Glynis heard a soft tread. Dear God, who now?

"Got some kind of problem?" The voice held no inflection. Without turning around, Glynis knew immediately to whom it belonged. Her heart thudded against her rib cage. Would he recognize her?

She twisted slowly sideways, so she could see Jacques Sundown directly behind her. He looked past her at the marshals.

"No, no problem, constable—not if you know these two ladies here."

Jacques's eyes brushed over Glynis and Kiri, then back to the marshals. "Yeah, I know them."

Glynis swallowed to force down the bile rising in her throat. Jacques still looked past her. "Hear you been asking about runaways," he went on. "Thought we cleared that up earlier this morning."

"Not exactly, constable," the marshal in front of Glynis said. "Wire just came through from the Auburn office, said one runaway had been picked up outside Oswego. There were four of 'em, so there's three more to go."

Glynis felt Kiri tremble beside her and squeezed the girl's arm again. She told herself to concentrate on Jacques. On the bloodhounds tied to a post a short distance away, watching with their mournful eyes Jacques's every move.

Jacques started to come around from behind her. But he

seemed to stumble, grazing against her skirt. As if he had thrown her off balance, he grasped her wrist and pressed hard, forcing her to step backward; in one maneuver he stood between Glynis and the marshals. The ploy had been so smooth, so fast, Glynis barely understood what happened. But apparently Kiri had seen, because she also stepped back to stand beside her. She herself remained close enough behind Jacques to smell tobacco, lye soap, the paint gelding. Whether he recognized her or not she couldn't be certain, but what just occurred could not have been accidental; Jacques Sundown, lithe as a cougar, did not *stumble*.

The marshal had been unrolling the handbill. Glynis could now see the drawing of a girl's face, short curly hair . . . She suddenly felt light-headed. Her body began to sway, as if the ground under her feet shook, and thunder roared inside her skull. To steady herself, hardly aware of what she did, she raised her hand to rest it against Jacques's back. She felt him tense instantly, but he stood facing the marshals as if he hadn't noticed. The men said something Glynis couldn't hear over the growing roar.

The noise must be blood pounding in her head. Was it possible to faint from fright? She couldn't do that . . . and leave Kiri alone. Trying to calm herself, Glynis concentrated on the triangle formed by Jacques's shoulders and back; the muscles distending his blue cotton shirt; the pulse beating steadily in the side of his neck.

The roar in her head became deafening.

"Aunt Glynis!"

Glynis jumped as Kiri's terrified cry broke through the din, and she saw the girl backing toward the station house. Glynis took a step toward her just as Jacques's arm shot around her waist, sweeping her away from the track as the train thundered in, sparks shooting, wheels screeching, soot flying like swarms of black insects.

Jacques stared down at her. His face came to within inches of hers under the veil, his arm still wrapped around her waist. "Get on the train," he said evenly, his voice low, lips barely moving. "Keep your faces covered. Don't stop, don't look around. Just go."

With an abrupt shove, he released her.

Glynis took a deep breath and shakily reached for Kiri's hand. Together they went quickly toward the brass-trimmed yellow passenger cars of the New York Central, passing through engine steam that blanketed them like thick smoke. When they reached the train steps, they had to stand waiting while passengers got off. It seemed to Glynis they stood there alone and exposed for hours. And in the meantime, where were the marshals?

Finally the way became clear. Kiri started up the steep steps. Halfway up, she tripped over her long skirt, reaching for a railing that wasn't there; she teetered precariously and for a moment Glynis thought she would topple sideways. Reaching for Kiri's wildly gesturing hand, Glynis felt herself lose balance. Then Kiri grabbed at the next step, steadying them both. She turned to give Glynis a frightened look; her bonnet ribbons had come untied and the veil had pulled partially away from her face.

A voice behind Glynis said, "Keep going." Jacques, right below her. "Don't look around."

Glynis gave Kiri a nudge, then followed her up the steps into the car. "Fix your bonnet now," she whispered.

When Kiri had it retied and the veil back over her face, Glynis said quietly, "Now just go down this aisle to the back of the car."

The dozen or more people already seated, from earlier stops on the line, gave them both curious glances as, struggling with their wide skirts, they edged sideways the length of the car. Glynis kept her eyes fixed on the seats, praying she'd find two together. They couldn't go back up the aisle the way they had come; they'd already drawn enough attention to themselves. And there were other passengers waiting behind her.

Kiri suddenly stopped at the very rear of the car. Glynis's heart sank. But then the girl slid sideways and Glynis saw the two empty seats. She waited for Kiri to seat herself next to the window, then slipped into the aisle seat beside her. Glynis took Kiri's gloved hand in her own, and the two of them sat without speaking, their heads turned away from the aisle to stare through the window. The bustle continued inside the car.

Kiri eased her head back against the seat; beyond her

Glynis could see the station house, where people still moved in and out. Jacques had disappeared, as had Deirdre Olivant, but as Glynis watched, Zeph came out through the front doors. He paused and seemed to be idly looking around, then thrust his hands into his pockets and leaned back against the station brick. Isaiah Smith appeared, rounding a corner of the building. After pausing to say something to Zeph, Isaiah went on inside—probably to pick up a shipment of fabric or thread for Lacey. Zeph had relaxed again, standing there for all the world as though he had just come to see the trains go by. But where were the marshals? Checking the other passenger car?

Glynis couldn't locate them and bent over Kiri to look more closely, just as Tavus Sligh emerged from the station house, carrying a large package. Dear Lord, had everyone in Seneca Falls chosen this particular morning to visit the railroad station? She'd thought it would be near-deserted at this time of day.

As she watched for the marshals, some commotion arose in the direction from which Tavus had come. With his mule and his wagon, Eebard Peck hove into view, heading toward the train. Glynis craned further forward over Kiri, who by now was also watching.

"What's going on?" Glynis whispered.

The girl shook her head. "Can't see anything but that crazy old man."

Glynis allowed herself to smile; the veil would hide it. "He is that, all right."

Eebard had begun gesturing with both arms to someone or something too close to the train for Glynis to see, then he tugged on the mule's harness, hauling the unwilling animal forward. People near him moved away—some shaking their heads, those closer to the train wrinkling their noses. The reason for this became clear. Several men appeared from the rear of the train, laboriously dragging a long baggage wagon toward Eebard. Piled high on the wagon were burlap bags, each about the size of a steamer trunk; the bags had stamped on them in large black letters: PERUVIAN GUANO.

Glynis came close to laughing out loud. Not appropriate behavior for the bereaved. She clenched her teeth, fighting the hysteria welling in her throat.

Beside her, Kiri whispered, "What *is* that stuff? In the bags?"

Glynis choked, reaching under her veil to cover her mouth. Kiri shifted on the seat to ask anxiously, "What's wrong?"

"Nothing. Nothing's wrong—it's just that . . ." Again the laughter threatened. Glynis gripped Kiri's hand, motioning with her head toward the bags now being tossed into Eebard's wagon.

"Guano is excrement—the dung of birds and bats." She heard Kiri gasp, then laugh softly. "It's used as fertilizer, believe it or not, but it must smell appalling because according to the farm journals, the best guano comes from fish-eating birds. Peru's been exporting it for decades, but I don't think it's hit Seneca Falls until today."

Glynis forced her hand as hard as she could against her mouth. Beside her, Kiri bent over, shaking, her hands under her veil.

"We're both getting delirious," Glynis whispered. "And no wonder." Still, it made her glad to hear Kiri laugh. A moment later, though, she gripped the girl's arm. "Shh, Kiri. Shhh."

Kiri's head came up. The two marshals had appeared at the far end of the passenger car, and now stood scanning the rows of seats. Glynis forced herself to look away and out the window. Eebard, hauling his mule with the wagon behind now bloated with burlap bags, trudged across the cobblestones in the direction of town. Deirdre Olivant stood near the station house doors, a man's valise on the stones beside her. Had Michael Olivant gotten off the train? Glynis had no memory of seeing him.

The marshals had progressed halfway down the aisle, still eyeing each passenger, when a long whistle suddenly blew. Clouds of steam whooshed from under the train. The bearded marshal turned to the other and shrugged; they scanned the car again, then made their way back up the aisle. After looking around one more time, they disappeared through the door.

Glynis let out a long sigh, and quickly turned back to the window to look for Jacques. Nowhere in sight, but somewhere close for certain. And she thought she knew now who the solitary rider watching the carriage had been the previous night. Just as six years before when, like an invisible shadow, he had known where to find her every minute. But it seemed strange; the man didn't appear to even like her. She twisted uneasily on the seat, recalling his hard back beneath her hand.

She *was* becoming delirious, she told herself, and turned away from the window where rain drops had begun splattering. The train steamed and chuffed. And finally, with a blood-curdling shriek of wheels, pulled slowly out of the station.

SOME SHORT TIME later, Zeph crouched just outside the doors of Boone's livery stable, concealed behind two large barrels of feed. He kept his head ducked just far enough under the open window to remain unseen by the marshals he strained to hear inside.

". . . so they got away. What d'we do now?"

"I'm not gonna do anything. Ridin' back to Auburn is all—after I wire the marshal's office in Rochester. That has to be where they're heading."

"What d'ya mean? Why Rochester?"

"He just said the Tryon woman had a sister there. So the Rochester marshals can meet 'em at the rail station. If not, they can find 'em at the sister's easy enough. Though it sure does beat the hell out of me, why all this fuss over one little slave gal. Somebody wants her real bad. Bad enough to pay extra."

"Who's complaining about more money? Not me—but when are we gonna get it?"

"How do I know? We'll go ask him about it before we leave. Now, c'mon, I gotta send that wire."

Zeph sank down behind the barrels as the marshals emerged. What should he do? Tell Mrs. Peartree? No; she couldn't do anything. More important, who was the "he" the marshals were talking about—the constable? But Sundown hadn't given them away when he'd had the chance at the station. Miss Tryon stood right behind him—he must have known it was her. But maybe not. Or maybe the constable wanted to trap them in Rochester, with leaders of the Underground Railroad there. But why? The man was Indian. An outsider. Didn't that count for something?

Zeph peered around the barrels. He could still see the marshals walking toward the telegraph office down Fall Street. The boy stepped from his hiding place into the shadow of the livery roof, then edged himself into the stables until he could see around the office door. No one. Zeph leaned back against a stall, kicking at loose straw with the toe of his boot. What could he do? There was the girl . . . and if what he suspected turned out to be true, he could be in danger himself.

Could Sundown be trusted? Nah, maybe he should just forget the whole thing. But there was the girl. And Miss Tryon—she'd be in trouble too.

Zeph moved again to the outside doors, watching until he'd seen the marshals enter the telegraph office. Then he started up Fall Street. He still wasn't sure what he was going to do. If anything.

"HOW LONG WILL it take?" Kiri murmured. The train had gathered speed as if preparing itself for a headlong dash across western New York. Which at twenty miles an hour wouldn't quite be the case.

"The traveling time is only about two hours," Glynis answered, "but what with stops, we won't get into Rochester now much before two o'clock. It's a good thing Harriet packed a lunch for us."

Kiri leaned forward, lifting her veil to peer out the window. Glynis glanced around the car; no one seemed to be paying undue attention to them, and Kiri must be blocked from view by the seat in front. The young woman seemed stronger, and somehow older, since they pulled out of the Seneca Falls station. Glynis decided she could probably stop worrying so much about her. That Kiri maintained enough composure to call her *Aunt* Glynis under such trying circumstances had been astonishing. Altogether Kiri had managed to keep her head very well—in fact better than she herself—during those tense moments at the station. Perhaps the change in Kiri had to do with her memory's brutal disgorging of the events of thirteen years before; she said later that she always feared she had somehow been responsible for her mother's death. At least now, tragic as the reality that emerged had been, the submerged phantoms could no longer haunt her.

Staring at the lovely profile outlined against the window,

Glynis became aware that she had just now thought of Kiri as a young woman, not as a girl. Not a child. She frowned at the alteration, confronted by her earlier superficial impression of Kiri, and looked beyond her at the countryside moving past. How different the late September landscape from that of February's train ride from Albany.

Leaves of deciduous trees were still lushly green, not yet turned to the lavish colors they could become after the first frost. Spans of forest stood interrupted only by clearings for farmhouses and barns, fields of wheat and corn, oats and buckwheat, and the large crops of rye and barley that supplied the state's hundreds of distilleries. The newer barns, Glynis noted, had been constructed well away from the railroad tracks; sparks flying from train engines had ignited more than one farm building and haystack. Several blackened and sagging skeletal structures along the way attested to this.

When Glynis turned from the window, Kiri seemed to be asleep, her head bobbing with the motion of the train; she slipped her arm around the young woman as her head slid sideways to rest against Glynis's shoulder. Glynis wished she herself could doze, but it would be too dangerous to let down her guard. She didn't know who might be on the train, or who might board at each stop. She couldn't be confident the telegram to her sister had gone through; or, if it had, that Gwen would figure out what it meant.

There seemed little question that someone in Seneca Falls had passed information regarding the fugitives to the marshals' office in Auburn. Glynis's earlier suspicion had been confirmed when, at the station, the marshal told Jacques there were *four* runaways: only someone in town could know that Kiri joined the three recently come in from the South. Who would do such a thing? And why the continuing all-out hunt for Kiri, which included printed handbills? Would the plantation owner in Virginia really go to all that trouble and expense just to retrieve one young female slave?

As the train began slowing for its stop at the Geneva station, Glynis rearranged the veil over Kiri's face, then checked her own. When they ground to a halt, she anxiously studied the few travelers waiting below on the platform, but failed to find a marshal among them. Still, she held her breath when they boarded, searching each one apprehensively. Perhaps the marshals had given up after all, and she worried over nothing. But she did not find this notion convincing, and although she let Kiri doze, she herself could not. Through three more stops she suffered in anticipation; three times she told herself she suffered from unreasoning fear.

Outside the train window, apple orchards began to appear, the first fall pippins and Early Joes being gathered by pickers. Even young children labored, dragging their lumpy canvas bags toward dray wagons mounded with the bright green fruit. Orchards of later varieties, especially the Northern Spies developed in western New York, were not yet ripe; on branches that drooped almost to the ground, their splotchy red-and-green skins looked from the train window like Christmas tree ornaments.

Finally, under a leaden sky, the oval drumlin hills southeast of Rochester came into view. In a few minutes the railroad tracks of the new northern route paralleling the Erie Canal would be visible. Cornelius Vanderbilt, a year before, had merged the numerous small rail lines into the New York Central; Rochester had now become one of the most important railroad junctions in the country. Trains rolled into the elegant new station from Albany, New York City and Boston, then on to Cleveland, Detroit, Chicago.

Glynis wondered why Allan Pinkerton hadn't chosen Rochester to open his new office. Trains from there could now move people and freight efficiently toward the still sparsely settled western states . . . but could that mean Cullen might eventually head even farther away? Cullen. She missed him as much that moment as she had the day he left. Her eyes began to smart, and she tried to ignore the well-known ache tightening her chest.

Beside her Kiri stirred, yawned, and straightened to peer through the window. "Is that Rochester up ahead?"

Glynis took a deep breath and managed to blink back the tears. "Yes; we'll be there in a few minutes. I didn't want to alarm you earlier, Kiri, and I hope I'm wrong, but I think we should be ready in case there are marshals at the station."

Kiri made a small sound of distress. "You'd think those

marshals would give up," she whispered. "How much longer do Ah have to run, Glynis?"

"Until you get to Canada, I'm afraid. But I think you'll be safe here in Rochester ... for the time being."

Before Kiri could ask more, a porter appeared up the aisle. "Next stop RAH-CHES-TER! Change trains for all points west!"

Over the rustling of skirts and conversation that followed, Glynis bent her head close to Kiri's. "After we pull into the station, we'll slip out through the rear door that will open." At least Glynis *hoped* it would open; it did the last time she'd made this trip, to allow the car to be cleaned. But if it didn't—don't borrow trouble, as Harriet would say. One crisis at a time.

As the train emerged from thick forest, the first houses of the city began to appear. Around them the stumps of cleared trees—oak, elm, maple, beech that had been cut hurriedly decades before—still stood in some places, rotting two and three feet above the ground.

Now ten times the size of Seneca Falls, the population of Rochester had grown to forty-four thousand; this just half a century after its settlement as a milling town on the banks of the powerful Genesee River, several miles upstream from where the river emptied into Lake Ontario. The Seneca Indians—westernmost nation of the Iroquois Confederacy—had called the lake O-hu-de-a-ra: great or beautiful lake. The river had been Casconchiagon: river of many falls. Genesee, the later name, derived from *genishau*, which meant shining or clear or open valley; it referred to the entire country of the original five-nation Iroquois through which the river flowed. During the centuries of Iroquois supremacy, Glynis thought, this must have been a magnificent site. But the river and its spectacular waterfalls were no longer visible, obscured by mills that processed wheat, corn and timber, the once-clear rushing water diverted into millraces and muddied by the discharge of factories and breweries.

It hadn't been so long ago that the city's bounty on rattlesnakes had been repealed. Rattlesnakes described as six-foot long and thick as a man's arm, they had thrived on the riverbanks of what became the center of Rochester. It hadn't been so much the danger—not after the Seneca shared the antidote effect of rattlesnake root—but rather the panoramic view of a hundred thousand snakes that had for a time put some damper on development. Now shoe and tailor shops lined Main Street on either end of the bridge over the Genesee; their new plate glass window fronts displayed high boots and slippers, jewelry and silver snuff boxes, silks and Leghorn bonnets, and colored prints of gentlemen in tight-fitting swallowtail jackets. With valises covered in rattlesnake skin.

The street scenes visible from the train window fairly vibrated with the energy of a young and growing and prosperous city. Glynis found herself reminded of an account written by Nathaniel Hawthorne several decades before, after a brief visit to western New York and Rochester. He too had been impressed with the vigor of the town. She couldn't remember all of his words exactly, but a portrayal of the city's crowded streets still rang in her mind. Crowded not only with pedestrians, Hawthorne had said, but horsemen, stagecoaches, gigs, light wagons, and heavy ox-teams all hurrying, trotting, rattling, and rumbling in a throng that passed continually, but never passed away.

Kiri's face pressed against the window; Glynis suddenly wondered if she looked for other Negroes. She wouldn't see many. The city's black population had dwindled since passage of the Fugitive Slave Law, as many of those who for years had lived there free fled north with the help of Rochester's Underground Railroad. Glynis recalled that runaways even walked to Canada in the winter across frozen Lake Erie—on the state's western border—which was shallower than Lake Ontario and therefore more apt to freeze. But most crossed Ontario on ships or ferryboats with either American captains sympathetic to their plight or with those of Canadian origin. Either way, their passage could be arranged by the city's abolitionists, the most important of whom being the *North Star* newspaper editor, a former slave himself, Frederick Douglass.

The train's speed had been decreased since it crossed the river bridge. Now the wheels screeched hideously as it rumbled into the year-old West Side station, passing under one of three brick arches; inside, the arches were loftier vaults, architecturally impressive even to travelers from the larger eastern cities.

Glynis suddenly drew in her breath and gripped Kiri's wrist; two marshals stood on the platform to which the train passengers would shortly descend.

She nervously reviewed the station's location. The passenger depot opened on the corner of Front and Mill streets; State Street, which held the big Central Market, ran one block southeast. She and Kiri might be able to lose themselves in the crowd of shoppers there, if they could first get past the marshals. Staring at the rear door of the train, she willed it to open.

"We'll wait as long as we can," she whispered to Kiri, motioning toward the door.

The aisle of the train filled with departing passengers. For the moment she and Kiri were relatively safe. But there could be no possible way to slip past the marshals who stood on either side of the train steps, scanning each descending passenger. Not if the lawmen were specifically looking for two women in mourning clothes. But could it be just a random check they were making, looking for someone else? Glynis didn't think she dared take that chance. She glanced anxiously toward the back exit. It remained closed despite her riveted attention.

In desperation she finally stood and edged toward the door. She stood before it facing those lined up and waiting in the aisle, and concealed her efforts by reaching behind herself to lift the door's latch. It wouldn't budge. She strained at it; still no movement. It must be barred from the outside.

She shook her head slightly at Kiri, who now for some reason stood on her toes in front of her seat, her back to the passengers in the aisle. Kiri made a gesture close to her chest, pointing toward the window on the opposite side of the car. Glynis stepped cautiously forward to look. Below her, between their car and the car of another train on the next parallel track, a walkway of concrete appeared to be about twelve feet wide. On this walkway an old Negro man leaned on a broom, his expression stoic. He gazed at the windows of their car, no doubt just patiently waiting until he could see that the passengers were gone.

But she and Kiri couldn't wait. Glynis frantically searched for a way of directing him to open the door. She couldn't very well stand there waving her arms at him without the other passengers noticing. And he probably had instructions not to start sweeping until all the passengers were off, so why should he open the door for her anyway?

Over her shoulder, Glynis looked back down the aisle, already half-empty. She had to try *something*. It might be a foolhardy tactic but there seemed no other way. Kiri had been standing quietly by her seat; Glynis now motioned the young woman to her side. Grasping Kiri's elbow, Glynis maneuvered her up close to the window. "Lift your veil," Glynis whispered, "and point toward that door. And pray, hard, that he's a friend."

When the young woman hesitated, Glynis gave her arm a tug. Kiri bent forward, her face close to the glass, and lifted her veil. Glynis saw the man below give Kiri a startled look as she pointed to the door. But he regained his stoic expression immediately and, turning away, faced the other track's car. Glynis's heart sank. Sank still further when the old man trudged off down the walkway and out of sight.

"He's gone!" Kiri shot Glynis a distraught look. "What'll we do now?"

Glancing back down the aisle, now close to empty, Glynis could imagine the marshals outside the train, just getting ready to board. Hope retreated in panic: they would both be captured. Publicly arrested and put on trial. She would be convicted and sentenced to years in a southern prison. Kiri would be returned in chains to slavery.

Glynis thought she heard behind her a muffled thump. She spun around, heart flopping, to see the exit door, creaking softly on its hinges, swing open.

The old Negro man stood just outside on the platform. As she and Kiri rushed to the door, he said under his breath, "Go round t'other train—takes y'all out to the street. Then head for the market. Livery's t'other side. And Ah ain't seen nobody."

He stepped aside to let them pass; they hurried by him, and as Kiri clambered down the steps to the concrete walkway, Glynis reached back to press the man's hand. He gave her a brief nod, his eyes flickering in the direction they should go. Then he stepped inside the car and closed the door.

Lifting their skirts nearly to their knees, they ran alongside the other train to its caboose, cut in back of it across the track, and emerged from under the station roof onto a crowded bustling street. Glynis smelled overripe fruit. Dill and onions and smoked sausage. Ahead were the stalls of the market, thick with shoppers.

"Quick, take off our veil!" she directed Kiri. "We'll attract too much attention otherwise." Her heart still pounding, she pulled off her own veil and looped it around her waist. Much as she wanted to, she didn't dare look back to see if the marshals followed but clutched Kiri's elbow and pulled her into the crowd.

She put her mouth close to Kiri's ear. "If we get separated, go to the livery. It's straight ahead of us, on the other side of the stalls. And don't look back."

Kiri moved her head slightly so her eyes, dark and frightened, met Glynis's. But her lips set firmly and she nodded.

"Let's go, then," Glynis whispered. They pushed forward. From the corner of her eye, Glynis saw carcasses of lamb hung from hooks in the roof of the stall they were passing. The lamb looked, she thought, exactly the way she felt. Following this thought came a surge of anger. That she should be made to feel like an animal led to slaughter, be made to run from the law like some dangerous criminal, because of congressmen who passed such an outrage to humanity as the Fugitive Slave Law—it was insane. The men of the United States Congress were insane! The men that she, a woman without the vote, was prohibited from throwing out of office. For like cause, and not all *that* long ago, tea had been dumped into Boston Harbor!

Blood again began pounding in her chest; she would probably have heart failure, but she preferred to die from anger rather than from fear. No! She would not give a bunch of lunatic congressmen that satisfaction.

Kiri beside her glanced at her anxiously. Glynis clenched her teeth and forced herself to smile. Hemmed in by the crush of people around them, jostled this way and that, they struggled to push through to the market's far side. Kiri began tugging on Glynis's arm and motioned to where, right beside her, a bin of ripe apples stood invitingly. Surprised, Glynis shook her head; she could hardly stop to fumble in her purse for coins. But heaven only knew when they would again have food available. What if they couldn't get to Gwen's until after dark? The anger bloomed again; she had never before in her life, until that moment, considered stealing food. Stealing anything, for that matter—but then, she'd never had to.

As she started to give Kiri a shake of her head, someone jostled her from behind, knocking her against the bin. Apples spilled out, rolling in every direction. While those around grabbed at the fruit, Glynis regained her balance and they quickly moved on. That could have been ruinous, attracting undue attention to themselves. She changed her mind about safety in numbers.

Hurrying by the last few stalls of fresh quince, plucked chickens, and baskets of brown eggs, Glynis felt something soft squash under her heel, then spatter her stocking. She didn't have room to look down. Now caught on her shoe, whatever it was continued to spurt juicily every other step, while Glynis fought down a rising hysteria. Then, at last, she and Kiri reached a point where the crowd thinned. Glynis viciously scraped her shoe against the cobblestones to dislodge the pulpy remains of what appeared to be green vegetable matter. While watching her, Kiri somehow managed a weak smile.

Ahead, the livery sign swung by chains over the cobbled alley in which they found themselves. Still grasping Kiri's arm, Glynis hurried her the last few yards. Only after they entered the livery stable did she look behind them. No marshals in sight. Perhaps they'd eluded them—if she and Kiri were the ones for whom the marshals had been looking. For the first time in hours, she breathed a long sigh of relief.

Some inner sense warned her, however, to be wary. This day was not yet over.

TEN

There was one of two things I had a right to, liberty or death; if I could not have one, I would have the other, for no man should take me alive.

—HARRIET TUBMAN

GLYNIS GLANCED UNEASILY at heavy gray clouds hovering overhead. She bounced hard against the carriage seat for perhaps the hundredth time since they started up the hard-packed dirt road bordering the west side of the Genesee River. Gritting her teeth, she held the reins in one hand, while the other gripped the side of the carriage until her spine stopped vibrating. When she had hired the phaeton, she anticipated rain, hence the parasol-like top that now rattled and wobbled in the brisk wind coming off the water. But a drenching would have been preferable to flipping over or lifting into the air like a balloon. The carriage swayed precariously.

Beside her, Kiri seemed surprisingly content, apparently enjoying the wind and the release from imminent danger. An occasional carriage passed them, traveling in the opposite direction, and once Glynis pulled the trotter to the roadside to let a six-horse omnibus with its driver and five passengers go by. She decided the marshals at the station must either have been searching for someone else, or were looking for two women on foot. And they could have assumed the two fugitives would head north, not south from the city as they now did. Glynis pressed her lips together; she hadn't, until that earlier moment at the market, truly felt herself a fugitive.

She turned the trotter east onto the Clarissa Street bridge and, after crossing the river, turned south again. Almost there. Her sister's family lived on this road; it ran between the fifty-acre Mount Hope Cemetery, and the three-hundred-acre Mount Hope Garden and Nurseries, which employed Gwen's husband, Owen Llyr, as chief horticulturalist. For some time, Owen and Gwen had been active in Rochester's Underground.

If Kiri for some reason couldn't stay with the Llyrs, they would know where she could stay.

Glynis flicked the reins over the trotter's rump, coaxing him up the rise of a small knoll. They had just reached its crest when, with a sharp intake of breath, Glynis drew up hard on the reins. Down the hill, she had seen two horses tethered at the fence in front of a rectangular, Federal-style brick house.

"What is it?" Kiri's voice rose softly in alarm.

"I don't quite know," Glynis said slowly. "Probably nothing."

Around the corner of the house appeared her sister's slim frame, the long honey-colored hair. When Gwen reached the front walk, she paused, and for a moment Glynis had the uncanny sense that her sister gazed straight up the road at the carriage. Two men appeared behind Gwen. She quickly turned to the south, shook her head, and pointed in that direction, walked a few more feet and again pointed toward the road south of the house. When she turned to face the two men, she placed her hands on her hips with an emphatic gesture.

With that, Glynis flicked the reins, steering the trotter to the right and through the open wrought-iron gates of the cemetery. She urged the horse up a tree-lined path just wide enough for the carriage to pass between headstones of marble and granite.

"Glynis, what all's wrong? Why are we in *here*?" Kiri whispered.

"I'm not sure what's wrong. My sister Gwen is slow to anger, but putting hands on her hips has always been a signal that she's reached her tolerance limit. I think she did that purposefully just now. To warn us."

"Those two men . . . ?"

"Are probably marshals," Glynis finished. "And we had better pray they haven't seen us."

Searching for some course of action, any action, Glynis headed the trotter farther up the path. Then, before the path dipped down again into a shrub-covered basin, she pulled the horse to a stop.

"I think first we should get rid of the carriage," she said to Kiri. "It's too visible, and we may have to hide—"

She stopped at Kiri's expression of distress, but there appeared little point in trying to soothe her with deceit—Kiri could see the situation as well as she. Those two men might not be marshals. But she couldn't take the chance. Glynis sat for a moment, squinting through tree branches where, in the distance, she could still make out Gwen's house. The three figures had remained on the front walk. They *were* marshals. Their very presence at her sister's—combined with Gwen's odd gestures, the men's obvious reluctance to leave, and something about the way they stood—made Glynis nearly certain.

Climbing down from the phaeton seat, she motioned Kiri to do likewise. They would be better off without the horse and carriage. Grasping the trotter's harness, Glynis quickly turned him around and led him a few yards back down the path. When the road was in sight, she gave the trotter's rump a sharp slap to send him off. He would find his way to the livery; it was only a few miles, and she hadn't known a horse yet who couldn't get back to his feed. If someone—someone like a marshal—spotted the trotter and the carriage heading *north* with "Carter's Livery" lettered on his side, so much the better.

Provided, of course, the marshals hadn't followed them from the train to the livery in the first place. But if that was the case, why didn't they make an arrest right there? Why go to Gwen's and, from the looks of Gwen's emphatic and fraudulent gestures to the south, ask about her and Kiri? No; either her telegram had been intercepted or someone in Seneca Falls knew about her sister and, guessing she and Kiri would head there, had informed the marshal's office in Rochester.

But who would do such a thing? Seemingly only Harriet and Zeph knew the plan. In her note to Jonathan Quant, delivered by Zeph to the library earlier that morning, Glynis merely said she needed to attend to some personal business. That she wouldn't be in for several days. Glynis looked above her to see Kiri waiting next to the path, anxiety written across her face. Glynis started back to her.

On either side of the path, gray stone markers thrust from

dark mounds of fresh earth. Which meant they were fairly
new graves, and this must be a new section of the cemetery.

Glynis glanced around to get her bearings. From Mount
Hope, the entire city, with its church spires and steeples,
could be seen, as well as the Genesee River winding its way
through the valley's rich farmland to Lake Ontario. Her mother's grave, and those of the infants, lay to the south and closer
to the road.

"Let's get off this path," she said to Kiri, "and find a better
vantage point—where we can keep an eye on those men and
the house."

They climbed ahead a few yards. Glynis scanned the slope,
the basin below, and peered down through the trees at her sister's house. To her horror, she saw the men had mounted their
horses and now looked to be heading across the road, toward
the cemetery.

"Come on, Kiri." She pointed beyond a copse of beech
trees. "We have to find a hiding place quick!"

Glynis started down into the basin, motioning Kiri to follow. They hiked their skirts as high as they could to avoid the
thickening undergrowth. The low clouds had at last begun to
clear off, and Glynis could now position a silvery disc of sun
ahead. Much good it did them. It wouldn't be dark, she calculated, for another two or three hours. And until then, they
needed somewhere to conceal themselves.

She decided that probably the only adequate hiding places
available to them were the mausoleums that stood scattered
throughout the hilly cemetery, and she began to try their door
latches while Kiri watched with a doubtful expression. The
first tomb that she found accessible smelled putrid, and Kiri
shook her head violently. The next, after they pushed open the
door, held skittering sounds very likely made by rats.

They walked hurriedly, constantly looking over their shoulders, moving from tree trunk to tree trunk. Glynis felt de-
fenseless, as though she and Kiri were stalked animals. Being
relentlessly, inexorably, driven closer and closer to a snare . . .

Suddenly she thought she heard, somewhere behind a
nearby knoll, the murmur of voices. Or just leaves whispering? Glynis quickly calculated the time; the sun had begun its

dip toward the horizon. But that still left too much daylight. They had to find a place to hide for a few more hours.

"Glynis?" Kiri clutched her arm. She must have heard the murmurs, too.

"Yes . . . over there!" Glynis pointed toward an iron fence enclosing a cluster of gravestones behind which stood a large marble-stoned mausoleum. The fence gate looked ajar.

They rushed through the gate, but when Glynis's fingers fumbled with the mausoleum's rusted latch, it wouldn't lift. She tried hitting it with her fist. The latch didn't budge. Looking over her shoulder, she imagined the marshals on the far side of the knoll, and jumped when Kiri nudged her with a fallen tree-limb. They each gripped an end and forced it under the latch. It finally shot up with a sharp ping. Glynis pushed at the door, but it stuck fast; putting her shoulder to it, she braced her feet, struggling against it. Suddenly, with a loud groan the door gave way. It flew open, pitching Glynis forward into the tomb. As she landed, behind her she heard Kiri shut the door with a soft thump.

"Are you hurt?" Kiri's whisper seemed to echo.

Glynis rolled over and got herself to a seated position. She peered into blackness, her hands groping for something solid. A musty odor of mold and something else she didn't want to consider rose from the dirt floor.

"*Glynis*, are you hurt?"

"No. I'm all right." Glynis got to her feet slowly, her tangled skirts all but toppling her again. At first it seemed completely dark, but gradually her eyes began to distinguish a faint light. It came, apparently, through a crack—probably some kind of vent—between the stones. "Can you see anything?" she whispered, trying to locate Kiri in the gloom.

"A little."

Glynis moved toward the voice and source of light. The mausoleum couldn't be more than ten or twelve feet across— where was Kiri?

Her groping hand finally encountered something soft. She reached out to grasp first Kiri, then a rough edge of marble; bending forward, she put her eye to the vent crack between the stones. Within her narrow field of vision she could see no one.

"This may not be the most ideal spot in the world," she said shakily, "but I think we'll be safe here."

"Glynis, Ah just thought of something." Kiri's voice sounded apologetic as well as frightened. "The latch outside was stuck. What if it does it, again—how'll we get *out*?"

Something exploded inside Glynis's chest, like a compressed spring suddenly released. Tears spurted into her eyes, followed by an overwhelming fatigue. How could this be happening? Cold sweat trickled down her back, but somehow she forced herself to move along the wall to the door, battling the urge to claw at it. Or to scream. Or kick.

How *could* this happen? Here they were, two women who had done absolutely nothing wrong, trapped like hunted animals. With marshals trying to capture them, for no reason other than some immoral law enforcing slavery. Couldn't people at least expect laws to be moral? Was that so unreasonable?

Gratefully, Glynis felt her panic begin to recede before the swell of anger. She took a deep breath. Her hand slid slowly up and down over the door, before encountering a hard protrusion. Please Lord . . . It *was* a latch! An inside latch. Well, of course—only a fool would make a door that could just be opened from one side! On the other hand, why put a latch *inside* a tomb? In case someone should want to reconsider their final resting place? Leave their coffin for a stroll through the cemetery? Bubbles of laughter threatened to burst in her throat.

Tears streaming down her face, she carefully began to lift the handle. *Slowly,* she told herself, clenching her teeth against a sudden noise; the marshals could be out there. The latch handle began to lift, then caught, refusing to move. Glynis jiggled it, pushed it, trying desperately not to panic again; abruptly the latch lifted and the door started to swing in. She grabbed its edge, to keep it from opening more than a crack. But light entered; a tiny ray of deliverance.

"Kiri," she whispered, listening for any sound outside, "we need to keep it from closing—it might stick for good the next time. Can you find something?"

She heard a muffled whack. Then Kiri's fingers touched her arm, found her hand, and placed in it a small piece of wood. A splinter from the tree limb Kiri had been foresighted enough to keep.

Glynis wiped away tears with her other hand. "Good!" she said, still whispering. "I'll wedge it in, down here next to the ground. No one should be able to see it from outside. There!"

She reached for Kiri's hand. It felt cold, but steady, no longer trembling. They lowered themselves to the dirt floor—to sit and wait.

They had heard nothing from outside. It was as though, inside the tomb, they were sealed off completely from the world. Glynis wondered whether Kiri could be as hungry as herself. They *should* have taken those apples!

"We'll wait here until it's dark," she said, squeezing Kiri's hand. "You know, for a minute back there, I really thought . . . To tell the truth, something horrible flashed into my mind, something I'd read once too often: 'and thrust deep, deep, and for ever, into some ordinary and nameless grave.' "

Remarkably, Kiri's voice held a small giggle. "Ah thought of that too: 'The Premature Burial.' "

"You mean you've *read* that? I thought . . ." Glynis paused in embarrassment. "That is, I guess I . . ."

"Thought Ah couldn't read? Most slaves can't. They can't learn how because it's against the law. But Ah learned. And Niles gave me Edgar Poe's stories."

"Poe? What could Niles have been thinking? Why not poetry—Keats, Shelley—or Jane Austen's novels?"

"Ah'd read Jane Austen—most all of her. Anyway, Niles said *you* like Poe."

"Not *that* Poe. But I do like his detective stories. Who taught you to read, Kiri, if it was against the law? If you don't mind saying."

"First Grandmere Masika—"

"Your grandmother?"

"Yes, she's my grandmother."

"Your grandmother lives on the plantation?"

"Not the same plantation Ah did. The one down the road: Riverain. My Mamma had been born there, but she got sold to Master St. Croix."

"But after your mother . . . that is, after you were taken

back to Virginia . . . well, why didn't they let you live with
your grandmother?"

Kiri hesitated, then she said, "Because Ah belonged to
Master St. Croix. And the masters mostly don't care about
that kind of thing . . . who your family is. Ah got to see my
grandmother though."

Glynis chewed on her lip. It was one thing to read abolitionists' tracts about the institution of slavery; quite another to
learn about it from one of its victims.

How could slavery be lawful in America? It couldn't be.
Glynis searched her mind, trying to remember the Constitution; she'd had to memorize it at Oberlin, but much of it had
since left her. But surely slavery wasn't provided for . . . and
even if it was, what kind of government would permit children to be separated from their nearest relatives? The same
government, she realized, that denied half its citizens the right
to vote.

'After a while," Kiri went on, "Mistress St. Croix, she gave
me things to read from the master's library. She wasn't supposed to, but she did."

"How could she? That is, where exactly did you live?
Weren't you with other slaves?"

"No, Ah lived in the big house, with her and Master St.
Croix. Ah had my own room, right off the mistress's."

"Why was that?" Glynis asked.

At first Kiri didn't answer. Then, as if to change directions,
she said, "Ah wasn't mistreated on the plantation. It's just
that . . . well, Ah had to leave. Ah just had to. Ah didn't want
to be what my Mamma and grandmere . . ."

"What, Kiri?" Glynis asked her. "What do you mean—
about your mother and grandmother?"

"Ah didn't want to be," Kiri answered slowly, "a white
man's concubine."

Glynis drew her breath in sharply. Did Kiri understand
what she'd said? Glynis decided that unfortunately she must.
And she herself didn't know what to say. She suddenly wondered if here was the answer as to why St. Croix persisted in
the hunt for Kiri—to retrieve a concubine?

Kiri had fallen into a long silence, and after some time
Glynis wondered if the young woman slept. Twisting to

squint through the door's narrow crack, Glynis saw that the
light outside had become dim. It would be dark soon. She'd
have to find the way through the cemetery back to the
road—to Gwen's and safety. And food!

She heard her stomach growling, then a faint rustling beside her. Kiri seemed to be pawing through her pockets. A
few seconds later Glynis felt something round and smooth being placed in her hand. And smelled the apple.

MORE THAN A crescent of moon, bright as it shone, pale
headstones like road markers on either side of the path allowed them to make their way. After climbing the last of what
seemed an endless series of knolls, Glynis saw the road below, and beyond it lanterns on the porch of her sister's house.
"Not too much farther, now," she told Kiri with a giddy relief. She had worried whether they headed in the right direction; even the moon's position in the east finally appeared
unreliable. But there it was: the house and the lights of sanctuary. Both she and Kiri shivered with cold, unable even with
the exertion of fast walking to shake the mausoleum's clam-
miness.

Kiri had finally broken her long silence and, for the final
minutes of their entombment, talked of how she and Niles
met. Theirs had not by any means been a customary court-
ship. At first it was reluctant—mostly on Kiri's part, as Niles
himself had said—then furtive, and ultimately very confusing
for Kiri.

It would be difficult for the two of them, no matter where
they went. That Kiri truly loved Niles, Glynis now felt convinced. Whether that love would survive . . . ? But then, who
could know that in any circumstance? As she listened to Kiri,
heard the caress in her voice when she spoke of Niles, Glynis
thought of Cullen. And asked herself, again, why she had let
him go to Ohio alone? It now seemed so wrong. But if she
had gone with him, would she then have regretted that decision?

They had stopped behind a clump of gray birch at the bottom of the knoll slope. Crouched there at the road's edge,
Glynis gazed across the warm blaze created by scores of
porch lanterns. In fact, there looked to be the household's en-

tire collection of lanterns either hanging from the porch roof or perched on the railing like bright yellow birds.

Twice Glynis started forward to cross the road; twice she stepped back into the concealment of the birches. Something didn't feel right. Were her instincts to be trusted, or could she be overly cautious?

"What all's wrong?" Kiri asked in a whisper.

"I don't know. Something. Let's wait a few more minutes."

Then she heard, or thought she heard, a faint mutter of voices somewhere to the right of the house. She motioned Kiri to quiet, then listened again. Nothing. Then suddenly the front door opened. From the house erupted a smallish brown spaniel and enormous, deep-chested black Newfoundland, barking together in two-toned yelps and growls as they hurtled down the porch steps. Close behind them came Glynis's brother-in-law Owen, who followed the dogs to the edge of the porch shadows. In the light of the myriad lanterns, Glynis could see the scene as clearly as if it took place on a theater stage. And her heart thumped against her ribs. Both dogs knew her; should they catch her scent, would they then barrel across the road in a clamorous welcome?

"HELLO?" her brother-in-law called. To Glynis's relief, Owen collared the dogs, hushed them and called out again. "HELLO THERE. CAN I HAVE A WORD WITH YOU?" Owen's voice rang out extremely loud. He walked a few more feet, adjusted his wire-framed spectacles, and waited. When the two men emerged from the darkness, their badges catching the lantern light, Glynis didn't recognize them, and didn't know if they were the same marshals she had seen at the Rochester train station. Behind her, Kiri gave a soft moan.

"Gentlemen." Owen's tone sounded cordial enough when he spoke to the marshals. "Don't you think all this spying is just a little overdone? If whoever you think you're waiting for was going to show up, wouldn't they have done it by now? It's *cold* out here. Or hadn't you noticed that?"

Glynis's sister Gwen came through the open front door, her hair now pulled back in a single braid that hung to her waist. In a distracted manner, she wiped her hands over and over on an apron. Behind her toddled a small boy, one hand clutching

Gwen's skirts, the other's thumb in his mouth. Two-year-old Harry, youngest of Gwen's and Owen's four children.

"Officers!" Gwen's high, usually sweet voice strained to shrillness. "You're frightening my children—sneaking around our house!"

In the doorway behind Harry, two more youngsters appeared. Twelve-year-old Seth. His younger sister Bronwen, chewing a braid of red hair. Where, Glynis wondered, could be fourteen-year-old Katy, the oldest? And her other niece, twelve-year-old Emma Tryon, come from Illinois to spend the summer with her cousins?

". . . have reason to think," one of the marshals had been saying, "that they're coming here."

"And I've *told* you," Gwen protested, "that my sister left our niece here, and went back to Seneca Falls."

Good for her, Glynis thought; Gwen *had* understood the wire. But the marshal to whom Gwen addressed her protest shook his head. "Your sister's not in Seneca Falls. Our inform— . . . our information is that she hasn't shown up."

"How long ago did you hear that?" Owen asked, his voice still loud but still cordial. "She probably stopped to visit friends on the way back. Decided to stay the night. It *is* getting late, after all."

The other marshal stepped forward; he had a bushy mustache that Glynis, watching the scene anxiously, could imagine quivering with anger. "Mr. Llyr—and you, too, missus—you *do* both understand, don't you, that you could be charged with obstructing the law? Miss Tryon is suspected of aiding the escape of a runaway slave. Interfering with the capture and return of valuable property."

"Property?" Gwen repeated. "You call—" She paused and turned for help to her husband.

"Officers," Owen began, his tone no longer so polite, "I'm asking you to leave *my* property. I have told you repeatedly that my sister-in-law is not here. Nor is any runaway slave."

Owen stopped, interrupted by the noisy sobs of young Harry; with the same result as a cork popped from a bottle, the toddler had pulled his thumb from his mouth and now poured forth wail upon tearful wail. Gwen bent down to scoop up her son and hold him against her chest. Glaring at the marshals, she said fiercely, "There—you see what you've done? Terrified my children!"

The face on young Seth standing behind her in the doorway confirmed his mother's words. Bronwen, however, looked not so much frightened as fascinated; she had stopped chewing her hair and regarded both marshals with eyes Glynis knew to be the gold-green of a cat.

At Gwen's outburst, one of the marshals had taken an uncertain step backward, and Glynis heard her brother-in-law seize the moment. "All right—you can take one more look around, and that's it!" Owen said icily. "I'll even help you, if it will get you out of here. After that, you can spend all night in the cemetery, if you so choose. Just keep away from my family!"

Snapping his fingers at the spaniel and Newfoundland, Owen began to walk from the house toward the tree-shadowed area to the south of the yard. The dogs trotted dutifully behind. Both marshals watched for a moment, then shrugged and started after him.

"Kiri, he's getting away from the house. Come on! Quick!" Glynis whispered. "Follow me."

She glanced back to see Kiri's frightened nod and motioned her to stay close. Again a nod. Half-crouched, Glynis scurried north along the road's edge, parallel to the Llyr yard, until she and Kiri came opposite the first trees of the nursery. She stopped then, taking as long a look as she dared back toward the house. The men were still out of sight. After one step forward to cross the road, Glynis felt herself checked, as her mind delivered itself a hundred reasons not to proceed. Stop. Think. But Cullen would say it could sometimes be disastrous to hesitate. Trust your instincts, and act!

Again a quick glance at the house. "Now!" she whispered, gripping Kiri's arm. "Fast!"

Hauling up their skirts, they started running, Glynis believing that at any moment they would hear shouts: *Halt or we'll shoot!* She and Kiri would be apprehended and dragged humiliated to her sister's house; they would be paraded like common felons before her nieces and nephews. Thrown into the Rochester Jail, then tortured for information about Underground Railroad members.

Glynis thrust this macabre image from her mind to concentrate on immediate danger. Their skirts hampered every short stride. Twice Glynis stumbled, but Kiri pulled her forward as they hobbled across a road that seemed to widen at every step. At last they reached the first fruit trees, ducked under branches and on into the concealing gloom of the orchard.

"Quick!" Glynis panted. "Under that apple tree!"

Hurriedly they lifted the tree's heavy outer branches to crawl under and toward its trunk, all the while dodging apples, which bounced and rolled like massive hailstones. Crouched under the tree, Glynis heard a whack followed by Kiri's muffled yip of pain, and the thumps of more apples hitting the ground.

"Kiri, we can't stay here," she whispered over her shoulder. "We have to get to the house!"

"How? They'll see us."

"Maybe not—if we can get around to the back kitchen door. I just hope I can orient myself so we don't have far to cross open ground. But we don't have much choice. Ready?"

Kiri made a soft murmur of assent before they crawled out of their shelter, moving cautiously lest they provoke another hailstorm of fruit. A few apples thudded softly behind them as they made their way around mounds of other fruit-heavy trees as if they maneuvered through a topiary garden's maze. At every step Glynis strained to hear the sound of voices. The smell of apples, reminding her of warm kitchens and pies and family gatherings, seemed to mock the peril she felt. But again, the surge of indignation at being made to skulk through the night, frightened unto death, helped her to keep moving. How far away could the house be?

And, she thought while they skirted smaller trees that smelled like ripe plums and undoubtedly were, this couldn't be any worse than what her grandmother and other pioneer women had gone through in the early years of settling western New York. Women obliged to leave their Massachusetts and Connecticut homes, their friends and their family, to head west with restless husbands. Whether or not they wanted to go. Her grandmother Tryon had endured blizzards and swamp fever; given birth alone, hundreds of miles from the nearest doctor, oftentimes miles from another white woman; fended off wolves and rattlesnakes; and with only a flintlock musket faced down a band of furious Seneca braves. Not that the Senecas didn't have good reason to be furious—the land held for generations being treatied right out from under them by arrogant white men—but that didn't make them any less dangerous to a lone woman. A woman with five children clinging to her skirts. A woman who could plainly see scalps of other settlers strung on canoes beached in front of the cabin she defended. How could men be allowed to put women into such impossibly perilous situations?

What was that? Glynis abruptly stopped moving, so abruptly that Kiri just behind her barely avoided a collision. They stood listening; then, pulling Kiri along, Glynis moved quickly behind a clump of bushes.

"Gly—Glynis?" Kiri stammered, her teeth chattering.

Glynis shook her head; had that been a flash of light she'd seen, somewhere in front of them? Perhaps she'd imagined it. No, there again; two flashes this time. She squinted into the darkness and saw an open expanse of grass lying just ahead. Beyond that, a large structure loomed. Again came the light flashes, followed with a glow as if by a lantern wick being turned up and down. When they were young, she and Gwen had signaled each other that way if one of them was out in the back garden. And supposed to be in bed. The two flashes had meant: *All clear. You can come inside.*

It couldn't be coincidence. Someone must be signaling from the Llyr kitchen, Glynis felt sure of it. But sure enough to risk Kiri's and her own safety? Alternatives crowded into her mind, all of them including the likelihood of pneumonia or capture. Not much of a choice, especially since she could hear Kiri's teeth chattering violently.

"We have to chance a run for it, Kiri. Across the grass to the house. Are you ready?"

Kiri's whispered "Yes" sounded more like a sigh.

"Don't stop until we get to the back door—then pray that it's open. All right? Then let's go. Now!"

Glynis gripped her skirt, again hauling it up to her knees. As she started across the grass, she slid on the wet dew underfoot; teetering, she caught and righted herself, and continued in the direction of the lights. But the flashes had stopped!

Her heart leapt to her throat. Could it be a trap? The marshals might have circled around and gone back to the house.

Glynis slipped again. This time Kiri's hand under her arm steadied her with a whispered "Ah think we're almost there." Kiri pointed ahead and Glynis saw brick steps a few yards beyond. But above the steps the house looked dark. If she'd been wrong—if the back door was latched . . . ?

They slid to a stop in front of the steps. From above came a spine-tingling creak, and a sliver of light appeared. A voice whispered, "Hurry! Inside!" The door swung open.

Glynis pushed Kiri ahead of her up the steps. At the top, hands reached out and pulled her into a warm dark room.

"Aunt Glynis! It's me, Katy." Her niece's voice. Glynis nodded, and caught the scent of lavender when a blanket was thrown around her shoulders.

"Kiri?" Glynis asked.

"She's already on her way upstairs," Katy said, "with Emma. Come on, Aunt Glynis! We'd better go, too. Those marshals with Papa could be back any time." Katy plucked a lantern from the windowsill, turning up its wick just enough to radiate a faint glow.

With astonishment at her seemingly unruffled niece—did this kind of thing happen often?—Glynis found herself propelled forward, hustled up the back stairs, and guided into a small rear bedroom. Three of the room's walls consisted of brown walnut paneling; thick draperies covered the windows of the fourth wall. Shadows from a single burning candle flickered across the faces of those in the room.

Katy positioned herself just inside the door. Kiri stood dwarfed inside in a thick quilt, her teeth still chattering. She managed a hesitant nod at Glynis, then lowered herself to perch on the upholstered arm of a stuffed chair. Emma, daughter of Glynis's brother, sat on the edge of a narrow bed with her hands clasped in her lap. Her dark gray eyes mirrored flecks of candlelight.

"Hello, Aunt Glynis. Are you all right?" Emma asked. Her expression looked more somber than her cousin Katy's. But Emma always looked serious. Too serious for a twelve-year-old—the way Glynis herself had probably looked when she'd been that age.

"I'm all right," Glynis answered. "Tired. Tired and frightened . . . and angry, but otherwise all right."

"Angry?" Emma repeated.

"Outraged, actually," Glynis said. "At being chased, Kiri and myself," she nodded toward the silent quilt-wrapped figure on the armchair, "as though we had committed some heinous crime. At laws that made the chase permissible. At—"

"Men!" came an emphatic young voice from the doorway, and Bronwen slipped into the room. Glynis often had to remind herself that Bronwen, although big-boned and tall for her age, was still only a child.

"Bronwen!" her sister Katy protested. "You're supposed to be downstairs."

"Nothing's happening down there," Bronwen announced calmly, belying the pink flush over her freckles. "Mama's just wringing her hands, Papa's looking mad, and Seth keeps pulling my hair. Besides, I wanted to see Aunt Glynis. And the runaway slave."

"Bronwen!" Katy blushed and turned to Kiri. "I'm sorry. My sister is not always tactful—" she frowned at Bronwen "—or polite."

Bronwen shrugged and continued to stare at Kiri with her cat-eyed curiosity.

They all jumped at a hard rap under their feet. It sounded as if someone was striking the ceiling of the room below. In alarm, Glynis looked at her oldest niece.

"Papa's signal," gasped Katy. "The marshals must have come back. Quick," she motioned to Kiri in the chair, "get up!" This as Katy raced to a paneled wall with a bookcase some six feet high and five feet long. She lifted two volumes from the end of a middle shelf, then reached into the narrow recess to fumble with something. A small click followed. A latch was lifted.

"Bronwen, help me!" Katy directed the younger girl, who had bounded to her sister's side. Together they gripped the end of the bookcase and pulled. With a rasp of hinges, the bookcase swung out into the room, revealing behind it a compartment that looked to Glynis to be about three feet deep.

"Get in," Katy directed Kiri. "You too, Aunt Glynis—you're not supposed to be here, remember?"

While Emma helped Katy cram Glynis's and Kiri's black skirts and petticoats into the compartment, Bronwen dashed to the doorway of the room. "I'll be lookout," she whispered loudly.

"No, you won't!" Katy snapped over her shoulder. "Just get back in here, sit in that chair, and be quiet!"

Bronwen's pointed chin lifted peevishly, but she did as she'd been told. Glynis heard the front door open downstairs. Men's voices floated upward as Katy and Emma pushed the bookcase back into place in front of the two fugitives.

Glynis heard the muffled click of the latch dropping back into place.

ELEVEN

Aliens are we in our native land. The fundamental principles of the republic, to which the humblest white man, whether born here or elsewhere, may appeal with confidence in the hope of awakening a favorable response, are held to be inapplicable to us.

—FREDERICK DOUGLASS

THE COMPARTMENT GREW steadily smaller, pressing in on her like Poe's "Pit and the Pendulum" dungeon walls. Glynis told herself if she had to stay squeezed into the diminishing space one more minute she would shriek. If only there were room to sit down. Her legs prickled, her back ached, and worst of all, she felt she couldn't breathe. Given the complete absence of light, where could air come from? She didn't know how long it took to suffocate, although how useful this fact might be just now eluded her. She did know panic interfered with breathing.

The bookcase seemed to effectively suppress sound coming from the outer room if, indeed, there was any sound out there. The eerie quiet added to Glynis's stifling sense of another entombment. But next to her, Kiri stood quietly. It crossed Glynis's mind that the young woman had been through something like this before ... but of course she had. Reverend Eames's wagon, Glynis recalled, had that narrow space under the bed of corn. She had thought when she saw it how horrible it must be to lie confined for hours, flat on one's back in a closed, cramped space, at the mercy of good will from total strangers. How did the runaways endure it? How unbearable must be the circumstances from which they were running.

In addition to the other discomforts, Glynis became aware of cold seeping through her; the compartment must be backed by an outside wall of the house. And now from somewhere came a low moaning. She thought for a moment it could be her own voice she heard, then realized it must be Kiri's. At the same time she felt the weight of the young woman, leaning against her heavily. Glynis wondered if Kiri felt as lightheaded as she . . . about to faint? But she didn't dare whisper to her.

Voices, muffled voices, suddenly penetrated the little compartment. Glynis thought she heard her sister Gwen's; given the soft quality of Gwen's ordinary speech she must now be talking very loudly—to warn Glynis and Kiri? Owen's voice also sounded forced, followed by another man's words, somewhat more muted. Glynis gave Kiri a small shake to alert her to the danger just outside. Kiri didn't respond. Her weight now seemed to be resting entirely on Glynis. Dear Lord, Glynis thought, what could she do? If Kiri needed air, if she'd fainted, how long could she . . . ?

A muffled yell reached Glynis. It scaled upward, startled, a young voice. There immediately followed a babble of sound, words jumbled together, unintelligible. What was going *on*? The only noise Glynis could distinguish now was a frenzied barking—the dogs must be close by. Would they smell her and reveal the hiding place?

Abruptly all went silent. Glynis strained to hear . . . nothing. Minutes, hours it seemed, went by. Still no sound. Had they all left? Left her and Kiri to die in their airless prison? A great wave of weariness broke over her; she slouched against the back of the compartment and closed her eyes. If she slept . . . would she ever awaken? She wished she could tell . . . Cullen . . . what did she want to tell him . . . it seemed to be important . . .

Glynis's eyes flew open. She felt a trace of air moving. A crack of light appeared, followed by a rasping sound. The bookcase in front of Glynis began to move; she pushed against it and staggered out into the room, gulping huge lungfuls of air. She saw her brother-in-law Owen, reaching past her to grab Kiri's body as it fell forward.

"Papa!" Behind Owen, Katy screamed. "Papa, is she dead?"

Glynis's knees crumpled and she fell to a kneeling position, arms wrapped around her chest, her head bent toward the floor. Still gasping for air, she became conscious of an arm encircling her shoulders. Emma had knelt beside her, pale young face full of concern. "Aunt Glynis?"

Coughing, Glynis bobbed her head. "I'll be all right," she choked. "But Kiri . . . ?"

Emma motioned to the chair. Gwen and Owen were bending over the fragile form, Gwen waving under Kiri's nose what appeared to be smelling salts. Glynis strained to get up, then collapsed back against Emma. Nausea threatened, then slowly receded.

Kiri at last began to struggle, attempting to push away the vial of smelling salts. She coughed several times, then opened her eyes. Taking deep shaky breaths, Kiri gave Gwen a grateful look; after several more inhalations, she curled her legs up underneath her skirts to huddle down in the chair.

Gwen sat back on her heels with a sigh of relief. "Thank the Lord," she said to no one in particular. Then she smiled at Kiri with what Glynis thought of as the warmheartedness so characteristic of her sister. Gwen leaned forward to put her arms around the young woman. "It's all right, Kiri—you're all right now. Just breathe deep, and you'll be fine." She looked up at her husband, who stood over her. "They were in that cupboard way too long, Owen. Think what might have happened."

"But it didn't, Gwen. *Don't* think about it." Owen reached down to give his wife's shoulder a squeeze.

Fine for you to say, Glynis thought, wondering if she herself could ever forget it. "Are the marshals gone then?" She cleared her throat, which still felt scratchy. "For good, I hope?"

"Yes," Owen answered. "We think so. But the strangest thing happened."

"Really strange, Aunt Glynis." Seth stepped into the room from the doorway where he had been standing. He ran a hand through hair the color of clover honey, the same color as his mother's and sister Katy's. "This man came, Aunt Glynis—he just appeared . . ."

"The marshals had come up the stairs," Gwen said. "They insisted on going through the house—there wasn't any way we could stop them without it looking suspicious. We've had runaways hide once before in there," she gestured toward the bookcase, "and we thought the men would just glance into the room from the doorway as they'd done that time. But one of the marshals actually walked in here." Gwen trembled, and stopped talking.

"I was behind them," Seth jumped in eagerly, "and all of a sudden there's this man behind *me*. Scared me like to death—I didn't even hear him come into the house. Or up the stairs. It was spooky."

Glynis felt hair rise on the back of her neck. Seth's words reminded her . . . She shook her head slightly; it couldn't have been him.

"Really, Aunt Glynis!" Seth protested, as though she had disagreed with him.

"It *was* odd," Owen said. "We none of us heard him. He suddenly just appeared."

"And what happened?" Glynis asked.

"He told the marshals that you," he nodded at Kiri, "had been spotted just north of Rochester, heading on foot toward the lake. He said it so offhandedly, so convincingly, the marshals didn't even question him. They took off down the stairs, got their horses and lit out."

"And the man?" Glynis said. "What did he do?"

"He went with them."

Bronwen came into the room behind her brother. "He had the biggest horse you ever saw," she said to Glynis. "Black and white, big as an elephant!"

"Bronwen!" said Seth, giving her a disgusted look. "It wasn't *that* big."

Glynis couldn't believe she'd heard correctly. She got to her feet and, with Emma's arm still around her shoulders, she asked, "What did he look like, this man?"

"Oh, Aunt Glynis," Katy sighed, "he was the most beautiful-looking man . . ."

"C'mon, Katy," Seth interrupted. "That's not what you call a man. '*Beautiful*,' " he snorted. "He was . . ."

"Handsome," Bronwen said. "He was handsome—the same color as our tea kettle."

Copper. Glynis groped for the chair, and sank down on its arm next to Kiri. "Did he say why he came here?" she asked.

"Yes," Gwen answered her. "He said he was a constable

and helping the marshals search for the runaway. Do you know him, Glynis? He said he came from Seneca Falls. But how could he—I mean, how did he get *here*?"

"Heaven knows," Glynis said. "Sometimes I think he's a spirit. Dagwunnoyaent."

"Dagwunnoyaent," Owen echoed. "Indian. Is he a Seneca?"

"I *knew* he was Indian!" Seth exclaimed. "I knew it, just the way he crept in here so fast and quiet."

"I guess I should have been more scared," Bronwen said soberly. "Does he scalp people, Aunt Glynis?"

"Bronwen!" Owen's voice held exasperation. It occurred with complete irrelevance to Glynis that her family said "Bronwen!" a lot.

Kiri sat forward in the chair. "Was that the man at the train station in Seneca Falls?" she said to Glynis. Glynis nodded. "Well," Kiri said, "after we left, couldn't he have put his horse on the next train to here?"

Yes, Glynis thought; that would be the only way Jacques Sundown could have reached Rochester so quickly. Quickly? It seemed as if she and Kiri had been running for days! Jacques must have persuaded Harriet to give him Gwen's address—but why did he follow them? Did he know that someone in Seneca Falls had wired ahead to the marshal's office in Rochester?

And that reminded her. "You figured out my wire, Gwen," she said to her sister.

Gwen smiled. "At first I thought it was a joke—you said you'd changed your mind about the railroad. Of course I thought you meant the *real* one. But then, it didn't make sense when you said you were arriving by train. So it must have been the Underground you meant—we've talked about it enough times, you and I. About how wrong you thought it was to break the law."

Glynis flushed but nodded; she'd relied on Gwen's remembering those conversations.

"And," Gwen went on, "the only niece you and I *both* have is Emma—and you knew she was already here."

Owen smiled at his wife with affection. He was an open man, and not reluctant to show how much he loved her.

Glynis always found great warmth in this house. Gwen and Owen had a good marriage. They fit. Gwen had always wanted nothing more than to raise children and take care of her husband.

"And *you* understood all the lights, didn't you, Glynis?" Gwen now said to her.

"Not right away," Glynis admitted. "But finally I realized that if you guessed Kiri and I were trying to sneak in unnoticed, the last thing you would do is have every lantern in the house blazing. Unless you wanted to warn us away. You saw the carriage earlier, and signaled me, didn't you, Gwen—put your hands on your hips?" Glynis smiled. "You still do that when you're getting mad?"

The youngsters in the room nodded vigorously.

Gwen laughed. "I'd been so afraid you wouldn't understand, or couldn't see me. And those marshals—but it's over."

Glynis wasn't so certain. "I don't think Kiri can stay here," she said slowly and looked at Kiri, who shook her head. "No, I think it's too dangerous for all of you."

"She'll be safe enough here tonight," Owen said, "with those marshals chasing their own shadows north. Tomorrow," he turned to Kiri, "tomorrow we'll get you to someone who'll know what's best to do next."

"Who's that?" Glynis asked.

"You've met him, I think. He's a friend of Elizabeth Stanton. Frederick Douglass."

WITH A BONE-JARRING bounce, the front wheels of the carriage left the cobblestones of Buffalo Street and hit the dirt road they would travel for another mile, to Frederick Douglass's farm, south of Rochester.

Glynis glanced beside her at Kiri. The young woman's face had again been concealed under silk tulle, but which now, rather than black, was a soft rose color, matching the big-brimmed velvet hat from which the veiling cascaded. They all wore hats: Glynis and Kiri, Gwen and her Katy and niece Emma. The width of the hats prevented them from moving their heads much in the confined space of the carriage; from a bird's-eye view, Glynis guessed they must resemble a clus-

ter of flat, brightly-colored mushroom caps, the stems of
which were invisible from the air.

Just ahead of the carriage Owen and son Seth rode horseback; they also had dressed as if visiting a head of state.
Gwen had insisted this would provide a flawless disguise,
should they need it. Who, she said, would suspect a well-
dressed family, riding boldly through the main streets of the
city, of hiding a runaway slave amongst them?

Bronwen had stayed at home with baby Harry. "Why do *I*
always get left," she had protested in her oddly robust young
voice. "The whole world goes by while I get stuck with a
baby. *You're* his mother!" she said to Gwen. "I don't see
why—"

"Bronwen! That's enough," scolded Owen. "And don't
speak to your mother that way."

"That's why you get left," added Seth. "Because you can't
keep your big mouth shut."

Behind her father's back, Bronwen had stuck out her
tongue at her brother.

Glynis clenched her teeth against the bumps in the dirt road
they now traveled, which had become narrower and more rutted. Ahead of the carriage, Owen and Seth abruptly turned
onto a private dirt road. Gwen steered the carriage after them,
and for a time the horses labored up a long hill. After passing
a clearing that held fruit trees and a plot of squash and beans
and corn, they entered another cleared area that contained a
good-sized farmhouse and barn.

As Gwen pulled the carriage to a stop, the front door of the
house swung open and a tall, strong-featured man came down
the front steps.

Kiri turned to Glynis. "Is that him?"

Glynis nodded. She had told Kiri earlier, "I think you'll
like Mr. Douglass. He was born into slavery too, and escaped
at about the same age you are now."

She didn't add, thinking that Douglass himself should tell
Kiri if he so chose, that his father had been white. As to exactly who his father had been, and although Douglass suspected his former owner, he couldn't be certain.

Glynis watched Kiri's face as Douglass came toward the
carriage. The young woman's eyes widened with his every

step. His skin was lighter then Zeph's, very nearly the same muted brown as Kiri's. His bone structure reminded Glynis somewhat of Jacques Sundown's, and Douglass had said he'd heard talk in his youth of an Indian ancestor; the Eastern Shore of Maryland where he was born had been wrested from Indians in the 1600s.

Now, as Frederick Douglass came forward to greet them, Glynis understood how deeply involved her sister and brother-in-law were with Rochester's Underground Railroad. Douglass spoke to them as if Gwen and Owen were much more than casual acquaintances. Although always gracious, Douglass had struck Glynis, the few times she had met him in the Stanton home, as a very private man. Just now, though, he seemed at ease, less guarded than she remembered him.

"Any trouble?" he said to Owen, the voice deep and rich as aged brandy.

Gwen, being helped down from the carriage by Owen, rolled her eyes skyward. "You'd best ask Glynis about that," she said.

"Miss Tryon." Douglass extended his hand to assist Glynis onto the road. "You came, I'm told, from Seneca Falls with your niece." His inflection on the word "niece" brought a giggle from Katy, and left no question in Glynis's mind that the Underground had a communication system that Western Union might envy.

"Yes," Glynis replied, turning to help Kiri down from the carriage. "This is Kiri, Mr. Douglass. And yes, I do feel at this point like her fond aunt. We've been through rather a lot together."

"*Rather* a lot?" Owen laughed. But Glynis suddenly wondered if Douglass found offensive the reference to Kiri as "niece," which might imply she thought of the young woman as a child. Which, she winced inwardly, she initially had.

If offended, Douglass didn't reveal it, but motioned them all toward the gray clapboard house. Glynis recalled that Gwen told her the Douglasses regularly held escaped slaves coming in from the South. The fugitives would wait there for a wagon, which after dark would take them either to be hidden in another house in town or straight to the lower falls of the Genesee. There they would be put on boats bound for

Canada. Members of the Underground estimated that some one hundred fifty runaways a year were now moving through Rochester.

Douglass stepped aside to let Gwen and Owen and the young people climb the porch steps. Glynis hung back. "Mr. Douglass," she asked, "I wonder if I might speak with you."

Gwen looked over her shoulder and nodded at Glynis, then proceeded to herd the others into the house. The smell of baking bread wafted out through the open door.

When the others were inside, Glynis said, "Mr. Douglass, there are several things I need to ask."

Douglass gestured toward the porch. As they went up the steps he said, "Although pleased to see you here with the young woman, Miss Tryon, I confess I'm somewhat surprised." He motioned Glynis toward wicker chairs. "Your sister and Elizabeth Stanton have said you've not been sympathetic to the Underground's work."

"No, but I've changed my mind," Glynis answered. "Although I must tell you that I don't feel good about breaking the law. On the other hand, I don't feel I can sit by and watch what has been happening ... well ... happen.

"To be truthful, Mr. Douglass, I probably wouldn't have become involved at all, if those I care about hadn't been threatened." She added lamely, "But from your vantage point, you probably can't understand my ambivalence."

"No. No, but I can understand your not wanting to break the law. It's a law, however, that has to be changed. I think that will happen. But when ... ?" His hands went into the air palms up. He was not, Glynis thought, a man who would shrug.

"In the meantime," Douglass went on, "we break the law that now exists and you are aware, I presume, that the penalties involved are harsh. That 'civil disobedience,' as my friend Henry Thoreau has called it, carries with it great risk. Since you're a librarian, Miss Tryon, you might be familiar with Thoreau."

Glynis nodded. She knew of Thoreau's defense of a private conscience against a majority's lowering of moral principles to expedite certain ends. At the time she first read it, several years earlier, she grasped how "Civil Disobedience" applied to the abolitionists, of which Thoreau himself was one, and she understood Frederick Douglass's reference now—but she wondered if what he really questioned was her resolve. Or if he didn't quite trust her. Well, she could hardly blame him. The risks *were* great.

Douglass was now studying her intently, as if probing for some visible proof. At last he sat back in his chair. "Tell me something about the young woman."

Glynis briefly related what she knew. "Kiri told me last night," she concluded, "that if it would be agreeable to you and your family, she'd like to stay here until Niles Peartree can come for her. Would that be possible?"

"*Will* he come?" Douglass again looked at her intently.

"I've no doubt of that. None at all. I've known him a good many years."

Douglass's face reflected little, but Glynis assumed he must have some reservation about Niles's intentions. About any unknown white man's intentions. "How long might that be," Douglass asked, "until the young man comes?"

"He told his mother he needed just a few days to complete the sale of his art gallery."

Douglass nodded. Glynis couldn't tell if this satisfied him. And she wondered if she had the right to ask him her next question. But the circumstances defied any etiquette with which she was familiar. "Mr. Douglass," she began, "I wonder if . . . that is, do you know any way in which Kiri's freedom could be legally obtained? I mean . . ."

"Bought?" Douglass asked. "Could her freedom be bought? Is that what you mean?"

"Yes. I understand that you yourself were born into slavery. That your freedom was . . . was . . . I'm sorry," Glynis stammered. "I really am having difficulty with the idea of 'buying' a human being," she murmured. She could feel her cheeks redden. Frederick Douglass must think her totally ignorant. Well, on this subject, she was.

To Glynis's intense gratitude, Douglass seemed to overlook her embarrassment. "It might be possible, if the young woman's owner wants to sell her. But has there been any indication of that?"

Glynis shook her head. "No. No, in fact quite the contrary.

But if Kiri and Niles flee to Canada, then neither of them will be able to return; I thought if Kiri were free, then they might at least be able to visit. As it is now, Niles's mother is heart-broken, as you can imagine." Glynis stopped. Considering what she had recently learned, she thought Harriet's misery might be considered by Douglass to be insignificant com-pared to what slave mothers had to endure.

She had underestimated him. "I think we should be able to make some cautious inquiries about Kiri," he said. "That's re-ally all we can do, though. It seems her owner is determined to have her brought back. Or someone else is."

"Why 'someone else'?" Glynis asked. "I say that," she ex-plained, "because I've wondered myself why a slaveholder would go to all this trouble and expense just to get one slave back. It seems totally irrational." She did not want to specify her suspicion regarding St. Croix's motive. "My understand-ing of the Fugitive Slave Law is that the owners must pay the expense for return of their slaves. Surely the cost of getting Kiri back . . ."

She paused because Douglass looked as if he differed.

"Not if the slaveholder is encouraged by other slaveholders to persevere," he said. "The man may have neighbors who don't want to see their own slaves getting any ideas about es-caping. Or he may want to see abolitionists discouraged in their Underground activities. Or . . ." Douglass hesitated. "Or there may be another reason entirely. Perhaps someone else wants her sent back." He looked at Glynis as if asking for her thoughts.

"I can't think why," she answered. "But I *have* had the dis-tinct sense that someone in Seneca Falls has been thwarting Kiri's escape. I think the Marshals' office in Auburn, for in-stance, has been notified of runaways in town."

Douglass sat forward abruptly, gripping the arms of his chair. "Miss Tryon, this is important. I have suspected for some time now that an informer is operating somewhere along the line—the line from Philadelphia to Rochester. Oth-ers believe that too; Harriet Tubman, for one." Douglass smiled fleetingly. "We're certain the problem is north of Philadelphia—most assisting runaways south of there are Ne-groes, or white people Harriet knows. But if the informer is, for example, in Seneca Falls, that might explain a number of recent captures."

Glynis stared at him. She hadn't completely believed it. Now it seemed possible.

"What can be done about this?" she asked him.

"Watch. See who in your town has access to telegraph messages. To trains going in and out. Someone who wouldn't look suspicious in the church organizations. Someone familiar with the free Negroes and the active abolitionists in Seneca Falls, or even with the livery stable that rents horses to lawmen chasing runaways."

The livery, she thought; Zeph had learned about the marshals there. But any number of people fit Douglass's description. "I still can hardly believe this," she said. "But yes, I understand what you're saying. We can watch for that kind of individual. In the meantime, what about Kiri?"

Douglass at last sat back in the chair. Did he seem a little less distrustful of her? "I need to know where she's from," he said. "Virginia, did I hear?"

"Yes; a tobacco plantation just outside of Richmond, Niles Peartree said. The planter's name is Victor St. Croix."

Douglass looked off. "Richmond. I think that's Henrico County. . . . Miss Tryon? Is something wrong?"

Glynis exhaled the breath she had drawn. Henrico County? Where had she heard that before? "Excuse me," she said, frowning. "I'm just trying to remember something. Please go on."

"There are several lawyers in Richmond," Douglass continued, "who are attempting to have the Fugitive Slave Law repealed. Who are working for abolition. When we go inside, I'll write down their names for you. If you know a good lawyer in Seneca Falls, he might contact them about Kiri."

"Yes, I'm sure Jeremiah Merrycoyf will help. Thank you."

A woman's voice from inside brought Frederick Douglass to his feet. "My wife Anna," he said, motioning toward the door. Then, with a curiously European flourish, Douglass swept open the door, bending almost imperceptibly from the waist. Not at all a servile gesture, it possessed instead a certain arrogance, something very close to mockery, which was not wasted on Glynis.

AFTER SEVERAL PITCHERS of lemonade and a dozen or more slices of warm bread, the Douglasses' five children with Katy, Seth, and Emma went out the back door, toting baskets to gather apples from the tree behind the house. Anna Douglass had been sitting in a rocker in front of the kitchen window. Mrs. Douglass, an ample, soft-eyed woman whose round face held an expression Glynis would have called melancholy, hadn't said more than three consecutive words all morning. Now, with a faint "S'cuse me," she left the kitchen, retreated to the back hall and disappeared. Owen and Gwen didn't act as if they found her reticence unusual. Perhaps it wasn't. Perhaps the quiet Anna Douglass found her husband's prominence overwhelming, even a reproof, as she herself had not, for instance, learned to read. In fact, other than their children, the two seemed to have little in common.

Glynis pulled her attention back to the parlor. Gwen had been asking after a former Rochester resident, a young woman with whom she had attended Celestia Bloss's Clover Street Seminary. After graduation Myrtilla Miner taught in a number of New York towns before leaving for Washington, D.C., to open a school for free Negro girls. In the three years since her school had opened, enrollment climbed from six to forty.

Gwen said she'd heard reports of opposition to the school, compelling three moves within two years; that Myrtilla taught the girls to ignore taunts, but during one hostile episode, she herself brandished a pistol to ward off the threatening mob.

". . . but she survived the threats against her school and has bought three acres and a building on the outskirts of Washington," Gwen said now. "Is that true?"

"Yes, although I tried to talk her out of it," Douglass answered. "Her health isn't good—you know how thin she is, her severe back problems—but Myrtilla's determined, has a will of iron, if you remember. Especially now, with the large donation Mrs. Stowe made the school from her royalties on *Uncle Tom's Cabin*—" Douglass broke off, turning his head toward the window.

The sound of galloping hoofbeats came from down the road. Frederick Douglass was on his feet instantly, moving to the back door. "Take Kiri to the cellar cupboard—now!" he called to his fifteen-year-old daughter Rosetta. "The rest of you, in here. Quick now!"

The youngsters rushed into the house as the hoofbeats approached, louder by the second. Owen and Gwen had already moved to the porch, but Glynis remained in the house, trying to think what she could say to the marshals. She realized Emma stood beside her, forehead furrowed, eyes wide with what had to be fear.

"It's all right, Emma," Glynis said, with a confidence she did not feel. "We'll think of something—all the people here are certainly smarter, from what I could tell, than two not very bright marshals. We'll talk our way out of whatever happens."

Glynis paused, thinking this approach might not be an appropriate thing to teach a twelve-year-old.

Emma stared at her. "Aunt Glynis, you are so brave. I could never be—"

"No, Emma," Glynis interrupted. "I am most certainly *not* brave. Far from it! I just try to act that way when I'm in trouble. I don't know if I deceive anyone else, but it helps me— not to panic. Of course," she added, trying to smile reassuringly, "it doesn't always work."

Returning a wan half-smile, Emma turned back to the window. Her smile vanished as the hoofbeats thundered closer. Both Glynis and Emma drew in their breath as a single chestnut horse suddenly appeared over the road's crest, galloping toward the house.

The figure astride the horse, although tall, looked much too slight for one of the marshals. Or any other man for that matter. Glynis edged to the door in time to hear her sister's low groan.

And Owen's angry "Bronwen!"

Now that she could clearly see her niece, Glynis had an immediate and vivid image of historians' accounts of Queen Boudicca in the first century A.D., leading her Britons to battle against occupying Roman legions. Tacitus described the Queen's Celtic coloring and red hair; her height and fierce expression. Glynis had to wonder if Boudicca might not have been an ancient foremother of Bronwen Llyr.

With one pale arm thrust in the air—in either defiance or

greeting—Bronwen's heels dug into the horse's sides, urging the chestnut toward the waist-high fence surrounding the Douglass yard. The horrified watchers on the porch stood dumbstruck. All that is but Gwen, who screamed "Bronwen! No!"

As the chestnut neared the fence it seemed, for a heart-stopping instant, as though he might balk, but then over the rails horse and rider soared. Bronwen's straw hat flew off, exposing the braids of red hair that had been tucked underneath. No one on the porch uttered a word.

Just in front of the house, Bronwen pulled the horse to a stop and slid off. She had ridden bareback, barefoot, and was dressed in what appeared to be her older brother's trousers pulled up under her armpits, the drawstring waist gathered across her flat young chest. A baggy shirt completed the image of a circus clown. But nothing about Bronwen seemed the least bit clownish, Glynis thought with a twinge of admiration. Poor Gwen and Owen. In a few years, this girl would be something!

If she lived that long. Owen, having recovered his voice, stepped off the porch step, his expression one of fury. "Bronwen! What are you doing here? Just what do you—"

Bronwen cut him off; gasping for breath, she yanked a paper from a trouser pocket. "It's a wire," she panted. "For Aunt Glynis."

"Where's my baby? What have you done with baby Harry?" demanded Gwen frantically as Glynis hurried down the porch steps.

"Oh, he's O.K.," Bronwen told her mother, the disgust in her voice barely concealed. "I took him to Papa's office—"

"My office?" Owen repeated. *"My office!"*

"Yeah, I left him with Mr. Ellwanger and Mr. Barry. Even took fresh nappies to them in case Harry—"

"Bronwen, that's quite enough!" Owen growled.

Glynis stretched out her hand. "May I have the wire please, Bronwen?" she said, fighting back the dread that always accompanied an unexpected telegraph.

"Oh. Oh, sure, Aunt Glynis." Bronwen relinquished the folded piece of yellow paper with a grin, shooting Glynis a look of conspiratorial intrigue. Glynis quickly looked away, afraid that despite her concern she might laugh.

Owen, however, took tight hold of his daughter's arm, and marched her toward the porch. "I'm sure you've enjoyed yourself, young lady! But perhaps you'd better think twice about . . ."

Glynis shut out the voices around her and stood next to the porch to unfold the telegram.

GLYNIS STOP HARRIET HAD ACCIDENT STOP INJURY NOT MORTAL BUT NEED YOU HERE IF POSSIBLE STOP DR QUENTIN IVES

TWELVE

*And ain't I a woman? I have borne thirteen chilern, and
seen 'em 'most all sold off to slavery, and when I cried
out with my mother's grief, none but Jesus heard me!
And ain't I a woman?*

—SOJOURNER TRUTH

HEN-RICO COUN-TY HEN-RICO *Coun-ty Hen-rico Coun-ty* ...
the train wheels clacked intrusively. Where had she heard that
name? And why did it seem so important? Glynis wondered
uneasily.

A long shrill whistle brought her head up with a jerk. For
a moment she could not remember where she was, until an
anxious glance through the window showed the familiar landscape of Seneca County moving past. She would be home in
a few minutes after having been gone, it seemed, for months.
Years. Surely not just two days?

Leaving Kiri had not been easy. Glynis didn't think anything but concern for Harriet could have pulled her away
from Rochester before Niles arrived. However, Kiri probably
would be as safe with the Douglasses as anywhere until he
did. But what had happened to Harriet?

An orange-splotched field of ripe pumpkins reminded her
that the Seneca County Agricultural Fair would be held the
first Saturday in October, just a few days off. Ordinarily
Harriet would now be finishing her fruit preserves; she won
a prize nearly every fair for her transparent golden quince
jelly.

And no wonder. The quince project was a Herculean one.
Each year, after picking, peeling, coring, and cooking the
fruit, the kitchen would become an obstacle course while,
dangling from hooks in overhead beams, white cheesecloth
bags plump with quince mash gently swung to and fro, drain-
ing into kettles. Then the yielded juice had to be strained once
again. A sweetly potent fragrance, at first delightful but

quickly as cloying as strong perfume, would permeate the house. For all Glynis knew, this year's quince might still be swinging, still be dripping; the white bags by this time, no doubt, as yellowed and wizened as aged ghosts. She groaned inwardly. She did not share Harriet's enthusiasm for elaborate food preparation. What could have *happened* to Harriet?

As the train braked, screeching down the last grade, the Seneca River-Canal glittered to the south, a shiny ribbon unwinding beneath a sunny, cloudless sky—a rare event in a western New York autumn. Glynis leaned forward for a better look and winced as her abused back protested. She felt exhausted. Glad to be home.

The rail station looked nearly empty; a far cry from the furor of two days past. Stepping from the train, Glynis came face-to-face with Mad Jennie muttering dementedly to the few male travelers. The sight of her never failed to leave Glynis miserable. What should the town do with the poor woman? No one seemed to know. Jennie resisted all efforts to shelter her, and none had the heart to force the issue until after the weather turned cold. Then every autumn the village council passed a resolution to confine her in the county asylum for the insane. Every year Jennie fought tooth-and-nail—Jamie would come home and she must be there to meet him—and every year the town capitulated. She slept in the rail station's baggage room. And townspeople gave her money, thus tacitly conceding to Jennie, and to themselves, that most anything was better than the asylum.

Glynis fumbled in her purse. Bobbing her head, Jennie grabbed at Glynis's coins; she jammed them into a pocket of her grimy skirt, her distraught eyes ever darting toward the train. For an instant, however, the eyes stopped to rest on Glynis with a startling lucidity before Jennie said, "Thank you, Miss Tryon."

This had happened before, and on those occasions Glynis had had an intuitive sense, as she did now, that Jennie had not yet been completely lost. But then, suddenly, Jennie's head jerked to one side; with a crab-like skittering she closed in on a young man walking past and thrust her face up into his. "Jamie? Is it you've come home then, Jamie?"

Heartsick, Glynis turned away, hurrying across the cobble-stones in the direction of Cayuga Street.

Duncan raced to meet her, shaggy hair bristling for joy, apparently much revived by cooler weather. Opening the front door of the house, the odor of quince assailed her. When she reached the kitchen, the first things she saw, lined up on the table, were dozens of glasses of clear gold jelly topped with thick layers of wax.

"Welcome home. What happened in Rochester?" Harriet sat near the window in a wing chair; against the chair leaned a pair of crutches. One leg rested on pillows piled upon a footstool—a splinted leg. The left side of her face looked swollen and bluish colored.

"Harriet! What happened *here*?"

"Fell off the chair I'd climbed on to put away those jelly glasses."

"Oh, Harriet, are you all right? Sorry, that's a stupid thing to say. You're obviously not all right. Is the leg broken?"

Harriet nodded. "Shinbone cracked, Quentin Ives says."

"Is it painful?"

"Not very. More nuisance than anything. I didn't want you to come back. No need for it—I can manage fine. But Quentin and Aurora Usher insisted I shouldn't be alone. They didn't know, of course, what you were up to, and I couldn't very well tell them that what you were up to was breaking the law!"

Glynis cringed. "Well, they were right to wire me," she said, pulling a chair away from the table and seating herself next to Harriet. "You *shouldn't* be alone . . . but where's Mr. Fyfe?"

"Still in Syracuse with his niece. Now tell me what happened in Rochester."

Glynis sighed. "It's a long story. Although, don't worry," she added quickly, "Kiri's fine. And safe. I have to wire Niles that she's going to wait for him there. Harriet, when did you do that to yourself?"

"Not long after you left, and I'd finished the jelly. Thought I should keep busy, keep moving, so I wouldn't fret. Ha!" She smiled ruefully. "As luck would have it, Zeph Waters came by to tell me you and Kiri got off safely, not without some

trouble though, I gathered. Anyway, Zeph found me on the
floor over there," she gestured toward the cupboard, "and got
me into a chair, before he raced off for Quentin. You know,
something's really wrong with that boy, Glynis. Not just his
sullenness—he seemed agitated. Worried."

"I imagine he *was* worried. You could have killed yourself,
falling like that."

"That's not what I meant," Harriet said. "He seemed worried about something else. Wanted to see you the minute you
got back. *If* you got back, he said, which of course scared me
half to death. What did he know?"

Glynis shook her head. What *did* Zeph know? Had he been
the reason Jacques Sundown appeared so fortuitously? She
shook her head again. "Let me make us tea and I'll tell you
what happened."

GLYNIS STRETCHED AND yawned, glancing at her bedtable
clock. She could easily sleep *another* ten hours. But Harriet
had just called from downstairs. The woman was simply
amazing; broken leg and all, she'd hopped about with the
crutches last night like a peg-legged sailor. Glynis had to
force her—threaten to sit on her and tie her down—before
she'd settle in one place. No wonder she'd outlasted three
husbands.

Sliding off the edge of the high four-poster, Glynis groaned
as her feet hit the floor. Her back complained sharply; then it
eased. But she walked gingerly to the head of the stairs to call
to Harriet, "Be down in a minute."

"Better put something on—you've got a visitor. It's Zeph
Waters."

By the time she splashed her face with water from the
pitcher on her commode, wrapped herself in a cream-colored
wool dressing gown—not that any lady should appear in undress before a man, but Zeph wasn't one yet—and went
downstairs, he had already seated himself at the kitchen table
with Harriet. They were eating muffins and—what else,
but?—quince jelly.

Zeph sprang from his chair. "Is the girl all right?" he asked
her. He rocked back and forth on his feet with his usual impatience. No; more than his usual, Glynis decided.

She said Kiri was fine, and Harriet added, "I *told* you that, Zeph." She raised her eyebrows at Glynis and reached for her crutches. "Beautiful day—I'm going out in the garden. Can't bear to watch this boy jumping around like a flea on a hot griddle."

Glynis glanced at Zeph; scowling, he shot her what he clearly meant to be a significant look, and mouthed at her behind Harriet's back, "I need to talk to you. Alone."

After they'd settled Harriet outside in the cast-iron garden settee with a mug of coffee, Zeph again eyed Glynis, again rocked on his feet, and jerked his head toward the house. Glynis, shrugging at Harriet's unspoken question, followed the boy inside.

"Zeph," she began, once they were in the kitchen, "what is the *matter* with you? You act like you're ready to jump out of your skin. Oh, and tell me, did you send Jacques Sundown to Rochester—"

"Didn't some marshals show up there?" he broke in.

"Yes, but—"

"Thought so. Yeah, I told Sundown they were going after you two—you and the girl."

"Well, thank you for what you did. It must have been hard for you, going to Constable Sundown. But why did you?"

"Guessed I had to trust him—with something I overheard at the livery. Figured he'd never let *you* get hurt. But Miss Tryon, there's somebody in this town oughta be strung up. Who's making runaways get caught."

"Yes, I'm sure there *is* someone. But who? And what did you hear?"

Zeph shook his head. "Don't know who, and anyway that's not what I need to tell you. It's something else." Zeph paused, then stared at the floor.

"Sit down, Zeph. Please, sit! It's obvious you're troubled. What's wrong?"

Glynis seated herself at the table and waited. Zeph ran the toe of his boot over the floor, then finally went to the window, probably to make certain Harriet remained out of earshot.

"Zeph?"

"O.K., O.K. Just let me think how to say this." He walked to the door, jiggling the latch as if to verify it was secure, then bent down to pick up an article from the floor. It looked like a bundle of shirts, or at least one large shirt wrapped around something else. Glynis hadn't noticed it until then.

Holding the bundle, Zeph returned to the table, throwing himself into a chair opposite Glynis. For some moments he just sat, staring intently at the bundle in his lap. When he finally looked up at her, his brown eyes had lost some of their customary hard wariness; they'd become very dark, almost soft and . . . and childlike, she thought, nonplussed by this unfamiliar Zeph.

He shifted in the chair. "You know how old I am?" he asked at last, voice nearly a whisper.

"Ah, well, I thought probably about fourteen, fifteen?"

He nodded. "Yeah, something like that. I don't know exactly."

"You don't know?" Glynis repeated. "You don't know how old you are?"

He ignored the question. "You weren't living here in town then—thirteen years ago? No, I didn't think so." His voice wavered. He took a deep breath. "You'll probably think this sounds crazy, but it's true. Really," he said earnestly.

Glynis nodded. Whatever had so upset him must be serious; she had better not interrupt or he'd never get it out.

Zeph fingered the shirt-wrapped bundle, and again breathed deep. "O.K. Well . . . you know my Mom and Pop Waters? They weren't . . . weren't my parents. Not my real parents. They said I got found. In the woods outside town. I don't remember any of it, though."

Glynis sat very still, hardly daring to breathe. She suddenly had an inkling of what was coming . . . no! No, it couldn't be. She must have shaken her head, because Zeph burst out, "See! I told you it sounds crazy. But . . ."

He stopped.

"No, Zeph, it doesn't sound crazy. Just . . . please go on," Glynis tried to encourage him. "But what?"

"I was just a baby, they said. And, well, you know my name? You know what 'Zephaniah' means?"

Glynis searched her mind. "It's biblical, isn't it? Means something like 'protected,' or—"

" 'Hidden by the Lord,' " Zeph murmured. He looked almost as if he might cry. "They named me that, Mom and Pop did; they said some people from town found me wrapped up in a blanket, about suffocating in leaves. They—the people—brought me to the Waters' cause Mom and Pop were black. Like me. And they didn't have any children . . ."

Zeph's voice caught, and he ducked his head. Glynis wanted desperately to say something to ease his distress. But what could she say? Without thinking, she reached across the table to cover his clenched hands with hers. When she saw what she'd done, she thought he might pull away. But he didn't.

"About the worst thing is," he finally went on, "is there were two other people in the woods. A man and a woman. And . . . and they were dead. They'd been shot. Dead."

Glynis gripped his hands as Zeph continued, "Mom and Pop told me never, *never*, to tell anybody about it. The people who found me promised they wouldn't tell—and I guess they haven't."

"Who were they . . . the ones who found you?" Glynis prodded gently when Zeph paused.

"Constable Stuart. And Lacey and Isaiah Smith. The Smiths said they went looking in the woods back of their house, 'cause some runaways were supposed to be coming and they hadn't gotten there, and Smiths heard something, so . . ."

Cullen knew. And he'd never told her. But he wouldn't—not if he'd given his word. That meant he also knew Lacey and Isaiah worked with the Underground Railroad, and he apparently looked the other way for years. But of course he had; runaways weren't caught, once inside the Seneca Falls village limits, until recently.

She believed what Zeph had just told her. But who else would—Kiri, for instance—unless there existed some proof, something tangible, that linked him to a runaway slave woman who would have been his and Kiri's mother?

"Zeph, what is that?" Glynis pointed to the bundle.

The boy sat forward and untied the shirt. It fell open to reveal a musty old gray blanket, flecked with dark, rust-colored stains.

Zeph turned back a corner of the blanket, motioning Glynis

to look at the eight letters, pale but still legible, embroidered into the frayed binding of the wool: JOLIMONT.

"Zeph ... Zeph, this means Kiri is your sister ... your half-sister," Glynis breathed. But he knew that; had known it several nights ago. No wonder he acted so strange. That and learning how his mother and father had been murdered. Glynis wiped at her eyes, seeing through a blur of tears that Zeph had buried his face in his blanket.

"If she's my sister, what it means," he said, his voice anguished, "what it means is that I'm a slave, too."

HOW COULD HE be a slave? How could that be possible when he'd lived in the North almost all his life? Glynis asked herself as she trudged up the long dirt road to Smiths'. Although it certainly made sense of the Waters' insistence that Zeph never divulge his history. But what concerned her most now was the possibility of a connection between the boy and Lyle Brogan's murder. Zeph had known for years that his birth name had not been Zephaniah Waters—but he said he didn't know what his name *had* been. Could it be, then, that Zeph was the Thomas Farley for whom Brogan had been looking?

After the boy had left the house, and she'd settled Harriet in the kitchen, Glynis sent Niles a cryptic wire about Kiri, one that couldn't be deciphered, she felt fairly sure, by anyone other than Niles. She then spent the remainder of the morning catching up at the library. Jonathan Quant had done his usual exemplary job, and nothing untoward had occurred in her absence. But she couldn't get Zeph's comment out of her mind. Lacey and Isaiah Smith might know something more. How *could* Zeph be a slave?

She smelled woodsmoke and heard Isaiah Smith's hammer before she could see him. The gray house and yard came into view with Isaiah at his forge; beside him stood a large black and white paint. And Jacques Sundown.

As Glynis approached the house she saw seated on the front porch, rocking back and forth, the tall black woman preacher who called herself Sojourner Truth. Glynis started for the porch.

"Afternoon, Miz Tryon," Isaiah greeted her, grinning. He let drop the horse's hoof he'd had between his knees. The horse pawed the ground several times before swinging its head toward Jacques.

Jacques rose from a squat, pulled coins from his trouser pocket and handed them to Isaiah. Then he ran his hand down the paint's near foreleg. "Seems O.K. now. Like I said, he's had some hard riding last couple days."

Glynis suspected the horse had indeed. "Jacques," she said, changing course and going toward him, "I appreciate what you—"

Jacques cut her off with, "I'll be back to have you check that shoe again," this said to Isaiah, "in a few days." He swung himself up on the paint, then at last seemed to notice Glynis. He gave her a brief nod.

"Jacques, would you wait a minute?" Glynis spoke quickly as he had turned the horse toward the road.

"Got to get back into town," Jacques said. With a flick of the reins, he rode off.

Glynis stared after him. Well, of course he didn't want to talk about the marshals and Rochester in front of Isaiah. She hadn't intended to say anything specific. Did the man really think her a total fool? Jacques Sundown had to be the rudest man who ever—

She realized her hands had clenched into fists, and turned to Isaiah, who watched her with what looked very much like amusement. He wore denim breeches and a long leather apron, its narrow bib the only covering over a massive chest. The muscles of his upper arms must be larger than her waist span, Glynis thought, somewhat awed; then, feeling more than a little ill at ease, just standing there staring at a man's naked torso, she moved away. "I'll just go see Lacey and Sojourner," she mumbled, as Isaiah went back to his forge with his amused look, she noticed, still intact.

"Tell Lacy I need somethin' to drink," Isaiah called after her, but Lacey had already come down the porch steps with a pitcher in her hands.

"Be right back," she said to Glynis. "Got Miz Peartree's shawl about done."

"That's not why I'm here, Lacey. I need to ask you about something."

"Well, go on up and sit yourself down, then," Lacey said over her shoulder. "You know Truth, I reckon."

Glynis climbed the porch steps to where Sojourner Truth sat rocking, scrutinizing Glynis over her metal-rimmed glasses. "Well, Missy Tryon, just what you be doin' here this day?"

"How are you?" Glynis held out her hand to the woman, who grasped it firmly and motioned her to sit down. "I've come to talk to Lacey, but I'm glad you're here, too," Glynis said.

She'd never seen Sojourner Truth in other than a plain gray dress, and white sunbonnet and shawl. The woman might be in her early fifties, or her late seventies, no one could tell from the smooth walnut skin and the shrewd eyes now regarding Glynis with interest. Sojourner Truth came through Seneca Falls frequently, lecturing on abolition and women's rights, with as magnificent a voice as Frederick Douglass's. She didn't have Douglass's sophistication, his well-read, urbane manner, but she possessed a compelling presence all her own.

Elizabeth Stanton knew the woman fairly well, and had repeated to Glynis one of her favorite comments of Truth: "Now I hear talkin' about the Constitution and the rights of man. I come up and take hold of this Constitution. It looks mighty big, and I feel for my rights, but there ain't none there. Then I says, 'God, what ails this Constitution?' "

Now Truth rocked forward, fixing Glynis with a long look. "I been hearin' some mighty peculiar things 'bout you, Missy Tryon," she said, starting to smile. "Seems like you been tearin' up the miles 'twixt here and there." She gestured vigorously toward the west.

Toward Rochester, Glynis thought. How could she possibly know? Jacques? But would *Constable* Sundown admit to anyone that he'd aided a runaway? No, it had to have been the Underground network.

Lacey just then returned to the porch and handed Glynis a glass of sun tea, warm and strong, the color of amber. "Know you don't need that shawl quite yet," she said. "It'll be ready, though—one, two more weeks now. But I got a room full of gowns and robes and crowns and whatever," Lacey gestured toward the house. "Got to finish them first. That Usher lady she is most persuasive, she is." Lacey laughed.

"You mean you're doing the *Macbeth* costumes?" Glynis asked.

"Yes, ma'am! I sure am. Seems like their regular costume maker, she upped and took off. Took off without even a by-your-leave, mind you."

Glynis sat forward. "Lacey, do you mean a woman named Luella?"

"That's the one."

"She just left?"

"Guess so. Nobody seen her, so that's what they think."

Glynis wondered what Jacques knew about this—not that he'd tell her, not voluntarily. She'd have to drag it out of him. Well, she wouldn't.

"Anyhow, don't you worry none about that shawl. I'll have it done by Miz Peartree's birthday."

"Oh, I know you will. As I said earlier, Lacey, I'm not here for that. I'd like to ask you some questions, if I may. About some things that I'm . . . well, I'm embarrassed that I don't know."

Sojourner Truth peered over her glasses to say, "Everybody don't know somethin'. Don't feel bad 'bout that. 'Sides, you done earned yourself the right to ask a few questions, I'd say."

"In that case," Glynis said, "can you tell me, is it possible for someone who has lived here in the North most of his life, to still be considered a slave . . . by his mother's owner in the South, for instance?"

A quick look passed between Lacey and Sojourner Truth. For a moment it seemed to Glynis neither would answer her, but then Lacey gave Glynis a searching look. "You asking about somebody in particular? Or you just want to know for yourself?"

Glynis hesitated. Lacey Smith certainly knew about Zeph's circumstances, but did Truth? "I'd just like to know," she said carefully.

"Was this here mystery person's mamma set free by her owner?" This asked by Truth.

"Ah, I don't think so. But I suppose his father could have been freed. I don't know that."

"Don't make no difference 'bout the father, anyway," Truth said.

Glynis must have looked puzzled, because Lacey added, "Depends on the mother. Children born of slave women, they're slaves too. That's the way it works. It's no never mind what the father is."

Truth gave a harsh laugh. "No, on account of too many bein' born by white men havin' their way. Wouldn't be enough slaves left if'n they was to count it like that."

"But that can't be, can it?" Glynis said. "I mean, what does the law say?"

Truth interrupted her with a loud chuckle. "Guess you *is* mighty ignorant, Missy Tryon. The law it say what them white men want it to say!"

Glynis sat for a moment, trying to remain calm; her head throbbed with the effort. "Lacey, I guess you probably know," she said finally, "who I'm talking about?"

Lacey gave her a brief nod. "Think I do. And while we appreciate you being careful, Truth here knows about the boy, too. Harriet Tubman told her about Zephaniah."

"You know 'bout Harriet Tubman?" Truth said to Glynis. "The one we calls the Moses of her people, leadin' them slaves out of bondage . . ."

Glynis didn't hear the rest, didn't hear past "Moses." Moses! That's where she'd heard about Henrico County—Cullen had told her, weeks ago, in connection with that old black man's death.

"Excuse me," she said now, "but how did Harriet Tubman hear about Zeph?"

"The boy's grandmother, Masika," Lacey said.

"Zeph's *grandmother* told Harriet?"

"No, no. Masika told Moses Rawlings to ask Harriet Tubman. Years ago, word traveled on the Underground—the grapevine telegraph we calls it—that a baby had been found, still alive, after those killings in the woods up here."

Moses Rawlings! "Ah, how did that come about?" Glynis asked. "How did Masika know Moses Rawlings?"

"Why, they both on the same plantation. Anyhow, near as

I can figure," Lacey said, "when Moses Rawlings got his freedom papers he headed up this way, 'cause he found out from Harriet Tubman that the boy was here'bouts—Harriet found out *that* from me."

"Did Zeph know that Moses Rawlings was looking for him—for his grandmother?"

Lacey shook her head. "No. Zeph don't know he even *got* a grandmother. We not about to tell him, neither—that boy's so hotheaded he'd likely shoot right down there to Riverain and get himself picked up and sold!"

Riverain . . . yes. Yes, that was the plantation next to St. Croix's Jolimont that Kiri had told her about. From where Kiri's mother had originally come before she had been sold to St. Croix.

"But," she said, "why didn't Moses Rawlings tell Zeph? Or hadn't Moses found Zeph before he—"

"Before he found himself in the canal? Dead?" Lacey spat the words. "Oh, he found him, Moses did. Come to ask us if we knew the boy workin' at the livery with him. He thought the boy was 'bout the right age, so's we, Isaiah and me, told him how Zeph was found in that woods and all. But Moses likely never got the chance to talk to the boy, 'cause that was the day he had his *accident*."

Glynis stared at her. "Lacey, the way you said 'accident'—do you think it *wasn't* an accident?"

Sojourner Truth made a scoffing sound. Lacey scowled at the woman, and again a look passed between them.

"Please, Lacey, if you know something about Moses Rawlings's death . . ."

"What do I know? Only that the old man was the best horseman in Henrico County. Ain't likely he go and get himself and his horse in that canal. No ma'am! Not unless somebody pushed him."

Glynis's head throbbed harder, trying desperately to keep this all straight. Lacey Smith was saying Moses Rawlings had been killed. And Glynis remembered that Cullen, too, had thought there was something odd about the old man's death. But why would anyone murder Moses? To keep him from finding Zeph? That didn't make sense. And Moses Rawlings's death *could* have been an accident. Or could have been caused by someone in town, God forbid! who simply hated Negroes. The same person informing on runaway slaves? Glynis's mind reeled.

"One more thing," she said to Lacey. "Since you seem to know everything else, I assume you also know about a young woman named Kiri? This Masika's granddaughter?"

"Course we do," said Lacey.

"Then tell me: that slave-catcher that was murdered here, about a week ago; is there a possibility that his death has something to do with all of this?"

Lacey shrugged. But Sojourner Truth stopped rocking to lean forward and ask Glynis, "Slave-catcher named Brogan, was it?"

Glynis drew in her breath. "Did you know him?"

"*I* didn't, thank the good Lord. But I can tell you this, missy: that there Brogan, he worked mostly for slaveholders in Virginia. That mean anything to you?"

"Could he have worked for the owner of Jolimont, this Victor St. Croix? Or Riverain, do you think? But more to the point, do either of you know a man named Thomas Farley?"

"Most likely Brogan did work for them owners," Truth said. "I hear tell he'd work for anybody'd pay him. Never heared of a Farley, though. You, Lacey?"

Lacey frowned and seemed about to say something. Then she shook her head, eyes flicking toward her husband. Glynis wondered why the woman hesitated; she looked toward the forge where Isaiah damped the fire. Could the blacksmith know something the women didn't? Probably not; he had been born a free man, here in the North. But Lacey hadn't, Glynis suddenly remembered. Lacey had run away from her dead mistress's son and therefore, it now dawned on Glynis, was still a slave. Had Brogan known about her?

She couldn't think, couldn't begin to deal with what felt like a hornet's nest of questions buzzing in her ears. Cullen. She needed Cullen. Who else could she talk to about this— two people murdered and possibly linked in some twisted, baffling way. But the important thing was: Did these murders mean danger for Zeph? Or Kiri? And from whom?

Isaiah came striding toward the porch. "You ladies just

gonna sit there gabbin' all day? Or is there a chance a man can get some food?"

Lacey threw him an annoyed look. "You so hungry, you just get yourself something to eat. We busy here."

Isaiah grinned, and climbed to the porch, then went inside. They could hear the icebox door clank open, and Isaiah's subsequent yelp of pleasure.

"Made rice pudding for him." Lacey chuckled. "Looks like he managed to find it." She turned and called toward the kitchen, "Don't you go eatin' *all* that, you hear? Save some for us *ladies*!"

Glynis stood and walked to the edge of the porch to see the sun. "I didn't realize it was so late," she said. "I have to go. Harriet Peartree's broken her leg, and I don't want her fussing over supper for us. Lacey, and Truth, can you think of anything else that might be important to Zeph—I don't mean about his grandmother. I won't say anything about her to him. But I'm afraid the boy might be in some danger. I really think I'm going to have to tell Jacques Sundown about all this. Unless," she paused, "unless you've already told him."

"Not about Zeph, we didn't. But that Indian, he's on to something, that's for sure. Oh, he won't turn in runaways—I s'pect you know that for yourself now," Lacey said, grinning at Glynis, "but he sure did ask a lot of questions about that Brogan."

"We couldn't tell him nothin' 'bout the man," Truth said, "'cepting he was the Devil's own helper."

Glynis said good-bye and started down the steps. At the bottom were Isaiah's big boots, clean and smelling of saddlesoap. The last time she'd seen them, she remembered, they'd been muddy. She paused a moment on the last step. Then she started toward the dirt road.

The last time she'd seen those boots was a sunlit Monday morning—following, she now pieced together, Lyle Brogan's murder the Saturday before. The Saturday night of the play, when it had poured rain. But after that downpour, it hadn't rained again for days.

Glynis turned back to wave once at the women on the porch, hoping she hadn't betrayed her anxiety. An anxiety that spoke only in shadows, unseen and unheard; anxiety that told Glynis that beneath the surface of her quiet little town, something evil had taken root, evil possibly sown years before. Perhaps even carried from another place, like seeds borne by migrating birds. Like slavery.

THIRTEEN

❧

Camptown Races sing this song, do-dah, do-dah
Camptown racetrack five-mile long, oh, do-dah day.
Gwine to run all night,
Gwine to run all day,
I'll bet my money on the bob-tail nag,
Somebody bet on the bay.
—STEPHEN FOSTER, "CAMPTOWN RACES"

AFTER NILES PEARTREE strolled past a four-story wooden building whose sign glinting in bright sunlight declared it to be a MANUFACTORY OF WHALEBONE, he paused to look out over New York City's East River. A steady breeze curled white-ruffled waves. In the distance sailboats darted here and there like small pale butterflies around three-masted schooners and a Fulton steamboat. Along the river's edge rose a jumble of masts; masts belonging to vessels from all ports of the world. Scores of muscled, sweating men in suspenders and shirtsleeves rolled barrels down ship ramps, stacking them with rhythmic thumps on sawhorses in front of waterfront warehouses, while the strong fish odor from Fulton's Market drew like a magnet the gulls wheeling overhead.

His last morning in New York. Niles experienced a pang of regret; he would miss the bustle, the noise, and the excitement of this city. Suddenly aware of a noisy clatter behind him, he leaped across the gutter to the sidewalk as one of a hundred horse-drawn omnibuses on the city's twenty-seven lines rolled by over the cobbled paving. The clamor was deafening. Once the vehicle had passed, Niles circled piles of garbage to reach the street again, then picked his way cautiously around mounds of horse dung. Every so often, some leading citizen would complain that the streets of New York had become cesspools of filth; with which complaint everyone would agree, shake their heads at the unmanageability of a city containing well over five hundred thousand people, and then go on about their business. Warily.

When Niles reached the west side of Broadway, a wide—indeed a broad—tree-lined street, he paused to stare up at the steeples of St. Paul's Chapel and Trinity Church. Although a Saturday, the faithful entered in a steady stream. It seemed a shame, Niles reflected, that he could never bring Kiri to see these churches, which did not, like their white southern counterparts, defend the institution of slavery. Kiri's downcast eyes might lift and dance, shaking off what Niles knew to be an armor of meekness: "I am nothing; not worthy of your attention" the lowered gaze telegraphed. This saved her, she once told him, from abuse that less servile women suffered. Kiri believed the religion of white men condemned slave women by its hypocrisy. By offering them no protection, and no sanctuary.

But Niles recalled that Glynis Tryon felt much the same about religion and unservile *white* women; reminded of her, Niles thrust a hand into the trouser pocket containing Glynis's wire. And suddenly whirled around. Just in time, *this* time, to spot two men dodging under a shop's sidewalk awning to disappear inside.

Niles hesitated. Should he enter the shop himself, follow those who had, he believed, been following him? Or could he just be imagining the footfalls behind him ever since he left his valises at the rail station and bought a ticket to Rochester?

He shrugged uneasily, then forced himself to grin at his guilty conscience; he only felt like a hunted criminal because he had broken the law. Simple. No one followed him.

Still, he kept one ear cocked as he proceeded down Broadway to his gallery, or rather his previous gallery. He had finally completed its sale, had warehoused those paintings he couldn't yet ship to Montreal, and now had only last sweeping up to do. Time enough before the train left for Rochester, and Kiri.

A few doors from his gallery, Niles stopped on the sidewalk under an open window of a boardinghouse from where he could see the back of an upright piano. The refrain of some sweetly poignant melody floated out to the street. The music stopped, repeated itself, and continued from Stephen Foster's temporary room. Temporary for lo these past many months. Man would starve to death, believing he could make money by writing songs. Niles grinned, and yelled up at the window, "So long, Foster. And good luck!" His response came in a fast flurry of notes that sounded like racing horses' hooves.

Niles laughed, took several more steps, and stopped to spin around. No one there. He could have sworn he'd heard footsteps. Well, naturally he had—he couldn't be the only person out walking on a sunny Saturday morning in New York City!

Even so, he peered at the next pane of glass, looking for a reflected follower. No ominous reflection, but instead Mathew Brady's mustached face grinned out at him, surrounded by the score of Brady's award-winning daguerreotypes hanging in his gallery's front windows. Brady abruptly vanished. He reappeared, opening his door to step out to the sidewalk. "Are you on your way, Niles, or do you have time for coffee?"

"*Coffee?* Is that what you call that swill?" Niles grinned. "*That* I won't miss. You—I shall! Actually, I may have time. Just let me clean up some in there—" he motioned to his own gallery next door "—then I'll be by."

Brady smiled and, nodding, went back inside.

Since Niles's gallery stood all but empty, awaiting its new tenant, he didn't expect to be there long. He swept, then lugged a few empty crates to the rear exit, which opened on a narrow alley. Pushing the door open with his foot, he turned, backing out to the cobblestones while juggling the crates. So intent was he on this maneuver that he didn't see the shadows of two men approaching, or hear them steal up behind him. Niles realized they were there only when they grabbed for him. The crates hit the cobblestones with the sharp crack of splitting wood as the men twisted Niles's arms behind his back.

Struggling to free himself, Niles yelled angrily. It didn't occur to him to be fearful; not yet.

"Shut up," one of his captors growled. He gave Niles's arm a quick upward jerk behind the young man's back. "Just shut up and it'll go easier for you—we don't want no big scene. That's why we waited till now."

Neck straining, Niles yelled again. Again the arm twisted behind his back was yanked upward, and the pain this time forced Niles to his knees. A man on either side hauled him quickly to his feet and shoved him forward.

The back door of the next gallery flew open. Mathew Brady started through it, then stopped, rocking back on his heels as a Colt revolver came up level with his chest.

"Matt, get back!" Niles shouted.

"Yeah, hold it right there, fella," one of the men said evenly to Brady. "We don't want no trouble with you. This here boy's got to go to Richmond to answer for what he done. So you go on," he motioned with the Colt, "you just walk back inside your place there, and close the door. Go ahead now. Move!"

Brady took a step toward Niles, then hesitated at the cock of a hammer and the click of a cylinder falling into place.

"Matt, go on!" Niles shouted. "There's nothing you can do." He broke off as the men began to hustle him forward. But he managed to twist in their grip, yelling over his shoulder, "Wire Seneca Falls . . ."

The men dragged him, still struggling, down the short alley. Mathew Brady followed a few steps but stopped as one man turned to raise the Colt again. Brady then caught the flash of silver on the man's shirt; he stood stock-still until the men rounded the building with their prisoner between them.

Brady ran back inside his gallery, raced to the front entrance and on out through the door. The street looked empty except for a few morning strollers who glanced curiously at his agitation. Brady leaped from the sidewalk just in time to see horses disappearing around the corner.

THE OPEN MEADOWLAND stretching from the road to the Seneca River lay scattered with large green-and-white-striped awnings. Although the awnings lent a festive look, they were needless; for just the second time in its thirteen-year history, not rain but sunshine poured over the Seneca County Agricultural Fair. Overhead the sky gleamed with the particular brilliant blue only October could grant, thought Glynis as she gazed up and over the fairgrounds. A warm breeze, lacking as yet autumn's bite, felt like that of spring.

In the distance Jacques Sundown sat astride his paint gelding. Hock-deep in goldenrod the horse seemed motionless, save for an occasionally switching tail, while his rider appeared to be scanning the meadow. Glynis rode with Harriet in the carriage that Zeph Waters guided up to one of the awnings. From long tables beneath the striped canopy drifted the fragrance of gooseberry, raspberry, and strawberry jam; cinnamon-spiced peaches and pears; pickles emitting a spectrum of smells from dill to watermelon to pigs' feet.

"This all right, Mrs. Peartree?" Zeph asked Harriet.

"It's fine. Now all I have to do is get down." Harriet handed her crutches to Glynis and began to swing her splinted leg over the side of the carriage.

"Wait a minute, Harriet," Glynis said, "until Zeph and I can find someone to help." She looked up and saw engineer Ian Bentham coming toward them. He appeared very trim, having lost some weight; probably from the past weeks' strain of dealing with Vanessa and The Usher Playhouse. "Good morning, Mr. Bentham. We could use your assistance, if you would."

"Glad to help."

After they'd settled Harriet with her jellies and companion cooks under the awning, Zeph, leading the trotter and carriage, went off to find his employer, John Boone. The boy would be riding one of the livery owner's horses in the late-afternoon cross-country race that traditionally closed the fair.

Glynis walked with Ian Bentham toward the central exhibition area, already thronged with farm families. Women stood draping their quilts carefully over frames for display. Quilts as original and intricate as any museum's artistry; designed and constructed during the previous months, they were still pristine, unscathed by a long winter's wear and tear. Glynis often wondered why quilts were not considered works of art like paintings and sculpture—could it be because they were not only beautiful but functional as well? Or because the artists were women, women who didn't have time and liberty to create objects other than those that had utilitarian value.

The voices of the crowd were those of a happy expectant morning; the disappointed, grumbling voices would come later. Over them all hovered a remarkable range of odors: fresh-baked apple and pumpkin pies; the tanned, polished leather of saddles; the pine of cabinetry for sale; and the omnipresent horse manure.

"I'd forgotten what fun these fairs are," Bentham commented. He gestured toward the first of many livestock pens rippling with the woolly backs of merino sheep; beyond were pens of large black Berkshire pigs and brown-and-white Ayrshire dairy cows. Glynis thought, Fun for whom? The noisy bleating and grunting and lowing from the pens indicated anything but pleasure in this fun-filled event.

Bentham motioned toward buntings of red, white and blue draping the sides of a raised platform—obviously erected as far from the livestock pens as possible—while lines strung overhead held banners fluttering in the same colors. "I suppose," Bentham said dryly, "that this is the grandstand from where we will have the opportunity to suffer endless speeches."

Glynis laughed. "And endless awards. Were you living in town the year the fair began, Mr. Bentham?"

"Yes, although it was much smaller. Not anything like this," he said with an expansive gesture. "But as I recall, we were spared the speeches in those early days."

"Well, the four new theater boxes will be auctioned between the speakers, or so Vanessa told me. Providing some comic relief, I'd imagine."

"Actually, there are only three boxes left now," Bentham said, "because I bought one of them myself a few days ago. Proving to all how safe and sturdy they are. Did you know that some crank wrote a letter to the *Courier* editor speculating that they might collapse? *My* boxes! This troublemaker went into grisly detail as to what would be the fate of those seated underneath. And of course Ephraim Penrod saw fit to print it."

"Oh, he *would*," Glynis agreed. "Anything to stir up the town and create more readers for his newspaper." She stopped as from the corner of her eye, she swore she saw bumping over the grass a greenish gray whale with warts. "What in the world?" she gasped, turning in disbelief.

Crossing the meadow, Eebard Peck strained mightily to haul forward a cart containing what surely must be the most enormous Hubbard squash ever borne by Mother Earth.

"Look at that thing—it's immense!" Bentham laughed.

"Produced, no doubt," Glynis added, "with Peruvian guano."

Bentham gave her an odd look. "I didn't see you at the train station the day Peck's guano arrived," he said.

How interesting, Glynis thought; she hadn't seen *him*, but given that day's dire circumstances, it probably wasn't so strange Bentham had escaped her notice.

The arrival of Vanessa Usher spared Glynis from answering Bentham's inquisitive gaze—why did he seem so curious about that day?—Vanessa who, in long-sleeved silky gown the right half of which was scarlet, the left half white, floated across the meadow as an exquisite harlequin. She looked as out of place among the fair's gingham and rough corduroy as would have Lady Godiva—well, no, not quite!

"Miss Usher," Ian Bentham said as Vanessa swept toward them, "that is truly a spectacular gown. Very dramatic."

Vanessa twirled slowly, first white, then scarlet; if she moved any faster, Glynis thought, she'd look like a candy cane, or a barber's pole.

"Isn't it something!" Vanessa said coquettishly. "It's my first act *Macbeth* costume. It expresses, as you see, Lady Macbeth's clashing dual nature. Her virtuous, conscience-driven self and her more . . . ah, shall we say, her more base desires. I want her duality to be quite clear."

"Well!" Bentham exclaimed, rather more loudly than called for. "Yes indeed, Miss Usher, I would say your gown certainly does do that!" He turned his face from Vanessa, the corners of his mouth twitching.

"What do *you* think, Glynis?" Vanessa twirled again.

"Oh, Van, it's really just . . . it's stunning is what it is." Whether or not it revealed Lady Macbeth's dual persona, or looked quite the appropriate garb for an agricultural fair, begged the question. The gown was magnificent. "Did Lacey Smith make it for you?" Glynis asked.

"Yes, of course," Vanessa said. "Who else but Lacey could do anything like this? You know, I really felt quite happy when that Luella person disappeared—although of course it was unforgivably irresponsible of her. But can you imagine *her* making something this fabulous?"

Glynis shook her head with sincerity. Ian Bentham shook his head.

"My dear Lady!" resounded a rich voice to the left of Glynis. Tavus Sligh came striding toward them: Macbeth made flesh. His ensemble included—Lord help us, Glynis said to herself—dark plaid kilt under long, fur-lined, black velvet cape; amulet and crown of bright brass; sword dangling from bejeweled belt; and black knee-high boots in which Tavus advanced undaunted through the swine and sheep droppings underfoot.

"Hail!" Macbeth saluted them. "And when does our auction begin?" He gestured toward the grandstand.

"The auction is why we're in costume," Vanessa informed those passersby stopped dead in their tracks to gawk.

"I'm certainly glad to hear that," Ian Bentham said in an aside to Glynis. "I had begun to think I'd lost track of time, and Halloween was already upon us."

Glynis choked back a laugh, as both Vanessa and Tavus were staring at her. "I *asked*, Miss Tryon," said Tavus sternly, "do you know how long we must wait for our auction? While enduring, I fear, long orations from political candidates?"

"No, I don't have any idea," Glynis said, wondering why on earth he thought she would. "But you've every right to fear—the candidates for the coming election will be offering their qualifications, and their platforms."

Bentham groaned quietly.

Tavus did not exercise like restraint. "Ah, then, 'So foul and fair a day I have not seen,' quoth Macbeth. Which means: We'll have to hear *ad nauseum* about their infancies, childhoods, schoolhoods, their grand and glorious war records—as if participating in war were some necessary proving ground for manhood. 'Accursed be that tongue that tells me so!' "

On that Glynis found herself for once in agreement with Tavus. Macbeth.

Ian Bentham, however, took an abrupt stride forward, fixing Tavus with a clearly contemptuous stare. "And Mr. Sligh, do you speak from your own military experience? Or from the far safer vantage point of the armchair observer?"

Tavus looked to be caught totally off guard; his high forehead furrowed, his mouth opened as if to retort. But he snapped it shut. Turning on his heel, he began to walk away.

"Just a minute, Sligh! I don't think I heard your answer," Bentham said, his voice tight. "To quote your Macbeth: 'False face must hide what the false heart doth know.' Or more specifically, Sligh, why don't you review your military history for these folks here?"

Glynis found herself gaping at Ian Bentham. He couldn't have startled her more had he whipped out a sword and challenged Tavus to duel. Which in fact was very nearly what he had done. People wandering by, their attention seized by Vanessa's and Tavus's costume, paused in anticipation. It was as if the affable Ian Bentham, like a harmless sleeping salamander, had suddenly transformed himself into a fire-breathing dragon. Tavus Sligh half-turned toward Bentham. He seemed, from his expression, to be just as startled as Glynis. Vanessa looked first confused, then stricken. There followed a long, tense silence while the two men glared at each other. At last Tavus muttered, "Why don't you ask that clown Eebard Peck the same question?" and stalked off. Vanessa threw Bentham an angry look before she whirled to follow the retreating Macbeth.

Bentham watched them with narrowed eyes. Then his shoulders relaxed, and he turned to Glynis and smiled; the dragon withdrawn into amiability. Glynis did not feel reassured. Plainly, an unpleasant history linked the two men. And Eebard Peck. But what could have so provoked Ian Bentham? To make her even more uneasy, during the men's exchange Calista Sligh stood to one side of the grandstand. Despite the hostile words directed at her husband, Calista had not once taken her eyes off Vanessa Usher. Eyes blazing hotter than those of the dragon.

BY MIDAFTERNOON MOST of the livestock judging had been completed. Farmers began leaving for home with their animals, relieving some of the inhuman racket on the fairgrounds. Harriet emerged from under her canopy with a blue satin ribbon pinned to a splint strap; reclining on a Cowing and Company hand-operated fire engine, she was towed to the grandstand area like Cleopatra on her barge by members of the Seneca Falls Fire Department. Although she looked drawn, as if her leg hurt, she laughed gamely at the spectacle she knew she made. And Glynis knew better than to fuss over her.

Most of the political candidates had by this time completed their speeches before a crowd that ebbed and flowed around the platform. Several speakers resented being forced to wait while the first two theater boxes were auctioned off, but as Vanessa pointed out, they could hardly dare complain about such a civic-minded postponement. The auctions had been surprisingly lively, Glynis told Harriet when she arrived, due in no small part to Vanessa's and Tavus's outstanding performance of a first act scene from *Macbeth*. During this, Glynis glanced around in vain for Calista Sligh; the woman seemed to have vanished.

Auctioneer Abraham Levy, owner of the small Levy's Hardware Store and ordinarily a rather reticent man, clearly relished his role of coaxing the town's leading citizens to compete against each other. Mercantilist Erastus Partridge, rumored to be Seneca Falls' wealthiest man, and Seabury S. Gould, president of Gould Pumps, Inc., were high bidders on the two boxes offered. The one box remaining would be sold after Michael Olivant's campaign speech, thereby underscoring Olivant's role in making The Usher Playhouse possible.

Olivant now stood on the grandstand. Deirdre sat in a chair on the grass below, her eyes locked on her husband. Deirdre had forgone her usual high-fashion look, Glynis noted with interest, and wore a simple linen gown and wide-brimmed straw hat. Without ostrich feathers. She gazed at her husband so intently, Glynis had the impression that if women had been allowed to speak before a mixed audience, Deirdre could have jumped in and finished word for word had Michael Olivant faltered.

Michael Olivant did not falter. In a firm, steady voice, he launched a vigorous assault on the Kansas-Nebraska Act, which had been passed, only after rancorous debate, by Congress earlier in the year. This controversial law allowed slavery in the Kansas and Nebraska territories, where it previously had not been permitted. In fact, as a result of this

recent law the new Republican party—on whose platform
Olivant ran—had been formed.

Glynis scanned the faces of the crowd. Elizabeth Stanton
and her husband Henry, Susan Anthony, Sojourner Truth and
Lacey Smith stood together in an attentive group. Olivant did
not mention working women's wages, but Elizabeth had said
he probably wouldn't. If brought up at this time, the issue
could hurt more than help him, he had told the women; once
he was elected, he promised to work for passage of reform
measures. His strategy might be the practical one, Glynis admitted. If he gained the support of Seneca County's male abolitionists, without alienating them over the "woman
question"—as newspapers had taken to calling the movement
for women's rights—Olivant could have a chance to win. Especially if his candidacy split the votes for his two major op-
ponents running on the American party and the Temperance
platforms. Moreover, the most passionate supporters of the
Temperance party legislation were women—who couldn't
vote.

Glynis wondered how Susan Anthony viewed this. She
had, after all, begun her reform activism in the temperance
crusade. Susan's experience in that effort proved similar to
Elizabeth Stanton's in the abolition movement: men allowed
women to do the drudge work of distributing petitions, writing letters, and organizing meetings. But when the meetings
took place, women were not allowed a voice in the proceedings. At one such meeting, when, after rising to speak, Susan
had been ordered to sit down—"Women are here *not* to speak
but to listen and learn!"—she had stormed out. She then orga-
nized the Women's State Temperance Society. That had been
in '52. The next year conservative women members were persuaded to admit men, with voting privileges, over the strong
objection of Susan; the men promptly used their votes to
throw out of office the society's one-year president, Elizabeth
Stanton. It had been this episode more than any other, Susan
said, that made her move into the women's rights arena.

Three years had now passed since Susan Anthony and Elizabeth Stanton first met on a street corner in Seneca Falls. Although both outspoken and passionate, they were very
different women: Elizabeth, short and plump, mother of

seven, outgoing and many-faceted; the tall, spare, unmarried Susan, possessed of a single-minded determination that made her seem at times remote. But together they formed a potent force. And the wellspring of their strength, Glynis decided, was the complement they were to each other. Elizabeth herself had said, "In writing we do better work than either of us could do alone. While Susan is slow and analytic, I am rapid and synthetic. I am the better writer, she the better critic. She supplies the facts and statistics, I the philosophy and rhetoric."

Glynis's thoughts were interrupted by sporadic bursts of applause. Above her on the platform, Michael Olivant had progressed to a recitation of his education, his investment successes and, as Tavus Sligh had predicted, his participation in the Mexican War. Deirdre jumped to her feet clapping, and she glanced around as if to record who exhibited support. And who did not. Glynis wondered if this obvious ledger of Deirdre's made others rise to their feet; it wouldn't do, certainly, to offend the wife of this candidate who was also a civic leader and bank president. Olivant might not only win *this* election, but march straight on to who knew where? A Senate seat . . . even the governor's mansion?

Deirdre Olivant looked every inch a candidate for New York State's first lady. Her expression that of a sleek, satisfied cat, almost she might have been purring. When the Olivants moved to Seneca Falls six years before, could Deirdre then have anticipated this moment?

As Michael Olivant stepped from the grandstand to grasp outstretched hands, a loud, good-natured voice suddenly broke through the commotion. "So when's to be the auction . . . for that last box? C'mon, me buckos—sure'n let's get on with it!"

Glynis turned with others to watch Brendan O'Reilly push his way through the crowd. Young Brendan O'Reilly, who had for the past several years been dubbed the town rake: Seneca Falls' Lothario. But since the winsome Brendan had a hard time holding down the same job for more than one month at a time, Glynis couldn't imagine why he now pursued the theater box. Nonetheless, Brendan now stood below

the platform, arms crossed over his chest, definitely waiting
to bid.

"What in the world?" Glynis heard Harriet say.

"Can you see over the crowd?" Glynis said to her.

"Well enough. What's Brendan O'Reilly think he's doing?"

"Apparently he wants to bid, Harriet. Although . . ."

"Although *what*?" Harriet asked; Glynis knew she recalled
only too well that Aurora Usher had been one of Brendan's
brief dalliances. That Aurora had been heartbroken.

Harriet now said coolly, "Does he think he's going to bid
with his good looks alone?"

The noise had dropped for no good reason to near silence.
Harriet's words rang clear. Not in the least abashed, she continued to stare at Brendan O'Reilly, who had turned around to
face her.

"Well, now . . . and g'day to you, Mrs. Peartree." Brendan's extravagant smile at Harriet flashed white, even teeth,
while he cocked a head of thick hair that shone like a black-
bird's crown. Glynis imagined she could hear the heartfelt
sighs of young and not-so-young females for yards around.
She supposed it had always been thus. A man as handsome as
Brendan O'Reilly didn't appear every day, and so he was forgiven a multitude of failings that in any other man would
have been grounds for outrage.

"Mrs. Peartree," Brendan's voice beguiled, "sure'n you
won't be grudging me the chance to bid now, will you?"

"Let's see the color of your money, young man," Tavus
Sligh demanded as he climbed onto the grandstand. For this
direct approach he earned a round of applause. With his eyes
fixed on Brendan, Tavus invoked Macbeth:

> *"If thou speak'st false,*
> *Upon the next tree shall thou hang alive*
> *Till famine cling thee."*

Hoots of laughter interrupted him; bowing from the waist,
Tavus executed a hand flourish, motioning auctioneer Abra-
ham Levy forward to the platform. Glynis had to admire
Tavus Sligh's bull's-eye calculation of his audience's mood.

Abraham Levy lifted his arm as though proclaiming from

the mountain. "One box, two seats, is what you get, ladies and gentlemen. Your last chance to own a piece of the mag-ni-fi-cent Usher Playhouse. You won't have to stand in line for tickets. You won't have to rub elbows with the great un-washed. No sir, you'll have your very own compartment. . . ."

Glynis mentally reviewed the present six boxes. When he'd seen Ian Bentham's original design, Michael Olivant had bought the first of the original two for thirty dollars. Then, to her and everyone else's astonishment, Eebard Peck had plunked down a like amount for the second box, stating it was "a friendly-like thing to do for that pretty Usher gal's the-ater." Vanessa had declared herself mortified with embarrass-ment, then quickly counted Eebard's money. Ian Bentham probably paid the same thirty dollars for his newly designed third box, and today the fourth and fifth had been sold at forty each. With that kind of patronage, Glynis guessed The Usher Playhouse should be on solid financial ground. But Brendan O'Reilly? Perhaps he just enjoyed putting on airs.

However, when Abraham's call for the bidding came, Brendan raised his voice first. "Twenty dollars!" High for a first bid.

All heads swiveled toward him. The thought suddenly oc-curred to Glynis that perhaps Brendan bid for someone else. Someone who couldn't be there, or who wanted to remain anonymous; Niles Peartree had once told her this was com-mon practice in the art world.

Another voice raised the bid to twenty-five dollars. Brendan went to thirty. The crowd grew. Glynis could hear an undercurrent of muttering from which she gathered that Brendan owed several of those present a good deal of money. Vanessa stood below the platform, wringing her hands; prob-ably in confusion over whether she should be happy about the potential amount of money coming her way, or worried about Brendan's ability to come up with it.

Abraham Levy's fist finally descended: "Once . . . twice . . . no more bids? Your last chance, ladies and gentlemen, to own a piece of your town's newest landmark! This theater box is now going . . . going . . . no more bids? Then—Gone! To Brendan O'Reilly for the grand sum of forty-three dollars and fifty cents. Cash on the barrelhead, Brendan. You just step right up here!"

A foreboding silence lengthened as Brendan hesitated. He played the crowd just long enough to bring forth a great sigh of relief when, pulling a leather pouch from his trouser pocket, he vaulted onto the grandstand. Grinning widely, Brendan thrust his hand with the jangling pouch of coins straight into the air for all to see.

Vanessa clapped, initially alone. Then others joined her, although everyone present still seemed bewildered at Brendan's unexpected wealth.

"Whose money you think it is?" came a voice to Glynis's right. She turned to find Jacques Sundown, climbed from his paint gelding to stand nearby with reins in hand, looking toward the grandstand.

It surprised Glynis. For some reason, she suddenly now realized, Jacques hardly ever spoke to her when others were present. "I wondered . . . well, I wondered that myself," she said by way of answer. "Maybe someone who wants to remain in the background."

It also surprised her to see Jacques in such proximity to the crowd; he usually stayed well on the fringe of any town activity. But the reason for Jacques's appearance became clear when the mayor of Seneca Falls climbed onto the stand.

"Horsemen participating in the cross-country race!" the mayor called through a megaphone. "Line up your mounts behind the grandstand! Race starts in five minutes!"

While some of the crowd moved aside to allow the competing horses through, many quickly dispersed to vantage ground along the perimeter of the meadow.

Over the ensuing commotion, the mayor shouted out the rules: "First leg of the race is one time 'round the fairground's track for a distance of one and a half miles. Second leg is east on the woods trail, across the stream and 'round the pond. Last leg is one time again 'round the fairgrounds track. All obstacles must be cleared by your horse—except the stream, which can be forded—and failure to do so means disqualification. First horse over the finish line wins."

The mayor lowered the megaphone to add, "O.K., boys, you can place your bets now."

While those betting rushed forward, the lining-up process began. It took some time for riders to position their mounts behind a thick rope held taut by men at either end. Every year at least one horse decided it wanted no part of this rigamarole, and every year the others pranced impatiently while the recalcitrant animal got coaxed into place. The horses never did quite all end up noses to rope at the start, Glynis recalled, and a few usually leaped off in a sideways direction, creating a free-for-all.

She stood beside Harriet, who was still seated on the fire-engine to one side of the grandstand, the start and finish of the four-mile race. Most of the dozen or so participating riders were veterans of past years' races; the new entries this year were Jacques Sundown, and Zeph on what he'd told her was his favorite livery horse: a smallish red-and-white-splotched roan mare.

Brendan O'Reilly had jumped from the grandstand to mount his big bay, whose reins were held by a lovely young farm girl. Isaiah Smith positioned his sturdy, newly acquired Morgan—the horse had better be sturdy, thought Glynis, given the smith's muscled frame—while Lacey sat on the grass, scowling at him as she did every year. With good reason: the race could be dangerous.

This year as for the past five, since a youngster died from head injuries, there had been a movement to eliminate the race. Led by mothers and wives. The men would have none of it. They had agreed only to institute an age limit of fourteen, which explained why, Glynis supposed, this would be Zeph's first race. He certainly seemed to be the youngest entry. She looked around for Dr. Quentin Ives; he sat at the other side of the grandstand, shaking his head at the riders' foolhardiness, as he always did. But she noticed that Ives nonetheless handed over a wager to the mayor.

At last, with the horses more or less lined up behind the rope, the mayor raised a shotgun into the air. The riders crouched. Into a tense quiet the gun roared. And the rope dropped.

The quiet converted into a bedlam of shouting and cheering. It appeared to Glynis that Jacques unaccountably held his paint back while the other horses thundered onto the dirt track, jockeying for position. Then came the traditional moment of chaos when one animal careened into several others, resulting in time lost until the horses disengaged.

When the dust settled, eight or nine horses could be seen as a close-packed herd of churning legs; two more followed at a short distance while Jacques's paint brought up the rear. This distribution held around the initial turn, after which the horses then began a long stretch parallel to the river. The first bales of straw were cleared by all but one, which pulled up short: Eebard Peck's dappled gray dug in his heels and refused to budge.

As those remaining came around the far turn, Glynis spotted Zeph's distinctive roan mare pulling somewhat ahead of the rest. After the little mare flew like a wind-borne arrow over the next straw bales, she and Zeph had gained several lengths on the others. They rounded the next turn to begin the long stretch parallel to the road. But suddenly, and seemingly from out of nowhere, Jacques Sundown's paint gelding appeared on the outside edge of the track, steadily gaining on the others who were now nearly a furlong behind Zeph.

In spite of her reservations about the race, Glynis felt her heart begin to pound; she found it impossible to resist the excitement, and she couldn't help but want Zeph to win. However, that seemed in immediate question as Jacques's paint gained ground stride by long stride, his hooves barely grazing the surface of the track. As Zeph's mare took the near turn, the paint galloped only a length behind. By the time they pounded toward the grandstand they were almost neck and neck.

As they neared, Glynis could see the two riders' faces; Zeph's deep frown of concentration, Jacques's enigmatic gaze straight ahead. She caught the instant Zeph's frown changed to disbelief as Jacques drew alongside. And then passed him when the paint swerved smoothly around the grandstand, and without a break in stride headed toward the woods. Zeph's horse couldn't take the turn as fast. By the time both horses disappeared into the trees, the paint ran a good furlong ahead of the little mare.

The remaining horses hammered toward the grandstand, led by Brendan O'Reilly's bay, followed closely by Isaiah

Smith's Morgan, then four others. So intent in the past minutes had Glynis been on Zeph and Jacques that she'd missed the elimination of three other horses. Balked at the obstacles, Harriet said, excitedly. "Do you think the boy has a chance?" she asked Glynis.

Behind them a voice answered, "Not likely!" Tavus Sligh went on. "That Indian's got something downright strange about him. Where'd he come from? His horse started out last!"

Glynis refrained from pointing out what she now saw as smart strategy on Jacques's part: he'd let the other horses use up precious energy fighting over the lead and setting the pace, while the paint, removed from the fray, just tagged along until Jacques felt ready to make a move. But why disabuse Tavus of the notion that Jacques might be strange? He *was* strange. Besides, she hadn't really thought anyone else could win the race. Even though she would like to see Zeph win, if she were a betting man, she'd have wagered her money on Jacques Sundown any day of the week.

Someone in the crowd who'd been timing with his pocketwatch said the race was "fast. *Very* fast! Constable and the livery boy should be out of them woods any minute now."

They waited. And waited. When the sound of hooves came, and the first horse emerged from the woods, the restless mass of people gasped as one voice. It was not the paint. Not Zeph's mare, but Isaiah Smith's Morgan. Close behind ran Brendan O'Reilly's bay. Three more men and horses appeared singly. When no other horses came out of the trees, Glynis's stomach knotted. What could have happened—some terrible accident involving both Jacques and Zeph? And shouldn't there be one more rider as well?

She heard over the uproar a few voices around her repeating her own fear. The rest of the crowd, riveted on the final leg of the race, yelled encouragement to their favorites. Glynis turned to Harriet, who looked worriedly after Quentin Ives. Ives had already begun moving into the woods on horseback.

A woman's voice cried out with relief as a man leading a limping horse emerged from the trees. Glynis counted on her fingers for the tenth time; eight horses had gone into the woods, the sixth had just come out. Which left only Zeph and Jacques unaccounted for out of the dozen that started the race. Something terrible *had* happened, she was certain of it.

She left Harriet and attempted to push her way through to the man with the injured horse. He might have seen Zeph or Jacques. But she couldn't get near enough. Those packed around the grandstand had closed in on delirium, screaming wildly, as the five remaining horses rounded the last turn and headed for home. Two now ran well ahead of the others—the Morgan and the bay. Men loosely holding either end of the rope finish line could barely keep themselves from pounding one another in frenzy as the horses raced toward them.

Glynis turned anxiously toward the track. It looked as if Isaiah's Morgan had tired; Brendan's bay closed the earlier gap, his head now alongside the Morgan's black flank. But suddenly Isaiah stood in the stirrups, gave a tremendous whooping yell, then threw himself face down into the Morgan's mane, his fists striking the horse's shoulders. The Morgan responded, surging forward. Despite her concern, Glynis's breath caught at the awesome beauty of the black man and the black horse hurtling through the air as a single source of power. They tore over the finish line a good two lengths ahead of the bay.

In the ensuing furor as the crowd rushed forward, Glynis found her way clear to the man walking slowly beside his limping horse. "In the woods," Glynis shouted at him over the din, "the constable—did you see him? Or the boy on the roan mare?"

When he nodded, Glynis moved closer to ask him, "What became of them?"

The man shrugged. "Don't know rightly—the boy was on the ground next to the stream. Constable was kind of, well, squatting beside him and looking under some bushes, I think. That's all I saw, 'cause next thing I know this horse of mine stumbled. And I went off. But I was a ways from the stream by that time." He shrugged again.

Glynis nodded, and turned back to Harriet in time to see Jacques Sundown riding from the woods. She hurried to him across the grass.

"Jacques, what happened? But Zeph . . . where's Zeph? Is he all right?"

"Yeah."

"Well, what *happened*? When you went into the woods—"

He cut her off by jumping from the paint and motioning to a small group of men who were walking back from the grandstand. They looked dejected, she noted distractedly; probably bet on Brendan's bay. But where was Zeph?

Jacques moved toward the group. "You men want to go help Doc Ives? He's got some trouble." Jacques pointed toward the trees. "You need a litter to carry . . . someone. Get a couple blankets. And keep it quiet—they don't need a crowd in there."

A litter to carry someone? Glynis barely managed to contain herself until the men started off in search of blankets.

"Jacques!" she said furiously. "Are you going to tell me what happened to Zeph? Oh, never mind! I'll find out for myself." She started toward the woods.

"Hold on." Jacques fell into step beside her, then moved in front of her, blocking the path. "Just slow down. I said the boy wasn't hurt."

"You did *not* say that! You said 'Yeah.' Now get out of my way!"

"He's not hurt. Got thrown off, is all, but he's O.K. Now leave him be. You want to embarrass him?"

"No. I do not want to embarrass him." Glynis bit off the words. The men were just returning, carrying several blankets, and Jacques moved aside to let them by.

When they'd passed, Glynis stepped forward to follow them, but Jacques again planted himself in her path, his arms crossed over his chest. "Wait. Just wait."

Pressure pounded behind her temples. Impulsively, she stepped forward to shove him backwards, out of her way. Just in time she caught herself; his feet were braced and if he didn't move, she could hardly stand there attacking him—the constable—in view of half the town. Glaring at him, under her breath she said tightly, "Move out of my way!"

He stood his ground. Keeping her voice down until the men were out of sight, Glynis said stiffly, "What is it I'm waiting for? So you can be more rude than you already have been?"

"Rude," Jacques repeated.

"Excuse me. Not rude. Obnoxious. Insulting."

Jacques looked away, off across the meadow. Then his eyes slowly swung back to her. "You don't want to go . . ." he began.

"How would you know what I want?"

"O.K., I don't want you to go. There's a dead body back by the stream. Been dead a long while."

Glynis instantly felt perspiration ooze from every pore, leaving her chilled, as if her blood literally ran cold. "Who?" she whispered.

"Don't know," Jacques said. "Not yet. Ives said it's been there maybe a week or more. Boy found it when he got thrown into the stream. You don't want to see it. But you know any woman wore big green stone earrings?"

"Green stone . . . it's a woman? You can tell it's a—oh! Oh, Jacques, I think I know who it is."

"Yeah. You likely do. I was going to ask you after I sent the men to help Ives." He paused, then said, "Before you went and got . . . insulted." The flat brown eyes stared down at her. Glynis began to feel foolish. But he *had* been insulting. Didn't he know that?

Still staring at her, he said, "All's we can tell is she's got reddish hair, red painted nails—"

"It's . . . was . . . Luella."

"Figured maybe. I got to get back there. You wait here. You understand? Don't go in there."

"No. No, I won't."

"But here," Jacques reached for his horse, and pulled a blanket roll from behind the saddle. "Hold onto this. Don't show it to anybody. And tell that actor character—what's his name? Sligh?—tell him I want to talk to him."

He climbed onto the paint and turned the horse toward the woods. "Stay here."

"All *right*, Jacques. I heard you the first time."

He rode into the trees.

Most of the last fairgoers began to amble away toward home; the men apparently had followed Jacques's instruction to "keep it quiet." Glynis saw Harriet off in a carriage with Vanessa and Aurora Usher, not saying anything to them about the body. She then told Tavus Sligh that Jacques wanted to talk to him.

"Why? What's he want?" Tavus said impatiently.

"I'm not sure. That is, he didn't tell me. But he seemed very emphatic about you waiting for him."

It was another few minutes before Zeph appeared on the mare. As Glynis rushed up to him, she noticed his peculiar grayish color, as if he had a layer of ash over his dark skin. When he climbed from the mare, his gait seemed unsteady. It must be shock. "Zeph, are you all right? Jacques Sundown told me about . . . well, about what you found."

He stood uncharacteristically still. His eyes looked very large, as they'd been when he told her about his parents. Glynis hardly knew what to say. "Zeph, I'm so sorry. You've been through such a lot. You don't have to act brave with me, though, you know. It must have been a terrible shock."

He nodded then, and looked around as if making sure he knew where he was. Glynis motioned toward the other side of the grandstand, now unoccupied. In fact, she saw to her relief, the only people still around were men clearing away the straw bales, and Tavus and Calista Sligh standing near the racetrack with several others of the theater troupe.

"Zeph, do you want to tell me what happened?" she asked him gently as they walked toward the stands. The little roan plodded along behind.

"The mare—she just pulled up at the stream," he said, jiggling the reins in his hands. "It was my fault," he added quickly. "I didn't expect it, and I wasn't ready. A better rider would have seen it coming."

"Zeph, I expect that could happen to anyone. You got thrown off?"

"Yeah. Head first into the water. Constable, he was way ahead of me already starting around the pond, but he looked over his shoulder—I don't know why he did. He turned the paint fast as you ever saw, and came back. Cleared the stream like a bird, that paint did. You know, Sundown was so far out in front, he could've won the race easy, but he came back for me." Zeph shook his head a little, as if still dazed.

Glynis didn't say anything; she realized, moreover, that she was not surprised. She had already begun to feel somewhat ashamed about the scene with Jacques. He had, after all, apparently been trying to spare her—but why couldn't he have just *said* that? *He* might be capable of mind-reading, but *she* wasn't.

Zeph stared silently at the ground. But his head came up as the men appeared through the trees, carrying the sagging blankets like a sling. They had tied kerchiefs over their noses and mouths. When Dr. Ives motioned toward a wagon, the men moved to it with their improvised litter, but as they approached the harnessed team, the horses strained at their collars, shying away from the smell of death.

Jacques walked up to Glynis and Zeph, saying to the boy, "If you're all right, you can head on back to the livery." When Zeph hesitated, Jacques said, "Go on, now. I'll stop by later."

Zeph threw Glynis a troubled look. "Zeph, why don't you come by the house a little later," she said. "Have something to eat with Harriet and myself. Please."

He stubbed the toe of his boot in the dirt, then gave the mare's reins a small tug. "Thanks." He climbed into the saddle and started toward the road.

Jacques watched him go. "Boy's got a lot to handle," he said unexpectedly. "Hard to be a man that young. No one around to teach him how."

Did Jacques know about Zeph's background? His remark struck Glynis as surprisingly sympathetic for a man she considered to be lacking in emotional responsiveness of any kind.

"Constable!" Tavus Sligh strode toward them. He stopped in front of Jacques and struck his warrior's stance. "Constable, Miss Tryon insisted I stay. Well, I've stayed—more than long enough—and now I'm leaving."

"I expect you can spare a minute or two, Sligh," Jacques said laconically. "It's too bad if you can't, 'cause then I'll have to tie you up and cart you to the lockup. Your choice."

Glynis wondered if she'd heard him correctly. But from the way Tavus stared at Jacques, she guessed she had. Calista Sligh, who had followed her husband, pressed her lips together as if restraining a smile. And she gazed at Jacques with frank interest.

Glynis realized Jacques had his hand out for the blanket

roll he'd taken earlier from behind his saddle. When she gave it to him, he unrolled the blanket to expose a dagger with an elaborately carved handle. "Ever see this before?" he asked Tavus.

Glynis recognized the dagger immediately, even without seeing the initials O.S.—Octavius Sligh—engraved on the handle. Calista stepped forward with a small gasp. Her hand flew to her mouth as she stared at her husband.

"So? You recognize this?" Jacques said evenly.

"Yes; yes, of course I do," Tavus answered. His voice carried across the grass and several actors some yards away glanced at him. Tavus lowered his voice. "I've been trying to find that," he said, pointing at the dagger. "Must have misplaced it. I'll take it now."

"No, I don't think so," Jacques said. "But maybe you can tell me where and when you think you lost it."

"I don't know where—that should be obvious," Tavus snapped. "And I don't remember when I first noticed it was missing."

"That so?" Jacques leaned back against the grandstand, turning the carved handle in his hands. "Couldn't have been the night that slave-catcher was stabbed, could it?"

"What? Oh, no you don't, Constable. Quit trying to trap me. You know damn well nobody's sure when that man was killed—at least I never heard. What are you implying?"

"Just asking. Anybody else know you lost the dagger?"

Tavus hesitated, then turned to Calista. "I told you I'd lost it, didn't I?"

Calista's eyes narrowed, then she lifted her shoulders. "Maybe you did. I really don't remember."

"What do you mean, 'you don't remember'?" Tavus said, a frown creasing his high forehead. "Calista—"

"Hold on a minute, Sligh," Jacques interrupted. "What're the odds, would you say, on somebody taking this dagger without you knowing it?"

"I suppose, my dear fellow, that anyone could have picked it up. I don't wear it all the time. Certainly not when I'm in costume. And I *was* in costume at the theater dedication. I don't think," Tavus paused, staring at the ground momentarily before he went on, "I don't think I've seen the dagger since that night. But I can't be sure."

"Can you be sure of where you were that night? Late—say after the theater party broke up?" Jacques said. His voice had no inflection. He might, Glynis thought, have been asking if Tavus remembered whether it rained that evening.

"Why are you asking me these questions?" Tavus said belligerently. "Surely you can't think *I* had something to do with that man's death? That's ridiculous!"

"Seems kind of strange that you haven't asked where this dagger of yours was found, Sligh. Or do you already know?"

"Of course I don't know. But all right, where *was* it found? In the woods back there, I assume?"

Jacques stared at Tavus before he answered. Reading his mind? wondered Glynis. Hadn't Tavus seen the men with the litter? Maybe not. At last Jacques said, "Found in a dead woman."

Calista moaned quietly. Tavus looked genuinely shocked, Glynis thought; but then, he was a very good actor. "What woman?" Tavus asked, his voice much less belligerent.

"Not sure yet. Been in the woods a while. Could be since that slave-catcher got killed. In case you forgot the question, you want to tell me what you did that night? After the party."

Tavus glanced at Calista. "I went back to the hotel. The Royal Hotel, where we—that is, the theater troupe—are staying."

"Yeah," Jacques said. "Anybody can vouch for that?"

"Of course!" Tavus bellowed. "For god's sake, man, you can't think I killed anybody. Calista, tell him, would you? We went back to the hotel after the party. Together."

Calista Sligh appeared even paler than usual. She looked at her husband for what seemed to Glynis a long time. Jacques just stood looking at them both.

Finally Calista said slowly, "Well, we didn't exactly go back together, did we, Tavus darling? I mean—"

"*What* do you mean, Calista?" Tavus broke in. "Look here—"

Jacques motioned him to silence. "Go on," he said to Calista. And almost smiled. Glynis watched with astonishment. Jacques Sundown smiling? But then she understood, knew where he had learned that disarmingly innocent look. From Cullen. Cullen who could coax a stone to speak with that almost smile.

Calista's eyes widened and her manner underwent a not-so-subtle change. She smiled with lavish sweetness at Jacques. "Well, Constable, if I recall that night," she then turned to her husband and shot him a very different smile, "dear Tavus said he needed to see *dear* little Miss Usher home. He said they had to go over some items about the theater . . ."

"Calista!" Tavus thundered. "You do *not* recall that night! Far from it."

"O.K.," Jacques said, his eyes still on Calista. "But tell me this. If your husband wasn't with you—"

"I *was*!" Tavus insisted. "Look, I don't know why she's saying that, but—"

"All right, Sligh. Now shut your mouth until I'm done." Jacques's tone hadn't altered. But whatever look he gave Tavus made the man take a step back. And Tavus didn't say more.

"If your husband wasn't with you," Jacques again asked Calista, "can you tell me where you were?"

"I went back to the hotel," Calista said, "right after the party broke up."

"O.K. So who'd you go to the hotel with?"

"Why, I went alone. It's not very far from the church grounds."

"Who saw you go? Anybody see you?"

Calista hesitated. Glynis wondered if the woman had lied about Tavus and Vanessa. If she had, did she realize that in doing so she'd left herself open to suspicion?

Calista gave Jacques another sugary smile. "Constable, in this business of ours," she extended her arm to graciously include her husband, "we don't always do what convention demands. I'm quite, *quite*, accustomed to getting around by myself. And I went back to the hotel that night *by myself*. I have no idea whether someone saw me or not. Now is that all? I'm really rather tired."

Jacques stared at her a moment longer. "You can go. Both of you . . . for now. Stay in town. Think you can remember that?"

Calista's eyes flickered before she nodded and turned to walk away. Tavus looked as if he wanted to say something, but Jacques had already moved toward his horse. Tavus took a step toward him, then he, too, turned and walked in the direction of the remaining carriages.

"I got to go to Doc Ives's. You have a way to get home?" Jacques said to Glynis, as he picked up the paint's reins. How odd that he would ask; he usually just walked off.

Glynis stood for a moment to watch the departing Slighs, who trailed vibrations of their antagonism behind them. She'd like to know what they said to each other, if indeed they were speaking at all.

She turned to walk beside Jacques, now leading the paint, and she felt somewhat uneasy about her earlier outburst. "Zeph left one of the carriages for me at the road," she said. "I can drive it back to Harriet's."

"You think they were lying, those two?" Jacques's eyes shifted in the direction the Slighs had taken.

"I don't know. It could be Calista just wanted to see Tavus made uncomfortable. She seems to dislike Vanessa intensely, and this could be a way of making her husband pay for the attention he gives Van."

"She'd lie to do that? She think this is a game? That was his dagger in the woman's body. I almost pulled him in on a murder charge. Still might."

Glynis sighed. "I know, Jacques. It's pathetic, pathetic and ugly, the things we say when we think we've been . . . misused." She gave him a sidelong glance.

He slowed his pace, but looked straight ahead when he spoke. "Misused. That anything like 'insulted'?"

Startled, she glanced at him again. "Ah, yes," she said. "Very much like that."

She kept thinking about his remark regarding Zeph. That Zeph didn't have anyone to teach him. She had known that about Zeph, that and his youth, and had always made allowances for him—for his sullen behavior, his angry eruptions. But she'd never made any allowances for Jacques Sundown, and she knew less about him than she did about Zeph. Maybe he didn't intend to insult her. All the time. Maybe he'd just never learned the rules. The codes of social behavior. It made life easier when everyone knew the same rules. But what if Jacques didn't know them? They were, it suddenly struck her, white men's rules. And why had she never thought of this before?

"Ah, Jacques . . . where did you grow up?"

He stopped walking. He not only stopped walking, he stared at her as if she were a total stranger. "Why? Why do you want to know?"

"I just wondered," she said, feeling embarrassed, as if she'd intruded on some private ground. But it wasn't, surely, such a profound question. . . . No, not to *you*, she told herself. "I'm not sure why I asked. I'm sorry if it offended you."

She would change the subject, go back to where they'd usually been on relatively safe, neutral ground. "You said you almost arrested Tavus Sligh for murder," she asked. "Why didn't you?"

"Can't think anybody'd be stupid enough to stab a woman, then leave their initialed weapon behind. Can you?"

"No," she said. "No, I can't. But maybe Tavus thought her body would never be found. And it might *not* have been except for Zeph's accident. Still . . ."

"Yeah. There's that dagger. Obvious. How many people have the initials O.S., you think?"

"Not many," Glynis agreed. They had reached the carriage, now the only one remaining, the trotter contentedly eating grass. Glynis walked to rest against the hitching rail. "It bothers me, though. Tavus Sligh may be a lot of things, but I don't think he's stupid. So, what if he is much cleverer than we give him credit for? That is, what if he counted on our saying just what we are: that Tavus couldn't be that stupid—someone *else* must have killed Luella with his dagger, and then left it there to implicate him."

"Too complicated for Sligh. Takes too much work to think that way. But . . . I guess it could be." Jacques sounded as noncommittal as he looked. "Why would he kill that woman? Or maybe his wife did."

"I don't know. It's horrible . . . poor Luella. Why would anyone kill her? For what reason—unless there's a connection with Lyle Brogan's death. And then there's that old man, Moses Rawlings."

"Reservation," Jacques said suddenly.

"What?"

"Where I grew up. For a while."

"Oh." Glynis experienced a hot sense of shame. Why hadn't she ever considered that?

"I didn't realize ... that is, I guess I've been rather high-handed," she murmured. She resisted the need to press her cheeks, to check the embarrassed flush she felt crawling from her neck to the roots of her hair. "It's just that ... well ... I've always thought you disliked me, Jacques. And it hurt my feelings. But I didn't appreciate our ... ah ... differences, and I'm sorry I said what I did earlier."

She looked up into his face, searching for some sign that he understood why she'd behaved as she did. That he forgave her her lack of charity.

He turned his head away, his gaze moving to some remote place. When his eyes swung back to her they had lost their cool brown flatness; something stirred in them, something quickened and vital, an alteration of color or light as when dark coals fanned by wind suddenly glow as if by sorcery with intense blue-green heat.

Glynis gripped the rough wood of the rail. Her lungs seemed to empty, her breath sucked from her by the same wind that lifted Jacques Sundown's mortal shell to reveal some mystic inner core.

Then the wind quieted and the light vanished, gone as swiftly as it had come. He turned from her to climb into his saddle and swing the paint toward the road. She heard an enigmatic quality in his voice when he said, "I'm going to see what Dr. Ives has. You'll get home all right."

Glynis stood, gripping the hitching rail for a moment longer before she got into the carriage. She fumbled awkwardly with the reins, her hands refusing to move. She looked down at them as if they belonged to a stranger.

Jacques sat in the saddle, holding the paint until she flicked the reins over the trotter's back. Then he wheeled the horse toward town and rode away.

GLYNIS TIED THE trotter to the Peartree porch railing; she hadn't even remembered driving home. She stood at the bottom of the porch steps, unwilling to go into the house just yet, when Aurora Usher burst out the front door.

"Glynis! Something terrible's happened. Hurry!"

"What's wrong?" Glynis asked as she rushed after Aurora down the hall to the kitchen. "Aurora, what's the matter?" She stopped in the kitchen doorway. Harriet sat in her chair, the crutches lying haphazardly as though they'd been dropped beside her on the floor. The woman had gone deathly pale, and her face reflected a fear Glynis had never before seen there.

"Harriet?" Glynis went to her. Harriet shook her head slowly. Aurora reached down and took the yellow paper from Harriet's lap, handing it to Glynis.

"This wire came from New York City about ten minutes ago. Read it, Glynis," Aurora said, her eyes bright with tears. "Read it."

Glynis felt her body sag with fatigue, when what she needed was the energy to flee, to leave behind this volatile day. She still felt unnerved by the strange episode with Jacques. By the glimpse into his . . . his what? His spirit? Or had she, in an overwrought state, simply imagined it? She shook herself slightly, brought back to the moment by the look on Harriet's face. And took the wire from Aurora.

MRS HARRIET PEARTREE STOP NILES SEIZED BY FEDERAL MARSHALS STOP TAKEN TO RICHMOND VA STOP MATHEW BRADY

FOURTEEN

The offense consists in continuing to secrete from the owner what the acts of Congress and the Constitution, as well as the laws of several of the States, treat, for certain purposes, as property, after knowing that claims of property exist in respect to the fugitive.
— UNITED STATES SUPREME COURT,
JONES V. VAN ZANDT

THOSE STANDING ON the Washington railroad platform backed hastily away from the tracks as steam belched from the awakening engine. The train would leave shortly, and Glynis looked anxiously through the passenger car window to the platform below for Jeremiah Merrycoyf. A few moments later the lawyer appeared at the end of the car. When he came down the aisle toward her, Merrycoyf's substantial girth slowed his progress considerably. He held the stem of a pipe between his teeth, but had secured his tobacco pouch in his frock coat pocket by the time he sat down beside her.

He removed the pipe to announce, "Just one more stop—Fredericksburg—then straight on to Richmond." Having finally settled himself, although not without some difficulty, in the narrow seat, Merrycoyf pulled a watch from his waistcoat. He studied the skull-and-bones charm on the gold chain threaded through a buttonhole before he looked at the watch face. "Four o'clock—train's on time. At least John won't have to wait for us."

Merrycoyf had wired former Yale Law School classmate, John Hamilton, the morning they left Seneca Falls—had that been only yesterday? thought Glynis wearily. They'd made ready to leave in just two short days after the wire from Mathew Brady, with Harriet initially insisting she must go to Richmond with Merrycoyf. Glynis finally managed to persuade her it would be impossible with a broken leg. But

Glynis's heart plummeted when the woman then turned on her with distraught eyes brimming a silent appeal.

Glynis let out a deep breath. "All right, Harriet—if it will make you feel better," she heard herself with disbelief saying, "I'll go, and I'll wire you as soon as we've seen Niles." It had occurred to her that perhaps she could meet Zeph and Kiri's grandmother Masika, as well as find out something more about Moses Rawlings. She couldn't shake the suspicion that the old man's death tied in somehow to those of Brogan and Luella and, if that was true, she felt uneasy about Zeph's safety. At least the boy had agreed, if with reluctance, to move in temporarily with Lacey and Isaiah Smith. Dictras Fyfe, who'd returned from Syracuse in answer to Glynis's wire, stayed with Harriet. And Jonathan Quant again ran the library. It seemed to Glynis that she'd spent much of the past month riding trains.

Merrycoyf welcomed her traveling with him to Richmond. "I'd have asked your assistance if Mrs. Peartree hadn't, and I will be most grateful if you would come," he had said. "I'll have my hands full practicing law in an unfamiliar state. Also, there won't be time to interview that young woman hiding in Rochester before I leave and you can fill me in on her background. Then there are the potential witnesses to interview in Richmond. Since I know from past experience how ably you collect information, you could be a help to me with the trial preparation. And," he had said finally, "I well remember your detection work of six years ago."

Glynis glanced at Merrycoyf now as the train pulled out of the Washington station. He stared off into space, fingering his full but neatly trimmed white beard; then, peering over the wire-rimmed spectacles perched on his plump cheeks, he pulled some volumes of law from a crammed valise. Glynis recalled the first time she'd seen the lawyer, and how Clement Moore's "A Visit from St. Nicholas" immediately leaped to mind, even though Merrycoyf's small nose wasn't usually cherry red. Perhaps Moore's St. Nick kept a flask of brandy stowed in his sleigh. But Merrycoyf enjoyed a nip now and then himself.

Glynis hadn't asked the lawyer point-blank before, but now

she said, "Just how bad *is* Niles's situation? Is there a possibility he'll be convicted, sentenced to prison?"

"Oh, yes, indeed," Merrycoyf answered, "there's every likelihood of that. The terms of the Fugitive Slave Law are not ambiguous." He shuffled through his bulging valise to extract another law book. "Here it is," Merrycoyf said, opening the volume to a marked page, "from the Thirty-first Congressional Record of September 18, 1850, Section seven. I've gone over it several times and, paraphrased, what it says is: any person knowingly hindering the arrest of a fugitive, or attempting to rescue one from custody, or aiding to escape, or harboring, shall be fined and imprisoned."

Glynis could only stare at him, hoping she hadn't heard correctly. She said at last, "That doesn't leave much room for argument, does it? That and the United States Constitution."

When she'd returned from Rochester, she read the library's copy of the Constitution again. And again; disbelieving, or not wanting to believe what she saw with her own eyes. Article I, section nine, paragraph one, read: *"The Migration or Importation of such persons as any of the States now existing shall think proper to admit, shall not be prohibited by Congress prior to the Year one thousand eight hundred and eight."* In other words, it upheld the African slave trade until Congress chose to abolish it.

There was also Article IV, section two, paragraph three: *"No Person held to Service or Labour in one State, under the Laws thereof, escaping into another, shall, in Consequence of any Law or Regulation therein, be discharged from such Service or Labour, but shall be delivered up on Claim of the Party to whom such Service or Labour shall be due."*

Nowhere did the Constitution *prohibit* slavery. Quite the contrary as the two sections she'd studied actually enforced it. And she'd also read that Thomas Jefferson's original draft of the Declaration of Independence had included an attack on the slave trade; South Carolina and Rhode Island delegates to the Continental Congress objected, and the offending section had been deleted from the Declaration's final draft.

That the United States Constitution was a flawed instrument had not been a new revelation to Glynis. Some time ago she'd recognized that a legal document purportedly framed to

create a republic that, from the moment of ratification, excluded half the population from participation in government—
and many more than half when Negroes and Indians were
tallied with women—had proved its defectiveness. She found,
however, that to even suggest such a thing in public brought
instant rebuke. The Constitution seemed to be held in the
same regard as the biblical word of God—more so, in fact,
since white male atheists likewise thought it omnipotent. She
did not find reassuring the usual argument that the Constitution could be amended, since it could be amended only by
those already empowered.

She pulled herself back to the immediate problem. "Mr.
Merrycoyf, how will you prepare for trial?"

"If you mean, how am I going to keep Niles Peartree from
prison, I can't say. But tell me this: Are you familiar with the
concept of positive law?"

"Well, yes," she said slowly. "I believe it has to do with
what Frederick Douglass and I talked of just recently. Isn't
positive law what the majority of people consider as necessary to sustain their interests? Or, perhaps, the requirements
of the majority?" Merrycoyf shifted in his seat to peer at her
over the spectacles. "Yes, for now that's a good enough def-
inition. So it could then follow, could it not, that positive law
may be not only different from, but actually opposed to,
moral law—or what we might call natural rights? Would you
agree?"

"*Who* might call natural rights?"

Merrycoyf sighed fulsomely, and laced his fingers over his
stomach. "Miss Tryon, let us not get into another debate
about women's rights, if you please. Not now. May we concentrate on the issue of positive law as it refers in particular
to slavery?"

Glynis nearly smiled. Merrycoyf had, of late, unhappily begun to admit that there might exist certain inequities between
the laws concerning men and those governing women. It had
taken a long while for him to concede this, being a staunch
participant in the legal profession's love of *status quo*. This
all must be very trying for Merrycoyf. But she agreed she
shouldn't sidetrack him. Thus she pressed her lips together
and nodded.

"I am hopeful," Merrycoyf went on, "that perhaps in the arena of natural law there will be some room to maneuver. . . ." His voice trailed off as he again stared toward his legal horizons.

Glynis turned to the window. Merrycoyf wanted her to talk with Kiri's former mistress to learn, for instance, what there had been about Kiri's circumstances at Jolimont that might possibly help Niles. But how, Glynis wondered, would she manage to find common ground with this woman of a Richmond tobacco plantation? She had previously told herself that life couldn't be so very unique for southern white women—surely their situations and their concerns must be similar to those of women in the North.

But now, as she watched the unfamiliar landscape south of Mason and Dixon's survey line pass her window, she didn't feel quite so confident of this. In New York, deciduous trees had already begun to turn, the leaves of birch and poplars alchemized to gold, those of maples flamed to scarlet and orange. But here in Maryland and Virginia leaves remained green, a more delicate silvery green than those at home ever were, and they had not yet felt a frost. She tried to reassure herself by thinking that except for the silvery cast, the countryside itself looked something like that of western New York in August—even to the swaths of ubiquitous daisies and black-eyed Susans along the track.

When she and Merrycoyf had changed trains in Baltimore to board the Richmond, Frederick and Potomac Railroad, the air felt as warm as that of summer at home. Sun-warmed fresh-mown hay and tall field grasses smelled the same. Since she'd never been farther south than Philadelphia, Glynis wished she could enjoy the experience more. But worry about Niles and Kiri and Zeph, to say nothing of the recent bloodshed in Seneca Falls, kept her continuously on edge.

Over and over she asked herself: What could possibly be the link, if there was one, between a southern slave-catcher, his actress paramour, and an elderly freed slave? And who could be the slaveholder sympathizer in Seneca Falls? Could this informer also be a murderer?

She stared out the window, searching for answers. But the

train rumbled through a dark covered bridge and all she could see was a vague outline of her reflection.

THE NEXT MORNING'S sunlight slanted through east windows of the Federal District Courthouse of Richmond; a flurry of dust motes rose and fell as if keeping time with the measured voice of prosecutor Richard Steele. Glynis sat inconspicuously, she hoped, in the rear of the courtroom. She held a tablet on which she had been writing her first dispatch to *The Seneca County Courier*.

Just before leaving Seneca Falls, she'd stopped to see editor Ephraim Penrod, offering to write an article on Virginia authors for the newspaper. But only under "Glynis Tryon." Penrod wanted the article but not her name. "You'll use the Japes pseudonym—same as always."

She'd turned to leave, too tired and too anxious for Niles to argue with him.

"Ah, wait a minute, Miss Tryon. I've just had a thought."

Glynis stood by the door while the editor's thought jelled. She wouldn't back down this time, she told herself without much conviction.

"How would you like to write an account of the Peartree trial?" Penrod abruptly asked.

Glynis felt her heart leap to her throat. Could she do that? Probably just as well as anyone else, she told herself, very nearly wincing at her bravado.

Ephraim Penrod, perhaps mistaking her expression for refusal, said promptly, "I'll pay you."

Glynis couldn't believe she then heard herself say, "How much? The same amount the men get for their dispatches?"

"I don't think so! You're not a man. Furthermore, you're inexperienced. Say, half their amount."

Glynis again turned to leave, but managed to swallow her dignity enough to object. "If I'm to be paid half, even though I *am* experienced in writing for you—and you know I can do it or you wouldn't be hiring me—then I use my own name. Not Sebastian P. Japes. And that's my last word, Mr. Penrod. Really it is."

Then, since she couldn't credit she'd actually said this, she reached for the door. Editor Penrod had glowered alarmingly, but then had given her a curt nod of his waxy bald head.

Glynis now put the tablet down on her lap to study the scene at the front of the courtroom. To the right of the judge's bench, and next to his former classmate John Hamilton, Jeremiah Merrycoyf stood, running the rim of a tall silk hat through his fingers.

Glynis sighed restlessly. The silk hat had required a frantic foray into the Richmond shopping district when Merrycoyf learned the dictated attire for a Virginia lawyer. He and Glynis left their rooms at the American Hotel on Eleventh and Main streets seemingly at the crack of dawn, Merrycoyf grumbling every step of the way down the block to the elegant haberdashery.

"Damnably silly if you ask me," Merrycoyf had complained. "As pretentious as the sacred wigs of the British."

And with lawyers Merrycoyf, Hamilton, and Steele lined up before Judge Artemus Trumbull, Glynis decided that but for Merrycoyf's girth, she couldn't have told them apart. All wore the same sober black suits, white linen with black scarf tie and black boots, and all held the irksome tall silk hats.

Hamilton first stepped forward to move for Merrycoyf's admission to the Virginia court—in order for Merrycoyf to appear there as counsel for Niles. Prosecutor Steele, his long face pinched-looking as though this proceeding wasted his valuable time, at last completed what Glynis thought to be an unnecessarily lengthy speech, since he apparently didn't intend to argue Merrycoyf's admission. If this proved customary for Steele, it would be a long trial.

Niles stood quietly to one side. His face looked drawn, pale and haggard, but not at all contrite. When he'd turned toward the prosecutor, his jaw clenched as if his teeth were grinding.

Some time earlier he'd been brought by two marshals in a horse-drawn omnibus from the Virginia Penitentiary. Merrycoyf had visited him there the previous evening while Glynis waited anxiously in her room. A gaslight under the hotel window allowed her to see across Eleventh Street to the offices of the *Richmond Enquirer*, a reporter from which had interviewed Merrycoyf earlier. Glynis sat in on the session and herself took everything down for the *Courier*.

When Merrycoyf had returned from the penitentiary, he hadn't much to say about Niles, save that "the lad seemed well enough." The lawyer *had* gone into great detail about the penitentiary itself, designed in part by Thomas Jefferson. It stood, a vaulted masonry fortress, rising alone like an ancient walled city atop one of Richmond's several hills.

"Same prison where Aaron Burr was incarcerated during his treason trial," Merrycoyf told Glynis with what sounded to her like misplaced satisfaction. Should Niles be expected to take some sort of pride in this association with Burr?

"Furthermore," Merrycoyf had concluded, smiling, "to everyone's surprise, Burr was acquitted."

Glynis came back to the present and the courtroom with a jolt when she realized prosecutor Steele had begun reading the indictment against Niles. ". . . The *United States* versus *Peartree* . . . in that the accused did aid and abet the escape of one female slave, property of Victor St. Croix."

Judge Trumbull leaned forward to look down at Niles. "How do you plead?"

Merrycoyf, who had gone to stand beside his client, said, "The accused pleads not guilty, Your Honor."

"Is there some reason why trial cannot commence immediately, counsel?" Judge Trumbull asked Merrycoyf.

"With Your Honor's permission, I request one week for preparation of my client's defense. I have just yesterday arrived in your picturesque city. And may I add, Your Honor, that it will be my great privilege to practice law in such venerable surroundings. I believe, for example, that Aaron Burr's trial was held here, was it not?"

Looking at the judge over the narrow spectacles poised on his cheeks, Merrycoyf's eyes—Glynis couldn't see them but she *knew*—conveyed the very essence of artlessness.

The corners of Judge Trumbull's mouth twitched. He seemed to study Merrycoyf for a moment, then brought his gavel down with a thump. "The trial of the *United States* versus *Peartree* will commence at ten A.M. one week from today."

"All rise," called the bailiff as Judge Trumbull left the courtroom.

* * *

GLYNIS AND MERRYCOYF spent the remainder of the morning
and much of the early afternoon in John Hamilton's law office. To prepare for Niles's defense, the lawyers drew up a list
of potential female witnesses for Glynis to interview in the
following days. At first Hamilton voiced doubts about this until Merrycoyf persuaded him Glynis would be capable and indeed had performed this function for him in the past. He
would vouch for Miss Tryon's competence, he said. Glynis
didn't know if she deserved vouchsafing, but had already
agreed to assist.

Leaving the two men, she wired Harriet a terse: Niles fine
Stop Do not worry Stop All will be well Stop, telegraphing a
confidence she didn't believe. Didn't believe one whit.
Merrycoyf would need to be a wizard to gain Niles's freedom.
She also hoped the lawyers could persuade Niles to present
himself with more humility at the trial then he'd exhibited
that morning; a southern jury would undoubtedly not find his
hostility appealing.

As she walked up Main Street toward the hotel, the price
of the gowns she passed in the shop windows astonished her.
They were half the cost of those in Rochester, and the cotton
frocks almost two-thirds less. No wonder the women of Richmond appeared so beautifully dressed. Beside them she felt
like a hayseed. She paused in front of a shop window then
walked on. After turning around for another look, she went
back to stand before the dressmaker's form draped in a yellow cotton frock she found irresistible. How could she therefore resist?

Visiting a strange city, she decided, granted one an
immediate anonymity—a sense of having no past with which
to be identified. No future in which to be held accountable.
No familiar persons to startle with one's unfamiliar behavior.
One could be whatever one chose to be. It was a heady sensation.

Waiting in the dress shop for the frock to be wrapped, she
overheard two lavishly gowned patrons speaking together in
hushed tones, their voices barely audible from behind a jungle
of greenery sprouting from brass pots on carpet lying ankle-
deep. But Glynis had recognized a name.

". . . that St. Croix trial . . . Yankee scoundrel kid-napped . . ."

Glynis tried to overhear more of the conversation by lean-ing unobtrusively into the foliage. She heard a sound behind her and jumped back, snagging a branch with her sleeve. The small Norfolk pine belonging to the branch tipped toward her to sway precariously. On the other side of the greenery, Glynis heard a sharp intake of breath; grabbing the slender pine trunk she pushed it back upright. She had just breathed a sigh of relief when, turning around, she found the shop pro-prietor standing directly behind her with the wrapped gown, regarding her with what Harriet would call a "fish eye." Glynis took her package and hurried from the shop.

When she reached the sidewalk, she straightened her bod-ice and plucked a few green needles from her dress. Embar-rassing as the incident had been, it served to remind her of something her sister Gwen once said: "When you want to know the latest gossip in town, just go to a ladies' hair dresser."

Gritting her teeth and affixing a look she hoped suitably contrite, Glynis stepped back inside the dress shop for infor-mation.

On a quiet shaded street off Main, a sign by the side door of a well-kept white house said:

HEADS DRESSED—in curls or otherwise, in the most beautiful styles, AT ANY HOUR. Shampooing done if desired. Mrs. P. keeps the Best and most Celebrated Hair Dyes. Also, LADIES' WIGS, Half-wigs, Madon-nas, Braids, Bands and Curls, made in the neatest manner.

The amazonian, henna-haired proprietor of the establish-ment wielded her instruments with such aplomb, along with a steady stream of conversation, that Glynis neglected to pay much attention to what the two-hundred-pound Mrs. Peel ac-tually did. She kept asking questions and Mrs. Peel kept twisting Glynis's hair around coal-heated curling irons that looked like something discarded by the Inquisition.

"Do you know the mistress of Jolimont?" Glynis inserted at one point in the operation. "Katherine St. Croix?"

"Oh, yes; she comes into town 'bout once a month. Poor woman suffers, Ah tell y'all, with that fine hair of hers. . . . And a' course she brings those twins along."

"Twins?" Glynis repeated.

"Twins. Y'all know what they are?" Mrs. Peel paused, waving the curling iron, which radiated heat. Glynis swiftly moved her head aside while concluding the woman must believe Yankees incapable of multiple births.

When she nodded encouragingly, Mrs. Peel went on, "Miz St. Croix, she had those twins from an earlier marriage. Not surprising her first husband died. He was an older fella, too old to be carryin' on producin' children! Unnatural, Ah call it."

Glynis didn't quite follow this, but asked, "Was her present husband also married before?" and flinched at the smell of smoking hair.

"Victor St. Croix? Oh my, yes, but that poor wife died in childbirth along with the baby. Tragedy it was, 'cause now he's got no children of his own."

Sometime later, while Glynis waited for the hotel doorman, she wondered how she'd ever had the nerve to ask so many questions. And she now felt some concern for her hair. Once inside the hotel lobby, she peeked cautiously around the silver-frame of a mirror and felt a twinge of disappointment that, with the exception of a few exotic-looking curlicues, it appeared much the same as usual. After very nearly risking her life with the iron-brandishing Mrs. Peel, she'd at least expected something more daring. But since she wouldn't have been brave enough to carry it off—not in front of Jeremiah Merrycoyf she wouldn't—she knew she'd have rinsed it out anyway.

She hurried up the staircase to her room, eager to finish her first *Courier* dispatch to Ephraim Penrod before supper. Somehow she must withstand the impulse to sign it: Glynis Tryon, a.k.a. Sebastian P. Japes.

THE NEXT MORNING, seated in a carriage with one of the Hamiltons' Negro servants driving—Jonah was a paid servant, not a slave, Faith Hamilton emphasized—Glynis looked around her with the realization that she'd been in Richmond two days and up to now had seen very little of it.

She'd gotten her first glimpse from the train of a beautiful city rising on hills above the James River. The river this morning looked like a sun-flecked strip of silk unrolling to the Chesapeake Bay and the Atlantic beyond. As the carriage rattled downhill, Glynis could see sailing vessels tied at the wharves below. Jonah pointed across the river to the south; what he said was the milling village of Manchester stood out-lined against soft green slopes.

From what she had read, Glynis thought of the country south of Pennsylvania as being almost solely agricultural. The iron factories and flour mills along the James surprised her, but obviously the falls of the river, like those of the Genesee at home, provided the power needs of the industries. She'd quickly gathered that this city possessed wealth; John Hamil-ton confirmed what Niles earlier said: that like others, Victor St. Croix had made his fortune in tobacco. Rows of the ware-houses stretched as far as Glynis could see.

Richmond, with a population of some forty-five thousand people, was about the same size as Rochester; this morning, it seemed at least half of them used the large square-stone sidewalks that fronted the Main Street commercial buildings. And even at this early hour, everyone seemed to be in high dress: women in light silk dresses, with hair ribbons or elab-orate satin bonnets; men in close-fitting, shiny black evening suits. And the hats. Nothing like Seneca Falls.

Some few miles past the city limits, Jonah turned the car-riage into a long cobbled drive and gestured to the two-story building up ahead. Glynis sat forward and shaded her eyes to see. By northern standards the white-painted St. Croix man-sion looked immense. A wide porch ran the length of the house front; supported by thick porch pillars, an equally wide balcony with ornate railing ran under the second-story win-dows. Six chimneys rose above the flat roof.

Beyond the main house stood clusters of small wooden buildings. Glynis wanted to ask Jonah if those were the slave quarters, but she wondered if he might once have been a slave himself, and she felt uncomfortable questioning him. Beside the small buildings were several squat wood cabins; from their chimneys curled thin smoke, fragrant with hickory even from the distance of the drive. And beyond them stretched row after row of long low sheds—for curing tobacco most likely.

As Jonah pulled the carriage up before the main house, Glynis felt a knot of anxiety form in her stomach. Jeremiah Merrycoyf insisted she be the one to do this, but she now thought herself completely inadequate. Only a determination to help Niles kept her from asking Jonah to turn the carriage back toward the city.

Jonah had jumped from the driver's seat to help her to the cobblestones. Glynis waited by the carriage while he climbed the wide front-porch steps with John Hamilton's calling card and a letter from his wife introducing her. In the distance Negro women and youngsters carried armfuls of huge drooping leaves into the curing barns. Since morning the outside air had grown warm and muggy; dark wisps of smoke rose from the sheds and Glynis imagined that inside where the tobacco dried it must be an inferno. How could anyone be expected to work in such heat?

The night before, John Hamilton had explained that tobacco planted in May was cut in September and left in the fields until the sun "killed" or wilted the leaves enough to become pliable; they could then be carried without breaking to the curing barns in early October. The leaves would be stripped in November and tied into hands of five leaves each. In December the dark fire- or air-cured tobacco of Jolimont would be packed for marketing in thousand-pound barrel-like casks called hogsheads. These hogsheads would be taken to market in wagons, or flatboats on the river, or rolled over the roads, in which case shafts for hitching horses were attached to the casks.

Hamilton said that the size of farms in this part of Virginia averaged about one hundred twenty acres, while big plantations like Jolimont had four hundred acres or more. One slave could work two to three acres. Supervised by the planter or an overseer, this slave labor was tedious but didn't require great strength and consequently could be done mostly by women and young boys.

The previous evening Glynis found she became more and more distressed with the neutral, almost offhand manner in which John Hamilton discussed slave labor. And yet, both he and his wife Faith were professed abolitionists. It was as if he believed in the principle of abolition, but refused to acknowledge the practice of slavery in his own state by men like Victor St. Croix—whom Hamilton appeared to regard with a certain admiration. This made no sense to Glynis. How could one condemn the institution of slavery without condemning those who held slaves?

She turned toward the plantation house when the wire-cloth screened front door opened. As the mistress of Jolimont descended the porch steps, Glynis met the guarded brown eyes inspecting her. The hem of Katherine St. Croix's hoop-skirted gown floated over the stone walk as she came toward the carriage to offer Glynis an extended hand and a cool half-smile. The woman's grip proved unexpectedly strong, with a palm rough and uneven. Glynis glanced down to see a reddened hand, which looked like anything but that of the pampered southern belle of whom she'd so often heard.

The woman's eyes followed Glynis's glance, and her smile tightened. "Ah'm Katherine St. Croix, Miss Tryon. Please come up to the porch out of the sun."

The woman stood somewhat shorter than Glynis herself, her form buxom but not obese. Smooth hair the same brown of the eyes lay parted in the middle and swept back from a softly rounded face, while the reserved half-smile added to a sixteenth-century, *Mona Lisa* quality.

After she followed Katherine St. Croix back up the steps, Glynis found herself waved toward a grouping of whitewashed wicker furniture, which looked cool and inviting in the intensifying afternoon heat. Katherine St. Croix reached for a cord and within seconds a sweet-faced young Negro woman appeared in the door. The woman gave a subdued "Yes, ma'am" to the brisk request for tea and disappeared back inside.

A large centipede—it must have been twice as large as any insect Glynis had ever seen before—skittered across the porch floor. She tried not to look at it, although Katherine St. Croix seemed not to notice. The woman sat forward in her chair, jangling a ring with scores of keys, which she detached from her belt to place on a small table between Glynis and herself. Glancing at them, Glynis pondered the existence of that many locked doors in one dwelling.

Katherine St. Croix apparently caught the glance. "The household supplies are in cupboards—the silver, the linens, sugar, spices and other foodstuffs. It's been found that they all don't disappear quite so fast if the cupboards are kept secured."

She gave Glynis an appraising look. Why? thought Glynis. Did the woman expect her to question why a home needs to be locked up tighter than a drum? She shifted slightly in the chair in an attempt to cover her irritation. The wicker, to her chagrin, gave a small but revealing creak.

"Mrs. Hamilton's letter said you are here in Richmond," Katherine St. Croix said smoothly, "because of the young man, Niles Peartree—and that she and her husband John would appreciate my speaking with you. Ah can't imagine what they think Ah might have to say. Young Mr. Peartree is in jail, Ah understand. Ah really don't know what Ah can add." The half-smile remained fixed, almost as if it had been painted there.

Glynis had the distinct impression that she was not only being sized up but also being patronized by Katherine St. Croix. However, to be fair, she was doing much the same thing herself. She smiled determinedly. "Mrs. St. Croix, I much appreciate your seeing me. As you might guess, Niles's mother is terribly concerned about her son—as we all are."

"Excuse me, Miss Tryon, Ah don't think Ah quite understand your interest in this . . . affair."

"Harriet Peartree, a dear friend of mine, is presently indisposed, and I've known Niles since he was a youngster. I wonder if perhaps . . . well, if you might tell me what happened here. We—that is, those of us in New York who care for Niles—don't understand why he *is* in jail."

"Miss Tryon, the laws of the United States have been broken by your friend's son. That is why."

Glynis started to speak, but waited as the Negro woman came through the door carrying a tray. After she had deposited the silver tea service on the table and returned inside,

Glynis decided to try a different approach. "Mrs. St. Croix I'm familiar with the Fugitive Slave Law. However, an offer to buy Kiri's freedom has been made to your husband. Were you aware of that?" Glynis thought she had her answer as the St. Croix eyebrows lifted ever so slightly. No; the woman didn't know that.

"Your husband hasn't replied to the offer," Glynis went on as Katherine St. Croix quickly bent forward to pour the tea, "and we wondered why."

"Ah expect we do things a little differently here in the South than you might be accustomed to, Miss Tryon. My husband doesn't discuss business matters with me." She paused, then said, "On the other hand, Ah imagine you have heard tell of southern women who sit all day on their verandas, drinking mint juleps, fanned by their slaves, and doing not much else."

Recognizing that her question had been rather skillfully deflected, Glynis felt her face flush as Katherine St. Croix extended her hands palms up. "As you noticed, these are not idle hands. The southern belle Ah just described doesn't exist except in some Yankee imagination. Oh, somewhere you may find one or two who fit that picture, but there are not many.

"Let me tell you what Ah and other planters' wives do with our time, Miss Tryon . . ." Her voice trailed off as she bent to the tea, handing Glynis a cup and saucer thin as eggshell, transparent enough to see the liquid through. As Glynis took them, she questioned why Katherine St. Croix felt the need to justify herself. Or did she just want to maintain control of the conversation?

The tea served, Katherine St. Croix said, "Ah'm responsible for running this house, and all the other domestic operations of this plantation. That means taking care of the needs of *all* who live here—clothing and food and shelter not only for my own family but for my husband's slaves."

She gave Glynis an intense look, and despite herself Glynis shifted uncomfortably under the woman's gaze—did her face reveal the surprise she felt at hearing Jolimont's Negroes described as "my *husband's* slaves"?

Katherine St. Croix went on, "Ah handle the household budget, which means dealing with local merchants. Ah get up every morning, *every* morning, at dawn to distribute supplies," she nodded at the key on the table, "after which the work begins: the gardening, the dairy activities, preserving the produce we grow, salting pork, preparing medicines, sewing rugs and pillows, linen and bedding and all the clothes for forty-seven slaves, as well as knitting socks, and making candles and soap. Ah have help with these, but Ah work as hard as the others. And just like northern women, Ah'd expect, Ah'm also subject to my husband's comfort and . . . needs. And the care of my children."

Katherine St. Croix sat back, still looking intently at Glynis as if challenging her to refute this inventory. In the air pulsed hostility very nearly palpable. Glynis shifted again in her chair, wondering how to turn the conversation around. She and Katherine St. Croix had gotten off on the wrong foot, or perhaps simply disliked each other on sight, but she had to get past that for Niles's sake.

Glynis tried to imagine how this woman might feel about a northerner judging her domain. She mustered every ounce of sincerity she could. "I feel rather as if we're talking with an ocean between us, Mrs. St. Croix," she said. "I suppose, though, it appears a bit forward of me to raise questions about your intentions—regarding Niles, I mean. And of course you're quite right; I'm not accustomed to southern ways. For one thing, I had no idea so much is placed on southern women's shoulders—but since that seems to be true for women everywhere, I shouldn't have been surprised. However, I hope you'll forgive my . . . I'm looking for the right word"—she smiled—"perhaps *ignorance* would explain my unintentional lack of manners."

Katherine St. Croix's eyes shifted away. When her gaze returned to Glynis, the woman seemed to have made some concession—her rigid posture eased somewhat. After a pause she said, "Yes, Ah do know you Yankees are more direct than we. When my husband and Ah visited New York City last year, Ah saw newspaper advertisements that would make the most sophisticated southern women blush. And Ah am an avid newspaper reader, Ah assure you."

Oh, Lord, she must mean the sarsaparilla ads, Glynis inwardly winced; she could just imagine what Katherine St. Croix had seen: *Dr. Townsend's extract—The Most Extraordi-*

nary Medicine In The World—expressly prepared for female complaints, invaluable for all the delicate diseases to which women are subject, like falling of the womb, irregular, painful and suppressed Menstruation, barrenness, as well as the "turn of life" and the numerous and horrible diseases to which females may be subject at this time, as well as the entire complicated train of evils which follow the female's disordered system . . .

Glynis risked a small laugh. "I would hate to think, Mrs. St. Croix, that you believe those newspaper advertisements represent the average northern woman—newspapers are not considered to be arbiters of good taste, and many of us Yankee women blush also, I can assure you."

The smile still in place, Katherine St. Croix nodded. "You must remember, Miss Tryon, that we live in our small rural communities here in the South. We don't have all your towns and cities." She seemed to be watching Glynis's reaction.

"I could see that, coming into Richmond on the train and then on the ride out here," Glynis answered. "I think I would find such isolation difficult—to live so far from other women . . . ah, friends and neighbors, that is." She swallowed hard, as after all, she could plainly see any number of black women on the plantation. But for a plantation mistress, those women could not be the same as female friends. Glynis suddenly understood that the institution of slavery must pervade every aspect of life here. Yet it wasn't an easy concept to grasp: that southern white women had more in common with their husbands than with other members of their own sex. Theirs must be a very lonely existence indeed.

"Ah believe Mr. Niles Peartree once mentioned that you are a librarian, Miss Tryon?" When Glynis nodded, Katherine St. Croix said, as if she had read Glynis's mind, "That would be a highly unlikely situation here in Virginia—that is to say, an unmarried woman, no doubt well educated, and employed as well. And financially independent. Highly unlikely."

Again Glynis nodded. It also seemed unlikely that the South, with its isolated farms, its absence of large towns and cities, would have those groups of women that in the North provided mutual support to one another. Groups of working-class girls, temperance and abolition associations, orphanages and homes for unwed mothers, and all the other charitable organizations becoming commonplace in the Northeast. Here women likely performed their charitable work within their own households. Or within their churches, and those, being male preserves, would hardly encourage the independence of females. These women were almost as confined, in one sense, as their slaves. Small wonder that the women's rights movement had been born far north of the Mason-Dixon Line.

So where might she find common ground with Katherine St. Croix in order to gain the information Jeremiah Merrycoyf needed? Perhaps an abrupt change of topic? "Mrs. St. Croix, did you know Kiri's mother, a young woman named Ama?"

Katherine St. Croix's smile remained frozen in place. Only her eyes betrayed her with a slight flicker of lashes. "Ah'm not acquainted with my husband's field slaves, Miss Tryon. They're quartered in the cabins down back, so Ah rarely if ever see them."

Again Glynis felt the frustration of having her question evaded. She didn't really blame Katherine St. Croix for protecting her own interests and for resisting what she must view as an invasion of privacy, but Glynis also knew how important these questions were to Niles's defense. She couldn't give up yet. Try something else, she told herself.

"Mrs. St. Croix, if Kiri was to be returned here, would your husband drop the charges against Niles, do you think?"

The smile suddenly wavered. Glynis saw with surprise that she had inadvertently blundered into an area that for some reason distressed the woman.

"Ah have no idea what my husband would do," Katherine St. Croix answered after a moment. Her smile then disappeared altogether. "Is that a real possibility—that the girl *would* be returned?"

Absolutely not, Glynis thought. "I suppose it could be," she said. Why did the woman seem so upset by this? Wasn't it the whole point of arresting Niles in the first place? But suppose that what Katherine St. Croix wanted and what her husband wanted were not the same thing? For instance, what if the woman suspected that her husband desired Kiri as his concubine? "Well, let me ask you this," Glynis said slowly, feeling her way blindly. "If Kiri was to come back, what would be her position in the household—the same as before? Would she live here in the main house with what would be . . . ah, well, her same duties?"

Again, Glynis saw her question provoke distress; Katherine St. Croix shifted in her chair, actually frowning, then abruptly looked off toward the white-fenced horse enclosures at the far side of the drive. Coming across the grass were two young people of almost the same height and same slim frame. Two blond heads shone in the sunlight. Glynis stared at them, realizing these must be Katherine St. Croix's twins by her first marriage. She had assumed that twins meant identical. But one of these blonds had long hair and distinctly feminine features. The other did not.

"Your children?" she said to Katherine St. Croix.

"What? Oh, yes." The woman suddenly sat forward to fasten Glynis's eyes with her own. "Miss Tryon," she said a little breathlessly, "it would be difficult to bring that girl back into this household. She is very lovely, soft-spoken and sweet-tempered. That kind of black woman is extremely attractive to men." She paused, then added, "To any man."

Glynis found herself gaping at Katherine St. Croix. What precisely had she just said? And again the woman's glance fluttered toward the pair strolling up the drive toward them. Now she spoke rapidly. "My son Andre is nineteen. You have mentioned yourself how isolated we are here. Think what it must be like for a young man . . ." she hesitated, but continued to hold Glynis's eyes.

Glynis knew a moment's confusion, and she needed to make certain she understood Katherine St. Croix's implication. But when she started to ask for clarification, the woman got to her feet, moving quickly to the edge of the porch.

"Ah'm afraid you will have to excuse me now, Miss Tryon. One of our slave girls is in labor, about to deliver, and Ah need to assist. Ah really must go."

The obviousness of the ruse, the abruptness with which it had been delivered, left no doubt as to her dismissal of Glynis and to the end of conversation. Uneasily, Glynis rose and followed Katherine St. Croix down the porch steps just as brother and sister neared the house. They strolled arm in arm, their bright heads thrown back in laughter.

Obviously Katherine St. Croix did not intend to introduce her children, because she called, "Antoinette! Andre! Please find the overseer for me—he's in the south field, and he took the key to the medical supplies this morning."

She turned to Glynis, saying quickly, "Ah'm pleased we have met, Miss Tryon. And now will you excuse me?"

Not even waiting for an answer, she hurried off across the grass to intercept the two slim figures, and together the three then disappeared around the corner of the house. Glynis stood staring after them. And Kiri's words again thrust back at her: that she didn't want to be like her mother and grandmother—forced to be a white man's concubine.

Could it be Andre and not Victor St. Croix to whom Kiri had alluded, as his mother seemed to have just done? Katherine St. Croix had managed to dodge most of Glynis's specific questions, but she had also revealed herself as protecting something. Her privacy, her son . . . or her marriage?

Glynis walked slowly to the carriage parked in the shade of a leathery-leaved magnolia where Jonah sat slumped, eyes closed, snoring softly in the driver's seat.

FIFTEEN

But what country have I, or any one like me, born of slave mothers? What laws are there for us? We don't make them,—we don't consent to them,—we have nothing to do with them; all they do is crush us, and keep us down.
—HARRIET BEECHER STOWE,
UNCLE TOM'S CABIN

THE NEXT MORNING'S overcast sky hung like a lofty gray ceiling above the carriage that Jonah directed toward the bustling Richmond wharves. The air felt muggy, as if needing to be wrung out, and it smelled of rain. Glynis tried to ignore the dull throb behind her eyes, a result no doubt of sitting with Merrycoyf in the dim candle-lit hotel lobby, he with his brandy, she with black tea, theorizing late into the night. They had arrived at no conclusion, save that Victor St. Croix's motive remained enigmatic. Could it be personal vengeance for Niles's theft of his "property"? Did St. Croix want Kiri for carnal reasons, or, hard as it might be to credit, was his an honest concern for Kiri's welfare, as prosecutor Steele claimed? Or might it be simply the slaveholder's desire to make an example of Niles, and thus discourage future assistance to fugitives?

Glynis suddenly became aware of escalating noise in the street and realized a crowd had begun to gather. She glanced around uneasily at the restless, milling people. "Jonah, why are we here on the waterfront? The sky looks threatening, and I need to get to Riverain plantation today."

Jonah half-turned on the driver's seat. "Yes, ma'am. But Ah thought on the way you might like to see this here part of the city."

He turned back to urge the horse up a short rise. At its crest Glynis looked down to see a one-story brick warehouse with its front abutting the street and which ran back almost to the river front. As the carriage drew near, a sign over the warehouse entrance became visible with the name of its owner and the words AUCTION WAREHOUSE conspicuously painted. On the entrance door itself hung a red flag carrying the advertisement "Auctions and Negro Sales." A young mulatto man walked in front of the building; in one hand he held yet another red flag, in the other a bell, which he swung back and forth. Over the strident clanging, he shouted, "Oh yea! Oh yea! Walk up, gentlemen. The sale of a fine, likely lot of niggers is now about to begin. All sorts, belonging to the estate of the late Mr. Wallace, sold for no faults, but to settle the estate. There be old-uns and young-uns, men and women, gals and boys. Walk up, now gentlemen!"

Glynis suddenly realized the carriage had stopped moving. She lunged forward to tug at Jonah's coat. "Jonah, please drive on. I want to leave. Right now, Jonah!"

The man's shoulders lifted in a shrug. "Sure 'nough, Miz Tryon. But yesterday you said you wanted to see the city." He raised his crop to point at the warehouse. "This here *is* the city."

Glynis stared down at her hands clenched together in her lap. Her head came up a moment later when the crowd's mood shifted from restlessness to expectation. A man had appeared who all but filled the doorway of the warehouse. Glynis heard the crowd's murmur of "auctioneer," and she stared at the bearded figure with his quick, cold black eyes. After reading loudly a formal announcement authorizing the sale, the auctioneer began to pave the way for good prices, Glynis assumed, by announcing that among the slaves to be offered were carriage drivers, gardeners, dining-room servants, farmhands, cooks, milkers, seamstresses, washerwomen, and "the most promisin', growin', sleek, and sassy lot of young niggers" he ever had the pleasure of offering.

And with that Glynis began to understand why Jonah had brought her here. He wanted her to see behind the beautiful Greek Revival architecture of the city's public buildings and their green parks, and the splendid new gas lighting on Main Street. Behind the tellingly inexpensive cotton frocks and rich-smelling cigars and pipe tobacco.

She had already learned that Richmond became a prominent slave-market city because Virginia was a slave-breeding state. Slaves were brought to Richmond's central markets for shipment and for sale to the Deep South drovers. John Hamilton said that it was common for planters to command their girl and women slaves to produce children, and that Negro girls were often sold off to the dreaded canefields simply because they didn't. A "breeding woman" was worth three or four times more than one who did not breed.

Hamilton told of a well-known Richmond planter who offered white men twenty dollars for every one of his female slaves whom these men impregnated. The offer, not an unusual one, had been made for the purpose of "improving" the stock, much as farmers attempted to improve their cattle by cross-breeding.

The editor of the *Virginia Times* newspaper estimated that about forty thousand slaves were sold out of the state in a single year, and the professional slave-breeders who sold them put into their pockets some twenty-four millions of dollars.

Glynis had heard all of this in the past few days, but found it impossible to believe. Either that or her mind simply rejected as unthinkable the magnitude of suffering that slavery created. But now, here in this place, she was forced to view the reality.

She wouldn't look—if she didn't, she could pretend this did not exist, and she could go home to Seneca Falls, to her relatively comfortable life there, and not have to feel as ashamed as she did that moment. But slavery wasn't her doing. She wasn't to blame. And yet . . . she *had* bought the frock, the frock she now recognized as having been made from the cotton picked by slaves. And for years she had turned the other way when desperate runaways came through her town seeking help. Perhaps worst of all, she had blindly accepted the laws sustaining slavery simply because they *were* the law—instead of looking behind them, as Jonah now demanded that she do, at the reasons those laws existed in the first place.

She had located the thread of Merrycoyf's positive law argument; positive law wove an acceptable disguise behind which the unacceptable could be obscured. An intricate legal web designed for the majority, which said: We will do it this way because *this* way protects our interests; but since this flies in the face of ethics, morality, and natural rights, we'll call it something high-minded: positive law. The ancient "might makes right," dressed up in oblique language. The emperor's new clothes.

Glynis lowered her eyes again. She, a woman and therefore lacking majority rank, should have seen this long before now. And white women existed nowhere near the depth of degradation that seemed to be routinely inflicted upon black women slaves. That she hadn't grasped this earlier created reason enough for her sense of shame.

She raised her eyes cautiously. In front of her Jonah sat motionless in his driver's seat, the carriage just far enough away from the crowd to allow a clear view of the coffles of chained Negroes shuffling from the warehouse. Many were women and children, children of all ages, some so young they clung to the women's hands or were clutched to their mothers' breasts. For a brief, agonized moment Glynis thought she saw Kiri, dark head bowed above drooping shoulders, feet bare, collared with chain that hammocked to the neck of the slave behind her. No; it wasn't Kiri. But it could have been.

"I've seen, Jonah—more than enough," Glynis whispered just loud enough for him alone to hear. "Now I want to leave this place. Please. Please!"

Jonah's head came up with a jerk, and he lightly flicked the reins. The carriage jolted forward.

THE MAIN HOUSE of Riverain plantation sat back from the road, perched on a small hill that rose from a bend in the James River. While the carriage bounced up the rutted drive, Glynis attempted to thrust away the image of the slave market—despite knowing it would be with her forever—to concentrate on cattle grazing over the hill, the ravens and turkey buzzards circling overhead. Chickens scratched in the dirt. Fences looked in need of repair and paint, the roofs of sheds sagged as if weary, and weeds grew over the drive.

John Hamilton had told her that Claude Dupont, third-generation owner of Riverain, had died two years before. Dupont's widow now ran the plantation with the assistance of Negroes who chose to stay on with her after she freed them—the day of her husband's funeral. Chantal Dupont had done this despite anticipating strong opposition from Claude's brother. But she'd registered the slaves' manumission papers with the County Court clerk before her brother-in-law discovered what she'd done. Louis Dupont retaliated by holding his late brother's wealth out of Chantal's reach; this in spite of Claude's will, which left all to his wife.

Women could not sign contracts or handle business affairs in the public sphere. But if circumstances forced it, women could manage internal plantation affairs without the advice or consent of males. This Chantal Dupont had been doing.

As the carriage neared the main house, the surroundings looked considerably less run-down. Just ahead at the top of the hill sat a well-proportioned, freshly painted, white wooden building with a columned portico that shaded the ground floor and first story. Wire-cloth screened windows looked out at the river.

As Jonah jumped from the carriage to deliver the calling card, a woman under a large-brimmed straw hat came around the corner of the house. From a distance she looked ordinary enough, but as she came nearer the carriage, Glynis saw strong features and a firm stride. The woman abruptly plucked off her hat, loosing an extraordinary tumble of white-blond hair, thick and curly as that of an Irish water spaniel. No genteel gown and hooped petticoats on this woman, but homespun blouse and indigo, ankle-length skirt of tight-woven jean cloth. Glynis climbed from the carriage and extended her hand to the approaching woman. "Mrs. Dupont?"

"I'm Chantal Dupont."

For a brief moment their eyes locked, and Glynis heard an inner voice that said that this woman, in spite of their differences, might become a friend. And she immediately noticed the near absence of drawl. John Hamilton said Mrs. Dupont had not been born in Virginia, but rather in northeastern Maryland; the way he'd said this made it sound as if the fact went far to explain the state of things at Riverain.

Chantal Dupont's grip proved as firm as her stride, her palm even more callused than that of Katherine St. Croix. Glynis had begun to wonder who, or what, had inspired the fantasy of the soft southern belle.

"I expect you're Glynis Tryon," Chantal Dupont said unexpectedly. Glynis must have looked surprised, because the woman added, "One of our young men—" she inclined her head toward a patch of crookneck squash being harvested by several Negroes "—was at Jolimont yesterday. News of strangers, especially Yankee strangers, travels fast here. I imagined you'd come to see us sooner or later."

A wry smile deepened lines around the woman's mouth and the fine wrinkles at the outer corner of her eyes. Eyes the indigo blue of her skirt, they were level with Glynis's own.

"How's the girl? Kiri, I mean," Chantal Dupont asked. "Her grandmother needs to know."

"I'm sure she does," Glynis answered, again startled by the abrupt directness. She found other southerners, especially the women, to be more circuitous.

"You look surprised, Miss Tryon. Masika is my friend; we don't have many secrets. But don't say anything you think only Masika should hear—although I would never report a runaway. Not that that makes me terribly well liked in Virginia. That and a few other things."

"Did you ever meet Niles Peartree?" Glynis asked as they climbed the stairs to the porch. No whitewashed wicker here, but instead pine rockers that looked as if they'd rested there several centuries.

"Sit down," Chantal Dupont said, settling herself with a sigh in one of the rockers. Glynis sat. "I saw Mr. Peartree once in town—from a distance," the woman said. "You should know that I'm not welcome, not welcome at all, at Jolimont." Again she smiled wryly. "A bad influence. But I assume you don't want to talk about me. I heard the young man's in jail, and I heard what for. Did you know I've been subpoenaed to appear for the prosecution?"

"No. No, I didn't." Glynis supposed in that case she should be careful about what she said, and wondered if Merrycoyf knew about the subpoena.

"At any rate, I'm not going to help their case much," Chantal stated flatly. "Theoretically, I don't know anything about Kiri and the young man. Theoretically. But you can ask away if you want. I should warn you, though, Miss Tryon: I may not sound much like a southerner, and I certainly have my differences with the institution of slavery, but since my marriage I have become a Virginian. And bound by certain social codes regarding behavior."

She gazed at Glynis, who wondered why she had been cautioned. She got her answer. "There are things that are simply not talked about," Chantal said, an emphasis on the "not." "There's no question," she went on, "that this perpetuates injustice. But that's the way it is. You can't understand it, I suppose, but you'll have to accept it."

Fair warning, Glynis thought, but what were the "things" to which Chantal Dupont referred? Very likely precisely those Glynis wanted to learn.

"Even so," Chantal said, running long fingers through her unruly mass of hair, "you will certainly want to talk with Masika. When I saw your carriage, I sent word to the weaving shed. She'll be along soon."

Glynis murmured a thank-you. She would save her news about Zeph until his grandmother arrived.

"In the meantime, let me tell you something about Masika," Chantal offered. "When she'd been with us for only a few months, I found her looking at a newspaper—which she held upside down—clearly trying to decipher the black chicken-scratchings my husband and I pored over every evening. So I taught her to read. I found her to be quick and bright. Do not underestimate her intelligence—or her courage."

The woman paused to look intently at Glynis as though conveying something vital. Glynis's mind immediately went to Zeph. So that's where he'd gotten it—the quick mind and the curiosity. And the courage. The boy needed to know his grandmother, know where he came from. But would that be possible? His grandmother might have been freed, but his mother had not. And it was from her that he derived his slave status. She and Merrycoyf had been over this a dozen times.

"My husband never knew that about Masika," Chantal abruptly added. "It's against the law to teach slaves to read, and he wouldn't have tolerated it. Whether Masika's daughter Ama learned to read . . . ?"

Her voice trailed off as Glynis's head came up with a start. Would the woman talk about Ama—Kiri's mother? But just then Chantal rose abruptly and went to look out over the porch railing. Perhaps she thought she had already said too much.

"Here she is now." Chantal turned back to Glynis. "Masika's just coming. You can introduce yourself." She started down the steps, saying over her shoulder, "I need to go check my vineyard—such as it is." She gave a short laugh. "My family came from Bordeaux and I'm still trying to duplicate the wine they made. But the climate and soil here are so different." She stopped on the last step to look up at Glynis. "I'll see you before you leave, Miss Tryon."

She walked away before Glynis had a chance to say anything more. It seemed clear the woman meant for Masika and herself to talk in private. Glynis heard Chantal greet someone as she went around the corner of the house, and a moment later a tall black woman appeared, walking toward the porch.

She must have been close to six feet, with a bearing that could have balanced a pitcher on her head; below the red turban covering her hair, large brass hoop earrings swung almost to her shoulders. Glynis tried to guess her age. It could have been anything from forty to sixty, as the woman's sleek blue-black skin revealed little. Had her daughter Ama been as stunning-looking? Masika's granddaughter certainly was, although Kiri's features were more fragile.

"I'm Glynis Tryon," she said as the woman glided up the porch steps. "You're Kiri's grandmother?"

"Ah'm Masika. Tell me how she is, my granddaughter."

Glynis told her. "And I'm sure Kiri's safe with Frederick Douglass," she concluded. She didn't think it necessary to add: for now. Masika nodded once and gracefully lowered herself into a rocker.

"I have some other news for you, Masika—something that should make you very happy. It's about your grandson."

The woman inhaled sharply and leaned forward to clutch the arms of the rocking chair. "Tell me—the boy, he's alive?"

"Yes." Glynis smiled. "Yes, he's *quite* alive. He's in Seneca Falls, in New York State. I know him as Zeph—Zephaniah."

"Hidden by the Lord." Masika's words were barely audible, spoken in a reverent whisper. "Ah knew it! Ah just knew he was alive. Been having that feeling ever since Moses—" the woman paused, seeming to search Glynis's face. "Moses? Did Moses Rawlings find the boy?"

Glynis hesitated, wishing there was some way to avoid telling her about Moses. But short of lying there wasn't. This woman did not deserve lies.

When Glynis finished, Masika sat very still, staring off into some other place, the skin over the knuckles of her hands gripping the chair pulled taut.

"I'm sorry, so very sorry about Mr. Rawlings."

"He never drove no horse into no canal. Never!"

Glynis nodded. "Others feel about that the same as you. But perhaps it will help to know that yes, Moses Rawlings had found your grandson." Glynis waited some before she said, "Can you think of anyone who would have had reason to harm your friend? He'd just arrived in Seneca Falls when . . . when it happened."

Masika didn't respond. She rocked back and forth, staring off, her eyes deep pools of brown, still and dark. After a time, she stopped rocking and sat forward to ask, "The young man—he all right?"

"You mean Niles Peartree?" When Masika nodded, Glynis said, "He's going to be put on trial. For helping Kiri to escape from Jolimont. That's another reason I'm here, Masika. Is there anything you can tell me, anything you know, that might help Niles's lawyer defend him?"

"What you want to know? The girl left with him. Ah knew she'd do it—she's smarter than me, smarter than her mamma. And that young man, he was her way out of here."

Now Glynis sat not speaking. She waited at length, and when Masika offered nothing more, she said, "Niles is in love with your granddaughter. He wants to marry her. I hope you believe that."

"Ah believe that. Wouldn't have told her to go, if Ah didn't. Think Ah wanted to lose her too? But she loves that man, so she'd better grab her chance, Ah told her. Time some woman outta this here place got what she needed."

For some moments the only sound came from a mockingbird singing the same phrase over and over from somewhere high in the seventy-foot sycamore growing beside the house. Glynis reluctantly broke the quiet. "Masika, I have to ask you—I wish I didn't, but it's important—Kiri told me that she didn't want to stay here and . . ." Glynis paused. How could she say this?

Masika said it for her. "Told you she didn't want to end up like me. Or her mamma. That what she said?"

"Yes. That's what she said. Can you tell me what she meant exactly? I've guessed at it, but I may be wrong."

Masika's eyes changed then, the still pools agitated by some inner force. She bent forward to say, "Two things you have to know, Miz Tryon. One is, Ah can't help that young man—it's the law that us Negroes can't speak against white men in court, you 'ware of that?"

Glynis hadn't been. "And that means you can't testify against Victor St. Croix, isn't that what you're saying?"

Masika gave her a long look. "That's what Ah'm saying." She began rocking, fast. "Next thing is, there's another law—not written down but just as powerful—says no black woman can name a white man as father of her child." She stopped rocking abruptly, again staring hard at Glynis. "Black woman do that, she liable to not say anything again. Or worse: get sent south to the canefields."

Glynis had heard this before. But did Masika mean she couldn't help at all? Or had the woman meant that she herself couldn't say, but someone else could?

"Masika, you know who Kiri's father is, don't you? I mean, you must. You are . . . were . . . Ama's mother. She must have told you who made her pregnant. And Kiri knows her father is white. I'm not sure if she has named him, even to herself, but she's certainly guessed."

"Can't say."

"But it's important!"

"Can't say."

In frustration, Glynis got to her feet. She moved to the porch railing to look out at the dusty fields beyond. This code of silence was what Chantal Dupont had referred to earlier. And she'd been right about one thing: Glynis *didn't* understand it. Nor could she accept it. How did these men get away with this?

But the answer came all too clear. Because their wives wouldn't talk, and the female slaves the men violated *couldn't* talk, in effect slaveholders—not all surely, perhaps not even most, but whatever the number it was too many—could do as they wanted, without anyone calling them to account. With one exception, apparently: she had heard that killing a slave intentionally violated the law. But since slaves couldn't testify against white men, this law must be hollow.

The echo of rattling chains in the slave market challenged the silence. But it had been for a purpose that Chantal Dupont told Glynis not to underestimate Masika, and now she went to crouch beside the woman rocking.

Placing her hand on the arm of the chair, she said, "Masika, I need to ask you some things. I hope for Kiri's and Niles's sake, and your grandson's as well, that you can find the wherewithal to answer. I don't believe Chantal Dupont will hold it against you if you do—in fact, I think that's why she left us to talk together alone. And no one else need ever know."

She rose from her crouched position, seated herself in another chair, and waited. The black woman sat rigid in the motionless rocker. Finally, after so much time passed Glynis wondered if Masika had heard her, the woman gave her a nod.

Glynis breathed a long sigh. "Your daughter Ama's father was white, wasn't he?" she began. "That's what Kiri meant when she said her mother *and* you?"

Slowly, Masika nodded.

"Did the man live here at Riverain?"

"Didn't live here no, but . . ." Masika shifted her body uneasily. Glynis feared the woman might refuse to say more, but then, "Ama was born here. She lived with me until she got sold."

"Sold to Victor St. Croix, Kiri told me."

Masika nodded again. "My daughter—just fourteen when she got taken from me. She never came back." The mother's eyes filled.

GLYNIS ESTIMATED THAT an hour had gone by before Chantal Dupont appeared at the bottom of the porch steps. Glynis stood, as did Masika.

"You have a good visit?" Chantal asked, coming up to the porch. She looked not at Masika but directly at Glynis.

Masika remained silent.

"Yes. Yes, we talked about your hot weather," Glynis answered. If she needed to play this charade, which the three of them knew to be a charade, she would. However, "If I might, I'd like to ask you both something before I leave?"

"You can *ask*," Chantal said with her ironic smile.

"Thirteen years ago, the slave-catcher involved with the death of Kiri's mother—I'm sorry, Masika: with your daughter—could that slave-catcher's name have been Lyle Brogan?"

Chantal Dupont's expression gave answer enough, but Masika spat, "Devil-man. Brogan."

"Well, Brogan's dead," Glynis told them. "Murdered. In Seneca Falls. I'm certain neither one of you will mourn him. But he wasn't alone thirteen years ago," Glynis went on, as if she hadn't seen the furtive look that passed between the two women. "That slave-catcher had someone with him, someone as responsible as Brogan for those deaths—the overseer that Kiri said brought her back to Jolimont."

"When Victor St. Croix found out what happened," Chantal interrupted, "he fired that overseer."

"Yes, so Kiri implied. But where is he now?" Glynis asked. "Do you know, either of you?"

Both women shook their heads. Then Chantal put out her hand. "Wait!" She frowned in concentration, then said slowly, "I think the last we heard he'd gone north—somewhere north of here. Yes; someone said they'd heard he signed up with the Army. But after that he disappeared, far as I know. At least no one's heard of him since."

Glynis, taken aback, stared at her; that hadn't been what she'd expected. A memory swam in her mind, flashed momentarily to the surface, then, before she could catch it, darted from view like fluid quicksilver. But it was there, the memory; submerged again for now, but there. Glynis said, "The overseer. What was his name?"

The plantation mistress glanced at Masika and another long look passed between the two women. As if debating with herself, Chantal shook her head slightly. But then she turned back to Glynis. "Farley," she said. "The overseer's name was Thomas Farley."

"AND SO YOU think, from what the women told you," Merrycoyf said, his voice lowered as he glanced around the American Hotel dining room, "that Ama's father might have been Louis Dupont." He lowered his voice still more. "Chantal Dupont's brother-in-law?"

Glynis took a sip of the excellent coffee before she answered. "That's what I guessed. It wasn't easy, because Masika spoke so indirectly. Covering up this sort of thing has been so ingrained in these women—not just slave women, but the wives of the men, as well—that it's a conspiracy of silence. No one will say anything explicit."

She put down her coffee cup, running her finger around its silver-banded rim. "But from what Masika *did* say, I believe, yes. It fits. Although he didn't live there, I gathered that Louis Dupont spent a lot of time at Riverain. Probably planning to take over the plantation when his older brother died—Claude had been ill for years before he finally succumbed. I'd wager that Chantal Dupont knows about Louis—about him and Masika. And that's one of the reasons she dislikes him so.

"But of course," she went on, "Louis Dupont is not the crucial element here, even though he's probably Kiri's grandfather. It's Kiri's *father* we're concerned with—and Kiri herself inadvertently, I think, exposed the path to him."

Merrycoyf nodded. "And Katherine St. Croix's twin children? Do they enter into this?"

"Well, one thing I learned is that Katherine St. Croix has tried to get the boy Andre away from Jolimont, and Richmond. She enrolled him to start William and Mary College this fall, but at the last minute he refused to go. Perhaps Katherine thinks that if Kiri comes back, the boy will never leave—at least that's the impression Masika gave me. And I think Kiri worried about Andre too.

"But . . ." She drew back from the next words in embarrassment, but there could be no other way to say it. "A black slave mistress is not uncommon—in fact, the practice appears to be tacitly acceptable. If you recall, Mr. Merrycoyf, Thomas Jefferson was rumored to—" She broke off, feeling herself flush under Merrycoyf's attentive gaze. "Well, anyway," she went on, "Katherine St. Croix may not find the practice at all acceptable. And she could want her son permanently separated from Kiri, or Kiri from her husband."

"You may be right," Merrycoyf said. "But there could be another reason why Katherine St. Croix doesn't want Kiri back here. Well, at least it's beginning to come together. Some of it. Whether I can use it, and whether it will release Niles Peartree . . . ?" His hands lifted in question.

"Mr. Merrycoyf," Glynis said, her finger now tracing the intricately entwined pattern of the lace tablecloth, "there's also the Thomas Farley matter. I believe it may bear directly on the recent deaths in Seneca Falls. As I said earlier."

Merrycoyf used his napkin to deftly remove pecan pie's whipped cream from his beard, then peered thoughtfully at her over his spectacles. "And?"

"And I've been thinking about it. Does the United States War Department keep records—well, they must—of those who serve in the Army? And are those records accessible?"

"I doubt if just anyone can get into them. Let me think a minute." Merrycoyf's forehead, under a short fringe of white hair, creased in concentration as he stared at the ceiling. The creases had smoothed when he looked back at Glynis. "*I* probably couldn't get access, quick access anyway, to those records and—" Merrycoyf smiled "—as you might suspect, it's even more unlikely that the War Department would let a woman in to look at them."

No doubt highly unlikely. Glynis pressed her lips together. "But then how might I find—"

"Let me finish," Merrycoyf said, his smile broadening. "I can tell you who probably *could* get access."

She waited, since when Merrycoyf chose, he could be almost as melodramatic as Vanessa Usher. Almost. Glynis did not find it his most appealing trait.

"I'm reasonably certain," Merrycoyf said, a grin now reaching for his sideburns, "that if you were to contact a detective agency, it could find the information you want." He sat back in his chair apparently to watch her reaction.

But her mind went blank. What was he talking about? "A detective agency?" she repeated. "How would I find a detect—? Oh. Oh, yes. Mr. Merrycoyf! You mean, I presume, a detective agency like Allan Pinkerton's?"

"Pinkerton's is said to be the best. And he certainly has some good men working for him."

Glynis's cheeks grew hot. Her chest tightened, and she hoped Merrycoyf didn't know how hard she strained to sit there and look serene. But of course he did. He'd known about her and Cullen for years.

She had received only one letter from Cleveland, and that when Cullen first arrived there. It had been just a short, stiff, almost formal note. She hadn't answered it. Mostly because she didn't know what to say. And every time she thought of something to write, she'd started to cry. Time went on, and then it seemed too late to answer. Because why hadn't Cullen written again? If he'd cared, he would have. Surely he would.

She glanced up to see Merrycoyf studying her with a bemused expression—at least he'd stopped grinning. She stared back at him, refusing to burst into tears. Which might be what she'd do if she opened her mouth.

Merrycoyf finally folded his napkin and sat forward to place it beside his empty dessert plate. "If I were you," he said, not looking at her but down at the plate, "I'd send a wire tomorrow, asking—well, whomever I happened to know at Pinkerton's—if he could find what you're looking for in the War Department records." He sat back again in his chair to knit his fingers across his stomach.

"I don't even know what it is, exactly," Glynis answered, "that I'd ask Cullen to find. Does the Army keep a ledger of some sort when they pay—they do *pay*, don't they?"

Merrycoyf nodded. "They pay. Sometimes money. More often in the form of land grants. And they certainly must keep records. Why?"

Glynis shook her head. "I need to find out not only whom they pay, but where they pay it—that is, where certain men went after they'd served." She smiled at Merrycoyf. And said no more.

Merrycoyf appeared to be disappointed. But he pushed himself away from the table to struggle out of the narrow chair.

"You've done an admirable job for Niles, and I'm somewhat heartened," he said to her as they left the dining room. "But there remains a formidable task before us. Let us pray, pray with diligence, that Judge Trumbull is at the very least capable of listening. With an open mind."

Sixteen

The clause in the constitution of the United States, relating to fugitives from labour, manifestly contemplates the existence of a positive, unqualified right on the part of the owner of the slave, which no state law or regulation can in any way qualify, regulate, control, or restrain.
—SECOND CONGRESS, SESS. II, CH. 7, 1793

"OYEZ! OYEZ!" THE bailiff bawled over the hum in the courtroom. He paused while the hum quieted. "The Federal District Court for the Commonwealth of Virginia is now in session; the Honorable Artemus Trumbull presiding in the case of the *United States* versus *Peartree*. All rise now!"

Glynis glanced around her as she stood with the rest of the courtroom. On this the second day of the trial, the number of those attending more than doubled that of the previous day's jury selection. The trial had been moved to take place in City Hall on Broad Street, fronting Capitol Square on Shockoe Hill, instead of the county courthouse, which was situated almost a mile away and undergoing repair. An elegant structure with a portico at each end of four Doric columns, City Hall's courtroom had a high white ceiling bordered by elaborately carved molding; on immaculate pale gray walls hung gilt-framed portraits of prominent Virginians—male Virginians—and paintings depicting Revolutionary War battles. To either side of the judge's bench hung two glass chandeliers.

Judge Trumbull entered by a side door and stepped up to the bench. His clean-shaven, resolute jaw thrust forward, and his shoulders under the black robe looked as broad as those of a dockworker.

"Be seated," called the bailiff. The court clerk hurried forward to a small table.

"Mr. Clerk," Judge Trumbull said, "has the jury been sworn?"

"Yes, Your Honor."

"Very well." The judge looked down at the lawyers' tables facing him. Niles sat between Merrycoyf and John Hamilton; his skin had taken on an ashen pallor, like that of someone too long in a sick room. His head turned, his eyes sought and found Glynis, and she glimpsed the dark shadows under them. The eyes themselves still flared angrily.

In an attempt at reassurance, she smiled at him before he turned back to face the judge. The smile froze in place, as if disconnected from her, since there seemed very little about which to smile.

"Mr. Prosecutor," Judge Trumbull said to Richard Steele, "are you ready to proceed with your opening statement?"

Steele rose and came around his table to stand before the bench. "Yes, Your Honor."

"Proceed, Mr. Prosecutor."

Steele nodded. "Thank you, Your Honor." Steele then turned his attention to the twelve men seated in the jury box. "Gentlemen. In this Federal Court the prosecution will prove that the female known as Kiri, so named in the indictment, has been a slave in the service of her master, the complainant Victor St. Croix.

"We will prove that Niles Peartree willfully violated Chapter Seven of the congressional action, approved February twelfth, 1793, entitled 'An Act Respecting Fugitives from Justice, and Persons Escaping from the Service of their Masters.' Furthermore, we will prove that the accused violated Section Seven of the amendment to the 1793 act—known as the Fugitive Slave Law—approved by the Thirty-first Congress, Session one, September eighteenth, 1850.

"We will show that Niles Peartree aided and abetted the slave Kiri to escape, thereby depriving her master, said complainant Victor St. Croix, of her service and therefore of his lawful property. We will prove that Niles Peartree harbored and concealed said fugitive, so as to prevent the discovery and apprehension of such person, and did knowingly hinder the arrest ..."

Steele's voice droned on. It seemed to Glynis that the man deliberately restated himself over and over to make it look as if Niles were guilty of breaking scores of laws. And it proved of some discomfort to her that she herself was as guilty as

Niles of the concealing-and-hindering-arrest portion of the law. Some discomfort—but not too much. Strange how, after years of considering herself a law-abiding citizen, she had so quickly become reconciled to civil disobedience—she preferred this term to *criminal activity*.

Muffled sounds of the city outside carried through large open windows. The smell of oiled wood rose from low-backed pews like the one that Glynis occupied, and from the railings around the jury box. The room felt extremely warm, and that, coupled with the prosecutor's monotonous voice, made her nod with drowsiness. She straightened and kneaded her neck muscles. Since her arrival in Richmond, sleep had become an unaffordable luxury.

She had spent all of one night composing a wire to Cullen, wording and rewording it for brevity, and still it had cost her a small fortune to send to Cleveland. A fortune obtained in part by the return to the dress shop of the beautiful yellow cotton frock. Knowing what she now knew, she could never have worn it in any event.

She continued to fret that the wire to Cullen had not been clear enough, while at the same time worrying that it had been *too* clear: would Cullen wonder if she had been waiting for an excuse to contact him? She sadly admitted to herself that might just be true; after all, Merrycoyf could as well have written it.

Then, after she sent her daily reassuring wire to Harriet, she also sent one to Jacques Sundown to alert him to Cullen's possible reply, in case it arrived in Seneca Falls before her. She didn't want to think about Jacques, and the fact that she had done so meant she left the telegraph office anxious and confused. And concerned. Concerned that whatever the evil at work in Seneca Falls, it might put Jacques at risk—Jacques and Zeph and whoever else might, even unwittingly, have a connection to the man Thomas Farley. Because he *must* be the link. Both Masika and Chantal Dupont confirmed that Moses Rawlings, longtime horsemaster at Riverain, had known the Jolimont overseer of thirteen years before. Lyle Brogan had been looking for Farley. And Luella? Had she known Farley too?

Prosecutor Steele paused to clear his throat loudly, and

Glynis determinedly set aside her speculations. There was nothing she could do right now about Seneca Falls. Except worry herself to distraction.

"And finally, gentlemen of the jury, we will establish that the slave girl Kiri was spirited away by the accused Peartree on the night of September nineteenth and taken to western New York State for nefarious purposes, after which her trail became lost and her present circumstances unknown. These circumstances are of grave concern to the complainant. It is Victor St. Croix's contention that this poor girl is being held against her will, to be ill-used by this northern adventurer."

Glynis heard Niles suddenly begin to curse, something immediately stifled by the lawyers on either side of him.

"In closing, gentlemen," Steele said at last, "we will establish by competent testimony and to your satisfaction the undeniable guilt of the accused Niles Peartree."

Steele gazed at the jury with what Glynis supposed meant rapt sincerity, then returned to his table and sat down. It might have been her imagination, but the courtroom seemed to breathe a sigh of relief. Steele's opening monologue had probably not been what most of the spectators came to hear.

Judge Trumbull pulled himself upright from a slouched position in his tall-backed chair. "Mr. Merrycoyf, Ah presume you want to make an opening statement?"

"Not at this time, Your Honor. However, I wish to reserve the right to a statement of the case for the defense when the prosecution rests."

Glynis knew why Merrycoyf did this. By the time the voluble Mr. Steele had finished with his case, the jury would have forgotten all of what Merrycoyf might now say. Better to have the stage to himself later, his words fresh in the jury's ears before they heard Niles's defense.

"Mr. Prosecutor," the judge said. "Call your first witness."

"Ah call Captain Hosiah Cutteback."

Glynis saw Niles's head jerk toward the aisle of the courtroom. He looked startled as a solid-framed man with black-and-gray-speckled hair and beard made his way forward to the witness stand. Passing a hand over his eyes, Niles leaned sideways to say something to Merrycoyf, while John Hamilton sat erect and silent, facing straight ahead.

When Captain Cutteback had been sworn in, Steele stepped forward to stand in front of the witness.

"You, sir, are the owner and captain of a bay sloop called the *Flying Gull*?"

"I am."

"And is your sailing ship out of the port of Baltimore?"

"That's right."

"Tell us, Captain Cutteback," said Steele, "where you ply your trade."

"I run between Richmond and Norfolk, up the Chesapeake to Alexandria and Baltimore. Sometimes south to—"

"That's fine, Captain Cutteback. At the moment we're concerned with your northerly routes." Steele smiled at the jury, as if inviting them to guess where he would head with the captain. "And do you ever follow the Atlantic coast as far north as Delaware Bay?"

"Once in a while."

"What kind of cargo do you carry, Captain?"

"Anything that wants carrying. Can't take real heavy loads; ship's not built for that."

"Can you be a bit more specific?" Steele asked.

"No. I think that about sums it up," Cutteback said.

Steele frowned momentarily and turned toward the judge; then, as if thinking better of it, he swung back to the witness. Recovering his smile, he asked, "Captain Cutteback, would you say that those who hire your boat are more interested in speed than capacity?"

"If you mean does the *Flying Gull* make good time, mister, where you think she got her name?"

Glynis heard a few chuckles, and saw several members of the jury smile. Good for the captain.

"Yes, Captain Cutteback." Steele frowned again, his pinched nostrils quivering like those of a rabbit. "Now, how many crew members do you employ?"

"Depends on the cargo, destination—lotta things. Small load, I can make do with two men."

"By a small load, what do you mean? Passengers, for instance?"

"I take passengers sometimes."

Merrycoyf laboriously got to his feet. "Your Honor, this is

indeed fascinating, this excursion into the shipping trade, but is it in any way relevant to the matter at hand?"

Judge Trumbull raised heavy eyebrows at Merrycoyf, then looked at Steele. "Mr. Prosecutor, defense counsel has raised a valid point. Are you intending to display some relevance soon?"

"Yes, Your Honor. Very soon, sir."

"In that case, proceed."

"Captain Cutteback," Steele said, moving closer to the witness stand, "where were you born?"

"Born?" Cutteback looked incredulous. "Where was I born?"

"Just answer the question, Captain," Judge Trumbull said, although he himself looked as puzzled as the witness.

"I was born in Philadelphia."

"And did you grow up there?"

"Your Honor," Merrycoyf sighed heavily. "I really must object to prosecution's digressions."

"Yes," Judge Trumbull said. "Truly, Mr. Prosecutor, Ah find this line of questioning very far afield. Get to the point, if you please."

Steele looked rather self-satisfied, Glynis thought with alarm, for a lawyer who's just been admonished. Had Merrycoyf's objection unknowingly given emphasis to some upcoming testimony?

"Captain Cutteback," Steele now went on, "is the name William Still familiar to you?"

The captain's eyes narrowed. "I might have heard the name."

"My dear sir, you are too modest," Steele protested. "In fact, you are an investor in the very successful Philadelphia coal dealership of the free Negro William Still—isn't that true, Captain Cutteback?"

"I make investments from time to time but—"

"And isn't it a fact, Captain, that this same William Still is a leader in the clandestine criminal activity known as the Underground Railroad?"

"Objection!" Merrycoyf rumbled. "The question is leading, irrelevant, immaterial and incompetent. It calls for a conclusion on the part of the witness. It's cross-examination, and has no bearing—"

"Mr. Merrycoyf, don't overdo it," interrupted Judge Trumbull, scowling at both Merrycoyf and Steele. "Ah agree with your objection, and Ah'll sustain it. Mr. Steele, may Ah remind you, sir, that the good captain's investment partners, whoever they may be, are not on trial here."

"Let the record show, Your Honor," Steele replied, "that Captain Cutteback is a hostile witness, testifying under subpoena. Ah'm simply trying to establish—"

"You're simply trying to prejudice the jury," Merrycoyf broke in. "Your Honor—"

"Yes, yes," Judge Trumbull said impatiently. "The jury is directed to disregard the prosecutor's last question of the witness." He bent forward over the bench to glare down at the lawyers. "Gentlemen, Ah don't care for this contrariness in my courtroom. Ah don't care for it at all. Now, Mr. Steele, you will proceed within the bounds of the case, without any more fancy footwork. That clear to you, sir?"

"Yes, Your Honor."

"Proceed."

Steele turned back to the witness stand. Captain Cutteback had sat motionless throughout the previous exchange, but Glynis had seen his eyes several times dart to the back of the room as if looking for an escape route. If Steele intended to rattle the witness, he'd apparently succeeded.

"Captain," Steele began again, "do you recognize the accused, Niles Peartree?"

Captain Cutteback's eyes brushed over Niles. "I couldn't say."

"Couldn't say?" Steele echoed. "Well, let me ask you this: have you ever seen this man before?"

"I may have." Glynis watched with concern the small drops of sweat forming on the captain's forehead.

"You may have. Well now, Captain, isn't it a fact that—" Steele moved to pick up several papers on his table, which he glanced at fleetingly "—that on the night of September nineteenth you gave this man passage on your ship?"

"I might have."

"You more than 'might have,' Captain. The prosecution has

located two of your crew members who have sworn in these affidavits—" he waved the papers "—to the presence of the accused on the *Flying Gull* the night in question."

Merrycoyf struggled to his feet and lumbered up to the bench. He scanned the affidavits, then returned to his seat.

"Do you have an objection, Mr. Merrycoyf," said Judge Trumbull, "to these being placed in evidence?"

"Ah'm prepared to call the crew members," Steele interjected.

Merrycoyf paused. Then, "No objection, Your Honor."

Judge Trumbull looked down at the witness. "Captain, Ah feel Ah should remind you of the law regarding perjury. And direct you to answer the prosecutor's questions. Proceed, Mr. Steele."

"Yes, Your Honor. Now, Captain Cutteback, isn't it a fact that the accused was on your ship that night?"

"Yes, if you say so. But there were several passengers aboard that night." The captain, to Glynis's relief, now looked more annoyed than nervous. But as she feared, his damaging testimony was not concluded. "He wasn't anything special," the captain went on, jerking his head toward Niles. "Paid his fare same as everybody else—no more, no less."

Steele strolled to the jury box, and rested his hand on the railing. Then he turned back to look at the witness.

"Isn't it also a fact, Captain, that the accused was in the company of a Negro slave girl?"

"Objection!" Merrycoyf half-rose from his chair, peering at Steele over his spectacles. "As the esteemed prosecutor well knows, it has not been established that the female named in the indictment is a slave."

"Objection sustained. The jury should disregard the question."

Glynis saw relief slide across the captain's face.

Steele went on, smiling, knowing full well, Glynis thought, that despite the sustained objection, the damage had been done as far as the jury was concerned. "Now tell us, Captain, on the night of September nineteenth, to where did y'all sail? North along the Atlantic coast?"

"As I recall, yes."

"And where did y'all put into port? The last port, where the passengers—excuse me, the passenger Niles Peartree in company with the female who has not yet been established as a slave . . ."

"Objection!" Merrycoyf bellowed. He was on his feet in an instant this time, and he looked as angry as Glynis had ever seen him. "Your Honor, I believe we may have grounds for a mistrial here if the prosecutor continues in this vein. He has repeatedly led the witness and prejudiced the jury."

"Mr. Steele," Judge Trumbull's voice sounded weary. "You have sorely tried the patience of not only your Yankee colleague, by myself as well, sir."

"Ah apologize, Your Honor," Steele said, appearing not in the least apologetic.

While the man might look prissy, and sound pedantic, Glynis realized she earlier had dismissed Steele as a threat far too readily. He now went to stand in front of the witness to say, "Captain, Ah have just a few more questions. Where did the accused and the female disembark your ship on that night?"

"At a Delaware River port."

"Which port?"

"I don't recall."

"You don't recall? How fortunate then that your crew does. Wasn't it near Wilmington in the state of Delaware?"

"I suppose it could have been."

"And how close, Captain, would you say that port is from your own fair city of Philadelphia? And your friend William Still—"

"Objection!"

"Sustained."

"One last question, Captain Cutteback. Are you now, or have you ever been, a member of the treasonous Underground Railroad?"

Over the babble that broke out in the courtroom, the angry objections of Merrycoyf, and the judge's perfunctory reproof of the prosecutor, Glynis could barely hear Captain Cutteback's last words: "I run a ship, not a train."

Judge Trumbull's gavel descended with a sharp crack. He gazed around the courtroom with an expression of disgust. "Ah won't have any more such outbursts in my court. Ah

hope y'all take me at my word. Now, Mr. Merrycoyf; you
may proceed to cross-examine this witness."

"No cross-examination at this time, Your Honor. I would
like to reserve the right to recall this witness, however, at a
later time."

Judge Trumbull stared at Merrycoyf as if were he to look
hard enough, he might see the basis of the lawyer's strategy.
Glynis doubted it was strategy; she guessed that Merrycoyf
just plain didn't want to cross-examine the captain, not just
now but ever, and risk compounding the harm already done,
albeit reluctantly, by this witness.

"So granted, Mr. Merrycoyf," Judge Trumbull said. "The
witness is excused, subject to recall. Now would the prosecution and the defense approach the bench?"

A relieved-looking Captain Cutteback stepped down from
the witness stand as Steele, Merrycoyf and Hamilton went to
stand in front of the bench; Judge Trumbull bent forward and
spoke in tones too low to carry beyond the three lawyers.
They were getting a dressing down for their behavior, Glynis
surmised. She just hoped Merrycoyf remained his usual san-
guine self. While she had every confidence in the lawyer's
ability, he was an interloper here; the Virginians would dog-
gedly defend their own. Although Judge Trumbull's rulings
had so far been surprisingly fair. But Merrycoyf must have
noticed his cocounsel John Hamilton's total silence. While not
hindering Niles's defense, Hamilton hadn't helped this morning, either. Uneasily Glynis remembered Chantal Dupont's
comment that while she might not agree with slavery, "I am
a Virginian."

The three lawyers now returned to their seats, none of them
looking particularly chastened. Judge Trumbull straightened
his robe and said, "Mr. Steele, call your next witness."

"Yes, Your Honor. The prosecution calls Mrs. Claude
Dupont."

Glynis turned to watch Chantal Dupont come forward.
Strands of white-blond hair brushed the woman's face, more
of them escaping tortoise-shell combs with her every step.
Another woman would have looked disheveled; the Widow
Dupont looked remarkably self-possessed. She walked as if
unaware that anyone else was in the room.

Once again Glynis wondered why white southern women were so often described as frivolous; perhaps this applied solely to the young and pretty ones who hadn't yet lived on anything but their own terms—and their fathers' money.

The truly astonishing fact Glynis learned, and one which belied all she thought she previously knew about the South, was that the majority, in fact the overwhelming majority, of southerners had never in their lives owned as much as one slave. And yet, the institution of slavery seemed to reach into every aspect of southern life—from the law to the marketplace—and most southerners defended its existence.

But only a few, those like Chantal Dupont, seemed to realize what it had done to them.

Glynis watched Chantal step to the witness stand. While being sworn in, the woman fixed her dark blue eyes on the clerk who tripped over the familiar words as if flustered by the woman's composure.

"Where do you reside, Mrs. Dupont?" Steele's tone seemed somewhat less arrogant with this witness.

"Riverain plantation."

"Is there a slave woman named Masika living there?"

"She's been freed, but yes, Masika lives with me."

"How long ago was she manumitted?" Steele asked, obviously surprised.

"Two years ago."

"Ah, well then, she was a slave for many years at Riverain, correct?"

"Yes."

"As her mistress, did you assist in the birth of this slave Masika's daughter, in the year 1820?"

"I assisted at Ama's birth, yes."

"Did you know that the slave Ama gave birth to a daughter herself sixteen years later?"

Chantal did not answer immediately and seemed to deliberate before saying, "I did not witness the birth of any child of Ama's."

Steele looked annoyed. "Well, then, Mrs. Dupont, did the slave Ama ever tell you that she had a daughter?"

"Objection!" Merrycoyf said. "Provisions of the Dead Man's Statute prohibit this testimony because cross-examination is impossible. The woman Ama is dead. Witness's answer would be hearsay."

"Your Honor—" Steele began, his voice a whine.

"Objection sustained, Mr. Steele," said Judge Trumbull.

Prosecutor Steele clearly looked frustrated. He must prove that Kiri was a slave or Niles's indictment would be meaningless. But suddenly Steele whirled toward the jury box to mutter, "The birthright of the girl Kiri is common knowledge—"

"Objection!" Merrycoyf rose to his feet, shoving back his chair with such vehemence that it crashed against the spectator railing. "Objection, Your Honor! I most strenuously protest the prosecutor's tactics with the jury—"

"The defense's objection is sustained," Judge Trumbull interrupted, scowling down from his bench. "Mr. Steele, I caution you against making prejudicial remarks in front of the jury."

The prosecutor's face reddened. "No more questions of this hostile witness," he said curtly. Glaring at Merrycoyf, Steele went to his table and sat down.

"You may cross-examine the witness, Mr. Merrycoyf," Judge Trumbull announced, still scowling.

Merrycoyf, as yet on his feet, ignored the glare and the scowl to amble toward the witness stand. Glynis thought she saw a faint smile dart across Chantal Dupont's face as the lawyer approached; if so, it disappeared quickly. But members of the jury plainly were not in so friendly a mood. Their antagonism toward the Yankee lawyer had become near palpable.

"Mrs. Dupont," Merrycoyf began, "how did you acquire the slave Masika?"

"My husband bought her as a wedding present for me."

"So she has resided with you at the plantation Riverain since the time of your marriage?"

"Yes, since that time."

"I understand your husband Claude, as the elder son, inherited the plantation from his father, is that correct?"

"Yes."

"Your husband Claude grew up there, did he not?"

"Yes, he lived at Riverain all his life."

"And did any other member of the Dupont family also live at Riverain, after your marriage that is?"

Chantal Dupont's pale eyebrows lifted momentarily. "Yes, my husband's younger brother Louis continued to live with us for more than a year."

"Yes, I see." Merrycoyf paused, letting this last statement hang there surrounded by silence. A man on the jury finally coughed. And Merrycoyf shifted his feet. "Now, Mrs. Dupont, you said that Masika gave birth with your assistance, and as the prosecutor so kindly established, the year was 1820. How long had you been married to Claude Dupont at that point?"

"Objection!" Prosecutor Steele's hands gripped his table. "The question is irrelevant and immaterial."

"Your Honor," Merrycoyf said, "I intend to establish a sequence of events here. The question is indeed relevant."

Judge Trumbull bent over his bench to scrutinize Merrycoyf, apparently trying to determine if the lawyer was simply naive and, as such, innocent of malice in probing this area. "Very well, Mr. Merrycoyf, but make sure relevance is clear."

"Thank you, Your Honor. Mrs. Dupont, do you recall the question, or shall I repeat—"

"No, I remember it. Claude and I had been married about a year when Masika's daughter Ama was born."

"Really. All things considered, did you think that time frame significant—"

"Objection!" Steele sprang to his feet. "Your Honor—"

"I withdraw the question," Merrycoyf said quickly. Steele remained standing, slightly crouched, as if ready to pounce on Merrycoyf if he persisted. And while the jury might be prejudiced, they weren't stupid. They had caught the inference, and all looked shocked. However, it surely would be Merrycoyf they blamed for their dismay—not Louis Dupont.

Judge Trumbull remained silent, staring at Merrycoyf with an inexplicable expression; it could have been anything from anger to apathy. Which made Glynis wonder if perhaps the judge's intention all along had been to give this Yankee enough rope with which to hang himself. And therefore his client.

But Merrycoyf went on, deceptively oblivious. "Mrs. Dupont, will you describe the baby Ama's appearance?"

"Objection! Irrelevant!"

"Objection overruled," Judge Trumbull said slowly. "You yourself brought up this area on direct examination, Mr. Steele."

"The baby Ama, Mrs. Dupont?" Merrycoyf prodded.

"Ama was a lovely, good-natured child." Chantal paused, her eyes moving to the courtroom ceiling almost as if seeking divine guidance. Then, quickly, she added, "And light-skinned."

"Would you describe her therefore as a mulatto?" asked Merrycoyf. "Of mixed blood?"

Chantal hesitated. Then, "Yes, I would describe her like that."

"Mrs. Dupont," Merrycoyf said slowly, "please answer me this: did you know who fathered the child Ama?"

"Objection! Objection, Your Honor," Steele barked, jumping again to his feet.

Chantal shifted her body to grip the arms of the witness chair. "I can't say—"

"Objection sustained!" Judge Trumbull said sharply. "Mr. Merrycoyf, you know that calls for a conclusion on the part of the witness. Now, sir, Ah direct you to move on."

Merrycoyf said, "Yes, Your Honor. But," he gazed levelly at Chantal, "Masika's child had mixed blood?"

Chantal did not hesitate again. "Yes, I would say so."

"When did Ama leave Riverain, Mrs. Dupont?"

"When she was bought by Victor St. Croix, and went to Jolimont to live."

"When was that?"

"After Mr. St. Croix's wife, his first wife, died."

"How old was Ama at that time, Mrs. Dupont? And please tell us the year Ama went to Jolimont."

Chantal said readily, "Christmas time in, I believe, 'thirty-five. So Ama would have been fifteen."

"Thank you, Mrs. Dupont. I have no further questions." Merrycoyf gave Chantal a brief nod, and went back to his table. Chantal stepped quickly from the witness box and proceeded down the aisle to the back of the room. As she passed, the woman gave Glynis a tight-lipped smile.

"Ah think since it's getting on to noon, we'll stop now," Judge Trumbull said, bringing his gavel down with a sharp report. "This court stands adjourned until two o'clock."

"Y'all rise now," called out the bailiff.

As he was escorted from the room, Niles threw Glynis a doleful glance. No, she silently agreed; things did not look good.

SEVENTEEN

ᐲᐳᐲ

*In deciding the question [of slavery] . . . we conceive it
ought to be decided by the law as it is, and not as it
ought to be. Slavery is sanctioned by the laws of this
State, and the right to hold slaves under our municipal
regulations is unquestionable. But we view this as a right
existing by positive law of a municipal character, without
foundation in the law of nature, or the unwritten common law.*
—Judge Mills, *Rankin v. Lydia*, 2 A.K. Marsh 467,
The Supreme Court of Appeals of Kentucky

LUNCH HAD BEEN a tense affair, mirroring as it did the impact of the morning's testimony. Merrycoyf, when not clink-
ing his spoon against a water goblet, rapping his knuckles on
the table, or pulling his watch from a waistcoat pocket to once
more check the time, displayed a short temper and left the hotel dining room as soon as he finished eating. John Hamilton
remained silent, toying with his food.

Glynis, who had had no appetite to begin with, now sat in
the courtroom, wondering if her stomach would growl for the
entire afternoon. She worried terribly about the apparent prob-
ability of Niles's conviction. Southern prisons were said to be
bleakly harsh places, and she couldn't bear to think of him,
sensitive and impulsive, being thrown in among the worst of
criminals.

And for one reason or another, she also found herself swept
with almost intolerable homesickness.

She glanced sideways at Faith Hamilton, who had just
slipped in beside her. The quiet, rather timid-looking woman
sat nibbling at her fingertips, reminding Glynis of an anxious
churchmouse. The only time she saw Faith Hamilton as less
than mousy had been when the subject of abolition arose. On
these occasions Faith Hamilton seemed more impassioned
than her husband.

Although Glynis remained uneasy about John Hamilton's reticence in Niles's behalf, she supposed it could have a pragmatic origin. Perhaps he didn't wish to interfere with Merrycoyf's strategy, probably as yet unclear to Hamilton. If this was so, the man wasn't alone, as the prosecutor and judge hadn't caught on either. It seemed more likely, however, that Hamilton's silence stemmed from a reluctance to alienate his Richmond friends and neighbors, and potential clients. Glynis observed that most Virginia abolitionists spoke cautiously, at least to outsiders, when they spoke at all. She couldn't help but wonder what these people's position would be if the worst happened: if the southern slave states at some point tried to secede from the United States, as they had more than once already threatened to do. Would Virginia abolitionists find their loyalty to be first with America, or with Virginia?

But surely it would never come to that.

Merrycoyf appeared to be lecturing Niles when the bailiff gave the command to rise. Judge Trumbull, when he entered, looked rather drawn. Small wonder, after the morning.

"Mr. Prosecutor, are you ready to call your next witness?"

"Yes, Your Honor. Call Mrs. Amanda Kettles."

A rather pale elderly woman with faded blue eyes came slowly down the aisle, constantly pushing her small spectacles back in place. The spectacles kept slipping down her nose as her head was bowed toward the floor. Glynis saw John Hamilton, who had turned to watch the old woman, suddenly frown and lean behind Niles to say something to Merrycoyf. Merrycoyf swiveled around to also peer at the prospective witness. He then nodded vigorously to his colleague. Hamilton rose and, looking neither right nor left, walked rapidly out of the courtroom. Beside Glynis, Faith's eyes followed her husband, a puzzled expression on her face.

After being sworn in, Amanda Kettles lowered herself carefully into the witness chair.

"Your name is Amanda Kettles?" asked Steele.

"Yes, sir."

"Where are you employed, Mrs. Kettles?"

"Ah work at Jolimont."

"How long have you worked there?"

The woman stared at the floor, then said, "Ah don't know—near to twenty years, Ah'd guess."

"And what are your duties at Jolimont?"

"Ah'm a midwife."

Glynis felt a prick of fear and looked ahead at Merrycoyf. She saw the lawyer's shoulders stiffen before he twisted around to look down the aisle toward the door.

"Ah wonder where John went," Faith whispered to Glynis.

"Mrs. Kettles, as a midwife, did you have occasion to—"

"Your Honor!" Merrycoyf had risen, after glancing again down the aisle, and he now went toward the bench. "Your Honor, I request some preliminary questions—to determine the legal competency of this witness, sir."

Steele turned from Mrs. Kettles to glare at Merrycoyf. He then turned to Judge Trumbull. "Your Honor, Ah most strongly object to this defense tactic, which is obviously meant to delay and obfuscate this proceeding. There are no grounds to question this witness."

"I should like to determine that for myself, Your Honor," Merrycoyf broke in. "I would be doing my client and my profession a disservice if I did not call upon my worthy cocounsel, a lawyer of outstanding reputation and . . ."

Glynis wondered how long the judge, to say nothing of Mr. Steele, would let Merrycoyf stall. Even she knew he meant to delay the proceedings. But just as Steele opened his mouth and the judge's gavel came down, John Hamilton strode up the aisle with a legal text in his hand. He nodded at Merrycoyf as he went to the lawyer's table and sat down.

"May it please the court, I should like to confer momentarily with cocounsel," Merrycoyf said.

Steele looked furious, Glynis thought, but he apparently couldn't think of a way to intervene.

"Very well, Mr. Merrycoyf," said Judge Trumbull. "You may have a *moment*."

Merrycoyf went to the text Hamilton already had open on the table. While the two bent over it, their voices too low to be audible to Glynis, the courtroom hummed quietly and Judge Trumbull got up and left by the side door. In the witness chair, Amanda Kettles looked small and scared.

Prosecutor Steele sauntered back to his table and managed to appear bored. While Glynis felt this man to be a near caricature of the mustache-twirling villain, when she'd mentioned this to Merrycoyf he had said, "There's no such thing as a good prosecutor who can afford sensitivity to the other side." Well, Steele might just be doing his job, as Merrycoyf insisted, but it seemed to be one he clearly relished.

Returning a few minutes later, Judge Trumbull brought down his gavel. "Mr. Merrycoyf, Ah direct you to ask your questions—briefly, sir."

"Thank you, Your Honor." Merrycoyf went to stand before the frightened-faced woman, the legal text in hand.

"Mrs. Kettles, I have just a few questions," Merrycoyf said to her, the tone of his voice unexpectedly gentle. "You reside, ma'am, at the Jolimont plantation?"

"Yes, sir."

"And were you subpoenaed by the prosecution to appear here today?"

"Ah didn't want to come, but they said Ah had to."

"Yes, I'm sure they did. Now, Mrs. Kettles, I must ask you this question: Do you, ma'am, have any Negro blood?"

The courtroom went silent. So silent that even tree leaves rustling outside the windows sounded loud.

Mrs. Kettles bowed her head and her answer came haltingly. "Well . . . yes . . . yes, sir, Ah do. My grandmother on my mother's side it was . . . yes, sir."

Merrycoyf shot Steele, who had become uncharacteristically quiet, a murderous look before he said, "Your Honor, I move to dismiss this witness on the grounds that a Negro cannot testify against a white man. Namely my client. The law of this state is unequivocal on this point, as ruled by the Court of Appeals of Virginia in *Winn* v. *Jones.*" Merrycoyf gestured with the legal text.

"So noted. Mr. Steele, do you have some comment?" Judge Trumbull asked, his annoyed face apparently expressing his own comment.

"No, sir. Of course, the prosecution did not know that Amanda Kettles—"

"Oh, no, of course not," Judge Trumbull interrupted, leaving it in doubt as to whether this intended sarcasm or agreement on his part. "This witness is excused. Mrs. Kettles, you may step down."

The courtroom exhaled a long-held breath, while Merrycoyf extended his hand to help the old woman from the witness chair. He must have said something to her, because Amanda Kettles gave him a grateful smile before starting for the back of the courtroom.

Glynis reflected on this ironic turn of events. A law designed by white slaveholders to protect themselves from accusations by their slaves had now been used to the benefit of an escaped slave and her rescuer.

Faith Hamilton bent toward Glynis to say, "Ah can't believe the prosecutor would try that. If the woman was a midwife, Mr. Steele should have known she could well be Negro. And he knows the law."

"But he hoped Merrycoyf didn't," Glynis answered. "And the ruse might have worked but for your husband." Even so, Steele managed to get a not-so-veiled implication of Kiri's birth to the jury, despite the judge's ruling. Still, Glynis felt comforted that John Hamilton had come through. Perhaps Steele's tactics angered the lawyer sufficiently to risk censure. Or perhaps the memory of Yale Law School with Merrycoyf had done it.

Judge Trumbull glanced at a tall clock standing against the near wall and brought his gavel down again. "Before the next witness—Ah can only suppose there *is* a next witness, Mr. Steele?" He leveled an enigmatic look at the prosecutor.

When Steele said "Yes, sir," Trumbull continued, "Then we'll take a short recess while Ah tend to some court business." He glanced again at the clock. "Court will reconvene in twenty minutes."

"Y'all rise," the bailiff shouted.

IT HAD BEEN by sheer chance John Hamilton recognized the light-skinned Amanda Kettles as a sister of the Negro gardener he'd employed. And while Steele's attempt to prove Kiri's birth as a slave had been legally thwarted, the jury could easily disregard his tactic and hear only his insinuation. In addition, there remained a last witness; who that might be, neither Merrycoyf nor Hamilton knew for certain. Both of them now appeared wary.

As she came back into the courtroom after a brief recess, Glynis looked at those sitting near the rear door. She'd seen Katherine St. Croix enter some time earlier, and now she located the plantation mistress seated in the last row. Katherine glanced up and for a split second her eyes met Glynis's. The woman looked away swiftly. Before Glynis moved on up the aisle, she glimpsed the profile of the man seated beside Katherine St. Croix. He looked much as she had pictured him from Kiri's description: medium frame, neither slight nor heavy, clean-shaven jaw, straight emphatic nose, and a thick shock of silver hair. Glynis went to her seat, wishing she'd had opportunity for a longer look.

Judge Trumbull seated himself and bent forward over the bench.

"Gentlemen," he addressed the lawyers. "We are well into the afternoon. Ah want to finish the prosecution's testimony today, so Ah'll ask that y'all move along without the cantankerous behavior as has been brought to this court so far. Do y'all understand me?"

He glowered with obvious warning. "Call your last witness, Mr. Prosecutor. And may Ah hope this *is* your last witness?"

"Yes, Your Honor," Steele replied. "The prosecution calls Victor St. Croix."

Over the whispering heads of the courtroom observers seated in front of her, Glynis looked at Merrycoyf. In profile to her, his expression appeared bland, but he must be heartened that his strategy had succeeded. He'd prevented the prosecutor from obtaining the testimony from his subpoenaed witnesses that Steele needed to prove Kiri's slave status, thus the prosecutor had been forced to call St. Croix. Merrycoyf himself could have subpoenaed the planter, but the lawyer would then be limited to direct examination, whereas now he could cross-examine the witness.

From his startled expression, John Hamilton apparently still hadn't grasped Merrycoyf's maneuver. And Steele must be certain that St. Croix could prove the prosecution's case. But Steele could very well be ignorant of the danger ahead for this witness—for which ignorance Merrycoyf had prayed. However, Glynis realized, Steele probably felt confident as to the jury's decision no matter what could or couldn't be proven. And he might be entirely justified in this confidence.

Victor St. Croix strode to the witness stand. His bearing looked self-assured, as that of a man would who had every belief in his right to be there. His right to regain his property as the law said he could do, and to see Niles Peartree justly punished for violating that law. There appeared to be nothing avaricious, nothing base or immoral about him, if such things could be read in a man's face and the way in which he carried himself.

In fact, Victor St. Croix looked to be altogether a decent human being. Glynis, after her week in Richmond, would have wagered he considered himself to be exactly that. A man who treated friends and neighbors fairly. Who took care of his family and their needs. Who made sure, from what Kiri had said, that his slaves were fed well and sheltered better than most. Who saw himself as doing those Negroes who belonged to him a great good, since he would be convinced they could not exist half as well without him.

From the lines around his eyes, and the deeper ones around his mouth, Glynis guessed the man had a sense of humor. A manner of kindliness about him. If she had met him under other circumstances she most probably would have liked him.

Prosecutor Steele came forward as the clerk with the Bible stepped back to his table. "Mr. St. Croix," Steele began, "did you own a slave woman called Ama?"

"Ah did."

"What were her duties in your household?"

"Actually, soon after she came to Jolimont, Ah put her in charge of the household. She learned quickly, and she behaved responsibly."

"While she lived at Jolimont, did she give birth to a daughter."

"Yes."

"And were you there, sir, when Ama's child was born?"

"No. She gave birth in the slave quarters, and the midwife Amanda Kettles assisted Ama at my direction. Ah did see the child soon after she was born."

"What was her name, Mr. St. Croix?"

"Kiri, her mother called her. Ah recall Ama saying it meant some kind of beautiful flower. Ah always thought it suited the girl." Victor St. Croix made a sudden shift in his position to gaze off toward the windows. Glynis sat forward, the better to see him, and what she saw looked unmistakably like sadness.

"Did there come a time," Steele asked, "when you invited the accused Niles Peartree into your home, Mr. St. Croix?"

"Yes. He was an art dealer with paintings Ah admired. He came as a guest into my home any number of times."

"And did you notice any unusual interest on his part in the girl Kiri?"

"Objection," Merrycoyf said. "Leading the witness. And the prosecutor's question is ambiguous—what, pray tell, would 'interest' be?"

"Ah'll rephrase the question," Steele said before Judge Trumbull could reply. "Did the accused spend much time in the company of the girl Kiri?"

"Yes. Yes, Ah found them together quite often. Ah suppose Ah should have been more aware—"

"That's fine, Mr. St. Croix," Steele cut him off. "So you found them together *often*. Did you suspect the accused was planning an escape?"

"Objection!" Merrycoyf sounded disgusted. "Leading the witness."

"Sustained."

"Mr. St. Croix, were you surprised when the girl and the accused—" The prosecutor paused as Merrycoyf made to object. Steele then said, "When the girl disappeared from your plantation?"

"Very surprised," St. Croix answered. "Ah thought Kiri was content with her life. She never complained, never wanted for anything—she simply didn't have reason to run away. She never had been mistreated in the slightest." He looked sincerely baffled, even wounded, Glynis thought, by this incomprehensible behavior on Kiri's part. And suddenly she believed that he truly was.

"So why do you think the girl ran away?" Steele asked.

"The only reason Ah can think of is that this young man—" St. Croix motioned toward Niles "—somehow talked her into it. Or frightened her. Or even possibly seduced her, Ah fear."

"Objection!" Merrycoyf said emphatically, grabbing at Niles as the young man leaped to his feet. John Hamilton took hold of Niles's shoulder to press him back into his chair.

"Your Honor," Merrycoyf protested, "it isn't bad enough that my client has been accused, wrongfully I might add, of breaking some ill-founded law? Is he now being charged with seduction as well?"

"Your Honor—" Steele began.

"Yes!" Judge Trumbull seemed to rouse himself with some enthusiasm. "Mr. Merrycoyf, Ah order you not to characterize the law of this land as 'ill-founded.' That is not a judgment for you to make and Ah will hold you in contempt of court, sir, if it happens again!"

Niles continued to glare at his accuser, St. Croix, but although fidgety he remained seated. Merrycoyf sat back in his chair to lace his fingers over his stomach. Glynis knew this signified either deep thought or considerable self-control.

Mr. Steele, his face a study in self-righteousness, said, "Ah just have one more question of the witness. Mr. St. Croix, sir, why did you report this action of the accused Niles Peartree?"

"Because Ah'm very troubled about the girl. Ah have grave concern, sir, for her safety."

"That's all, Mr. St. Croix," Steele said, with a broad smile. "Thank you."

St. Croix did not return Steele's smile.

"I assume you want to cross-examine this witness, Mr. Merrycoyf?" asked Judge Trumbull.

"Yes indeed, Your Honor." Merrycoyf rose to stand behind the table. "Mr. St. Croix, would you kindly tell the court again why exactly you initiated the charge against Niles Peartree?"

"Objection," Steele said. "Witness has just answered that."

"Ah'll allow the question by defense counsel on this point," ruled the judge. "Answer if you please, sir."

"Ah didn't know—still don't know—what Niles Peartree's intentions were toward the girl," Victor St. Croix said. "He never disclosed them to me. And Ah know that some slave women are taken north for immoral and illicit purposes—Ah feel responsible to protect the girl from that."

Peering over his spectacles, Merrycoyf studied the man at length before saying, "Did it occur to you, sir, that Kiri might have preferred to take her chances with that which you have just described? Preferred that to the likelihood of becoming what her mother and grandmother did—a white man's concubine?"

Victor St. Croix reared back in the witness chair, his expression stunned, as if he had never considered such a possibility.

Steele meanwhile had leaped to his feet, shouting, "Objection! That conclusion on the part of defense counsel is entirely speculative. And irrelevant in any event!"

"Sustained!"

Merrycoyf sighed. "Very well, Mr. St. Croix. Then let us proceed. You unfortunately lost your first wife some years ago, sir, is that true?"

St. Croix seemed to have somewhat recovered himself, although his expression remained guarded. "Yes."

"When exactly was that?"

"In the autumn of 'thirty-five."

"Mrs. Claude Dupont has previously testified," Merrycoyf said, glancing down at his notes, "that later in that same year you bought from her husband the beautiful young Ama. Is that correct in your recollection, sir?"

"Yes."

"You have stated, Mr. St. Croix, that you put the fifteen-year-old Ama in charge of the entire household. Did that mean she lived in the main house?"

"Yes."

"And how long did she live in the house?"

St. Croix looked off toward the windows as he answered, "Ah . . . Ah don't recall."

"Did there then come a time, sir, when Ama was forced from that house?"

His gaze returning to Merrycoyf, St. Croix's forehead creased in a frown. "Well, Ah wouldn't use the word 'forced.' "

"What word would you use, Mr. St. Croix?"

"She ... she moved elsewhere is all, sir."

"She *moved* to the slave quarters on your plantation?"

"Yes."

"And would you tell the court what prompted this move?"

"The occasion of my marriage—my second marriage."

"I see. On the occasion of your second marriage you felt that Ama should no longer live in the main house, so you forced her—pardon me, sir; you *moved* her to the slave quarters, is that correct?"

"Objection, Your Honor. The question is immaterial."

"Sustained. Move along, Mr. Merrycoyf," Judge Trumbull directed.

"And how long after Ama moved to the slave quarters did she give birth to her daughter Kiri?"

"Objection! Immaterial!"

"Sustained," Judge Trumbull scowled. "Mr. Merrycoyf—"

"Wasn't it just five months later that Ama's child was born?" asked Merrycoyf rapidly, his voice straining over the shouts of Steele's continued objection and the thud of Trumbull's gavel.

"Mr. Merrycoyf, Ah have sustained the prosecution's very proper objection, and Ah direct you to leave this area of questioning!" Judge Trumbull glowered down from his bench. "Do you understand me, sir?"

"Yes, Your Honor," Merrycoyf replied amiably, as if delighted to comply. He glanced down at his notes and then said, "Isn't it true, Mr. St. Croix, that some time later—" Merrycoyf looked down again "—that some five years later, the woman Ama attempted an escape from your plantation, together with her daughter Kiri, and the male slave Sam, and a male infant?"

While Merrycoyf spoke, Glynis watched a series of expressions streak across Victor St. Croix's face: surprise, disbelief, then dismay. He answered, "Yes, Ah'm afraid that's so, sir."

"Why do you think this escape attempt was made?"

St. Croix hesitated. "It could have been ... that is, because of the depression in 'thirty-nine, Ah had some need of cash, so Ah had to sell some slaves. And one of them going to sale was Sam. Ah figured, later on, that's maybe why they ran."

"And what became of this escape attempt?" Merrycoyf asked.

St. Croix looked at Steele, whose gaze concentrated somewhere on the ceiling. If the witness expected an objection to rescue him, he apparently had mistaken Steele's purpose, Glynis decided. It was, in fact, to the prosecution's advantage to have this earlier escape brought up—but she felt certain that Steele didn't, or couldn't, anticipate St. Croix's explanation.

Judge Trumbull looked at the witness. "Sir, the question was—"

"Yes. Yes, Your Honor, Ah heard the question. When Ah discovered my slaves gone, run away, Ah sent the overseer after them."

"The overseer," Merrycoyf repeated. "And who might that have been?"

"A man named Farley. Thomas Farley."

"And did Thomas Farley bring the fugitives back?" Merrycoyf asked.

"No, sir, not all of them. He brought Kiri back, but . . ." St. Croix paused and his jaw clenched. "But Ama and Sam, and Ama's other child, were killed."

The word "killed" reverberated before it drowned in the courtroom's cumulative sigh. Glynis expelled her own breath in relief, as apparently St. Croix knew nothing of Zeph's survival. But her sense of uneasiness about the boy's welfare lingered.

"Were you told how they died?"

Glynis expected this question from Merrycoyf to bring an objection, but Steele looked as absorbed—and in fairness to him, as shocked—as everyone else.

"Well, my overseer explained that a slave-catcher he'd hired to help with the search . . . that the slave-catcher shot them. By accident."

"Your overseer Farley told you this. Did you believe him?"

"Ah've never known if Ah believed him or not. But Ah fired him right then."

"And the slave-catcher's version of this dreadful event?"

"Ah don't know—he was gone. Long gone. And Ah told Farley to get out of Richmond fast or Ah'd have him charged with those deaths. Farley was responsible, no matter who held the gun."

"Yes, I completely agree," Merrycoyf said. He went on, "But what then happened to the child Kiri . . . after her return?"

"Poor little thing didn't talk for days. She just trembled, Ah remember. Ah felt sorry, so Ah brought her into the main house to live."

"And from that time forward did Kiri live in the main house?"

"Yes."

"What were her duties?"

"Oh, Ah presume my wife saw to that."

"I see," Merrycoyf said. "Would you say then that the girl's duties were not taxing or burdensome? Were not even observable, since you yourself apparently didn't notice what the girl was required to do in your household—if, in fact, she did anything at all?"

"Objection," Steele said, frowning. "Irrelevant. Ah don't even know what the lawyer for the defense is asking. Does he?"

"Ah'll sustain the objection," Judge Trumbull, also frowning, said. "Go along now, Mr. Merrycoyf—Ah believe you have established to everyone's satisfaction that the girl had nothing demanding to do. Though why you are helping the prosecution's case, Ah'm sure Ah don't know."

Merrycoyf smiled. "I'm always happy to cooperate, Your Honor."

Glynis swallowed a laugh: That would be the day! But since Merrycoyf now smiled, the end must be in sight.

"I have a few more questions," Merrycoyf said, "about that time before your second marriage. The time period when Kiri's mother Ama stayed in your house. Tell me, Mr. St. Croix, since you have stated that Ama lived there, did you mean that she also spent the nights there?"

Did St. Croix hesitate, for just the flick of an eye, before he answered? Glynis couldn't be sure.

"Yes; yes, of course she did," St. Croix said. "She was a house servant," he added.

"How many other house servants did you have—sleeping in the main house?"

"Your Honor—" Steele began to object.

"Mr. Merrycoyf, Ah believe we previously covered this ground. Are you sure your question is relevant?" Judge Trumbull asked.

"Yes, Your Honor. Extremely relevant," Merrycoyf said.

Judge Trumbull stared at him before nodding. "Very well. For the time being you may continue."

"I'll repeat my question. Mr. St. Croix. How many servants other than Ama slept in the main house?"

"Why . . . Ah don't remember . . . it was a long time ago."

"Yes. Well, let me ask this, Mr. St. Croix. Were the sleeping quarters in the main house, the bedrooms that is, all on one floor?"

St. Croix altered his position slightly before answering, "Yes."

"The upper floor, perhaps?"

"Yes."

"So we may conclude then that Ama slept in a bedroom on the upper floor, as did you yourself?"

A pause, then "Yes."

"And were there connecting doors between all the bedrooms?"

"Objection! Irrelevant! Immaterial!"

"Ah don't think Ah have to answer that," St. Croix said to Judge Trumbull.

"No, sir, you don't! Ah sustain the prosecution's objection of irrelevance."

"Your Honor, the question is entirely relevant," Merrycoyf declared. "The birthright of the girl Kiri is a material part of my defense—"

"Mr. Merrycoyf, approach the bench!" Judge Trumbull interrupted. "You too, Mr. Steele."

As the lawyers went forward, Glynis shifted for a cautious look back at Katherine St. Croix. The woman stared straight ahead, the expression on her face unreadable. Glynis wished she could muster more indifference toward this plantation mistress. With Niles at such risk, anything like the sympathy she now felt seemed entirely inappropriate. But it hadn't been

Katherine St. Croix who made these laws—and from what Kiri said, the woman had been kind to her. Even taught Kiri to read in defiance of the law, and her husband. Yet married to a slaveholder, Mrs. St. Croix must bear the consequences of slavery. Must now keep her silence while Merrycoyf did his best to publicly humiliate her husband and, in so doing, herself.

The men's voices at the front of the room had risen. Glynis could see Judge Trumbull regarding Merrycoyf with what looked to be a powerful antagonism. And now he said, "Mr. Merrycoyf, Ah reaffirm my ruling sustaining the prosecutor's objection to your last question."

When the lawyers had returned to their tables, the judge said, "You may continue cross-examination, Mr. Merrycoyf—with caution."

"Your Honor, I have one final question of this witness." Having said this, Merrycoyf then stood silent, staring off for a time toward the windows. When he turned back to St. Croix, his voice contained little satisfaction when he said, "I ask you for the truth, sir—are you not the girl Kiri's father?"

"Objection!" Steele snarled, leaping to his feet. "Objection, Your Honor! That question is irrelevant, immaterial and incompetent!"

The stillness that followed became so absolute Glynis could hear the stirring of ghosts, an uneasy rattle of bones, in the nearby Richmond graveyard. The rustle of a parchment copy of the United States constitution in a glass case outside the courtroom. A keening cry that rose like fine dry dust from the soil of Virginia to cover plantations and tobacco warehouses and wharves along the James River to the Chesapeake Bay and the ocean beyond, where great slaving ships had once sailed, heavy with black gold bound for America.

Into this stillness, which endured long after the prosecutor's shouted objections, Victor St. Croix finally spoke. "Ah am not free to answer that question, sir."

Prosecutor Steele then continued to voice objections. But Judge Trumbull, who had not stirred during all this time, bent forward and said, "Mr. Steele, Ah have heard your objections. Now be silent. Mr. Merrycoyf, what is the purpose of this line of cross-examination? The purpose, sir, of your last question?"

"Your Honor, it is the defense's belief that Victor St. Croix is the father of young Kiri. I submit that under moral and common law a father may not enslave his own child."

Expressionless, Judge Trumbull stared down at Merrycoyf. "It is the law of this Commonwealth that the birthright of a slave child is governed solely by the status of its mother."

"And that law is immoral," Merrycoyf argued. "The first Negroes brought to this country were not slaves, but servants—an impermanent condition, as was that of white indentured servants and captured Indians. But when the law, the *positive law* of Virginia, decreed that children of slave mothers would themselves be slaves, no matter the position of the fathers, slavery in America became an inescapable, timeless condition; a ghastly inheritance. One based on race. And therefore discriminatory. Contrary to moral and natural law."

"Mr. Merrycoyf," Judge Trumbull said, his face beginning to flush, "whatever their history, the laws and dictates of the Commonwealth of Virginia are binding on this court, and must be applied. Furthermore, Ah am sworn to uphold the Constitution of these United States, article Four, section Two, of which says: 'No person held to service or labour . . . ' "

As the judge spoke, Glynis knew with terrible certainty that Merrycoyf's defense could not work. And it would be the long reach, the intertwined labyrinth of slavery itself that would defeat him. Because it was not only slaves who were not free: Victor St. Croix said he was not free to answer; Judge Trumbull said he was not at liberty but sworn to uphold the Constitution, whether, he implied, he wanted to or not; the women like Katherine St. Croix were not free to challenge their husbands' license to father slaves. The many-faced Hydra of slavery consumed all obstacles in its path. How could Merrycoyf expect to escape it? His only hope had been a presiding judge who might listen to argument, might have some abolitionist leanings, might take into account the real reason St. Croix wanted Kiri back.

It had not happened.

" '. . . labour shall be due,' " finished Judge Trumbull.

"And so, Mr. Merrycoyf, I ask *you* how does your argument answer the U.S. Constitution and the law of Virginia?"

"I answer that this case must be determined on the basis of moral and natural and common law, which says a child's status should be determined by its parentage, and that said child is entitled to all the rights and privileges that flow from such parentage."

"Except," Judge Trumbull said, "in the circumstance of a slave. Which, yes, you correctly state is positive law in this commonwealth. But then again, sir, Ah am also bound to uphold the Constitution, which all Americans honor and revere, and which *does not prohibit slavery*!"

"But nowhere," Merrycoyf asserted, "nowhere in the Constitution does it deny the natural birthright of a child."

For a long moment Judge Trumbull looked down at Merrycoyf. He then turned his gaze toward the windows. The clock pendulum, relentlessly sweeping away time, seemed to be the solitary sound in the hushed courtroom.

As if the pendulum had at last captured his attention, the judge swung his gaze to the clock. "The hour is late, so Ah am going to call a recess." Judge Trumbull cleared his throat and sat forward. His expression appeared to be one of discomfort, or possibly fatigue. "Ah will take your argument under advisement overnight, Mr. Merrycoyf, and will make my ruling when we reconvene as to whether you may proceed with your last question. Court stands recessed until ten o'clock tomorrow morning."

The gavel came down. The bailiff jumped to his feet. "Rise, y'all!"

THE HAMILTONS' PERFUNCTORY supper invitation had been refused by both Glynis and Merrycoyf. Now in the hotel dining room, she sat opposite the lawyer, who stared at the ceiling. His plate with its fragrant, cured country ham, fried okra and candied sweet potatoes remained untouched. Merrycoyf had not so much as noted its arrival. Glynis herself ordered only tea, but this was not the first time here in Richmond her appetite yielded to anxiety. *Fear,* she corrected herself. And in all the years she'd known him, she had never before seen Merrycoyf so troubled. There seemed to be little or no doubt, he'd said, as to what Judge Trumbull—given the man's convictions—would *have* to rule.

Glynis found it ever more terrifying to contemplate what might happen to Niles in a southern prison. How could she go back to Harriet with the dreadful tidings that they had failed her son? And what would become of Kiri? Would St. Croix resume the hunt? To say nothing of *Zeph's* vulnerability. Glynis covered her face with her hands, unable any longer to keep tears at bay.

Merrycoyf abruptly shoved back his chair from the table. "I'm going to retire now." His sole words before he lumbered off toward the staircase.

A few minutes later Glynis, miserable, followed him up the stairs. As she stepped inside her room, she heard a crackle of paper and glanced down to see a white envelope, undoubtedly a note from Merrycoyf slipped under her door.

She turned up a lamp wick and sat down on a corner of the bed. Frowning slightly at his insistent formality in gracing the envelope with "Miss Tryon"—who else did he think might be in her room?—she tore open the sealed flap. It was not from Merrycoyf.

Dear Miss Tryon,

   I offer no explanation for my actions. God alone may pass judgment on me, for I fear no other.
   Before tomorrow's trial session, I sincerely request that you and Mr. Peartree's lawyer go to the Henrico County Courthouse, and there examine the book which registered freed persons of color in the year 1835. I believe you will find what it is that you need.

Glynis turned the page over several times and again examined the envelope. Neither carried a signature.

MORNING SUNLIGHT SLANTED through the windows of City Hall, casting long golden rectangles across the courtroom. Glynis hid a yawn behind her hand, wincing as with every movement her back complained. During the early-dawn trip to the mile-distant Henrico County Courthouse, Jonah had urged the horse and carriage over cobbled streets at breakneck speed. But the haste had been essential. Locating the sleepy clerk at that hour meant more tense moments. This clerk became less than happy with the subpoena then handed him. He now sat, probably still vexed, two rows in front of Glynis. She could barely see him; Mr. Ash was so small, she wondered if his boots reached the floor. At least he shouldn't have to sit there too long, swinging his feet.

Between the heads of those seated in front of her, only Merrycoyf's head and shoulders were visible, and they twitched with impatience. When Niles arrived with his two-marshal escort, Glynis watched to see if the lawyers would tell him what had transpired. Apparently not, as neither Merrycoyf nor Hamilton seemed to give Niles more than a cursory nod of greeting.

"Y'all rise!"

When Judge Trumbull entered, Merrycoyf stood immediately with a request to approach the bench. As he and Hamilton, and then Steele, went forward, Glynis fought down a surge of anxiety. She didn't know what had been the outcome of Merrycoyf's hastily called conference with the prosecutor. Both Merrycoyf and Hamilton appeared grim-faced, as did Steele, when they had emerged from an adjacent room just minutes before.

"Your Honor," Merrycoyf now said, "I ask the court's permission to interrupt the testimony of the present witness, Victor St. Croix, to allow testimony of the county court clerk to be taken out of turn at this time."

Judge Trumbull looked irritated. "Mr. Merrycoyf, can you *assure* me, sir, that your request, if granted, will advance this trial?"

"Yes, Your Honor. You have my assurance."

Judge Trumbull turned with obvious reluctance to Steele. "Do you have an objection, Mr. Prosecutor?"

Glynis sucked in her breath.

"No, Your Honor. No objection."

She exhaled gratefully. Could it be that Steele would actually, voluntarily, cooperate? But unless he wanted the trial to go on for days, he had little choice, she supposed.

"Will you so stipulate?" Judge Trumbull asked Steele.

"Ah will."

"Very well. You may proceed, Mr. Merrycoyf. Call your witness."

The courtroom sat forward in a soundless wave.

"I call Mr. Caleb Ash."

The diminutive Mr. Ash came forward, carrying a large leather-bound volume. When he had been sworn, Merrycoyf asked him, "Are you, Caleb Ash, the duly elected clerk of the county of Henrico?"

"Ah am, yes."

"In your capacity as such, do you maintain records of vital statistics, pertaining to residents of this county and of the commonwealth of Virginia?"

"Ah do."

"Is one of the records you maintain, Mr. Ash, a registry of manumission?"

"Yes."

"In that registry, for the year 1835, is there filed a manumission, granted to the one described therein as a yellow woman, five feet three inches high, with a long scar on her right shoulder, fifteen years of age, by the name of Ama— Ama Dupont?"

The judge's gavel hammered sharply over the courtroom buzz. "Ah want it quiet in this room!"

While the noise settled, Glynis wondered, as she had earlier that morning, about the name "Dupont." Ama must have taken the name of her first owner—and her mother Masika's owner—Claude Dupont. It also became even more probable that Claude Dupont's brother Louis had likely been Ama's father. To acquire the name of an owner, however, would not have been uncommon for a slave. When questioned about the "yellow woman" description, Mr. Ash had said this simply indicated a mulatto.

"Mr. Merrycoyf, continue," Judge Trumbull now directed, still scowling at the room of restless spectators.

"Was this Ama Dupont's manumission signed by her master at that time?"

"Yes, sir," Mr. Ash replied. "The clerk in 'thirty-five, James Cavendish, set his hand—his signature—and seal of the court, under the given hand of the woman's owner."

"And whose given hand is on that register of manumission granted to Ama Dupont in the year 1835, Mr. Ash?"

"Victor St. Croix."

The initial gasps in the courtroom quickly escalated to more substantial noise. Judge Trumbull's gavel banged a number of times. "Order!" he demanded. When the bailiff rose to stand in the aisle, most noise diminished immediately.

Judge Trumbull nodded at Merrycoyf to continue. "And was Ama Dupont's manumission," Merrycoyf asked Mr. Ash, "conditioned on her leaving the state within a limited period of time?"

"Yes, sir, it was. Within one year of the manumission date, sir. The restriction was standard practice then."

Earlier that morning, Glynis and Merrycoyf learned from Mr. Ash that the practice of stipulating a time limitation to manumissions had been to prevent recently freed slaves from inciting those still enslaved to revolt—after Nat Turner's bloody rebellion of 1831, the fear among whites of slave insurrections became frenzied. Thus freed slaves had to leave their region or risk losing their newly gained liberty. She, and Merrycoyf too, all but lost heart when they heard this. Because, of course, since Ama had stayed in Virginia until her attempted escape five years later, the one-year restriction would make Ama's manumission worthless.

The courtroom now waited while Merrycoyf paused, dramatically clearing his throat, before he said, "What occurred just last year, Mr. Ash, to change this—that is, to change what you called the 'standard practice' of restricted manumission?"

"The Richmond Court of Appeals, in January of 'fifty-three, held in *Forward* versus *Thamer* that the time period which restricted manumissions was invalid."

"In other words," Merrycoyf said, "the Richmond court ruled that a slave once freed is forever free; is that correct, Mr. Ash?"

Mr. Ash bobbed his head. "Yes, sir—or words to that effect. Otherwise, the court said, a manumission could be withdrawn at any time by the slave's owner, or the owner's estate. And that would conflict with the purpose of the manumission statute."

"As indeed it would," Merrycoyf said, looking up at Judge

Trumbull. "Now, Mr. Ash, would you please produce the document in question?"

The clerk opened the registry volume to a previously marked page, and thrust the book toward Merrycoyf.

Merrycoyf smiled. "No; I've already studied that sufficiently, Mr. Ash. Would you be good enough to hand it to the judge?"

Judge Trumbull reached for the registry, then for several minutes studied the page. "So noted," he said finally. "Mr. Steele, do you wish to question this witness?"

To Glynis's acute relief, Mr. Steele answered, "No."

"Then, Mr. Ash," said Judge Trumbull, "you are excused with the court's thanks."

As Mr. Ash stepped from the witness box, Merrycoyf and Hamilton both said something to Niles, who had sat as if in a state of shock during the clerk's testimony. Now he just shook his head in apparent bewilderment. Merrycoyf rested his hand momentarily on the young man's shoulder, before he came around the table to approach the bench.

"Your Honor," he said, "I move to dismiss the charge against Niles Peartree on the following grounds . . ."

Glynis bit down on her lower lip in an attempt to check pent tears. It proved futile. Merrycoyf became a large blur, distinguishable only by his voice. Frantically pulling a handkerchief from her sleeve, she wiped at her eyes in order to watch Judge Trumbull. While glancing periodically at Merrycoyf, the judge looked again at the documents in front of him.

When Merrycoyf finished, he returned to stand beside Niles. They all waited; Niles, the lawyers, the jury, and the rest of the still courtroom, while Judge Trumbull studied the trial record of the previous days' testimony with great deliberation. When he at last put the papers down, Glynis could have sworn she saw something resembling relief cross his face.

"There appears to be no question," Judge Trumbull began, "that the slave woman Ama had been manumitted in the year 1835. Therefore her daughter Kiri, born to a freed slave, was herself free at birth and at the time of her departure with the accused from Jolimont. That being the circumstance, there is no basis for indicting Niles Peartree under the Fugitive Slave Law. He is not guilty of aiding a slave to escape. He may be guilty of something else, but that is for his conscience to determine. Case dismissed."

In the ensuing noise, Glynis wiped furiously at her eyes. Her joy wasn't just for Niles and Kiri. By virtue of his mother Ama's manumission, it meant Zeph, too, had been born into freedom.

Her elation had to be tempered, however, by the almost certain conviction that Kiri and possibly Zeph were still in danger—of another kind.

For Glynis believed she knew why three people had been murdered in Seneca Falls. The question now remained: Would the murderer need to kill again?

EIGHTEEN

❧

O Conspiracy!
Sham'st thou to show thy dangerous brow by night,
When evils are most free?
— SHAKESPEARE, *JULIUS CAESAR*

NILES LEFT THE city of Richmond immediately, bound for the Rochester home of Frederick Douglass. Despite the reservations Glynis voiced, he remained determined to bring Kiri back to Seneca Falls—to see his mother one last time before he and the young woman left for Montreal. He dismissed Glynis's warning of possible danger to Kiri with, "We'll only be there for a day. Two at the most. Don't worry, I'll take care of her. She's free—what could happen?"

Glynis had been torn between her admiration for Niles's swift rebound from near-catastrophe and her frustration at his assumption that he could control circumstances that she viewed as having the potential for great peril.

Late Friday afternoon, Glynis and Merrycoyf sat once again on a train, steaming north for home. Their departure from Richmond had been rushed, leaving undone something she very much wanted to do: speak with Katherine St. Croix. When Glynis walked out of the courthouse that morning, she'd tried to find the woman. But Victor St. Croix and his wife managed to vanish into the crowd as soon as Judge Trumbull rendered his decision—or so Chantal Dupont told Glynis on the steps of City Hall, where they stood in the warm October sunshine for their farewells.

"I won't ever forgive Victor St. Croix," Chantal vowed angrily, "for all the tragedy that occurred. And so much of it without cause."

"I suppose Masika must have known her daughter had been freed by him," Glynis said.

Chantal nodded. "Masika said she tried everything to convince Ama to leave Jolimont, and Richmond, immediately.

But pregnant with Kiri, where would Ama have gone? Her mother lived here, and this was the only place Ama had ever known. She did understand the restriction placed on her manumission, but during that year, the one in which Kiri was born, Ama fell in love with Sam—and love does have a way of overpowering good sense."

At least for the young, and the young in spirit, Glynis reflected sadly. The young were so fearless, reckless, running with caution tossed to the winds, unaware of how much a misstep could hurt them. And suddenly the perception of her own aging, her own missteps, of what she had lost and what she had kept, brushed her with unexpected pain.

Chantal too seemed to feel this pain, for she sighed, saying, "The young, they believe they're different from all those gone before! Still, I don't think Ama would ever have left Jolimont if it hadn't been for the desperate fear that Sam would be sold."

But leave she did. And for that act of desperation she and Sam died. But their tragedy had not been the end of it. For Glynis suspected their deaths set in motion the spinning of a tangled deception now coming unraveled, thirteen years later, with still more tragic consequences. The long reach of slavery.

"Do you think Victor St. Croix knew about last year's Richmond court decision?" Glynis asked Chantal. "Knew the old manumission restrictions had been voided?"

"Lord, I hope not." Chantal flinched at the implication. "I'd hate to think that he did and that he still persisted in his search for Kiri under the assumption no one would find Ama's manumission record. But . . ."

"But we'll never know, will we?" Glynis completed. "Just as we'll never know what Judge Trumbull's ruling on Merrycoyf's question would have been."

Giving Glynis her wry smile, Chantal said, "Oh, I didn't believe Artemus Trumbull would concede, for *any* reason, that his beloved Virginia might be guilty of moral failure."

And apparently Katherine St. Croix hadn't believed it either, Glynis thought.

Neither she nor Merrycoyf disclosed from whom they concluded the unsigned note came, but surely Victor St. Croix

could guess. Who but Katherine, other than Masika and
Chantal—who, if they'd thought it still pertinent would have
told her—could have details about the manumission of Kiri's
mother? Katherine herself had told Glynis she read newspapers avidly, so in all likelihood she had seen in them the
court's decision of a year before.

Katherine's motive had not necessarily been a charitable
one. She had, after all, two children who might have to
share Victor St. Croix's wealth if Kiri returned to Jolimont,
as there was little doubt in Glynis's mind that Victor St.
Croix did have feelings for the young woman. Now, because Katherine had found strength enough to breach the
wife's code of silence, he would presumably never see his
only child again.

"You'll accept my invitation, then—mine and Harriet
Peartree's?" Glynis asked, as Chantal climbed into her carriage. "You and Masika will come to Seneca Falls for a Yankee Thanksgiving?"

"With pleasure," Chantal said, smiling. "But you're sure
now, if you tell the boy we're coming soon, it will keep him
from dashing down here to his grandmother? It just isn't safe
for him, you know."

Glynis had nodded vigorously. "You don't have to tell *me*
that. I'll do my best, but whether I can convince Zeph of the
danger . . ." She had shaken her head.

The clack of wheels, the wail of the train whistle, now reminded her of the February trip from Albany with Elizabeth
Stanton and Susan Anthony. It seemed years ago. But it had
been then, Glynis recognized, that for her this all began.
Began when marshals dragged that young black man from
the train. Those marshals were informed about where to
find him, she felt convinced. And could the informer also
be a killer?

IN LATE AFTERNOON of the following day, she and
Merrycoyf arrived at the near-empty Seneca Falls railway station. When they stepped from the train, the air felt as crisp as
the texture of a fresh-picked apple. Leaving Richmond in
summery heat, Glynis now missed the woolen cloak short-
sightedly packed in the bottom of her valise. The sun beyond

the canal already sank low on the southwestern horizon, and oaks and a few sugar maples still bore leaves that mirrored the sunset of red and orange and rust. A perfect autumn twilight—or it would be if a wire awaited her. The thought of word from Cullen made Glynis happier than she would have believed possible.

Merrycoyf, who had stopped to haul their valises off the baggage cart, looked with curiosity to just beyond the station house. "What on earth?" he muttered, adjusting his spectacles.

Glynis followed his gaze. Jennie Terhune, Mad Jennie, stood shaking her fist in the air, shouting something too garbled to catch. But there appeared to be nothing unusual happening. In fact, nothing at all happening, other than Eebard Peck again abusing his mule. The unfortunate animal had settled on its haunches and now brayed dejectedly, while behind it sat a motionless farm wagon, which, piled with bags of guano, looked too heavy for a team of mules to pull.

"Poor beast," Merrycoyf said. "You know, that Eebard Peck puts me in mind of the slavedrivers we saw in Richmond."

Glynis had been thinking much the same thing but, to her distress, she also remembered coffles of chained Negroes.

Jennie, still shouting, just then whirled around and eyed Merrycoyf. Glynis saw his shoulders stiffen to ready himself for Jennie's approach. But surprisingly, it instead was Glynis she came toward.

"Bad man!" Jennie said loudly. She thrust out an arm to point toward Eebard. "He's a bad, bad man." Pushing her face close to that of Glynis, she said again, "Bad."

"Why, Jennie?" Glynis said, expecting no answer but feeling compelled to respond in some way. "Why bad?"

Jennie's thin fingers plucked at Glynis's sleeve, and she, off balance, took a step backward. "Jennie, what is it?"

Jennie's eyes, looking into her own, had become clear and lucid. Rational. Glynis didn't expect the lucidity to last, however. From the corner of her eye, she glimpsed Merrycoyf watching with interest.

"That is a bad man," Jennie said now. "He ... he hurts."

Glynis thought Jennie must mean the mule. "Eebard Peck is hurting his animal?" Glynis asked her. "Well, yes, I'm afraid he is, but—"

"No!" Jennie cried. "Not that. He hurts Jennie, he . . ." she stopped to look about wildly, pointing at first to herself, and then to Eebard Peck. "He takes money . . . he should go away. Like the others."

"Like the others?" Glynis echoed, the words chilling her. "What do you mean, Jennie—what others?"

At that moment, Eebard came up behind them. "Hey now, what all's that there crazy woman sayin' this time?"

Jennie's lucidity instantly retreated to some inner refuge. She backed away from Eebard, then turned to skitter off around the corner of the station house. Eebard watched her with a scowl. "She oughta be put away, 'fore she does somebody harm."

"Speaking of harm, Peck," Merrycoyf growled, "why don't you leave the mule be? Animal can't possibly pull the load you've got there."

Eebard snorted noisily and started back to the farm wagon, but he continued to glance toward the station house. Glynis felt a strong misgiving. What could Jennie have meant—or had it been nothing more than the confusion of a poor demented woman? But Glynis, recalling Jennie's eyes, didn't think so.

Hoofbeats interrupted her thoughts. Coming around the far side of the station house, Jacques Sundown sat astride his black and white paint.

"Well, Constable Sundown," Merrycoyf said, picking up his two valises. "What's happened here in town since we left? No more deaths, I hope?"

"No. No more death," Jacques answered, not looking at Merrycoyf.

"And Zeph?" Glynis asked, not quite ready to meet Jacques's steady gaze. "He's all right?"

"He's all right." Jacques dismounted and reached for Glynis's valises. "You going home?" He swung the valises up behind his saddle.

"Oh, yes," Glynis sighed. "I certainly am."

"Miss Tryon," Merrycoyf said, "I now leave you in good

hands. It's been . . ." He paused, then continued, "It's been a most interesting experience, wouldn't you say?"

Tired as she was, Glynis managed a thin smile. "Yes, Mr. Merrycoyf, I surely would sat that."

Behind the spectacles, Merrycoyf's eyes glimmered briefly before he nodded and began to amble toward Fall Street.

Hearing nothing then but quiet, Glynis looked around; Eebard had apparently persuaded his mule to pull the wagon, because he and they were nowhere to be seen.

Jacques gave the paint's reins a light tug and, with the horse plodding behind, he and Glynis began to walk toward Harriet's. It was then she realized she hadn't been at all startled to see Jacques Sundown.

For a time they walked without speaking. "Jacques," she said finally, "did you get my wire from Richmond?"

"Yeah."

"And have you . . . ah . . . heard from Cullen?"

"No."

Disappointment welled up into her throat so swiftly it made her chest ache. Blinking furiously, she wiped at her eyes, terrified she would begin weeping right there in the middle of Cayuga Street. What made her so prone to tears lately? And why should she have expected anything from Cullen anyway? He most likely thought her wire simply an excuse to contact him. Or thought she had lost her mind—wasting words, and money, on the Department of War for heavens' sake. He and a lady friend probably had a good laugh over that! No, that wasn't fair—it wouldn't be at all like Cullen to make fun of anyone.

For once she found herself grateful for what Cullen used to call Jacques's "eloquent Seneca silence." The man must be embarrassed by her lack of dignity. Well, so was she. She clenched her hands together as if she could press the disappointment back inside herself.

The smell of smoke lingered from burning leaves; those remaining blanketed the road, so footsteps made the soft whispery sounds of autumn. The sounds comforted her somehow, blunting sharp edges of the awareness that Cullen was truly gone.

When he finally spoke, Jacques's voice seemed oddly muted, unlike his usual monotone, as if he too were experiencing some kind of sorrow. It could be the unsolved murders. But his next words surprised her. "Guess you thought you'd hear from him by now."

Had Jacques ever before, in all the time she'd known him, made to her a personal remark? She thought not. Glancing at him sideways, Glynis saw him studying the leaf-strewn road ahead as if to avoid looking at her.

With effort, she made herself say evenly, "I thought I might get a return wire. I'd asked Cullen to look for something that probably no one else could get to—at least not quickly. But tell me," she asked him, determined to change the subject, "have you discovered anything more about the . . . the murders?"

"No. Nothing that makes sense."

"Oh, Jacques, when has murder ever made sense? But in any case," she said, taking a deep breath, "why don't we start trying to sort through this. In Richmond I found out some things . . . and I have an idea or two. Maybe between us we *can* make some sense of it. For instance, would you be able to go to Waterloo, to the courthouse, and check some deeds I think might be recorded there?"

Something about him changed. He moved through the rustling leaves almost silently as if without weight, as if a sadness had been lifted. As if he were unaccountably pleased.

"O.K.," he said. "Let's hear what you've got."

SUNDAY MORNING, GLYNIS walked back down the hill from Lacey and Isaiah Smith's, yawning with fatigue. Her head still felt logy, even though she had slept twelve hours straight. Harriet let her sleep, but the woman herself had been wide awake, ecstatic over the outcome of the trial and the prospect of seeing her son and Kiri.

With effort, Glynis shook off her fatigue—she had no right to be tired, not when something so wonderful had just occurred. She'd told Zeph of his freedom, and of his grandmother Masika. And reminded him—as if he needed reminding!—that he had a sister also free. The boy at first looked disbelieving. His face expressed the wary uncertainty of one never before offered much joy.

But when Glynis assured him of the truth, when she swore it, Zeph's face transformed utterly with the first genuine smile she had ever seen from him. She herself, of course, wept again. As did Lacey, while Isaiah pummeled the boy with rough gladness. The single melancholy note sounded when they were reminded that Lacey had not been freed—remained still legally enslaved. God grant that no one with evil intent knew it. Particularly the unknown informer.

But now, as Glynis reached the bottom of the hill, she had to ask herself how far Isaiah Smith might go to protect his wife were someone ready to expose her background. Or threatening to take her back south. Reluctantly Glynis brought to mind Isaiah's muddy boots, and that she'd seen them the Monday after the murder of the slave-catcher, Brogan. Surely it had just been coincidental. Isaiah could have gone anywhere that night! She wouldn't think about it.

When Glynis stepped inside the *Courier* office, Ephraim Penrod glanced up to give her only a cursory nod, then gestured to the edge of his desk nearest to her and went back to reading. She picked up the envelope with her name on it. It would be unladylike to count the money now, but the issue seemed critical enough—she needed the money—to disregard propriety. She opened the envelope.

Riffling the bills inside with her index finger she counted silently. It was so little. For so much work.

"Mr. Penrod," she began tentatively, "I'm not sure—"

"Your dispatches were quite satisfactory, Miss Tryon," he interrupted. "So you've been paid what we agreed on."

Agreed? "Ah, Mr. Penrod, I think there's not quite enough here. That is, I know you pay the men's transportation expenses."

"First of all, Miss Tryon, it was my understanding that you were going to Richmond anyway. Isn't that true?"

"Well, yes, but—"

"There aren't any buts about it. Second, the men are entitled to expenses. They have families to support—wives and children to feed. Now that's not exactly your circumstance, is it, Miss Tryon?"

"No. No, but I did a satisfactory job—you just said so, and I think—"

"If that's all," Penrod said, glowering, "I have work here to do."

"Is that your last word?" Glynis asked. "Because if it is, I should tell you that I won't be doing any more *free* women's columns for you. If you want them, you'll have to pay for them."

Had she really said that? She must be angrier than she'd realized. And more aware of what the term "to slave" meant.

Penrod stared at her for what seemed forever. She could feel her face flushing, and turned to go.

"Ah, just a minute, Miss Tryon. As it is, your columns have been fairly well received, so I suppose I could consider giving you a small stipend."

She felt a glow of victory—extinguished immediately by his next words. "Of course," he said, "you'll have to write them under the Japes names as usual."

Just as she opened her mouth to protest, Penrod shut it for her. "That *is* my last word, Miss Tryon! Take it or leave it."

She supposed she'd have to take it. After the costly train trips of the past months, she needed the money. And she wanted to do the columns, because no one else would.

She could hear Harriet saying "Half a loaf is better than none." But then, Harriet was a woman. Accustomed to half a loaf. Glynis sighed heavily and nodded at Penrod. He went back to his reading after sending her a scowl as she turned to leave.

When she at last reached The Usher Playhouse—so announced by the splendid marquee erected over the original oak entry doors—she heard through an open window the murmur of rehearsing voices inside, and the occasional rap of a hammer. But a handful of actors seated on a nearby rectory's front steps were remarkably untalkative. Probably saving their voices for a more notable audience than themselves.

Pushing open one of the church doors, Glynis stepped inside. And could scarce believe her eyes.

It was a theater! Gone the church; only the stained-glass windows and long, mahogany pews gave witness to the former sanctuary, although the hard seats had been softened by cushions of wine red velvet. Wool carpet of the same rich color had been laid by just now departing workmen, apparently the source of the rapping sounds. The walls, at least those few portions not containing box seats and rear balcony, had been painted a dove gray, and pewter chandeliers swung over the stage area and center aisle of the audience section. Pewter wall sconces held tall tapers as yet unlit.

Along the stage left and right, double-wick oil-float lamps sat behind large glass containers of red-colored liquid. When Glynis walked down the aisle toward the stage, she could see on an apron just above the shallow orchestra pit more glasses of the colored liquid, positioned in front of flickering torches. Just behind the torches were metal reflectors. The effect created a pulsating blood-red glow over the entire stage area.

Now halfway down the aisle, just beyond the edge of the balcony overhead, Glynis shuddered involuntarily—no doubt precisely the desired response to this ingeniously macabre lighting. Even the boxes along the side walls had a bloody hue.

From the stage floor itself rose massive, gray stone columns—at least they looked like stone but were probably hollow—to either side of wide stone steps that climbed to another level at middle stage. More columns and stairs disappeared behind a canopy of red velvet. Tavus Sligh had obviously dispensed with the typical Elizabethan four-story stage house, designing instead a castle facade. And this also meant no curtain to raise and lower. The play would take place on the center stage and on the two extensions at either side.

For the dramatically sinister impact of the set, Glynis silently applauded Tavus's choices.

Suddenly, in the near-empty theater, thunder roared, then slowly rumbled away. Even as she jumped, Glynis knew the effect to be made by shaking a piece of sheet iron, and rolling a keg filled with sand. Silk rotated over a slatted cylinder now produced an eerie whistling wind.

She turned to look up for the origin of a light beam that had just illuminated a small portion of stage right. From its front balcony position, Glynis thought the source of the beam must be a "lime": developed several decades before, it consisted of a calcium block heated to produce the soft but brilliant light that could be directed and focused from an adjustable stand.

She whirled back to face the stage. From the corner of her eye she had caught movement in three mound-like objects she had previously assumed to be large rocks. In the beam of limelight the mounds now swayed, as in a slow uncoiling they rose to become three aged crones draped in gray. In harsh tones they spoke:

> "When shall we meet again?
> In thunder, lightning, or in rain?"
> "When the hurlyburly's done,
> When the battle's lost and won."

Drawn into the scene before her Glynis edged into a pew, disbelieving instantly that these three wraiths might be Calista Sligh's elderly female relatives. They were witches!

The spell they cast, however, proved brief. The three had barely begun to chorus: "Fair is foul, and foul is fair/Hover through the fog and filthy air," when, with a raucous belch, smoke began to pour onto the stage. The witches coughed, flung their gray-robed sleeves over their faces, and ran off with out-of-character sprightliness.

Tavus Sligh could be heard swearing backstage with awe-inspiring originality. The high-pitched wails could only be coming from Vanessa: "Oh, no! It's not working . . . there's too much smoke! Stop fanning it, you fools, and put it out!"

Glynis started to laugh—*Out, damned smoke!*—but choked as the air thickened. Trying not to inhale, she moved with head down to the entrance doors, managing somehow to pull them open and get outside before bursting into laughter. In

her haste she collided with someone who stood directly before the doors; head still down, her apology spluttered to a
pair of tan leather boots. Unwilling to stop laughing—
laughing for the first time in months—Glynis straightened
and looked up.

Into the face of Cullen Stuart.

For one terrible moment Glynis believed she must be as
mad as Jennie, who saw her lost Jamie's face on every man
she met. But this was no hallucination. This was really Cullen.

He stood looking down at her, his initial smile starting to
wane. Glynis attempted a shaky step forward as Cullen began to waver, fading in and out of fog like an apparition.
She waved her hands before her as though moving aside
cobwebs.

He caught her hands to steady her, saying, "Glynis, you
fainting isn't exactly the reception I'd hoped for—maybe
you'd better sit down."

She started to nod, light-headed, and swayed backward.
Cullen dropped her hands to grip her shoulders. She tried
reaching up to touch his face, but it had become a blur. Cullen
made an indistinct sound as his arms went around her, and
pulled her tightly against him. Glynis wasn't aware of tears
streaming down her face until she felt the dampness of his
shirt under her cheek.

SHE HAD NO idea how long they stood there. But at last she
heard people's voices coming toward them, and Cullen released her. Still standing so close his breath ruffled her hair,
he said quietly, "Think now you can manage 'Hello'? Or if
not, just a nod will do."

Glynis nodded. "I'm sorry . . . it's only that you were so
. . . so unexpected."

He took a step back. "Why unexpected? I came straight
from Washington."

"Oh. I guess I thought you would just wire. I didn't
think . . ." She stopped as she realized what she'd been
about to say. But what difference did it make—how important could her pride be—now of all times? Hesitantly, she

went on, "I thought after what happened, that . . . well, that you wouldn't want to see me again. Ever. And Cullen, you didn't even write." She felt tears again sliding down her face.

Cullen had begun to frown, but his face cleared as he ran his fingers over her wet cheeks. "I did write, Glynis. You didn't answer."

"I couldn't. I didn't know what to say."

"And you thought I *did*? If I remember correctly—and I'm positive I do—you were the one who . . ." He paused, and shook his head. "I don't think we need to go over this now, do we?"

"No!" she agreed, much too loudly, and quickly glanced around to see actors strolling by them on their way into the theater. But they gave her and Cullen only the briefest of looks, no doubt accustomed to weeping women in melodramatic scenes.

Cullen nonetheless said, "Let's walk along the canal. Less of an audience."

He took her hand and they went down the slope to the towpath. When they were on level ground, he said, "Your wire sounded to me as if there's a fairly nasty situation here. You don't think that old negro man's death, right before I left, was an accident, do you?"

"No. I'm almost certain it wasn't." She felt herself recovering, more in control, grateful to talk about something other than the two of them. But somehow she must keep herself from asking, or even thinking, about how long Cullen planned to be in Seneca Falls.

"I think Moses Rawlings was murdered," she said, "for the same reason that a slave-catcher and an actress were killed some weeks later. But Cullen, did you find what I asked about? Could you get into the War Department?"

He smiled, and she recognized with pain just how much she had missed that warm smile; one that lightened an otherwise serious face. "Allan Pinkerton has connections all over," he said, "Washington included. So, yes; I got into the department records."

He started to pull an envelope from the pocket inside his frock coat, but Glynis put out her hand to stop him. "Much as

I want to see what you've found," she said, "I should tell you all that's happened first. I think I know why the murders were committed, and I may know by whom. But while I'm telling you, I don't want to be influenced by what you might have there." She pointed at the envelope, saying, "*If* I'm right, that should only be confirmation."

Walking beside her, Cullen looked puzzled but agreed to what she asked.

They came to a place where several large oaks grew at the edge of the towpath. Leaves still clung brown and curled to long horizontal branches reaching over the canal, recently drained for the coming winter. Brushing away fallen leaves, they exposed an outcrop of flat bedrock they remembered to be underneath.

When they were seated on the rock, Glynis said, offhandedly she hoped, "Was your September weather in Cleveland as lovely as it was here?" She immediately felt uncomfortable, and even devious; she asked only to learn whether he had spent the month with someone else. A female someone.

"I wouldn't know what the weather was like," said Cullen, scowling. "I spent the whole month indoors, moving paper around an office desk. You wouldn't believe how much paper—" He broke off, the scowl lingering. "I missed our September picnics."

"I missed them, too," Glynis blurted before she could suppress it. She felt tears surface and caught her lower lip between her teeth, but stopped when she remembered Cullen knew why she did that. Small acts of pride weren't very effective with someone so familiar, someone who knew so much. She smiled at that, the tears retreating.

Cullen, who had been looking at her intently, exhaled sharply as if he'd been holding his breath. Then he smiled and lay back, stretched out with his hands under his head to gaze at the sky. Sun filtering through the oak branches played patterns of light across his face. Glynis wished she could just sit there and watch him, etching him in her memory against the time when he would again leave. But he said, "So let's hear it. All of it—start from when I left."

"That's not the beginning, Cullen. It started thirteen years before that."

* * *

IT TOOK A long time to tell. Long enough for the sun to dip toward the canal bed, where shallow water left in the bottom glittered in the slanting light. Occasionally Cullen interrupted her with questions, but otherwise he remained quiet until she finished.

"I think that's all of it," Glynis sighed, overwhelmed by the memories she'd had to resurrect. "Have you talked to Jacques Sundown yet?"

"Haven't talked to anyone. Soon as I got off the train, I went to the livery with my horse, then straight to Harriet's. She told me where to find you. Why, what does Jacques think of your theory?"

"I haven't told him all of it. Some of it just came to me last night. What do *you* think?" Glynis asked.

"What I always thought," Cullen said, sitting up and taking the envelope from his pocket, "that you're a very smart woman—that is, at least, about most things."

Too impatient to deliberate on this comment, she took the envelope to extract several sheets of paper with Cullen's handwriting. Reading rapidly, she found what she looked for at the bottom of the second sheet. "I was right," she breathed, gazing at Cullen, then back at the paper again. "I thought it must be so."

"Apparently," Cullen said, giving her a long look. "You going to tell me *how* you came up with this?"

"As I said earlier, it came last night when—believe it or not, and please don't laugh, Cullen—when I reread *Macbeth.*"

"Macbeth?" Cullen repeated, not laughing.

Glynis nodded. "It sounds bizarre, I know. I tried to ignore it, but I kept thinking of the play, frustrated by a nagging feeling it held something important, if I could only find it. It didn't make sense, but I went to the library anyway, mostly to distract myself and take my mind off the murders."

Cullen laughed now. "That *is* bizarre, Glynis. I haven't read Shakespeare since college, but I remember enough. *Macbeth* is one murder after another!"

"Yes, precisely. And believe me, there are some uncanny parallels to our situation—which, I guess, is why we still read

Shakespeare two centuries later. Some things never change. Motives for instance. Take all those allusions to masks in *Macbeth*: 'False face must hide what the false heart doth know,' and 'Make our faces vizards to our hearts, disguising what they are.' There are several others, but those are the two I can recall right now."

"Recall? Glynis, how in God's name . . . ?"

"It's my job to know these things—I'm a librarian, remember? Anyway, what finally jogged my memory enough were those ironic lines of Lady Macbeth:

> 'The sleeping and the dead
> Are but as pictures;
> 'tis the eye of childhood
> That fears a painted devil.' "

Cullen looked baffled. "What does that have to do with . . ." his voice trailed away as he shook his head.

"Although it wasn't what she meant at that particular point in the play, in the end it was a child, or children, that Macbeth most had to regret—and fear. Remember the witches' prophecy that Banquo would beget a line of kings, whereas Macbeth would not?"

"Glynis?"

She grasped the hand he put up to stop her. "Just a minute, Cullen; please hear me out. Both Kiri and her grandmother Masika referred to the slave-catcher Brogan and overseer Farley as 'devils.' That's what I needed to remember. Because it made me think: What if someone, someone here in Seneca Falls, had believed the past to be dead, and not any threat, as in Lady Macbeth's context. And then suddenly, a person—or persons—were to appear; persons who knew exactly what the past could do if exposed?"

Cullen took the papers from Glynis's hand. Scanning them, his puzzled look faded. "Yes, I see what you mean," he said slowly. "Thomas Farley."

"But the problem is," Glynis went on, "how can it ever be proved? Some kind of trap is the only way I can think of, but it would have to involve Kiri, and could put her in terrible danger." She broke off to see if Cullen followed her.

He understood, unfortunately too well. "I think we could handle it so she wouldn't be in danger," he said. Then, when Glynis frowned, he added, "Well, at least not much."

"I don't believe 'not much' is good enough, Cullen. And even if you and I think so, you can wager that Niles won't. He wouldn't ever agree to Kiri's being used as bait."

"Look, Glynis, there are three of us—you, me, and Jacques—plus Niles Peartree. What could happen to her?"

Glynis moaned. "There are plenty of things that could go wrong, like—"

"But that's not even the point," Cullen interrupted her. "Kiri won't ever be safe, anywhere. She'll be in danger until Farley is caught. And besides," he said after a pause, "shouldn't Kiri have something to say about it?"

He was probably right. And Glynis had already thought of all this herself. But it didn't make her feel less afraid.

Cullen got to his feet, brushing leaves from his shirt. He preferred action, Glynis was reminded. How had Allan Pinkerton managed to keep this man behind a desk?

"When will Niles be back here with Kiri?" Cullen asked, extending his hand to help her from the rock.

"Tomorrow morning. But Cullen, we don't know if Kiri can recognize Farley. Thirteen years is a long time, and she was only five years old then. 'The eye of childhood,' " she added.

"But you said he took her back south. They would have been together several days. Maybe Kiri could tell from his voice—voices don't change all that much over time. You could walk her around town tomorrow; she might spot him."

"But what if she can't?" Glynis protested. "What's worse is that he will be able to recognize *her*—Kiri's face has been on handbills all over western New York. And you know, Cullen, I think he's the one who kept the search for her active, even after Victor St. Croix gave it up as hopeless. Farley could be on guard by now. If he thinks we're at all suspicious of him—"

"Then we'll find another way; one that will lower his

guard and smoke him out." Cullen stopped. His forehead furrowed in thought. "Smoke," he said again, now looking in the direction of the theater. "When does that playhouse open?"

"Day after tomorrow—Halloween—and I'm afraid of what you're thinking, Cullen. Remember, Farley's surely aware that Kiri might be able to identify him. He's already killed three people for that very reason."

"That's exactly why he needs to be stopped." Cullen frowned in concentration. "Tomorrow they'll be here, you say?"

She nodded, biting her lip. She knew that look of his: he would think on it, then want to start out immediately.

Cullen thought a minute longer. "Then we don't have much time to set things up. We'll have to move fast."

Glynis sighed. "I'm telling you, Cullen, Niles will not go along with this. Ever."

"He won't have a choice."

NINETEEN

> *Hail to you gods . . .*
> *On that day of the great reckoning.*
> —THE BOOK OF THE DEAD

ALLHALLOWS EVE—HALLOWEEN—the old Celtic festival marking the end of summer, remained as balmy as the day preceding it. Sunday night had delivered a hard frost and the first flakes of snow, but the next two days brought a reprieve of soft warm air and sunshine. Indian summer did not occur every year, but when it did, Glynis thought of it as a benediction: one last blessing from the gods of summer as they retreated before winds howling down from Canada across Lake Ontario, and the days that came short and bleak and cold.

If Vanessa Usher had been allowed to choose the weather for opening night of her playhouse, she couldn't have chosen fairer. "It might be a good omen," she said with the caution of the superstitious.

And they needed all the good omens they could get, she declared uneasily, considering the curse that followed the play—Vanessa studiously avoided speaking its name—since its earliest performances. Hence, the fair weather indicated the gods *might* be pleased. She would go no further.

The night air held so still that torches along the towpath sent their flames straight into the sky. Lanterns positioned on posts along the path to the theater illuminated carriage after carriage bearing the audience; all seats had been sold and, to Cullen and Jacques's concern, the side aisles would be stacked two-deep with those willing to stand.

On the way to the theater, Glynis tried to reassure Kiri. "Kiri, we have an advantage tonight in that Farley can't suspect we know he's a murderer. It's important, should we come face-to-face with him, that you remember he has no reason to . . . to . . ."

"To attack me?" Kiri finished.

"Well, yes," Glynis admitted, wishing Kiri had found another word. "Although I was going to say *distrust* you," she added. "No reason at all."

"But Ah'm not sure he *needs* a reason, Glynis. He's killed a lot of people." She hesitated, probably thinking of her mother, then said, "Ah don't expect Farley's very reasonable to begin with."

Glynis could hardly argue that. "Please just remember, Kiri—he doesn't know that *we* know who he is!"

Kiri slowly nodded; she didn't look at all convinced.

"You can choose not to go through with this, Kiri. No one would blame you."

"We went over that," Kiri sighed. "Ah'll always have to be afraid, if we don't catch him now."

And they left it at that.

Harriet was at home, mourning her son's latest imprisonment, as Niles had been arrested for the murders of Lyle Brogan and Luella. Harriet, though, knew full well why Jacques had clapped Niles into jail.

When they first arrived at the theater, Glynis took Kiri ostensibly for a peek backstage, where Lacey Smith calmly made last-minute costume adjustments. Isaiah sat close to his wife, clearly enjoying every minute of Lacey's celebrity; he nodded and winked at Glynis, an indication that he would watch backstage for danger to Kiri coming from that direction.

Cullen initially opposed allowing so many in on the conspiracy to snare Farley, but it was the only way Glynis would agree to take part. Besides, Isaiah Smith had not really been a murder suspect, since Glynis finally recalled Lyle Brogan's words to her on Fall Street that September afternoon: *"Could you tell me if theah's a gentleman in town name of Farley?"*

At the time she jumped to the wrong conclusion: that Farley must be a runaway. Now, after being in Richmond, it seemed inconceivable to her that a man like Brogan, a brutal slave-catcher, would refer to any male Negro as "a gentleman."

She and Kiri slipped into their pew seats early enough to observe those entering the theater. Kiri had failed to recognize Farley on their afternoon walk through town, and Glynis questioned whether the young woman could identify him that evening—and this was the main reason they risked her exposure. Nonetheless, Glynis knew Farley was there. As Farley must also see Kiri.

Interest in the former church's metamorphosis occupied the audience before the first act, interrupted briefly as newcomers were greeted, and by a flurry of commotion attending Brendan O'Reilly's arrival with a woman swathed beyond recognition in a fashionable, ostrich-plumed hat and veil. This must be the person, members of the audience were heard to theorize, for whom Brendan successfully bid on the box seats at the fair. Whispered speculation as to who she might be leaped from pew to pew. However, when the woman declined to remove her hat, it appeared that the town's curiosity was not to be satisfied that evening.

Glynis herself had guessed the woman's identity when she sashayed in on Brendan's arm. There could be only one female in Seneca Falls who possessed that arresting sway of hips, enough money of her own to purchase the box seats, and a sound reason for anonymity: Serenity Hathaway. Seneca Falls madam Serenity Hathaway. Glynis, scanning the theater diligently, gave herself a second quick look up at Serenity's box. She had to smile at the woman's boldness. Her sheer impudence. Vanessa, had she known who sat in her audience, would have perished many times over.

And not just Vanessa; had Serenity not remained veiled, half the audience might have walked out. Although it shouldn't have been a surprise to anyone to find the madam at *Macbeth*. The time had not been so long ago, Glynis reflected, when the theater was considered thoroughly disreputable—and women appearing on stage just one notch above those who worked the brothels.

When the steady stream of those arriving slowed to the few latecomers trickling in, and with the box seats occupied, it seemed that most of Seneca Falls' wealthies and well-knowns had come—as well as aspiring lesser-knowns—whether to see Vanessa's project fall flat on its face, or to be seen themselves. Each and every politician standing for election managed to look as if he personally were responsible for the new theater; even Michael Olivant and wife Deirdre appeared wholly proprietary—which must be a surprise to Ian Bentham. Glynis looked for the contractor; earlier she'd seen him in his box, but he had since disappeared. He could be attending to last-minute details, she supposed—like reassuring Vanessa of the structural safety of her playhouse.

Another group of middle-class residents, including Elizabeth Stanton and her husband, were no doubt simply eager for some good theater. Eebard Peck fidgeted alone up in his two-seat box, characteristically glaring at those below. Glynis's gaze kept flicking back to him.

Kiri sat quietly, scrutinizing all with care. So far, to no avail.

When it appeared the playhouse could not hold one more body—only the center aisle remained empty—a woman behind Glynis gave an abrupt *tsk-tsk*, followed by, "Why I never!"

Glynis turned to see what had prompted this. She looked up the aisle, then looked again: she nearly had not recognized her young assistant librarian.

His unruly hair now parted and slicked down, swallowtail coat trim and pressed, Jonathan Quant strolled down the aisle with no other on his arm than Vanessa Usher's sister Aurora. Well, this was just too lovely, Glynis smiled to herself. So it wasn't Vanessa after all whom Jonathan wanted to impress. Glynis decided she'd not given him near enough credit. And she allowed herself to experience a moment of vicarious pleasure in this otherwise disturbing evening—until behind her she heard, "Well, really! Talk about robbing the cradle. Aurora Usher must be old enough to be his *mother*!"

Other voices echoed this condemnation.

Why was it, Glynis wondered sadly, that men could choose women half their own age, women young enough to be their granddaughters—it happened all the time—but let a woman do the same and it became "unnatural." Seduction of the helpless innocent male by woman as temptress. Scandalous.

Well, good for Aurora. And Jonathan.

At last actors costumed in velvet doublet and hose came forth to snuff the wall sconce tapers, and a trumpet's plaintive notes announced the first act of *Macbeth*. The limelight had been positioned to reveal the witches, already on stage in their "rock" formation. After delivering their opening lines, they were lowered from center stage by means of the platform trap, accompanied by trumpet and drums from the orchestra pit to drown the noise of the mechanism's creaking ropes and rasping timbers.

Tavus Sligh's entrance as Macbeth took place on one of the tree-dressed side platforms. Glynis could barely keep her mind on the play, but she admired Tavus's staging skill—by clever use of the limelight, and without awkward pauses for lowering and raising a curtain, the action flowed smoothly from scene to scene. She knew she would have loved this production if there hadn't been the constant reminder of Farley's presence—and Kiri's vulnerability. Again Glynis desperately wished she had more strongly protested Cullen's strategy—but she couldn't come up with one better. Or any safer, she now thought miserably.

If Farley was to rise to the bait, he would have to do it soon. The rumor had been put out, all over town, that Kiri must leave the next morning. Niles's arrest, this rumor implied, could only hasten her departure, since she might be implicated in the slave-catcher's death. Thus Cullen expected Farley's hand would be forced. The man had shown sufficient ruthlessness in ridding himself of any witness to the bloodshed thirteen years before. And he couldn't know Kiri was unable to identify him.

Prophetic enough to chill Glynis through and through were Macbeth's closing lines of act three:

> *"I am in blood*
> *Stepp'd in so far that, should I wade no more,*
> *Returning were as tedious as go o'er."*

Tavus Sligh had wanted to stage the shortest of Shakespeare's tragedies in its entirety without a break. But Vanessa persuaded him to suffer an intermission after act three. In consequence, the audience now thronged the canal slope where trestle tables groaned under the burden of pears and grapes, rounds of pungent cheese, roasted chestnuts, apple juice, hard apple cider, applejack, and German-brewed beer: Vanessa's tribute to Apollo.

The mild weather and impressive first three acts of *Macbeth* were not, however, the sole topics of intermission conversation. Niles Peartree's arrest had raised Seneca Falls to near-fever pitch; it even pushed the coming election, one week away, off the front page of *The Seneca County Courier*'s special evening edition.

Standing just outside the theater entrance Glynis glanced at Kiri beside her. Something had happened to the young woman during her time in Rochester. She no longer looked a portrait of meekness, but carried herself with the same sure grace of her grandmother Masika. And while she must be aware of the gossip about Niles, and worried about her own welfare, one would never guess this from her appearance.

Glynis, now looking beyond Kiri, spotted Cullen standing in the shadows of a birch clump; she couldn't see Jacques Sundown, or the bloodhounds, but they must be somewhere nearby. However, despite people's normal inquisitiveness about the young mulatto woman and the lingering glances her beauty produced, so far nothing unusual had been noted by either Glynis or Kiri.

The bell in the steeple now rang the end of intermission. Glynis gave Cullen a last glance, and took Kiri's arm.

"I imagine you've been seen by everyone now," she whispered as they made their way back to their seats. Kiri just nodded, her face fixed in a smile, though Glynis knew she must be even more apprehensive than she herself was. But Cullen had repeatedly said, "No harm can come to her—Jacques and I will keep Kiri in view every moment." So he had said.

Act four opened with the witches preparing their ghastly stew in a cauldron placed on the platform trap. The red hue cast by the footlights proved spectacular, especially when, in reply to Macbeth's demand for prophecy, the crones conjured the specter of a child. Glynis couldn't be sure how this was done, although feathery wisps of smoke—smoke now somehow under control—made the blood-dripping clay head of a child appear disembodied.

Did Farley recognize the analogy? Or was he too engrossed in other plots?

Drums rolled to cover the cauldron's noisy descent to the nether regions. Even without the supernatural, *Macbeth* would reek of evil, Glynis thought, suppressing a shudder. Evil let loose upon Scotland, ravaging and destroying in its grisly path. Surely she couldn't be the only one of the audience aware of Shakespeare's seventeenth-century lines made starkly contemporary by the reality of slavery in America:

> *"I think our country sinks beneath the yoke;*
> *It weeps, it bleeds, and each new day a gash*
> *Is added to her wounds."*

Again and again Glynis's eyes swept over the theater. She didn't really believe Farley could act now—but if not now, when? As soon as the play finished, the curtain calls and speeches over, she and Kiri were to meet Cullen and Jacques at the entrance doors. Still, she knew she had to be on guard against the unexpected. Glynis breathed easier, knowing the end of the play was near—by this time she knew *Macbeth* by heart—when Tavus in jeweled crown strode front and center:

> *"Tomorrow, and tomorrow, and tomorrow*
> *Creeps in this petty pace from day to day*
> *To the last syllable of recorded time,*
> *And all our yesterdays have lighted fools*
> *The way to dusty death."*

Glynis drew in her breath and apprehensively glanced around; Kiri grasped her wrist to give her a distressed, questioning look. Glynis shook her head slightly, quickly directing her gaze back to the stage to reassure Kiri, but in truth she had just experienced a spine-tingling sensation that Farley watched them both. Readying himself to move. It must be a false premonition, she told herself, brought on by the prophetic element in the play—nothing more. She must stop alarming Kiri. Yet she could barely sit still in the pew. Please let this be over.

And finally it was. Almost. Macduff entered with a long wooden pike upon which was impaled Macbeth's head—or a reasonable imitation in molded clay. Following enthusiastic applause, Seneca Falls' mayor came forward to deliver a lengthy speech. Then Vanessa, flushed and clearly buoyed by success, came forward to center stage. In the meantime Glynis noted uneasily that Tavus Sligh had not returned to the stage with the rest of the cast after the last bow.

". . . and to thank you all for this splendid reception," Vanessa said.

She waited for the applause to ebb, then continued, "It has always been a dream of mine to play Lady Macbeth. Now that I have done so, I will return the part to the far more talented actress who so kindly and graciously stepped aside for this performance. You have seen her tonight in the secondary role of Lady Macduff, but please welcome her return as Lady Macbeth: Calista Sligh."

Vanessa extended a hand to Calista at stage left, whose face as she came forward was a palette of inner conflict: jealousy, confusion, hostility, and gratitude—the last probably being the most galling for Calista. But yes, Glynis conceded; Vanessa did have her finer moments. The crowd's response to Vanessa's grand gesture crackled through the theater. Applause became a prolonged thunder.

This applause prevented Glynis from immediately comprehending what next occurred. She felt a sudden vibration, followed by an explosive roar that slammed her back against the pew. For the length of a heartbeat there followed an eerie silence. Then shouts rang out, cries of disbelief, the rising screams of the disoriented and the terrified.

Glynis grabbed for Kiri. Overhead a chandelier swayed wildly before it came crashing down into those seated directly in front of her; lighted candles flew like lethal birds, scattering sparks everywhere.

In the blood-red light from the stage, she saw Kiri struggling in the aisle, in danger of being swept away in the panicked stampede for the doors. But Glynis's glance shot beyond Kiri, and froze. A short distance up the aisle, Farley had materialized, his face unmasked by an expression of cold, restrained malevolence.

She screamed at Kiri, but a second explosion shook the theater again, hurling her to the floor. While groping frantically for Kiri's outstretched hand, she sensed someone behind her. Before Glynis could turn, her head burst with pain.

OUTSIDE THE DOORS of the theater Cullen Stuart, thrown to the ground by the force of the first explosion, slowly got to his feet. The second blast again flattened him face down.

He lay dazed until he felt something wet nuzzle the back of his neck. "What the hell . . . ?" He rolled over, spat dirt, and looked up into the woeful eyes of a bloodhound. Groggily, he lifted his head to see Jacques Sundown crouched a few feet away, gazing toward what had been the rectory.

Cullen leaned on the dog to help himself to his feet, then stood shakily, following Jacques's gaze. The rectory had become a smoking mountain of rubble. And a potent smell made Cullen's eyes water. It seemed to be a familiar enough odor, but it shouldn't be there. Cullen shook his head, realizing he still felt dazed.

What was that? He cocked his head to listen, thinking he'd heard a cry—a very faint one—coming from under the smoldering ruin. Jacques had sprung upright, and was at a run before Cullen steadied himself enough to follow.

"Someone inside?" Cullen yelled to him while stomping out fingers of flame beginning to curl around the collapsed timbers.

"Yeah, I think so," Jacques said, kicking away other pieces of lumber before they ignited.

Cullen paused beside Jacques. The rectory had fallen in on itself, and it would be next to impossible to quickly locate the source of the sound. Cullen again registered the disturbing smell, then heard the faint cry repeated.

He whirled around to shout at a few of the audience who had managed to get through the theater doors. "Hey! Over here! Give us a hand!"

Jacques had begun heaving timbers from the wreckage. But he abruptly stopped and bent down to pick up a short length of charred, hollow cord.

At the very edge of the rubble, one of the hounds whined, pawing at its muzzle. The other dog tossed its head and began to sneeze violently. Cullen stood staring at the dogs' reaction to the acrid odor, then shook his own head again to clear it.

And suddenly knew what had taken place. And almost surely why.

"Gunpowder!" he yelled. "It's gunpowder, Sundown— somebody blew up this place! Get to Glynis and the girl!" He turned to find Jacques gone. Cullen squinted through the smoke-hazed darkness to see him tearing toward the theater, deerskin boots barely touching the ground. The bloodhounds barked at his heels.

Cullen bent over to pick up the length of fuse Jacques had dropped in his flight and waited impatiently just long enough to direct the first men who straggled toward him. He pointed to the rectory debris. "Someone's under there! A few of you, go get the fire equipment—the rest start clearing away those timbers."

By the time he reached the front doors of the theater, he found them blocked with people trying to shove through. There were shouts of "It's the rectory!" He quickly searched for Glynis among those few outside, then dashed around the building to the backstage entrance. Jacques stood there, quietly eyeing the closed doors. He seemed to be listening.

"Dammit, Sundown!" Cullen shouted. "What's the problem with the doors?"

"Barred from inside."

Jacques's gaze suddenly jerked away from the theater, and he stared intently toward the canal. "It doesn't matter, anyway," he said softly to Cullen. "They're not inside."

"What d'you mean, they're not inside?" Cullen said brusquely. "They must—where the hell else could they be?" But he knew Jacques Sundown. If the man said they weren't there, they weren't there.

Jacques gave a slight shake of his head. "Don't know." He glanced down at the bloodhounds, which watched him expectantly, and said to Cullen, "You got that glove?"

Cullen scowled at him. "Glove? Oh; that! Yes." He pulled a black leather glove from his pocket. Thank God, Glynis had thought of getting it to him. Jacques finished tying a double lead around the necks of the bloodhounds, then took the glove from Cullen to wave it slowly under their noses.

The dogs sniffed at it furiously. They thrust their noses into the air, sniffed the glove again, and gave several joyful barks. Pulling at the lead in Jacques's hand, the dogs lunged toward the front of the theater.

GLYNIS HEARD HER name spoken over and over. Her head throbbed painfully. She just wanted to be left alone, but while swatting at the hand on her shoulder, she recognized Kiri's voice. Cautiously opening her eyes, she found herself stretched out on the carpeted floor. Kiri bent over her.

"Kiri," she mumbled, "what happened?"

"Get up!" Kiri whispered urgently. "He's around here somewhere—Farley is. Please get up, Glynis."

"How long have I been . . . like this?"

"Just a minute, Ah think," Kiri said.

Glynis could barely hear her over the shouts coming from the entrance of the theater. She sat up, rubbing the back of her head. Then holding the end of the pew, she pulled herself upright. Dizzy, her head aching, she stood there, staring at what surrounded them: a scene set in Hell.

Men whacked their swallowtail coats at candle sparks, while attempting to stamp out the small flames that licked the pews and apron of the stage. Red-tinged threads of smoke rose as the oil lamps continued to flicker diabolically. Several people lay groaning under the smashed chandelier; others, attempting to disengage them, cringed at the victims' sudden shrieks of pain.

Shadowy figures darted here and there, seeking some way out, and Glynis then saw that the entrance doors were hopelessly blocked by those who in panic pressed themselves forward against those trying to pull the doors open. Why don't the doors open *out*? thought Glynis distractedly—why hadn't Ian Bentham thought of that?

Kiri tugged at her sleeve, her voice anxious. "Glynis, we have to get away from here. Farley was the one who hit you. Then somebody yelled at him and he . . . Ah don't know what happened to him. Ah'd ducked behind the pew."

With a jolt, Glynis remembered Farley. They *did* have to get away from here. She thought frantically. Then twisted around to look for Serenity Hathaway. When she finally located the woman, Serenity was already halfway down the center aisle and moving toward the stage. Glynis took a step forward but, woozy and slightly nauseated, nearly fell. She paused to take several deep breaths.

"Kiri, go ahead of me. We have to get to that woman." She pointed up the aisle. Kiri brushed by her to run forward and grasp Serenity's arm. Glynis couldn't hear what Kiri said, but Serenity turned, waiting until Glynis, now weaving around those milling helplessly in the aisle, caught up.

"Miss Tryon—you want me?"

"Serenity," Glynis whispered, "we need your help . . . and I think you know how to get out of here. I can't explain now, but she—" Glynis motioned to Kiri "—may be in terrible danger." Glynis glanced around for Farley. But he was not to be seen. At least not yet.

Serenity's winged eyebrows lifted as her veil fell away from her face. Glynis heard Kiri's small sound of surprise— Serenity Hathaway was probably the most ravishing-looking woman on which Kiri had ever laid eyes. But Serenity rearranged her veil after a searching look at Glynis, as if to measure her sanity.

"Miss Tryon, I hope this is not going to involve something expensive," she said dryly. "The last time I got mixed up with you it lost me a lot of business—and a lot of money!"

All things considered, Glynis didn't know if she should apologize for this or not. "Serenity," she said quickly, "we really need your help. Please."

"All right then, c'mon," Serenity said just as quickly. "Up on the stage. And grab yourselves a light!"

They hoisted their skirts to climb the steps, and after scooping up oil lamps, Glynis and Kiri followed Serenity to the deserted center stage. The platform hung in its trap. It appeared to be positioned halfway between the stage floor and the basement below.

"How can we operate it from up here?" Glynis asked with urgency, glancing back down the aisle. No one seemed to be paying the least attention to them, but she expected at any moment to see Farley with a dagger in his hand.

"Can't," Serenity answered as she took hold of one of the ropes holding the platform. She pulled on it hard, apparently testing its strength. To Glynis's astonishment, the platform began to rise.

"Hallo, down there," Serenity shouted into the trap. "Just you wait now till we get on." She motioned to Glynis and Kiri. When they all three huddled on the platform, Serenity called, "Lower away, my boy!"

Kiri gasped as the platform wobbled, then jerked downward. Glynis would have gasped, but her breath caught in her throat. She gripped the edge of the descending platform until with a shake it came to a stop a few inches above the basement's dirt floor. From beside their perch, a handsome male face grinned at them.

"Good lad," Serenity smiled, stepping off the platform to pull back her veil and cover Brendan O'Reilly's grin with a swift kiss. "Now you just shinny back up that rope—same way you got down—and help those folks above. But you cut those ropes when you get up there, you hear me? Don't want anybody following us."

"But Serenity—" Brendan protested.

"Go ahead, now," Serenity urged. "Get your sweet ass moving—begging your pardon, Miss Tryon. Well, get now, Brendan. You'll get thanked proper later."

She gestured for Glynis and Kiri to follow. Clutching their lamps and their skirts, they squeezed through a small door, all but concealed in the basement wall, to climb down a short flight of rickety wooden stairs. A narrow, stone-lined tunnel stretched before them.

They entered it single file. As Glynis ducked her head to accommodate the tunnel's less-than-five-foot height, she wondered how many runaway slaves this had protected since its construction. The stones glistened with moisture; she, Kiri and Serenity must now be far underground. Where would they emerge—at the canal towpath?

Just ahead of Glynis, Serenity called over her shoulder, "Never thought I'd see you in such an unlikely situation, Miss Tryon. Compromising, some might say."

To Glynis's startled "What?" Serenity laughed, answering, "You wait and see where we come out."

Some minutes and a short ascent up stairs later, Serenity paused to push open a door. They stepped through it into a candle-lit room that smelled strongly of perfume and whiskey. Heavy red draperies and ornate, velvet-cushioned chaise lounges confirmed what Glynis had already guessed: they were inside Serenity's Tavern. And not only the tavern. They were now standing in what had to be the brothel's downstairs. Glynis winced.

"Didn't you ever get to wondering," Serenity said as she removed her hat, "how that randy ole man-of-the-cloth ever got over here from the church without anybody spying him?"

Glynis, swallowing her dignity, said, "Yes, as a matter of fact, I did."

Serenity laughed. Kiri managed a wan smile.

"When I bought this place, owner said the tunnel had been built for runaway slaves. Guess we better get you ladies out of here though, before you earn yourselves a reputation." Serenity glanced around the deserted room. "Probably they're all upstairs, anyway."

She went across the room to another door. Stopping to peer through the open window beside it, she said, "This'll let you out in back of the tavern. Nobody's there now. But you mind telling me," she said, turning to Kiri, "who's chasing you? You a runaway, maybe?"

Kiri shook her head. "Ah'm not a slave," she said, "least not anymore." Her voice broke off, and she looked at Glynis. "Ah heard Farley," she said abruptly. "Ah heard him inside the theater. He didn't think Ah saw him hit you, and he started talking to me—told me he could get me out."

Glynis moved to take her hand. "You recognized his voice?"

Serenity looked at her with a puzzled expression. But naturally she did, Glynis thought; Serenity couldn't know who Farley was.

"Yes," Kiri said. "Ah knew his voice then. He had a way of talking that sounded steady, sort of like a drumbeat. Ah finally remembered it back there," she motioned toward the theater, "and Ah *did* see him early on today, when Ah was with you. Ah just didn't recognize his face then."

Kiri stopped, interrupted by a sudden burst of air as the outer door flew open.

Farley stepped into the room.

"Well, well," said Serenity, looking greatly surprised, "fancy seeing *you* here. But sorry, all my girls are busy tonight. And these two are sure not for hire!"

The man smiled. Glynis could feel Kiri tremble, and she squeezed the young woman's hand. But she could also feel her own fear soaring and fought it down, telling herself he couldn't kill all three of them.

"I'm not here for that, Miss Hathaway," he said. "I happened to see these two ladies leave the theater."

And he obviously knew where they were going. But how . . . how did he know about the church tunnel, and that it led *here*? Glynis asked herself. Then with awful realization she remembered: of course he would know.

". . . and I thought," he was saying, "they might want an escort to more suitable surroundings. I have my carriage just outside."

Glynis felt herself go stone cold. *The man was mad. Evil. "In blood stepp'd in so far."* But she knew that, thankfully for her, this cold meant numbness. That now she would be all right. That her voice wouldn't shake when she said brightly, "Oh, how very kind. And thank you, but we're waiting for the constable."

She turned to look intently at Kiri. "You remember, don't you, Kiri? I told Constable Sundown we were coming here?" To Serenity's? The man would never believe that, but it was the best she could do.

Kiri's expression didn't alter. Only her eyes did, widening for an instant before she nodded.

"Really, Miss Tryon, I insist," he said. Then reached for Kiri's arm. "Let me at the very least get this young woman home. No offense, Miss Hathaway, but this is hardly the place for a lady." Gently, almost imperceptibly, he began to draw Kiri toward him.

Kiri braced her feet and shrank back against Glynis, clutching her hand tightly. Serenity, whose eyes had narrowed as the man spoke, now looked at him closely. "If Miss Tryon says she wants to wait, mister, then—"

She paused at a sound outside the window; the shrill penetrating sound of dogs baying.

Please Lord, let them find us; Glynis's inner eye moved to the towpath. Jacques must be there, and Cullen too. But how far away were they?

The man might remain calm, she reasoned, believing no one knew of his past. That he had no reason to fear. Or would he, still gripping Kiri's arm, be thrown into panic? Glynis stared past him at the open window. Through it she could hear the dogs' exhilarated howls, and she thought of five-year-old Kiri's night of terror in the woods, and of the irony in blood-hounds now tracking *him*.

He might have been thinking the same thing, because his face had grown pale under a sheen of perspiration. Still, his voice sounded steady enough when he said to Kiri, "Apparently the constable had the same idea as I. But since my carriage is right here, I urge you to take advantage of it. Please do come with me."

Kiri shook her head. Her doe eyes glittered, were unnaturally dark, and Glynis feared for her strength. This man, *this man,* had had her mother killed, and the man her mother loved, right before her eyes. Her infant brother had been left for dead. How much more of this could Kiri endure?

The baying came closer. By now the dogs must smell their quarry ahead. Still holding Kiri, who twisted in his grasp, the man stepped uncertainly toward the door. Glynis could almost see the indecision in his mind—should he rely on his social position and stand his ground, or cut and run? Hurry! her mind directed Jacques. Hurry!

Kiri gave a faint cry as the man abruptly pulled her behind him through the door. But she didn't resist. Good, Glynis thought; just try to delay him. Stall him long enough—

Serenity followed the man and Kiri through the door, saying, "Hey, hold on a minute there, mister!"

"Serenity," Glynis whispered, plunging through the door to seize the woman's arm. "Don't! Don't alarm him. He's dangerous."

"You said it, lady—he acts crazy!" Serenity stated loudly.

The man turned toward them, his face now flush-colored by the moon that had just appeared over trees on the far side of the canal. A blood-red, nearly full, harvest moon. Hanging huge in the night sky, it looked unreal, nightmarish, and Glynis suddenly felt disoriented, as if she were on a stage somewhere, taking part in a Halloween drama. Halloween: the night the witches ride. The netherworld of dead souls and goblins released for vengeance. And the Devil let loose on the land.

"Farley!" came Cullen's shout from the towpath. Glynis couldn't see him yet, but the dogs' panting sounded close. The man whirled around just as they became visible, emerging from under low tree limbs—the hounds, Jacques, and Cullen.

Behind her, Glynis heard Serenity Hathaway draw breath sharply, her skirts swishing as if she shook them in annoyance. Then, with the loud clear voice of logic, Serenity announced, "This is bad for business! I'm going inside."

She stormed back into the tavern, the door slamming shut behind her.

"Farley!" Still yards away, Cullen paused on the towpath. "Farley, listen to me."

The dogs stood whining softly, while Glynis prayed the situation might yet be controlled. Maybe the man would just give up. Surrender now that he'd been exposed, his real name known. What did he have to gain by resisting, or by hurting Kiri?

Cullen stayed where he had stopped. "Farley, we need to talk."

"Why?" the man asked. "What's the matter?"

"Well, for starters," Cullen said, his voice almost matter-of-fact, "I'd like to see you let go of that girl."

"Just going to give her a ride home," the man answered. He shoved his right hand into his coat pocket, still holding Kiri's arm with his left.

Glynis stood closer to him now than anyone, close enough to see that Kiri had begun to shake. Didn't the man realize Cullen had called him "Farley"? That they all *knew*?

"I don't think," Cullen said reasonably, "that the girl wants to go anywhere with you."

"No!" Kiri suddenly screamed. "No. Let me go!"

Stumbling forward, she squirmed from the man's grasp but, when Glynis took a step forward to reach for her, he snatched Kiri from behind. Thrusting his arm over her left shoulder he grabbed her wrists; with his right hand he pulled a knife from his pocket, shoving the blade against her throat.

As Kiri cried out Glynis started toward her again, but the man jerked Kiri between them. "Stay there! All of you—just stay where you are." With this he backed up against the tavern, Kiri locked against his chest.

"What is it you want?" Cullen asked. He'd managed to move a little closer, and Jacques had stealthily inched a short distance to Cullen's left. Behind the two men, the dogs now lay quietly, heads on their front paws, their tongues lolling.

"What d'you want?" Cullen repeated. "Because it's over, Farley. Finished. We know about you—almost everything there is to know."

Glynis watched Cullen take several, almost invisible, steps forward while he continued talking. "The cabin where Brogan was found," he went on, his voice as level as if he carried on a normal conversation, "sits on land the bank owns. Bank owns the fairgrounds where you hid the woman's body—and we've got the deeds to prove it. Why'd you kill her? You afraid Brogan told her he meant to blackmail you? And that poor old man. He would've recognized you, wouldn't he?

"You can't just walk off, you know—not with those murders on your hands, you can't. To say nothing of blowing up the rectory with somebody inside. That was some diversion, that was."

The man didn't appear to be listening; his expression indicated he might already be a hundred miles away. "Let me get to my carriage," he said, although his voice sounded less steady now. "Let me leave with the girl. I'll let her go when I'm sure you're not following me."

"No, afraid not," Cullen said. "You want to go somewhere else, lose yourself out west maybe, and change your name again? No, this is it. Right now. You release the girl, and come forward. I guarantee you a fair trial—that's all I can do. And that's more than you gave those folks you killed."

The man gave a harsh laugh. "You sound as if you think I enjoyed it," he said. "I didn't want to kill them. I *had* to."

Dear God; he sounded like Macbeth. Glynis fought hysteria, and the overwhelming need to flee. But the tension couldn't be borne by any of them much longer, not without someone doing something reckless. She knew Cullen, steady and resolute, would continue trying to talk Farley into surrendering, but the man held a knife against Kiri's throat! He had little more to lose by killing her. And when would he remember it was Kiri brought him to this pass, this turn-around of fortune? He had been so close to power . . . when did he go mad with wanting it?

Cullen took a step forward, his hand brushing the Colt in his holster.

"Stand back!" the man shouted. "I'll cut her throat, I swear I will. Should've done it back then, years ago. But I . . . I'm not an animal like Brogan. Couldn't bring myself to kill a child." He laughed again, a harsh bark of sound. "And just look what that brought me!"

He shifted the knife against Kiri's neck. Then he seemed to freeze in place as from up the towpath came the rapid drumming of hoofbeats. Cullen didn't take his eyes off the man and Kiri. He didn't look around even when Isaiah Smith reined in his sweating Morgan. Jacques, now crouching silently, kept his eyes fixed too on the killer, waiting for the opportunity to strike. But if he did, even as fast as he was, would Kiri survive?

"Found the one trapped in the blown-up building," Isaiah said as he dismounted.

"Stay back," Cullen said to him sharply.

Isaiah stood where he was. "She'd died by the time we got to her," he said. "Killed *her*, too, he did." Isaiah turned aside and spat. "Bastard killed his own wife!"

"No," the man murmured. "No, not Deirdre . . . no." His voice came with anguish, his face contorted in what had to be grief. The knife flashed, and terror swept Glynis as she saw a dark trickle spill over Kiri's collar. Kiri went limp. She sagged against the man's arm like a rag doll.

In his distress, he'd taken several steps sideways, so he now stood backed against the open window. Suddenly an arm shot out through the opening, grabbing the man's knife hand to pull it away from Kiri's throat. In an instant, Kiri had bitten down on the arm holding her. With a yell, the man released her and, shoving her aside, he spun to face the window. Reaching through it, he dragged out a struggling Zeph.

Glynis's clenched hands flew to press against her mouth. They had all told Zeph to stay away! He must have followed Cullen and Jacques, then crept round to the front of the tavern—and Serenity must have let him in.

Jacques had stealthily crept forward and in the moonlight Glynis saw his knife blade glint. His arm lifted, poised, then hesitated.

"Jacques, don't!" Cullen shouted. Zeph's back was to them while he fought to keep the man's raised knife from his throat. The boy's knee jerked up into the other's groin, and the knife plunged down as Zeph wrenched to one side, away from the blade. Then the two locked together as one. Glynis pressed her mouth in a mute scream. Suddenly a dreadful groan rent the near-silence. She couldn't tell which one had made the blood-chilling sound. As Cullen and Jacques both rushed forward, Zeph staggered a few feet, then sank to his knees.

Glynis got to him first. She knelt and gathered him to her, conscious of warm blood on her hands as she rocked him gently back and forth. Zeph's stillness seemed as if it would last forever. But after a long moment, he pulled himself back from her. "I'm O.K., Miss Tryon. I'm O.K. Just got cut on my arm." He held it up for her to see, the blood already beginning to congeal over the wound.

A short distance from them, the man they had known as Michael Olivant lay sprawled face up. Blood seeped from his mouth to froth over his lips, and his breath came shallow and fast. Jacques bent over him to pull the knife from his chest.

Getting to her feet, Glynis turned away. Then looked for Kiri. The young woman stood at the edge of the towpath, leaning against an old tree trunk, her face lifted like that of an awed child's as she gazed at the moon. But Glynis could see her shoulders shaking, the wetness of her cheeks glistening, and she assumed the boy standing beside her could see this too.

"Zeph?" Glynis said, gesturing to Kiri. He took a step toward the towpath. But then he hesitated and shook his head.

"Go to her," Glynis whispered. Zeph looked bewildered,

his eyes bright with tears, and Glynis reached for his hand. "It's over, Zeph. It's really over. The past is dead. Your mother and father have been avenged—and you are finally, and truly, free. But Kiri . . . Kiri needs you, Zeph."

And nodding, he went to his sister, and folded her inside his arms.

TWENTY

∽

The wind blows to the south and goes round to the north
                                                —ECCLESIASTES

REVEREND EAMES'S WHITE clerical collar encircled his neck
in a chaste embrace. He ran a finger inside the linen band and
cleared his throat. " 'Man, that is born of a woman, hath but
a short time to live, and is full of misery. He cometh up, and
is cut down, like a flower; he fleeth as it were a shadow.' "

Standing inside a dilapidated wrought-iron fence, on a low
hill overlooking the Seneca River, Glynis drew her cloak
tighter as a sharp gust of wind sliced through her. Cullen beside her pulled up the collar of his black frock coat. Around
the pallbearers lowering two coffins into the ground, a few
snowflakes eddied like small pale leaves. Indian summer had
at last fled south with the gray geese. The November twilight
now shifted relentlessly toward winter.

" 'And the places that knew them shall know them no
more.' "

They were burying Deirdre and Michael Olivant the day
following their deaths: All Saints' Day. Glynis wondered if
any of the very few gathered at the old neglected burying
ground recognized this one final irony. She looked up at
Reverend Eames, who stood with his *Book of Common
Prayer*, its pages ruffling in the wind, beside the two freshly
dug piles of earth. This was a good man, she thought. A
man of God. No other minister had offered to perform even
this briefest of rituals, or so Deirdre's uncle from Auburn
had told her earlier while they followed up the hill the pallbearers that he'd hired.

" 'Earth to earth, ashes to ashes, dust to dust.' "

As they started the walk back to the road, Glynis glanced
at those present. Other than Reverend Eames and the pallbearers, and herself and Cullen, only the Auburn uncle and Deirdre's housekeeper had come. A sparse gathering indeed.

Especially since she and Cullen were there solely to find the last piece of the puzzle that had been Thomas Farley/Michael Olivant.

Once she learned the man's history, Glynis regarded his moving to the very place where he'd been involved in the murder of Kiri's mother as nothing short of incredible. In fact, it had been the one thing that initially kept her from believing her own theory about Olivant. It was just too improbable a coincidence, she'd told Cullen.

It hadn't been, though. A calloused move, yes, but not coincidental. Deirdre's family, after all, were Virginia Rochesters, and the Rochesters had settled in a number of western New York towns. Deirdre's uncle owned land in Seneca Falls, which he'd deeded to his niece and nephew-in-law as a wedding present. And had loaned Michael Olivant the money to buy into the Red Mills Trust.

As they reached the foot of the hill, Glynis saw Jacques Sundown on his paint, waiting beside the carriage in which she and Cullen had come. He would no doubt ride back with them. She would have no chance to ask Cullen the question foremost in her mind: when he planned to leave for Cleveland. He had not yet said a word about this himself.

Starting back into town, they all three were silent for a time. Cullen drove the carriage horse slowly while Jacques rode alongside, and Glynis, glancing up at him, thought he had a faraway look. She sensed a sadness about him, as on the afternoon she'd come back from Richmond. But with Jacques it always proved so hard to tell.

Finally Cullen, beside her on the carriage seat, turned to ask, "When did you first believe Michael Olivant might be Thomas Farley?"

Glynis thought a moment. "I guess on the train, returning from Richmond. Yes, it was then, because I recalled an angry scene at the agricultural fair between Ian Bentham and Tavus Sligh. It seemed clear to me, from what Bentham and Sligh said that afternoon, that both of them—and Eebard Peck, too—had known each other previously. Later I learned they'd served in the Army together at the time of the Mexican War.

"In his campaign speech that day at the fair, Michael

Olivant lauded his own war record, and at the time there was no reason to question it—I just assumed that he'd served with the Fourth New Yorkers. But when I asked Ian Bentham if he'd known Olivant then, Bentham said he hadn't. Nor, when I later inquired, had Tavus Sligh. This really didn't mean a great deal to me then. Olivant might simply have been in a different New York division."

Cullen's hands tightened slightly on the reins as he turned the trotter onto the canal towpath. For a moment it looked to Glynis as though Jacques didn't intend to ride into town with them, but then the paint swerved to walk alongside the carriage once more. And it seemed odd; whenever possible, Jacques usually went his own way. Glynis felt uneasy. Could Jacques sense that Cullen would be gone from them shortly?

"Chantal Dupont told me in Richmond," she went on, "that she'd heard Thomas Farley served in the Army during the Mexican War, and had afterward disappeared. Of those men who had come to Seneca Falls since that war ended, Bentham, Sligh, Peck, and Olivant were the ones I suspected might be Farley. But since your notes, Cullen, confirmed that Tavus and Ian Bentham and Eebard Peck had a shared history, it meant that none of them could have changed his name during or since the war.

"Michael Olivant had by far the most to lose should his history be revealed. Running for political office on the ticket of the new Republican party, with its strong abolition platform, Olivant would have been ruined had his past been made public. He had no doubt changed his name precisely for that reason, before he and his wife came to live in Seneca Falls."

There *was* the matter of Tavus Sligh's dagger, but Calista Sligh had belatedly verified her husband's account of the weapon's disappearance. She'd apparently decided, after Vanessa's magnanimous gesture at the theater, that Vanessa had no serious designs on Tavus. But Calista had certainly managed to frighten her husband badly that day at the fair, and Glynis found the woman's retaliation for her husband's roving eye rather apt.

Of course, Olivant could have taken Tavus's dagger at any

time. His presence would not be questioned anywhere; he was a leading citizen, a candidate for political office, a bank president. And, as she'd remembered last night, naturally Olivant knew about the Underground tunnel—his bank certainly had the architectural plans for the church, because it had owned the building for some time.

"Both of you," Cullen nodded to Glynis and Jacques, "apparently suspected the murder weapon had been left in the woman's body to implicate Sligh—after it was used to kill both her and Brogan that night. But why'd you think it was Olivant who did it?" Cullen glanced up at Jacques.

Jacques grunted softly. "She—" he looked at Glynis "—told me to check land deeds in Waterloo. Found out the bank owned the land that cabin was on. Olivant must have told Brogan to stay there. Maybe even said he'd meet Brogan there next morning."

"Yes," Glynis agreed. "Olivant must have planned to kill Brogan when they first saw each other the day of the theater dedication. So Olivant probably *insisted* Brogan use the cabin," she added, "as the least he could do for his old 'colleague.' After he'd murdered Brogan, Olivant went after Luella. Since they had been together that night—and Olivant had plenty of opportunity to see them, as I did—he assumed, as you guessed, Cullen, that Brogan had let Luella in on his blackmail scheme. And Olivant couldn't take the chance that Luella knew about him."

The proof of Olivant's name change came when Glynis wired Cullen asking him to see if the War Department records showed a discharge bonus paid to a Thomas Farley—probably in a Virginia Division, she speculated. And this had proved to be the case. The records disclosed this payment had been made, as Jeremiah Merrycoyf predicted, in the usual form of a land grant.

Most important, however, the records showed that the land grant awarded to Thomas Farley in 1848 had three years later been sold. The seller's name on the deed: Michael Olivant. Current address: East Bayard Street, Seneca Falls.

They had him. But as Glynis said to Cullen: how could they prove that he'd murdered?

"Do you think Brogan traced Farley—Olivant—through

the War Department like you did, Cullen?" Glynis asked now.

"I doubt we'll ever know," Cullen answered, scowling somewhat—Glynis knew he didn't like unknowns. "He certainly could have," Cullen went on, "or seen the western New York newspaper stories following Olivant's political candidacy—in Brogan's eyes, a candidacy for blackmail."

Earlier, while driving to the burying ground, Cullen insisted Deirdre must have known of her husband's past. Glynis tended to agree. And while they had been married in 1849 under the name of Olivant, Deirdre had been as ambitious as her husband. If she knew of his past, she also knew it could come back to haunt him: Banquo's ghost at the feast. She would hardly oppose a change of name before their marriage.

As to whether Deirdre had known of the Seneca Falls murders—either before or after they were committed—Glynis and Cullen disagreed. Cullen argued, "She must have; she was his wife!"

As though they'd been joined at the hip! thought Glynis, frowning. Cullen believed too that when Michael Olivant blew up the rectory, he knew his wife was inside. She had either gone with him or followed him there after the play, during the speeches, when he apparently lit the fuse. It might be possible, Cullen conceded, she'd gone there to dissuade him; or to extinguish the fuse after he left. In that case, the rectory blew before she could escape.

Glynis thought this last could be plausible. Despite Michael Olivant's murderous ambition, he had seemed genuinely shocked, and grieved, to hear of his wife's death. But it seemed equally plausible that, after Kiri arrived back in town, Deirdre realized the deception was unraveling. That her husband would probably hang, and her humiliation be more than she could bear. She might, therefore, have preferred death to disgrace. This wouldn't have been a unique preference.

They would never be sure of that, either. Glynis sighed, watching the first houses of Seneca Falls come into view. Cullen gestured ahead in the direction of The Usher Playhouse. "Seems like the theater came through the explosion all right."

"Yes," Glynis said. "I saw Ian Bentham and Vanessa this morning and Bentham said, rather proudly, that there'd been no structural damage. Just a few cracks." She gave Cullen a small smile. "But Vanessa vowed that 'that play' would never be performed in her theater again! The whole disaster, she's positive, can be traced directly to the curse of *Macbeth*. She's convinced of it."

Cullen shook his head and glanced up at Jacques, although Glynis noticed that Jacques again seemed elsewhere. "Well, at least," she said, "no one in the theater got seriously injured. Broken bones only, Dr. Ives said, from the falling chandelier."

She almost took back her words, changing them to "physically injured." Elizabeth Stanton had been heartbroken, as had other women and men, when she learned of her candidate's murderous history. Glynis now believed Olivant had been using women's concerns—and their husband's votes—to gain election, and had no intention of honoring his campaign promise to them. It certainly wouldn't be the first time a political candidate had done this.

Cullen now pulled the trotter to a stop in front of the library. And Glynis realized he still hadn't said when he would be leaving Seneca Falls. She felt desperation, which she resolutely stifled. She was, she thought, probably like any other woman who watched a man readying to do something that she was powerless to stop.

THE NEXT AFTERNOON Glynis dipped her pen into the leaded-glass inkwell on her library desk, then signed the just completed letter. A letter to Chantal and Masika at Riverain.

She sat back and rubbed her eyes, then with her fingers felt her head gently. The small lump still hurt. Shivering slightly, she pulled her fringed shawl more tightly around her shoulders. November had the shifting moods of April. Tomorrow it could be warmer again. But today the tall windows were shut fast against a blustery wind. Even as she watched, a few fat snowflakes pasted themselves to the panes.

She picked up the letter lying on the desk; what might she have left out—other than the identity of the contemptible person informing on runaways? That had not been resolved. The threat remained constant, Glynis worried, gazing again toward the snow-flecked windows.

She glanced at the letter a last time. Masika would already know that her granddaughter and Niles had left for Montreal to be married, and Glynis had enclosed the address of Niles's new gallery. And wrote that she'd told Zeph to expect his grandmother in Seneca Falls for Thanksgiving. Now, Glynis thought dejectedly as she sealed the envelope, she had nothing else to distract her, no reason to put off thinking about Cullen's departure.

She didn't know how she could survive another parting.

On a gust of biting air the library door suddenly burst open, and Glynis looked up to see Zeph sprinting toward her desk. Behind him loped Jacques's two bloodhounds. Nearly out of breath, he panted, "Miss Tryon, you need to go to the railroad station, right now!"

"Zeph, why?"

"Constable Stuart wants you. C'mon!"

Zeph backed away, then turned and ran to the door. After another *"C'mon!"* he dashed out, dogs galloping at his heels, banging the door behind him before Glynis could gather her wits to question him further.

"I'm sorry, Jonathan," she said, taking her cloak from a hook, "I have to leave—again! This time I'll be back soon."

Hair once more like a rat's nest, Jonathan smiled happily and gave her an absentminded nod. He'd already turned back to his file cards when she tore out the door. It had suddenly occurred to her that Cullen might be leaving.

AT FIRST THE wind whipped the cloak around her ankles; but it gradually calmed, as did the flurry of snow, by the time she reached the station house and saw a handful of six or seven people gathered outside. Their faces, what she could see of them, looked positively grim. Jacques Sundown stood a short distance away, holding the harness of a mule. A mule?

And where was Cullen?

Although now approaching dusk, no last train was in sight.

Had Cullen already left—without even saying good-bye?
Frantically she looked around, and drew a shaky breath of relief when she saw him standing with Dr. Ives. But beside him
sat a valise.

Spotting her, Cullen motioned her forward. When Glynis
got to him, she found Jennie there, strangely silent and staring
at Cullen's badge. The small crowd had separated to allow
Glynis through, and now she could see a man's body
sprawled face up on the cobblestones.

Although Glynis could see no blood, Eebard Peck didn't
appear to be breathing.

"Cullen?" The numbness of shock returned. All this death.
All in a few short months. "Cullen?" she said again. "What
happened?"

"Look at his head," Cullen gestured at Eebard's prone figure. "Left temple."

She looked, turned away, then slowly turned back for another look. On Eebard's temple was a dull red half-moon that
looked carved into his balding head. The outline had become
somewhat swollen around its edge, but there could be no mistaking what it was: a hoofprint.

"Seems as though Eebard's mule finally got fed up," Cullen said.

"Are you serious?" Glynis asked. How inane—of course
he'd been serious. He wouldn't joke about such a thing.

And Dr. Ives's face looked anything but humorous when he
stated, "Must have been quite a blow! Wonder what brought
it on?"

Glynis then looked at Jennie. "Were you here when this
happened?"

Jennie blinked.

"She won't talk," Cullen said. "Hoped she might tell you,
but I guess not. You folks can go along now," he told those
standing around to view Eebard's misfortune with morbid interest. "You can read about it in the paper."

As all, including a reluctant Zeph and the hounds, straggled
off, repeatedly looking back over their shoulders, Cullen
turned to Glynis to mutter, "They can if we figure out how
this happened, that is. Quentin," he said to Dr. Ives, "you ever
hear of this kind of thing before?"

"David and Goliath," Quentin Ives declared soberly.

"What?"

"Bible . . . Old Testament. Boy killed a warrior with a pebble and slingshot. Blow to the temple. It'll do the job, all right."

"Quentin, that mule is no boy with dead aim. You really think—"

"Mule kicked him," Jennie said suddenly.

"Yes, that's what must have happened—a freak accident," Ives agreed, obviously not reacting to Jennie's words with the same surprise Glynis experienced.

"Jennie," she said, "can you tell us why . . . why the mule kicked Eebard Peck? Was he hurting it?" But that would be nothing new.

"Yes, he hurt it. They wouldn't give him money."

"Who, Jennie? Who wouldn't give Eebard Peck money?"

"Them." Jennie walked up to Cullen and poked at his badge.

"Lawmen, right?" Cullen said to her.

Of course . . . of course!

"What's she saying?" Quentin Ives said, staring at Jennie.

"I think what she means," Glynis explained, "is that for some time now Eebard Peck had been receiving money—blood money—from U.S. marshals in return for information about runaway slaves. And after all his abolition posturing. What a vile hypocrite!" She gazed down at the man on the cobblestones, realizing but not in the least regretting she'd just done the inexcusable in speaking ill of the dead.

Nonetheless, she continued a bit less imprudently. "Jacques and I've suspected it might perhaps be Eebard, so we—that is, I—started to do some investigating. Through a friend."

"I don't think I want to know who," Cullen said.

"Well, I wasn't going to tell you anyway." Especially since it had been Jonathan Quant's cousin; a teller in the Red Mills Trust.

"On second thought, who was it?" Cullen said.

Glynis thought she'd best ignore this. "It seems that

Eebard Peck had a large—a very large—amount of money in his bank account. I checked the dates of the deposits."

"How did you get those?" Cullen demanded. "Glynis, that's confidential information and—"

"Do you want to hear this, Cullen?" she interrupted.

He scowled at her, but nodded.

"The dates of Eebard's recent deposits, since February that is, matched up roughly with the dates I knew runaways had been caught. I suspected Eebard mostly because of his sudden prosperity—which I did not attribute to the magic of fertilizer, as he claimed—and because he found reason to visit this rail station so often." She added, "Frederick Douglass told me to look for someone like that.

"But it wasn't until about a week ago—the day I got back from Richmond, and Jennie said something queer about Eebard—that I was anywhere near sure."

She took a deep breath. "But we still don't know what happened here today." She turned to Jennie, who stood apparently listening. "Does what I just said about Eebard Peck, does that sound right, Jennie?"

Jennie bobbed her head.

Cullen looked skeptical, however. "O.K. So let's say Peck was an informer. And I agree it sounds like it. But why'd his mule kick him in the head?"

"He kicked the *mule*," Jennie said. "He got no money. From them." She pointed again to Cullen's badge.

"Eebard got mad?" Cullen said to her, "so he kicked the mule? And the mule kicked him back?"

Jennie's head bobbed. "Throwed out a back leg, that mule did . . . hit the bad man in the head." She looked down at Eebard, and a peculiar expression, both poignant and reflective, crossed her face. "He's dead, isn't he?" she asked Glynis abruptly.

"Oh, he's certainly that," Quentin Ives said.

But Glynis, who had been watching Jennie's eyes, didn't think she meant Eebard Peck. "Yes, Jennie," she said now. "Yes, Jamie is dead. I'm so very sorry, but he is."

Jennie's eyes widened, and her thin body seemed to jerk into rigidity. For a long moment she resembled a stick figure in a child's drawing. But when Glynis stepped toward her,

Jennie shook herself and, jabbering something incoherent, skittered off to disappear around the corner of the station house.

In distress Glynis stared after her, while Cullen and Jacques went about loading Eebard's body into his wagon. Quentin Ives climbed to the seat, and gave the reins a light flick over the mule's back. The mule brayed softly. Without hesitation it began plodding toward Fall Street.

From up the track came a long whistle. Glynis suddenly remembered Cullen's valise: he must be leaving on the incoming train!

Jacques Sundown disappeared into the station house, as she walked to Cullen. What could she do? She couldn't keep him here, and she couldn't go with him. Unless she married him . . . and maybe he didn't even want that anymore. But if he asked her again? She might reconsider—yes, she might do that.

She gazed up at him, not aware until then that he'd been talking to her.

". . . and it was a mistake," Cullen finished.

A mistake? What mistake? thought Glynis with cold anxiety. Was he saying it had been a mistake to come back?

"I shouldn't have done it," Cullen said emphatically, his face buffeted to a ruddy glow by the wind, his eyes in the dim twilight almost black.

Tears spurted predictably, but Glynis swiped at her eyes, trying to conceal her distress.

"Glynis, what's wrong?" Cullen said. "You know, I don't think I remember you crying so much before."

"I *didn't* cry much before," she blurted. "It's only been since you left!" The last remnant of dignity gone, her pride in tatters, she whirled toward the street.

"Glynis!" Cullen grasped her arm and stepped in front of her. "What the hell . . . ? I just said it was a mistake! Now listen to me and I'll say it again: *It was a mistake.*" He shook her gently. "You hear me now?"

Though the words came indistinctly, she heard them. Blinking tears back, she said, "What was a mistake?"

Looking frustrated, Cullen sighed heavily. "Pressing you to marry me. It was wrong. I should have known better, you've told me enough times. And you've got every right . . . not to marry. As I said, I won't bring it up again!"

Glynis abruptly felt an inexplicable disappointment.

"If you'd listened a minute ago," Cullen said, his voice patient, "you'd have heard me tell you I handed in my resignation to Pinkerton—two weeks before I got your wire."

She forced herself to keep joy at arm's length, for fear she had misunderstood him.

"You mean," she said hesitantly, "you're not going back? You're staying here?"

"Didn't you notice my badge?" He pointed to it. "How could you miss it, what with Jennie and all?"

How *could* she have missed it? Had she been that distraught? "But Cullen, what about your valise? I saw *that*," she added.

"Valise? What valise? Oh, that!" he said smiling. "It's Jacques's."

"Jacques's? He's leaving? Why? Where is he going?"

Cullen shrugged. "You know Jacques. Dagwunnoyaent—his spirit goes where the wind takes him. And he probably figures that since I'm back, he's out of a job. Which isn't true, but try telling him."

He said this as Jacques, a train ticket in his hand, emerged from the station house.

"You really going to do this?" Cullen said to him. "It's not necessary—town's big enough now for two constables."

Stunned, Glynis found herself babbling, "Yes . . . yes, Jacques, we *need* two constables. I mean . . . well, just look at what's been going on around here. . . ." Her voice trailed off. That hadn't been the most sensible thing to say, but then, this made no sense.

Jacques looked up the track where the train had come into sight. He reached down for his valise, and took a few steps away from them.

Glynis followed him. "Jacques, why should you leave? And besides, what are you going to do with your dogs?" But as soon as this left her lips she knew the answer.

"Gave 'em to the boy. It seemed right."

"I don't understand this, Jacques. You shouldn't leave."

Jacques stared down at her. "Why?"

"Because . . ." She found herself without words. Why indeed shouldn't Jacques leave? Why did she care what he did? "Well, because," she finally offered, "we need you here. And where will you go?"

Jacques took a deep breath and she thought he wouldn't answer. Then, "To see my mother."

His mother? "I didn't know she was still alive, Jacques." What *did* she know about this man? "Where is your mother?"

"Reservation."

"Oh. Well, after you've seen her, are you coming back here?"

"Don't think so."

She fell silent as the train roared in and screeched to a stop. A few passengers got off. Jacques walked to the bottom of the steps and Cullen followed to put a hand on his shoulder. "Take care of yourself," Cullen said quietly.

The conductor climbed back up onto the train platform, where he stood staring pointedly down at Jacques. Jacques nodded once to Cullen. And looked at Glynis. Her breath caught when she thought she saw again the intense blue-green warmth appear behind his eyes. If so, it vanished in an instant.

"Jacques," she said softly, "I wish you would consider coming back."

He turned to mount the steps. When he got to the platform, he took a step into the passenger car, then hesitated, and turned back to look down at Glynis.

"I'll consider."

Then he was gone.

They stood watching as the train began to pull out. Now almost dark, inside the passenger cars gas lamps flickered, but when Glynis searched for Jacques, she couldn't find him. She leaned back into the surety of Cullen's shoulder, solid and warm.

Glynis felt him pull taut. Following his gaze, she looked up at the train windows to see a Negro man standing inside a slowly passing car. A young man, healthy and strong-looking, he swayed in the aisle with the motion of the train. Two white men stood close to him, one on either side, and the badges on their jackets reflected the yellow lamplight.

Then the train moved on.

When Cullen took her arm, they walked without speaking toward Fall Street. The air still held a smell of burning leaves. Overhead the moon broke through thin clouds, and silhouetted against it, Glynis saw a large night bird circling. Then, with a dip of dark wing, it changed course.

To escape a sudden bitter wind from the south.

HISTORICAL NOTES

❧

BRADY, MATHEW (C. 1823–1896)

Born in upstate New York, Mathew Brady is known primarily as the Civil War photographer. However, his career prior to the war was also renowned. In 1845 he began the extensive project of taking portrait photographs of all "great" citizens, both male and female, and his daguerreotype exhibition in London won him a medal in 1851. He did indeed own a New York City gallery on Broadway in 1854.

THE CLOVER STREET SEMINARY

Mentioned in Chapter 11 as having been attended by future educator Myrtilla Miner (see the paragraph about her, below), the Clover Street Seminary is included here as representative of the many private schools existing in nineteenth-century western New York that either allowed girls to attend with male students or were exclusively female. Celestia Bloss (1812–1855) became the driving force behind the Clover Street Seminary, but she was not unique: a number of women in the Rochester area pioneered in advocating advanced education for women in an age when most men believed that girls needed none. The author believes the emphasis on female education was a primary factor not only in western New York's producing an astonishing number of outstanding women, but in its acceptance (albeit a wary one) of female accomplishment; an acceptance that made the area a fertile ground for innovative women to walk. This in turn nurtured an uneasy tolerance of such social issues as women's rights and abolition. It also may be of interest to note that the first U.S. four-year colleges for women, Elmira College and Ingham University of Leroy, were fruits of western New York.

COWING AND COMPANY

Fire prevention and good fire-fighting equipment were almost unknown in the early nineteenth century. Damage from fire was costly, disastrous and frequent. In 1850, partly as a result of two catastrophic fires involving its own factories, the Seneca Falls–based Cowing and Company began manufacturing hand-operated, wheel-mounted fire engines in addition to the company's regular pump business. Cowing fire engines were said to be unsurpassed in workmanship, power and efficiency, and by mid-century, they were sold throughout North and South America.

COURT CASES

With the single exception of the fictitious *United States* v. *Peartree*, the legal citations in the trial chapters of *North Star Conspiracy* involve actual, historic cases. Fictional attorney Jeremiah Merrycoyf's argument regarding positive law anticipates the actual dissenting minority opinion of Supreme Court Justice John McLean in the *Dred Scott* case, which would be brought before the court in 1857. McLean wrote that: "All slavery had its origin in power and is against right." The majority of justices (five were southern, including Chief Justice Roger Taney) did not agree. The point Merrycoyf raises concerning the birthright of a child was never resolved—in fact, to the author's knowledge it was never presented in a court of law in connection with slavery—but it is interesting to speculate what the historic consequences might have been if it had.

DOUGLASS, FREDERICK (1817–1895)

In 1851, Frederick Douglass renamed his *North Star* newspaper *Frederick Douglass's Paper*, but this name is rarely used by historians. At the time of its first issue, December 3, 1847, there were four other newspapers being edited by African-Americans. While lecturing on antislavery, Douglass urged his listeners to subscribe to his paper—appeals that helped greatly with the cost of production. In fact, he was selling his paper in Seneca Falls when he attended the first women's rights meeting in 1848. Douglass became a staunch supporter of rights for women until the time of debate over passage of the Fifteenth Amendment, which provided for enfranchising black men, but no women. When Susan B. Anthony and Elizabeth Cady Stanton asked Douglass to insist upon inclusion of women, his refusal created a rift never fully repaired, given the support his antislavery cause had received from these women. However, the arguments of either side for their positions were compelling, and while history has proven Douglass wrong in his assumption that once black men were granted the vote, women would immediately be granted theirs, it remains a complex issue.

ELLWANGER, GEORGE (D. 1906), AND BARRY, PATRICK (D. 1890)

George Ellwanger and Patrick Barry established the Mount Hope Garden and Nurseries of Rochester, New York, in 1838. These nurserymen led Rochester into an era of international fame as a supplier of fruit trees and ornamentals, which were shipped worldwide, and ultimately changed the city's nickname from "Flour City" to that of the "Flower City."

FARM JOURNALS

Before 1819, little in agricultural literature was being published other than *The Farmer's Almanac*. But by mid-century, due primarily to the more progressive view being taken by farmers, there were large amounts of literature available. *Moore's Rural New Yorker*, a weekly newspaper that began publication in Rochester in 1850, became one of the best known.

FOSTER, STEPHEN (1826–1864)

Born in Pittsburgh, Stephen Foster had moved to New York City by 1854, the year he wrote "Jeanie with the Light Brown Hair." For the most part unschooled in music theory, he nonetheless began writing songs as a child. In 1848 his "O Susanna" was published, becoming immediately popular during the California gold rush. This success earned Foster a commission to compose in the style of the southern Negroes for E. P. Christy's minstrel show. Ironically, though much of his music deals with the culture and people of the South, he visited there only once. For most of the 190-some songs he composed, he did the words as well as the music. His best-known songs, like "Camptown Races," "Old Folks at Home," "Old Black Joe," and "Beautiful Dreamer," were published between 1848 and 1862. Niles Peartree's prediction proved to be wrong: Foster earned large sums of money on royalties. However, he died penniless in New York City.

MACBETH CURSE

It is widely believed that Shakespeare's tragedy *Macbeth* is among the unluckiest to perform. Various mishaps during productions of *Macbeth* have, over time, led to a superstition that one must never say the name of the play aloud in rehearsal or dressing rooms. It is further said that the witches' song has the power to raise evil. The superstition regarding *Macbeth* is said to have begun on August 7, 1606, when a boy actor by the name of Hal Berridge, who was to play Lady Macbeth, took ill an hour before the performance. He later died in a tiring room during the middle of the play. Since scholarly consensus indicates that Shakespeare wrote *Macbeth* in either 1606 or 1607, the above was likely one of the play's first performances.

MINER, MYRTILLA (1815–1864)

Born in New York State, Myrtilla Miner became a pioneer in teacher education for Negro women. She attended, among other schools, the Clover Street Seminary in Rochester, where after graduation she stayed on as a teacher herself. With one hundred dollars donated by Quakers, Myrtilla went to Washington and, in December of 1851, opened the Colored Girls School. This school provided possibly the only schooling beyond the elementary level accessible to Washington Negroes before the Civil War. After the War it became known as the Miner Normal School and was renamed in 1929 Miner Teachers College. After the 1954 Supreme Court decision outlawing school segregation, it become part of the District of Columbia Teachers College.

MOUNT HOPE CEMETERY

Established in 1836, the beautiful Mount Hope Cemetery of Rochester includes among its hundreds of gravesites those of Susan B. Anthony and Frederick Douglass, and the Rochester family plot of Colonel Nathaniel and his wife Sophia.

O.K.

Readers of *Seneca Falls Inheritance* have questioned the appearance of "O.K.," frequently used by Cullen Stuart and Jacques Sundown, as perhaps anachronistic. But it is one of the oldest and perhaps most durable of Americanisms. At least one of the stories surrounding its origin involves the 1840 presidential campaign of Martin Van Buren; Van Buren's birthplace was Old Kinderhook, New York, and became his nickname. His campaign was supported by O.K. Democratic clubs in New York. (Van Buren lost.) The more favored explanation, however, is that it began as an abbreviation of *oll korrect*—"all correct." In any case, O.K. originated early in the nineteenth century.

OPIUM USE

Glynis's mother became a victim of what was known as opium eating, or opophagia, a not uncommon fate for middle- and upper-class women of the nineteenth century. Although Americans' use of opium did not peak until late in the century, 150,000 pounds of the Turkish poppy from which the drug was derived was being imported annually by the end of the Civil War, in addition to the considerable amount grown in the New England states and the Southeast. Physicians routinely prescribed it for women suffering depression, sleeplessness, menstrual pain or "nervous disposition." Druggists sold it in the form of laudanum, paregoric, morphine and tonics. Opium could be found in cough medicines, healing tinctures, lotions, poultices and liniments. Opiates were introduced to alcoholic beverages. It has been theorized that the social stigma attached to women's use of alcohol pressed many to use opium preparations, which could be taken under the acceptable category of medicinal.

PINKERTON, ALLAN (1819-1884)

Born in Scotland, Allan Pinkerton emigrated to the United States in 1842. In 1850 he left the Chicago police force to form a private detective company, The Pinkerton National Detective Agency, specializing in railway theft cases. The company became one of the most well-known and successful of its kind. During the Civil War, Pinkerton headed a spy group that obtained military intelligence in the southern states. He also had a station on the Underground Railroad in his cooper's shop outside Chicago. The agency eventually became famous for violent strike-breaking.

REPUBLICAN PARTY

The Republican party was born early in the year of 1854 in Ripon, Wisconsin, by antislavery men bitter over passage of the Kansas-Nebraska Act. The Republicans ran candidates throughout the North in 1854. Even Seneca County's November election that year included a Republican candidate (not the fictional Michael Olivant) as well as those of the American and Temperance parties.

THE RICHMOND CONNECTION

Readers may find incredible, as did Glynis Tryon, all the traffic in *North Star Conspiracy* that occurred between Virginia and western New York. However, the actual historic connection is a strong one. The Rochester family indeed originated in Virginia (see "Rochester, Colonel Nathaniel and Sophia," below). The Underground Railroad forged a link by means of the Tear family, which operated a wheelwright shop near Richmond, and a Seneca Falls "station" said to be run and supported by nearly all the families in the village, including that of Elizabeth Cady Stanton. The Tear Underground was possibly one of the longest in existence as well as one that deeply penetrated the South. The Tears' operation must have been exceedingly risky, but they apparently avoided suspicion until the beginning of the Civil War. The Tear family was forced eventually to move North.

ROCHESTER, COLONEL NATHANIEL (1752–1831) AND SOPHIA

Nathaniel Rochester was born in Westmoreland County, Virginia. He moved to Hagerstown, Maryland, where he established himself successfully in business, and it was from there that he left with his family for western New York. They arrived in the spring of 1810 after traveling 275 miles in Conestoga wagons containing all their belongings; the colonel, five sons, and a daughter preceded the others on horseback. Sophia was five months pregnant, and gave birth to her last child after arriving in Dansville. The family was said to have journeyed north over nearly impassable mountains and along Indian trails, camping at night beside streams whenever possible. Ten slaves traveling north with the family were freed immediately upon arrival. Colonel Rochester had previously bought land along the Genesee River, and although he lived in Dansville five years—establishing the first paper mill in western New York—eventually he took steps to lay out a village on this property, which became the city bearing his name. He moved his family there in 1818.

ROSE, ERNESTINE L. (1810–1892)

The Boston Examiner said of Mrs. Ernestine L. Rose that she was "An excellent lecturer, liberal, eloquent, witty, and we must add, decidedly handsome." Rose had left Poland and her Jewish family soon after her mother died and her rabbi father remarried. Glynis had heard several accounts of why Ernestine emigrated. Some said her father insisted she marry someone whom she despised—and that her refusal to do so came after a substantial dowry had been committed. Others said a dispute with her father over her rejection of Jewish teaching as to the inferiority of women, and her subsequent renouncement of the Jewish faith, forced her to leave. Before she left, as a gesture of her independence, she turned over most of a sizable inheritance to her father. She moved to Berlin, where she supported herself by inventing and selling a household deodorant. After marriage she and her husband lived in New York City, where she spent most of the remainder of her life working for abolition, temperance, and women's rights. She died in England, having never returned to Poland.

SARSAPARILLA

"Dr. Townsend's Sarsaparilla—The Most Extraordinary Medicine in the World": This advertisement, quoted in part in Chapter 14, appeared in the August 4, 1848, edition of the *Seneca County Courier*. Dr. Townsend's ad was but one of many glorifying the root of this plant. American sarsaparilla is a member of the ginseng family and was probably first used by Native Americans in North, Central, and South America. It enjoyed something of a national phenomenon status in the United States in the mid-1800s as a tonic to scourge poisons from the blood, and to remedy all manner of ills from rheumatism, gout, ringworm, colds, fever and flatulence to the "numerous and horrible diseases to which women are subject." One of the reasons for sarsaparilla's great popularity may have been the substantial amounts of alcohol often contained in its tonic.

SENECA COUNTY AGRICULTURAL FAIR

The annual Seneca County Agricultural Fair began in October of 1841, and for a time alternated among the various towns in the county, which included Waterloo and Seneca Falls. In 1848 it was decided to hold the fair each year in the town that raised the most money. After 1870 the fair was held annually in Waterloo. And yes, there were not only horse races, but mule races as well.

STILL, WILLIAM (1821-1902)

William Still was a successful coal merchant and an important black leader in Philadelphia's Underground Railroad. Still's carefully kept day-to-day records, published in 1872, constitute some of the otherwise extremely sparse written maerial on the Underground, as secrecy was essential to those operating it.

STOWE, HARRIET BEECHER (1811-1896)

Harriet Beecher Stowe was the author of *Uncle Tom's Cabin*, originally published in forty installments of the antislavery newspaper *National Era*, for which Mrs. Beecher was paid three hundred dollars. It was issued in book form in March of 1852. The book remains one of the most successful in the history of American publishing—within a year it had sold more than 300,000 copies. Stowe's character of Eliza was modeled on the actual bondswoman Eliza Harris from Kentucky, who crossed the Ohio River in winter, leaping from one ice floe to the next, while carrying her child. Harris did reach the opposite shore and the safety of the Ohio Underground.

THEATER, WESTERN NEW YORK

By the time of the War of 1812, theater had been well established in western New York. In 1823 the top floor of a Syracuse tavern was converted into a makeshift stage. Despite appeals that such wickedness be prohibited, in 1824 a theater was constructed in Rochester. The following year saw a playhouse open in Buffalo, with a traveling troupe that visited nearby towns. By the 1830s New York City had replaced Philadelphia as the country's theatrical center, but towns from Albany to Buffalo presented many of the same plays as New York and attracted the same actors and actresses. The standard repertoire consisted primarily of Shakespeare and seventeenth- and eighteenth-century English drama. The Usher Playhouse is fictional, as Seneca Falls did not have a theater in 1854.

TRUTH, SOJOURNER (C. 1797-1883)

Born Isabella, and a slave in Ulster County, New York, Sojourner Truth was freed under the New York Emancipation Act of 1827. She said that from early childhood she had conversed with God, and in 1843 a spiritual voice told her to take

the name of Sojourner Truth and travel as an itineran
preacher. She became a dynamic lecturer on abolition an
women's rights. Her journey for God took her from the Nev
England states west as far as Kansas, often sharing the plat
form with Frederick Douglass, whose effectiveness she wa
said to rival.

TUBMAN, HARRIET (1820-1913)

Born a slave on a Maryland plantation, at age twenty-nin
Harriet Tubman fled after learning she was about to be sol
south. Not satisfied with her own successful escape, she re
turned to Maryland to lead others of her family to freedom
Over the next decade it is said that this woman, known as the
"Moses of her people," conducted some three hundred fugi
tive slaves along the Underground Railroad to Canada. He
forays into Maryland became increasingly dangerous, a:
slaveholders offered rewards for her capture amounting even
tually to forty thousand dollars—a fortune at that time. Afte
nineteen trips north she settled in Auburn, New York, where
she had taken her fugitive mother and father. During the Civi
War Tubman served as a scout and spy as well as nurse fo
the Union forces. She died in Auburn, where her house stil
stands.

UNDERGROUND RAILROAD

Arch Merrill's "The Underground" says the following:

*When his slave disappeared, seemingly into thin air, a
Kentuckian—or so the story goes—was heard to say:
"He must have gone on an underground road." The
name caught on and because the first American steam
railroad had just been completed, it was twisted into
"the Underground Railroad."*

Although in the North the people most often associated
with the Underground were Quakers, many individual non-
Quaker women and men were involved as well. One minister
from Naples, New York, was sentenced to eleven years in a

southern prison for his participation. Today western New York is still dotted with hundreds of homes, taverns and inns, and former carriage houses with concealed compartments that once hid fugitive slaves. Often these are not discovered until a structure is being razed for some locale's newest parking lot.

WEATHER

Glynis didn't just imagine the severity of the heat in Chapter 2. According to the National Weather Bureau, western New York's summer of 1854 was the hottest on record (as of 1992), with an average temperature of 73.1 degrees Fahrenheit.

WHEATLEY, PHILLIS (C. 1753–1784)

Born in Africa, Phillis was as a young girl sold in Boston to John Wheatley, a tailor. She was tutored with the Wheatley children, became fluent in English, and eventually mastered Greek and Latin. Encouraged by her mistress, she began to write poetry. Her first book, *Poems on Various Subjects, Religious and Moral*, was published in 1773 in London. But it was not until the beginning of the abolition movement in the 1800s that this first of America's outstanding African-American women poets received attention.

Items that appeared in the Historical Notes section of *Seneca Falls Inheritance* have for the most part not been included in the above, although some may also be pertinent to *North Star Conspiracy*. Since there is frequent historical overlap, this choice was made to avoid repetition and to prevent these sections from eventually becoming longer than the novels themselves.

A Sir John Fielding Mystery

JACK, KNAVE AND FOOL

BRUCE ALEXANDER

Putnam